THE SIBERIANS

Fire on the Ice

A Siberian family's
extraordinary tale of
survival through revolution
and civil war

Simon J. Carey

jf
publishing

Jack Frost Publishing

Published by Jack Frost Publishing

22 Tingara Close, Yanakie, Victoria 3096, Australia

ABN: 74268410414

First published in Australia 2023

ISBN: 978-0-6459676-0-9 Paperback

ISBN: 978-0-6459676-1-6 E-version

Cover design by Britt Wilson – Author Services, Australia

Formatting by Author Services, Australia

Typeset in Adobe Garamond Pro

A catalogue record for this book is available from the National Library of Australia

Praise from Readers for
The Siberians Fire on the Ice

A closely imagined narrative of one family's struggles as they are caught up in momentous events. Political events form the backdrop to what people do and say, and the power of this book lies in the action on the page propelling the individually drawn characters from one dramatic event to the next.

John L. – Retired English Master and Russian scholar.

What a fantastic, fascinating book!! I just finished Isabel Allende's "Violeta", also gripping, but this beats it for sure.

Hans B. – Retired chemical engineer - Portugal

Well researched and couldn't put it down. Now I have to wait for the next book.

Patricia L. – Launceston Book Club

The historically detailed story is a compelling read of one family's struggles. I look forward to reading the next book in the saga.

Dr Sue L. – Retired radiologist - Perth

I read it in three sittings and was absolutely engrossed. I loved the caricatures the author created, and also the history.

Helen B. – Fashion house proprietor - Melbourne

I loved it - it was fascinating and thoroughly enjoyable. I felt connected to the characters, their struggles and failings. Beautifully written, transporting me to the communities, the townships, landscapes, and the brutal, unforgiving times.

Mark A. – Founder of Fish Creek Children's Literature Festival

I knew little about Russian history and found the book fascinating. It would make a fabulous movie.

Di McK. – Retired - Tasmania

Arlette (Sukhov) Cykman

1941 — 2021

The great-granddaughter of Pavel Dmitrievich Sukhov.

Born in the International Concession, Shanghai.

Arlette asked me to write this book,
propelling me on the journey of a lifetime.

Without her, this book would have never happened.

Simon J. Carey
Author

There are no monsters in this world

And no saints

Only infinite shades woven into the same tapestry

Light and dark

One man's monster is another man's beloved.

The wise know that.

Katherine Arden
The Winter of the Witch
A tale of Russian folklore

Author's Note

MORE THAN TEN years ago in Thailand Arlette Cykman, the last remaining member of the Sukhov family, approached me with a remarkable account of the family's struggle for survival during the Russian Revolution of 1917 and the horrendous four-year civil war that followed. Her request was simple – to write her family's story before she died. She was already old and in declining health.

Arlette was born in Shanghai. Her mother, Vera Sukhov, was Russian and born in Siberia during the civil war. Arlette's father was an Egyptian-Armenian who met Vera in Shanghai. Arlette took the surname of Cykman from her Polish-American stepfather after her mother remarried following World War Two.

I interviewed Arlette over several months at her home in Thailand. Her detailed oral history was richly augmented from diaries, files of documents, newspaper clippings, family photograph albums, and mementos. Amazingly, all of this had remained intact during the family's repeated flights to safety through three countries, trying to survive the major wars and revolutions of the twentieth century. Now Arlette, the last in the direct Sukhov line, had become the custodian of this extraordinary family archive.

The Sukhov family had been in Russia at the time of that country's involvement in World War One, and one of the family members fought against the Germans and Austro-Hungarians. They witnessed revolution sweeping through the country, and they were involved with the "White" coalition that fought against the "Red" Bolsheviks in the civil war.

Written histories of the Russian Revolution mostly focus on the events leading up to October 1917 and their underlying causes. The Bolsheviks saw the revolution itself, as depicted by the symbolic storming of the Winter Palace, as the ultimate victory. For the rest of the population, those not living in Petrograd (St. Petersburg) or Moscow, but spread across the vastness that is the Russian nation, this was far from the reality they experienced in their own region.

Little has been written about the civil war and there is good reason for this. The conflict pitted Russian against Russian; it was not so much about territory lost or gained as a vicious clash of diametrically opposed political ideologies. The true death toll will never be known. The best estimates suggest more than 250,000 died – from the fighting, and from disease, hunger and the bitter cold. The "Red" Bolshevik forces ultimately prevailed after four long years; but the death toll was so high, and the divisions within the population so deep, that the new rulers of Russia desperately wanted to "paper over the cracks" and pretend it didn't happen. Even in Russia today the civil war is a subject to be avoided, and museums and archives have deliberately expunged most references to the conflict.

Similarly, the Western Powers wanted to downplay their role in the civil war. Largely for their own political and economic interests, they supplied the White forces with armaments, and even put their own troops on the ground in Siberia and the Crimea. But when it became apparent they had backed the losing side, they withdrew and left the crumbling White forces stranded and set up for defeat. The intense residual bitterness felt by the Bolsheviks over the Western Powers' involvement gave birth to the "Cold War", underpinning the hatred and distrust between the East and West to this day.

Books by Western authors have been written about the civil war, but these mostly attempt to unravel the complex military and political history of the conflict. There is little about the effect on the general population, apart from horrifying statistics of death and disease.

The Sukhovs were a middle-class Russian family, a family of moderately wealthy merchants, as well as factory owners and small landowners who had established themselves in Siberia over three generations. They lived in the town of Barnaul in the southern Altai Krai, a long way from the political cauldron of the cities in Western Russia on the other side of the Ural Mountains.

During the revolution their awareness and comprehension of events would have been limited to letters from family, the hearsay of travelers, weeks-old newspapers, and occasional information coming in over the telegraph. But the conflicts and political upheaval going on in their own town and, in the countryside around them, were real and present. They could hold on and survive for a while, but sooner or later they would need to decide what to do – stay and fight with all the inherent risks, or abandon everything and flee for their lives.

This is not written as a family history, nor is it a documentary treatment of the conflict, but it is their story as re-imagined by a writer in another country from another time.

Riga
Petrograd
Mogilev
RUSSIA
Ural Mountains
Moscow
Perm
Yekaterinburg
River Volga
River Ural
Chelyabinsk
River Ob
River Yenisei
River Lena
SIBERIA
Upper River Tanguska
OKHOTSK SEA
River Amur
Omsk
Novonikolayevsk
Tomsk
Lake Baikal
Stretensk
Khabarovsk
BLACK SEA
River Irtysh
Altai Railway
Barnaul
Chita
MANCHURIA
Irkutsk
Harbin
Vladivostok
CIRCA 1917
Semipalatinsk
CASPIAN SEA
TRANS-SIBERIAN RAILWAY
SCALE OF MILES
0 100   300   500   1000
MONGOLIA
KOREA
Pekin
Port Arthur
YELLOW SEA
CHINESE REPUBLIC
N NE NW E W SE SW S

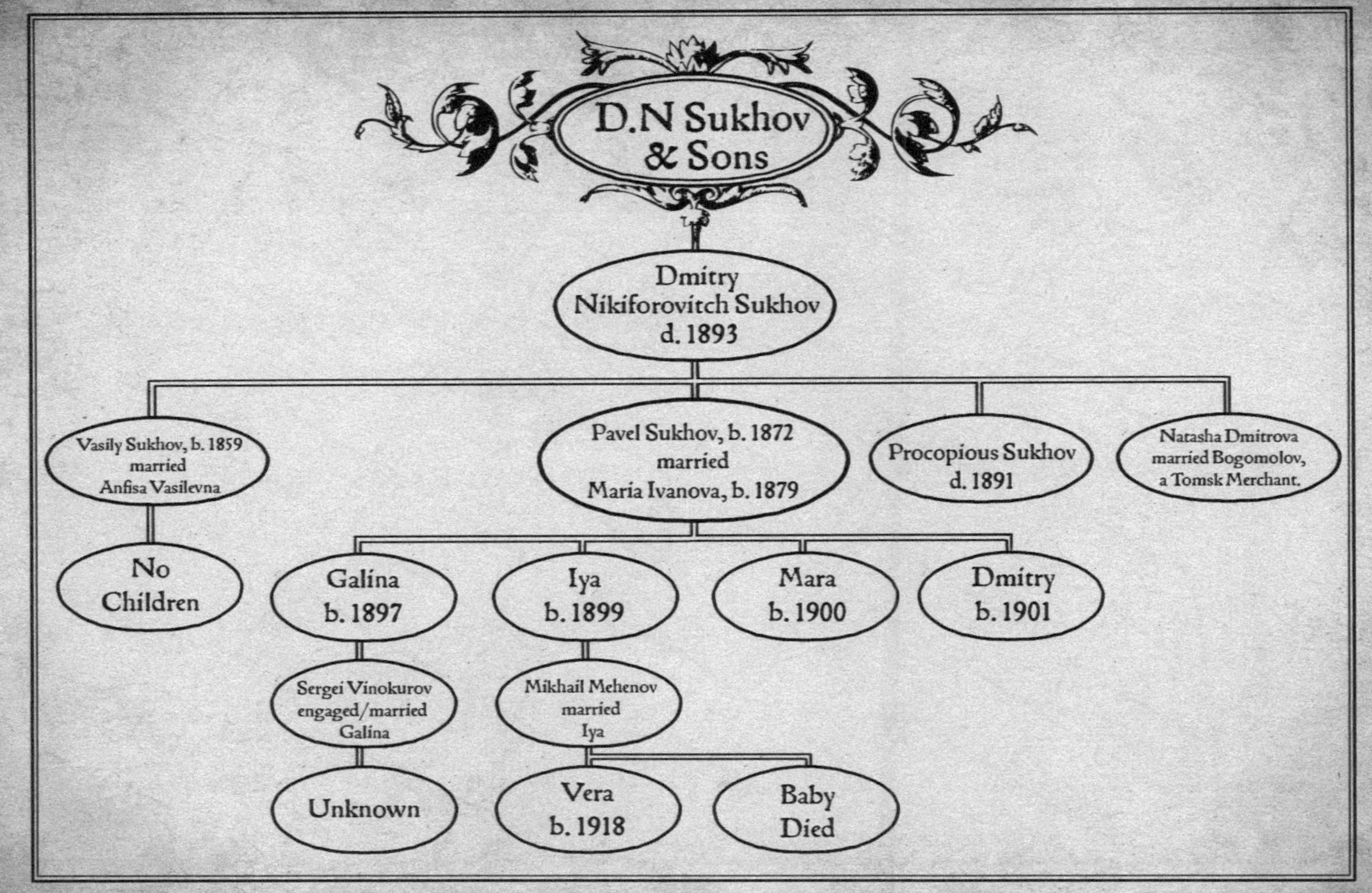

D.N Sukhov & Sons
Dmitry Nikiforovitch Sukhov d. 1893
Vasily Sukhov, b. 1859 married Anfisa Vasilevna
Pavel Sukhov, b. 1872 married Maria Ivanova, b. 1879
Procopious Sukhov d. 1891
Natasha Dmitrova married Bogomolov, a Tomsk Merchant.
No Children
Galina b. 1897
Iya b. 1899
Mara b. 1900
Dmitry b. 1901
Sergei Vinokurov engaged/married Galina
Mikhail Mehenov married Iya
Unknown
Vera b. 1918
Baby Died

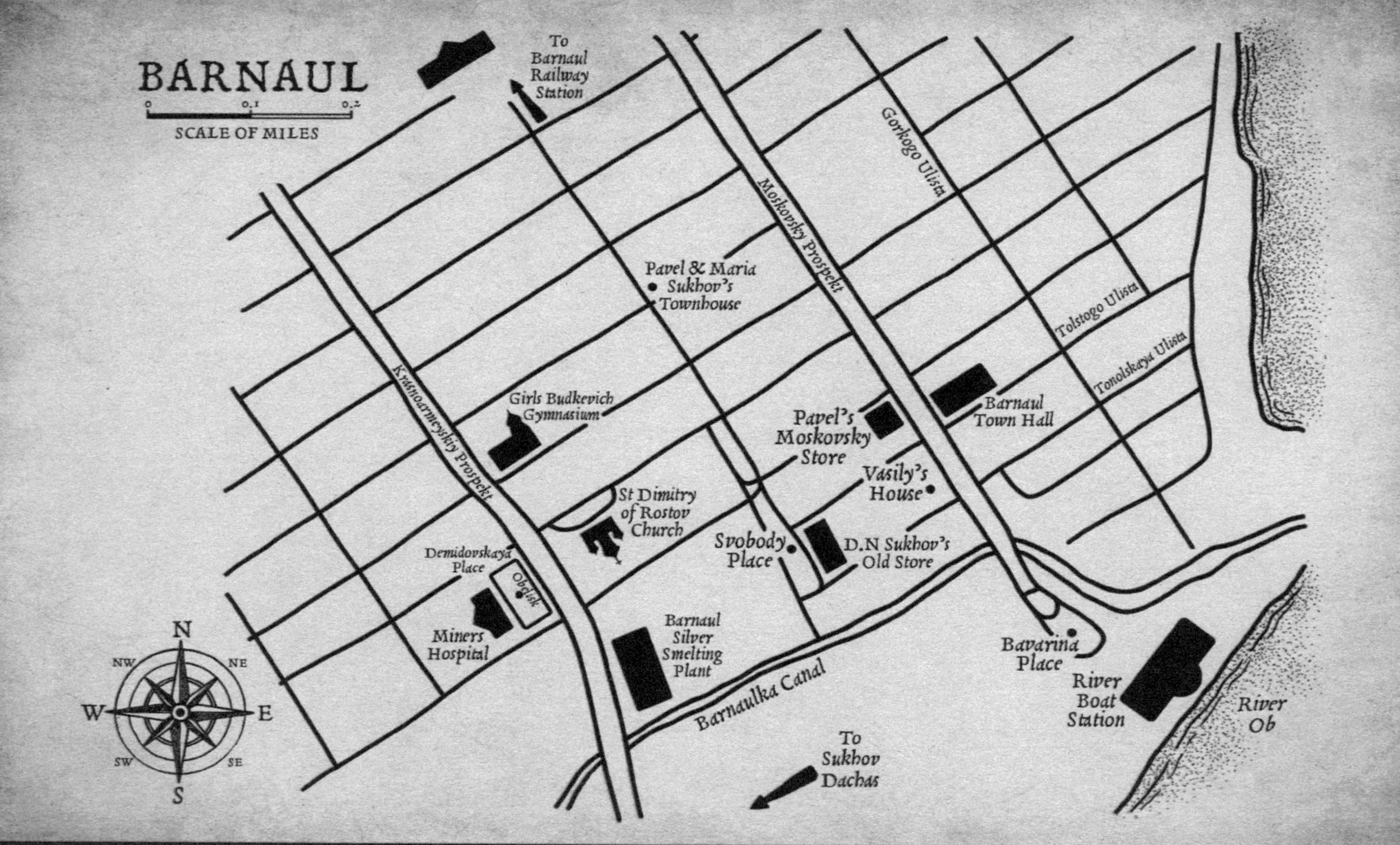

BARNAUL
SCALE OF MILES
0   0.1   0.2
To Barnaul Railway Station
Pavel & Maria Sukhov's Townhouse
Gorkogo Ulista
Moskovsky Prospekt
Tolstogo Ulista
Tonolskaya Ulista
Girls Budkevich Gymnasium
Pavel's Moskovsky Store
Barnaul Town Hall
Vasily's House
Krasnoarmeyskiy Prospekt
St Dimitry of Rostov Church
Svobody Place
D.N Sukhov's Old Store
Demidovskaya Place
Obelisk
Miners Hospital
Barnaul Silver Smelting Plant
Barnaulka Canal
Bavarina Place
River Boat Station
River Ob
To Sukhov Dachas
N
NW   NE
W   E
SW   SE
S

Chapter 1

THE DESERTERS

April 1917

PAVEL DMITRIEVICH SUKHOV stifled a yawn. He had been standing beside the troika for some time, gazing at the sinking sun reflecting off the chestnut sheen of his Don horses as they grazed the paddocks, and following the flights of the swallows as they swooped and dived for the evening insect rise over the grasslands.

It had been an early start at his store and, on an impulse, he decided late afternoon to make the journey to the stud farm. He always felt reinvigorated when he got out into the countryside. The grime, the poverty and despondency of the Siberian town, weighed down with more bad news from the war in the west, wore on him after a while. Somehow, the serenity of the countryside and the broad expanse of the steppes remained a constant, unchanging except for the seasons.

Pavel stood legs slightly apart leaning forward with both hands resting on the silver top piece of his black ivory cane. But he was neither aged nor decrepit, a man in his mid-forties with steely determination in his eyes, like a prizefighter about to step into the ring.

Pavel swept his hand back through his hair, tugged down on his old blue peaked cap, and pushed back his gold-rimmed spectacles. All was good with the world, at least his world out with his Dons.

He reached into his waistcoat pocket, pulled out his fob watch, and checked the time.

'It's almost seven o'clock, time to head home,' he said to his driver, as he climbed back into the carriage.

'Will that be back to town sir, or to the homestead?'

Pavel looked up at the sky. The first signs of pink on the western horizon heralded the approaching end to the day.

'It's too dangerous on the roads after dark, and we wouldn't make it back to town before sunset. Anyway, Maria Ivanova is expecting us, so the farm tonight, then we'll drive in to the Moskovsky Street store first thing in the morning.'

Anticipating as much, the driver touched the peak of his cap and flicked the reins. The three horses tugged at the traces and sensing the direction, wheeled the troika around and down the track leading towards the homestead.

The troika jolted and swayed as it bumped over the hardened grooves of the dirt track. With a clear sky overhead, and the sun quickly dipping towards the horizon, the temperature was dropping. Pavel could feel the fresh dampness in the air, and the grass was already glistening with evening dew.

'Head by way of the top paddock,' Pavel instructed the driver. It was something of a whim, but he always enjoyed surveying the view from the highpoint of the farm and, even with the light rapidly fading, he felt secure within his own domain.

Off in the distance came the faint hoot of a train whistle. The locomotive was out of sight since the track ran through the tree line on the far riverbank, but Pavel could make out the train's progress by following its trailing plume of smoke.

'The train from Novonikolayevsk,' commented the driver. 'It's on time for a change.'

The two of them followed the white smoke plume as it headed towards the Ob Bridge that would take it across the broad river into the town of Barnaul. Pavel gave a quiet grunt of satisfaction. The driver looked around and nodded.

'If it wasn't for that connection to the Trans-Siberian line, where would we be today? All the work of your father.'

'Budkevich and the Polyakovs also had a hand in it,' Pavel answered. 'But its unfinished business; the Altai line still hasn't been pushed through to Turkestan.'

'When the Altai silver was mined out,' continued the driver, 'we wouldn't have survived without the railway.'

Pavel grunted an acknowledgement knowing the driver was correct. The line joining Barnaul with the Trans-Siberian at the Novonikolayevsk junction had transformed the town when the mines and smelters closed. The local crop growers and merchants now had an alternative. When the river froze each November and the river barges were locked in by ice, they could still get their produce through to the cities in the west.

But today the train link was a mixed blessing. The trains coming east from Moscow in European Russia were crammed with destitute families fleeing hunger and the imminent danger of German invasion. There were also soldiers from the front – the wounded, the maimed, the disfigured and, mingled with them, thousands of deserters fleeing the war. Adding to this were trainloads of German and Austro-Hungarian prisoners of war destined for the internment camps scattered throughout the area.

Politics, from the intrigues of Petrograd and Moscow, moved eastwards along the train routes with agitators spreading their political creed and formenting dissent among the local population.

Bolsheviks, Mensheviks, Social Republicans, Kadets – all the political hues were present, but more often it was the Bolsheviks' simple unambiguous message "Peace, Land and Bread" which struck a chord with the starving, the landless, and people simply tired of countless years of war.

❧

The driver went to say more, but Pavel put up his hand, preferring to relish a few moments of quiet solitude as dusk gathered over the land. The sky had turned into a deep gunmetal blue and the dark green of the *taiga* was now a mass of black, twisted trunks impenetrable to the eye. On the far eastern horizon the pale bluish-grey of the Altai Mountains and their snow-capped peaks had turned a faint pink as their western flanks caught the last rays of the setting sun.

But as Pavel gazed at the changing light of the sky he glimpsed something else. Silhouetted in the sky were the black wheeling forms of large birds, their giant saw-toothed wings riding the air currents and circling in tight formation.

'Buzzards,' he exclaimed, pointing with his cane. 'Damned carrion-eating buzzards!'

The driver squinted skywards. 'Yes, I see them, sir. I reckon they're probably Crested Honey Buzzards.'

'If they're circling over our land, it means something's either dead or dying. Let's head over and find out.'

The troika crested a small rise. Pavel leaned over and rapped his cane sharply on the seat beside the driver. 'Stop! Stop here!'

The driver reined in the horses and looked back at Pavel. 'Sir?'

'Look over there. Who are those men, and what's that lying on the ground?'

Pavel was now standing to gain a better vantage. A few hundred meters away, down the slope, three men stood around the carcass of a partially dismembered animal. One of the men was swinging a heavy double-headed axe. It rose and fell rhythmically, cleaving limbs and rough chunks of raw flesh from the carcass. The other two men stood back to avoid being sprayed with blood.

'The bastards – how dare they!'

The driver looked back at Pavel. There was fear in his eyes. 'Should we get help?'

'By the time we return with help they'll be long gone.'

Pavel pulled out his rifle from its leather scabbard. 'What the hell are we waiting for? That's one of my horses down there!'

The driver flicked the reins and, with a loud yell, cracked the whip. The men looked up. The one with the axe stopped his butchering and rested the axe-head on the ground while the other two brought their rifles up to the ready.

The driver reached under his seat, pulled out his own rifle, and worked the rifle bolt and released the safety catch. Pavel stood upright, gripping the back of the driver's seat for balance, as it jolted and swayed down the slope.

The men glanced sideways at each other and nodded. The large man with the axe was dressed in the tattered uniform and stiff leather apron of an army sapper. The long apron, reaching almost to the ground, was dripping with blood. Nonchalantly he hoisted the axe onto his shoulder. The other two aimed their rifles at the approaching troika and waited with grim, fearless faces. They each wore grubby woolen astrakhan hats and mud-encrusted greatcoats with collars turned up against the cold, and a faded red ribbon pinned to their upper sleeve.

Pavel tapped the shoulder of the driver who sharply reined in the horses and stomped hard on the brake. The wheels locked and skidded, and the troika shuddered to a halt fifty meters from the men. Pavel was momentarily thrown forward against the back of the driver's seat but managed to steady himself. He held his rifle out of sight behind the seat.

'Keep your rifle down until I tell you,' he whispered to the driver.

There was an eerie silence as the two groups stared at each other. The only sound was the nervous snorting of the horses and the fading tinkling of the harness bells. The driver was straining at the reins to keep the horses under control; each of the three, harnessed line-abreast in the troika-style, was straining at its traces.

'Keep them still,' Pavel instructed the driver.

'I'm trying sir, it's not the rifles, they are upset seeing one of their own dead on the ground.'

Pavel glanced past the men at the steaming carcass, one of his prized horses, now reduced to a butchered mess of raw flesh and blood and guts. He could only feel revulsion and rage yet, strangely, was free of fear.

'What the hell do you think you're doing?' he shouted. 'This is *my* land and that's *my* horse.'

The large man with the axe stepped forward. He gave Pavel a sneering grin and glanced sideways at his companions. 'This fine upstanding gentleman says it's his land and his horse. I think he's saying we're just a bunch of no-good trespassers. Never mind that we were taking a simple short cut across the paddocks on the way back to the camp and we stumbled across this dead animal. Isn't that right, comrades?'

The two riflemen shuffled their feet, looking nervous and unsure, but kept their rifles trained.

Pavel glanced down at the steam rising from the still-warm carcass. *You bastards, you killed my horse.*

The axe man, appearing emboldened, continued. 'And since people at the camp are starving, should we have left it here for the buzzards and wolves, or take back some horseflesh? Would you begrudge us some sustenance?'

'You could have asked rather than kill and steal.'

'Come cap in hand begging for charity?' The axe man spat on the ground. 'When was the last time you landowners, or the Zemstvo Council in town, or even the townsfolk themselves, did anything for us? You hoard your food and we're left to starve in the forest with only these to help.'

The axe man held up two dirty calloused hands.

'We always keep a pot of soup at the back door for needy wayfarers.'

'Do you expect our children to walk for hours to your door for one measly bowl of soup? We don't want charity, we'll just take what is our due.'

Pavel pointed to the red ribbon on the man's sleeve. 'You make out you're Bolsheviks, but you're really deserters. You've chosen your way and it's your decision to end up in the camps. You've walked away from the war, and the motherland. At least we've still got enough brave and loyal men willing to hold the front.'

The two groups still remained forty meters apart. Pavel was thinking about the odds should they not back down. He noticed their rifles were bolt-action Mosin-Nagants. He and the driver both carried fully loaded repeating rifles and there was a chance they could down a rifleman each before the axe man could reach them.

But whether to start a fight was the question Pavel was carefully weighing. The Bolshevik camp was full of armed and desperate men, and the threat of retribution was real. The killing of these men could easily escalate into an all-out war, one in which Pavel and his farm workers would be heavily outnumbered.

This is going nowhere, Pavel thought to himself. Something had to happen before it spiraled out of control. Pavel took a deep breath. 'Just get the hell off my land,' he said, 'and don't come back. If I catch you here I'll shoot you on the spot.'

The axe man took one more step forward, noisily cleared his throat, and spat sideways on the ground.

'You bastard *Kulak* landowners are always trying to tell us what to do. While we fought your bloody war, you sat back here on your fat arses making fat profits. The Tsar and his German bitch can't protect you now. It's our turn, the people's turn. And whose land is this anyhow? It's now the land of the workers and the peasants, or haven't you read the proclamation?'

'That's just Lenin's proclamation. As far as I'm concerned, he's an agent in the pay of the Germans and is hell-bent on undermining the war effort. And you how dare talk about the Tsarina like that! You Bolsheviks are a minority in the Duma – you are not the government, a mere *proclamation* is not law, and this isn't Petrograd or Moscow. This is my property and that's my horse you've slaughtered. I won't tell you again, get off my land!'

Pavel whispered to the driver out the corner of his mouth, 'Let's take out the ones with rifles first. The left one is yours, the right's mine. Leave the one with the axe until last. On my count, fire.'

Pavel raised his rifle, thumbed off the safety catch, and squinted down the barrel. The gaunt brown face of the rifleman swam into focus. He took aim at the bridge of the rifleman's nose. *Lower, allow for the rifle kick.*

'I'm going to count to ten,' Pavel shouted, 'If you don't leave, then we'll fire. One, two, three . . . '

The axe man laughed and bowed in mock submission.

'Just this time you can have it your way, *Kulak*.' He turned to his companions. 'Come on, let's get out of here.'

Nonchalantly he raised his axe, and with a final swing, cleaved off a partially severed leg from the carcass and hefted it onto his shoulder. With one hand balancing the leg and the other his axe, he turned his back and trudged towards the distant spiral of smoke from the camp in the forest.

The others hesitated, their rifles still raised and facing the troika, till they too turned and jogged to catch up with the axe man.

'And if I were you, *Kulak*,' the axe man had stopped in his tracks and turned to shout back at Pavel, 'I'd get out now; your time is over. And don't try to come after us, we know where you live, just remember that.'

Pavel thought to reply, but instead slowly lowered his rifle. He told the driver to do the same. As they watched the men walk away Pavel tasted bile in his mouth, a feeling of frustration and helplessness, and a rising anger that they could do this to him with impunity.

Despite the chill in the air, he could feel rivulets of sweat trickling down his back. It took a few minutes and several deep breaths to steady himself.

'When we get back to the yard,' Pavel said to the driver, 'tell Ivan Nikolayevich to move all the horses out of the river paddocks first thing tomorrow morning. Tell him to bring them into the yards and the paddocks closest to the homestead. These bastards aren't going to get one more animal of mine.'

'Yes, sir,' replied the driver, looking up at the darkening sky. 'Shouldn't we be getting on our way?'

'One minute.'

Pavel got down from the troika and walked over to the remains of the carcass. He leaned over and ran his fingers through the soft chestnut mane of the Don and then gently rubbed his hand down its muzzle. He stood upright and had one final glance in the direction of the retreating figures. They were now almost lost against the darkness of the trees at the edge of the forest.

'Call themselves Bolsheviks, the lying bastards.'

Pavel slowly climbed back up into the troika. 'Come on,' he said to the driver, 'let's get the hell out of here.'

Chapter 2
BARNAUL TOWN

Monday 02 May 1917

MINUTE FLECKS OF dust danced in the filtered light of the town house hallway. Pavel could feel the rising warmth of the day creeping through the unshuttered windows as he stood in front of the tall mirror carefully brushing his frock coat and adjusting his cravat. Maria Ivanova, short and matronly in her dark blue skirt and white embroidered apron, came up the hallway from the kitchen and took charge of the clothes brush.

The day after the confrontation with the deserters Pavel had insisted the family move back into Barnaul. He usually lived in the town house alone during the week, apart from the housekeeper, and returned to the farm for weekends after completing his work at the stores and tannery. It was smaller than the homestead, and felt cramped with all the family here, but the farm was isolated, and he now was forced to confront the danger from the camps.

'Are you going to Moskovsky Prospekt or the new shop?' Maria asked as she finished adjusting the collar on his coat.

'The Moskovsky store.'

'Are you sure you don't want to take the troika? It's going to be hot today.'

'I'll be fine,' said Pavel, tugging at one of his sleeves. 'It's only a short walk to the store and I need the exercise. Dmitry will be bringing in my horse after lunch. We'll ride out to the tannery this afternoon to go over the books with the accountant.'

'Please be careful,' said Maria. 'You'll have to ride through all those camps of horrible people on the outskirts.'

Pavel leaned over and softly pecked Maria's powdered cheek. 'They're not all horrible. Let's not allow a few bad ones to make us forget most of them are here because they were starving in the cities. Anyway, Dmitry and I can easily avoid them if we choose our path carefully.'

Pavel took one final look in the hallstand mirror, adjusted his spectacles, and reached for his hat and cane.

'I'd better get going since it's market day. Make sure you lock the door behind me.'

'I trust business is good today,' said Maria, making the sign of the cross. 'Stay safe, and God Bless.'

Pavel paused on the stoop until he heard the reassuring clunk of the door bolts sliding into place. He descended the steps and turned left, heading across town towards Svobody Place. The slight breeze still bore the coolness of the night, but the soft azure blue of the sky, with its scudding puffs of white clouds, signalled the day would be fine and hot in a few hours.

He started down Tolstoy Street. There were a few people about, mostly heading to the marketplace in the center of town, a good sign for business. The ever-present beggars were taking up their stations at street corners and a group of army deserters huddled around the fire they had lit in the vacant land on the other side of the road.

Several carriages bumped and splashed their way along the street and heavy carts loaded with produce were tugged slowly forward by straining oxen teams.

Pavel walked quickly, avoiding the beggars and the soldiers, as well as the puddles of dirty brown water and the splashes of passing carriages. It was spring and Barnaul had nearly cast off the heavy cloak of winter. There were still dirty patches of old snow left in shaded areas, and the gutters ran with snow melt.

Elm trees lined the street on both sides. The branches were still black and bare, but tiny buds of green were already pushing their way through the frost-hardened bark.

Tolstoy Street was a main thoroughfare lined with double-story timber houses with white fretwork eaves. The thick hewed timber log walls were stained creosote black, and the cracks between the logs stuffed with sheep's wool to keep out the cold. The houses had a uniformity pleasing to the eye, with their small lace-curtained windows and blue shutters hooked back to let in the sunshine.

There was an unassuming feeling of prosperity, and the rows of solid houses seemed to symbolize Barnaul, just a medium-sized town, but an important outpost strategically located on ancient trading routes close to the border with Mongolia, Turkestan and China.

Rather than take the direct route to his main store Pavel cut off left down Gor'kogo Street towards the River-Boat Station and then turned right along Tobolskaya. The street ran parallel to the Barnaulka Canal, built to cut through a sweeping bend in the Ob River, and wide and deep enough for barges to navigate and load. Here the buildings were more solid, industrial in nature, and made from local red-brown bricks. The old silver smelter was here, but was now closed and falling into decay.

He paused and looked over the golden domes of Prince Volodymyr's Chapel in Bavarina Place to the low, whitewashed wooden structure of the boat station and the river beyond. The Ob had risen further, the blue-grey spring melt running strongly and the lowlands on the far eastern shore now partially flooded, with clumps of silver birch standing like marooned islands in the swirling current. A passenger ferry was pushing its way, in crab-like fashion, as it fought the current, heading for the wharves on the west bank where lines of barges lay tethered together.

Workmen from the Zemstvo council were sweeping up rubbish with straw brooms along the riverbank. Yesterday, the 1st of May, had been the traditional holiday celebrating the first day of spring, but for the first time it had been renamed Labor Day. Pavel smarted at the Kerensky Government's decision to appease the minority left-wing parties in the Duma, anything to maintain its tenuous grip on power. But begrudgingly, and finally in good humor, Pavel closed his shops for the day.

It had been a clear, warm spring day on the banks of the river. A fair was set up near the waterfront, picnic rugs spread, and the town band played in the rotunda in the park near the bridge. Young children, freed from the shackles of winter, ran and laughed between the strolling groups of people.

For one day the town's residents set aside thoughts of the blood-soaked trenches of the Western Front and the deprivation and strikes in the big cities. Call the day what they may, this was Siberian Russia's welcoming of spring.

But the gaiety of the day had an undercurrent of sadness. The war had touched every family in some way. While laughing groups of girls, twirling brightly colored parasols, strolled along the embankment, young men or courting couples had become a rarity. Those few young men in evidence were being pushed around on the graveled pathways in cane wheel chairs or hobbling along on crutches.

Pavel left the riverbank and the workmen with their brooms and resumed walking along Tobolskaya, at first briskly, but slowing when he came to the start of the commercial district. The aging red brick building on the corner of the large open square still had the sign painted high up on its brick façade. The words were faded but still legible, "D. N. Sukhov & Sons", his grandfather's original store.

The family had lost the store when the business went bankrupt and, although they retained some of their wealth, it was a blemish on the family's reputation. It had taken years of struggle, but Pavel had methodically and resolutely rebuilt the family business, and now had two new stores in Barnaul, besides the tannery on the town's outskirts, the horse stud, and a stake in a gold mine in the Altai Mountains.

Pavel still had a residual bitterness about the bankruptcy, but it had taught him a valuable lesson about the tenuous hold people had on wealth and status and how external factors could easily wipe out years of toil and effort. Money, so hard earned, but so easily lost.

A merchant stood leaning against the doorframe of the main entrance to the building; the old store had been broken up into an arcade with numbers of smaller shops. Pavel recognized him at once and tipped his cane to his hat. The man waved back and grinned. He had a broad, jolly face perched on top of a rotund body, wore a blue collarless shirt with rolled up sleeves, and was enjoying a cigarette in the spring sunshine.

'Good morning, Pavel Dmitrievich,' the merchant called out, 'and what brings you to this part of the town?'

'And good morning to you Nikifor Trifonovich, it's such a lovely day I thought I'd go for a stroll before we open up.'

The two men knew each other through the Merchant Guild and enjoyed an air of familiarity. They didn't see each other as competitors; Pavel dealt more in supplies to the surrounding farms, while the other traded in tea and fur with the Chinese, Mongolians and the Buryats.

Nikifor took a final puff of his cigarette then flicked the butt onto the dirt street.

'How's business with you?' asked Pavel.

'Slow as usual, but then we have the war. Not too many people in Petrograd can afford mink or sable anymore.'

'But your tea trade must still be going well. Russians can always be relied upon to drink tea.'

'We're still waiting for the first caravans to get through after the melt, and then hope the buyers arrive. Even then, I'm not certain what they're prepared to pay if demand has slumped in the cities. When people are starving and queuing for bread, will they have money left for tea?'

'Cheer up. The horse market is on today and hopefully that will bring us some good business.'

'Probably you more than me, I think. And how is your brother, Vasily Dmitrievich, I hear he's been unwell?'

Pavel nodded. 'He doesn't seem to get out of the house much these days. It's why I'm here, I'm heading over there now.'

'Wish him well from me. He's always been a good man; the town, the church, and the schools have a lot to thank him for when he was Mayor.'

Pavel lifted his hat. 'I must go. I hope you have a successful day Nikifor Trifonovich. Let's see if we can loosen the purse strings of these horse traders.'

Many people had come into town from the surrounding countryside for the May Day festivities and would stay on to obtain provisions before returning to their farms. There was also the monthly horse market today in Svobody Place, close to Pavel's main store, where native Buryats with their dark brown weathered faces would be selling their sturdy Altai Krai horses to traders from the west, traders hopefully with pockets stuffed full of rubles and in need of provisions.

Pavel did not offer his Dons at the local market, preferring instead to sell them direct to the army where they were much sought after by the Russian cavalry regiments. It was always a quandary for Pavel knowing his horses would be destined for battle in some far-off land, and their chances of survival were never high, but he had convinced himself supplying them was at the least a patriotic duty.

Pavel set off, retracing his steps, and quickly rounded the corner into the broad avenue of the imperious Moskovsky Prospect leading up from the river and bisecting the town. His brother Vasily's house was there, close to the bottom of the avenue nearest the river. Pavel noted the lace curtains were pulled closed and some of the heavy winter windows remained shuttered despite the early morning spring sunshine. There appeared to be no life or movement within the house.

Pavel hesitated, and was about to knock on the front door, when he noticed a man standing on the grassed island dividing the middle of the avenue and gazing at the upper section of Vasily's brick house. The man spotted Pavel and turned towards him. Pavel recognized the pallid features, the slicked-back hair, and large waxed handlebar moustache. The man's smile was forced, and when he did smile, displayed an uneven set of yellowed teeth.

'Pavel Dmitrievich, a fine good morning to you.' Pavel ignored the greeting. Whatever it was about Matvei Tsaplin there was something unsettling. Perhaps it was the way he never looked you in the eye when he spoke, or the sweaty palm of his handshake, or the contrived flamboyance of his appearance. He always seemed to be scurrying about town in his threadbare black suit with a small black briefcase tucked under his arm, always in a hurry, and with the determined countenance of a man on important business.

'A fine building and a good location', continued Tsaplin, outwardly untroubled by Pavel's lack of return greeting.

'It's my brother's house and, in case you're wondering, it's not for sale,' replied Pavel, rather curtly.

'Oh, you must have misunderstood me', replied Tsaplin, 'I've no intention of buying private property.' There was something disquieting about the way he said the word *private* that jarred with Pavel.

'It's property,' continued Tsaplin, 'which seems to singularly define the problems of Russia. Can Russia ever break the shackles of the past? Or will it remain, as one poet put it, "Russia is a country of masters and slaves".'

Pavel had no desire for a political debate with this man, but before he could respond, Tsaplin lifted his hat, 'Good day to you Pavel Dmitrievich. Sorry, but I must rush, I have a meeting to attend.'

Without waiting for a reply Tsaplin clapped his hat back on, turned and hurried up the Prospekt towards the City Duma offices.

'Bloody busy for a weaver, isn't he?' a voice boomed from behind. 'As the self-appointed leader of the local Bolsheviks he's undoubtedly got a lot on his plate. Also attended some of their conferences in Moscow, I hear.'

Pavel swiveled around and smiled.

'Alexei Alexandrovich Vinokurov, I thought it might be you.'

The two men embraced. Alexei, a tall man with a large barrel-chest, stood a full head height over Pavel. He had a deep tanned outdoors face topped with a shock of unruly light brown hair streaked with grey. His clothing was that of a farm worker – a rough collarless shirt and braces holding up old woolen trousers thrust into dirty riding boots.

'You're in for the horse market, I assume?' asked Pavel.

'It's a bloody four-day ride in from the Tyumentsevsky Stud. I'd almost forgotten how far it is but I needed to get them to market. I'm getting too old for this sort of thing, but I don't have much help these days.'

'Is your son Sergei still away at the front?'

Alexei laughed. 'You should know. Sergei and your son-in-law are in the same regiment.'

'Yes of course,' answered Pavel. 'Mikhail has mentioned Sergei a few times in his letters.'

'I suppose we all have the same problem', said Alexei, 'the army conscripting most of our workers and leaving us with old men, women and children to run the place.'

'Have you brought in many horses?' asked Pavel.

'A good few – whatever the army commissars haven't stolen for a few kopeks. We were lucky with the mild winter; the mares foaled well so I'm selling the older stock before the bastards steal them as well. And how's business with you?'

Pavel wobbled his hand. 'Up and down as usual, there's not a lot of money in people's pockets, and all these people flooding in from the West can barely afford to feed themselves.'

Alexei smiled. 'But they always seem to find money to buy vodka.'

'Mostly from illegal stills, just a couple of kopeks and you can drink yourself to death.'

Alexei shook his head. 'I've seen all those drunk deserters hanging about the streets – aren't you worried?'

'We're careful, and there are places in town you just don't go alone. And after dark it's worse, but we manage. And it's not just the danger, they'll steal everything that's not tied down.'

'I'm glad I live in the country,' said Alexei, 'we're so isolated out there the troubles haven't reached us.'

'You're lucky. How long are you staying in town, would you like to join us for dinner tonight?'

Alexei shook his head. 'We're so short-handed back at the stud I need to get going as soon as the auction is finished. But that's not before I visit your store.' Alexei patted his pocket. 'My housekeeper has given me a long shopping list. I'll see you after the market.'

'More than happy to be of service,' said Pavel, doffing his hat. 'Just come before midday. Dmitry and I are riding out to the tannery this afternoon.'

Alexei looked at his watch. 'I'd better be off. The auction starts soon and those bloody horse traders from the city will be trying to get good horseflesh for nothing unless I'm there. I'll see you later at the store.'

Chapter 3

THE MOSKOVSKY PROSPEKT STORE

Monday 02 May 1917

A SMALL QUEUE WAS already forming outside the entrance to the P.D. Sukhov Store on Moskovsky Prospekt. Pavel checked his fob watch as he walked up to the main doors. It was still a few minutes before the 8 o'clock opening time. Pavel nodded to several familiar faces in the queue, excused himself, and stepped past them through the front door.

His manageress, Katrina, a tall handsome mature woman with a ramrod straight back and a stern countenance, had already organized the shop floor staff and loaded the tills from the safe. The three servers, dressed in brown serge ankle-length dresses with white, starched pinafores and matching white caps, stood in line behind the scrubbed wooden counter extending the full width of the store. Behind them were shelves of tinned goods, bulk food items in open barrels, and columns of small drawers with polished brass handles holding all types of knick-knacks and small essential items.

'Good morning,' Pavel said to Katrina. 'Looks like a busy market day. Better not keep the customers waiting any longer.'

He didn't wait for a reply but hurried up the stairs to his office at the back of the store. From this vantage point, through half-frosted glass windows, he could look out over the shop floor, while through the rear windows he could look down into the warehouse and its rows of sacks, barrels and cartons. He could see men at the loading dock sweating in the early morning sun, as they unloaded a cart stacked high with sacks of grain.

Pavel murmured a quick 'good morning' to his main bookkeeper and clerk and hung his frock coat on the coat stand. He heard the faint tinkle of the front doorbell as one of the staff unlatched and opened the main doors. He checked his fob watch again and nodded approvingly.

A samovar bubbled away on a small table in the corner of the office. The clerk was already filling a large porcelain mug of steaming tea and brought it over to Pavel's desk along with a small crucible of liquid honey and a silver spoon. In his black tea he preferred a drop of honey to sugar.

The clerk handed him his mug of tea and the newspapers.

'I collected them this morning from the station. They came in on the morning train from Novonikolayevsk.'

Pavel leafed through the broadsheets while he sat sipping his tea. He glanced briefly at one, the *Investia* and threw it aside. It was the popular organ of the Bolsheviks and full of the usual propaganda and photographs of mass demonstrations, Lenin's speeches, and meaningless banner headlines. There was little real news. The *Vecherniy* was the local Novonikolayevsk evening paper and a little more informative, if rather out of date. The photograph on the front page was of the abdicated Nicholas and family having a picnic in the grounds of the Tsarskoe Selo (Summer) Palace outside Petrograd. The photo looked somewhat dated, perhaps taken in happier times in an attempt to convey the impression that everything was well with the royals. There was no mention of the fact they were actually under house arrest.

The bulk of the stories were about the war – articles accompanied by maps with lines and arrows, and photographs of stoic Russian soldiers in trenches. Not a lot seemed to have changed, and to Pavel, the front had reached a sort of static hiatus. He scanned the long list of local casualties, but not one name jumped off the page. There was news about strikes in the major cities and photographs of banner-carrying marchers. It was all a bit depressing, but Pavel devoured every sentence. News from the west was scarce in this part of the world.

Pavel had just finished his tea and pushed aside the newspapers when Katrina appeared at the office door.

'Excuse me sir,' said Katrina, 'it's the Fire Chief. He's after more credit to buy supplies and ammunition.'

Pavel looked across to his bookkeeper, 'Is it a problem?'

The bookkeeper nodded affirmatively, and then shook her head and silently mouthed, 'No more'.

'What do you want me to say to him?' asked Katrina.

'I'll come down', answered Pavel.

The Fire Chief, a stocky robust man with a red face and large bulbous nose, was standing with his hands on his hips. He looked aggrieved and angry. 'What's the problem?' he demanded.

Pavel took him by the elbow and gently led him aside.

'It's your credit limit. You have already exceeded it and you've not paid us anything for months. We've tried to be as flexible as possible.'

'It's the Zemstvo,' said the Fire Chief, referring to the local council. 'They haven't paid me, or any of the station staff, for months. How can we survive? Don't they know we've got mouths to feed?'

'I've also got mouths to feed, and there's wages to pay,' answered Pavel.

'Look,' said the Fire Chief, lowering his voice, 'with the river in flood there have been islands formed on the higher ground.' He indicated towards the river, 'There's boar and deer trapped by the water. We're going across to hunt them. I'll share the game with you to help pay back the money.'

'How sure are you they're there?' asked Pavel.

'One of my men's cousins lives across there, he's seen them with his own eyes. Dozens are trapped on one large island, and there's more.'

'How long do you need?' asked Pavel.

'Three days, and then we'll be back.'

'I'll give you until the end of the week, and we share the game equally. Do we have an agreement?'

The Fire Chief nodded.

Pavel turned to Katrina, 'Can you show me the list please?'

The hand-written list ran over two pages.

'You've enough provisions here for a month, and ammunition that could start a small war. And why these tins of gasoline?'

'It's for my motorboat, how else am I going to get across?'

Pavel handed back the list to Katrina, 'Half the provisions and half the ammunition, but both tins of gasoline.'

He turned back to the Fire Chief, 'Do we have an agreement?'

The Fire Chief clamped Pavel's hand with both his hands and shook it vigorously. 'You're a good man, Pavel Dmitrievich. We have a deal.'

Pavel turned to walk back upstairs but hesitated.

'What about the Fire Station while you're away?'

'Only a couple of men are coming with me; the others are staying. Anyway, it's not summer yet and there's little chance of fire.'

Pavel was unsettled about the answer, however decided not to challenge him. After the Fire Chief had left he asked Katrina, 'Did we do the right thing?'

'It's a chance to get some of the debt paid down, compared to getting nothing at all. We know the Zemstvo hasn't been receiving money from the regional government. All the taxes are going to pay for the war.'

'I'm nervous about letting half the Fire Brigade disappear for days.'

'Could we have stopped that? If we hadn't supplied him, one of the other merchants would have. You would have to think the Chief must have cleared it with the Zemstvo; he reports to them after all.'

Pavel looked at Katrina, and nodded, 'Yes, of course you're right.'

Dmitry arrived at the store just after midday and tethered the two horses to the hitching post directly outside the front entrance. He considered walking into the store to deliver his father's riding boots, but when he looked at his boots covered with thick black mud from the horse paddock, he thought better of it and handed the boots through the door to one of the assistants.

There was a bench outside the store. He sat there, stretching out his legs and enjoying the sunshine. It was a busy market day with people coming and going in the street. Some of the passers-by tipped their hats to him for he was Dmitry Pavelovich, son of Pavel Sukhov.

There were many farm folk in for the market, the men with their old rough rumpled clothes, leather jerkins and baste shoes, and their women in long, embroidered dresses and often carrying babies on their hips. The married ones wore kerchiefs on their heads, and the single girls had their hair in long plaits.

A group of kerchiefed women had spread squares of cloth on the pavement to sell their meager offerings of fresh vegetables – mostly cabbages, carrots, potatoes and other winter root vegetables. But there were few customers and the women mostly squatted on their haunches behind their produce and gossiped amongst themselves.

Groups of soldiers in muddy, tattered greatcoats hovered around street corners, smoking and furtively passing bottles of vodka around. They shared the same unwashed and unshaven look, with matted, lank hair and red-rimmed eyes. Some were hoping to find work, but most to beg or steal.

The Zemstvo had been running soup kitchens for the soldiers, and some townsfolk tried to help them. But most people were afraid of the unpredictable bursts of drunken violence and gave them a wide berth.

Dmitry watched with casual interest a chattering line of young student girls from the B.F. Budkevich Girls' Gymnasium walking up Moskovsky

Prospekt from the boat station. They were being met with wolf whistles and lewd catcalls from the deserters across the street. The girls, all dressed in white blouses, blue capes, long dark blue skirts and straw boaters, were shepherded along by two elderly female tutors. Their school, with its ornate wooden structure and distinctive turret and spire, was just around the corner on Krasnoarmeysky Prospekt.

Several girls gave Dmitry sideway glances and whispered to each other behind cupped hands. One of the older girls, a tall pretty brunette with long thick plaits, gave him a shy smile and a tentative wave before giggling and hiding her face in her hands. The peasant women laughed and pointed. Dmitry blushed and stared at the ground in front of him until they had turned the corner and were out of sight.

It was a relief for Dmitry to see his father finally come out of the store. He was with another man.

'Alexei, I would like you to meet my son. This is Dmitry. Dmitry, this is Alexei Alexandrovich Vinokurov, Sergei's father. He has come in from his stud farm out at Tyumentsevsky for the horse market.'

They shook hands, formally. 'I'm very honored, sir. My brother-in-law, Mikhail Mehenov, writes to us about Sergei all the time.'

Alexei leaned back and laughed. 'Then perhaps you can ask your brother-in-law to get Sergei to write to his father? My only son, and I hardly know if he's alive.'

Alexei looked Dmitry up and down. 'And how old are you, young man?'

'Seventeen years, sir.'

'And what are your plans, follow your father into the business?'

'I want to join Mikhail and Sergei in the regiment.'

Alexei shook his head. 'So, you think fighting for Russia is a great adventure? Well, I'll tell you young man, the reality is very different.' He waved his hand towards a bunch of soldiers. 'Just ask those damned deserters over there, they would tell you. And there's this Lenin person sneaking back into the country with the help of the Germans to stir up anti-war sentiment. If his Bolshevik friends have anything to do with it, the war may be over before you get there.'

'Kerensky should have Lenin arrested', said Pavel, 'it's nothing less than treason.'

'What would Kerensky do about it?' said Alexei, 'He's just a typical windbag lawyer. He claims it's all about civil liberties and free speech. That man will do anything to appease the Bolsheviks.'

'Anyway,' said Pavel, 'we don't think Dmitry will get called up by the regiment anytime soon. He still has the limp from when the horse fell on him last year and broke his leg. We're thinking about sending him to study medicine at Tomsk University next year.'

'What, a doctor?' bellowed Alexei, 'The Sukhovs have always been merchants. I knew your grandfather, Dmitry Nikiforovitch, and his father before him when Barnaul wasn't even on the map.'

Pavel held up his hands, 'All we care about is not having another soldier in the family. Both our families have contributed more than our fair share, and they've taken most of our able workers to boot. What would we achieve by sending another into that maelstrom just when the Bolsheviks are threatening to pull Russia out?'

'But those bastards are not in power – not yet anyway. Besides, the General Staff want to keep carrying the fight to the Germans.'

'Look around you, Alexei. The rank and file of the army is already voting with their feet. Kerensky's government and the generals may want to stay in the war, but half of their soldiers are here. The Bolsheviks want to negotiate a ceasefire with the Germans, but we know what they're after – the food of Southern Russia and oil from the Caucasus. We're hardly in a position of strength and they'll rip us to shreds at the negotiating table.'

Alexei laughed. 'Didn't Napoleon once say you could never win at the negotiation table what you haven't already won on the battlefield?'

'And look what happened to him,' answered Pavel, 'the Russian winter got him. But will *General Winter* save the day for us again? I don't think so.'

Alexei waved a hand in the air, 'Enough of the damned war, but pray tell me, if Dmitry goes off to Tomsk, who will follow you into the business?'

'I've got one of my daughters, Mara, who could be interested. She's the musical one of the family, but she's outgoing and likes dealing with people.'

'And what about this Galina of yours?' asked Alexei. 'Your eldest, and still unmarried.'

'Riding and shooting,' answered Pavel. 'She's very keen on horses.'

'Now, that's the type of woman I like,' laughed Alexei. 'We could do with someone like her out on the stud, especially since Sergei's mother passed away, God bless her.'

'Look, you'll have to excuse us,' said Pavel, 'Dmitry and I are due out at the tannery.'

'If it's all right with you,' said Alexei, 'I'll accompany you some of the way. There's safety in numbers until we get past those camps on the outskirts. We'll turn off at the Pavlovsk Trakt and head west. Besides, I'm not that keen about the smell of your tannery.' Both men laughed.

Alexei mounted his horse and waved to his men with the loaded wagon to follow. Pavel and Dmitry mounted up and the group moved off at a slow walk along the west riverbank road.

Once outside the town, Alexei walked his horse up alongside Pavel's.

'You know, I'm glad I live out in the Tyumentsevsky District, there's not even a hint of problems out my way. My workers know nothing about Bolshevik politics, and we don't get many visitors. No newspapers, and, let's face it, most of them can't read anyway. If you treat them well, then they're content with their lot in life. But mark my words, you're going to have serious trouble around here.'

Pavel nodded in agreement. 'Up until now we've managed to avoid the worker riots they've had in the big cities, but it's our womenfolk I worry about. They can't go outside the house unless accompanied, and most town folk literally barricade themselves inside their houses for fear of looting and violence.'

'Look,' said Alexei, 'if there's any trouble you know there is always room at the stud. Even if you just send the women out, they would be welcome.'

'Thanks for the offer,' answered Pavel, 'but we're all right for the moment. We've had a few issues, but nothing we can't deal with.'

Alexei clapped Pavel on the shoulder, "Well, the offer's still there.' He turned in his saddle to check the progress of his wagon.

'I think you have a fire back in town,' said Alexei. 'Look over there, down by the riverbank.'

Pavel pulled on his reins and turned his horse. Rising up from the far side of town, closest to the river, a thick dark plume of smoke was spiraling skywards.

'It's probably just one of those wood-fired saunas down on the riverbank, they're always catching fire.'

'That's a damned lot of smoke for a sauna fire,' responded Alexei.

After a moment's reflection Pavel called over to Dmitry,

'Forget the tannery. Just in case they haven't seen it can you ride over to the Fire Station and raise the alarm? Then go to the house and check the women are safe. I'll ride back into town and see what's going on.'

'I'll come with you,' said Alexei. 'The wagon can go on without me. I'll catch up with them later.'

Chapter 4
THE FIRE

02 May 1917

PAVEL AND ALEXEI spurred their horses towards the spiraling black smoke. It took them fifteen minutes to reach the fire at the edge of town where a large group had gathered on the riverbank to watch the fire and more were running out from surrounding houses and shops.

Two old houses and one large warehouse along the waterfront were well alight and the fire was threatening other nearby buildings. A brisk southeasterly breeze coming across the river fanned the flames, pushing the fire in a northwesterly direction towards the heart of the town. The fire sprang from building to building at an alarming rate, the creosoted timber exteriors accelerating the spread. Swirling streams of glowing embers ignited ground fires and spread the conflagration.

It was just after noon, but the plume of acrid black smoke filled the sky, blotting out the sun and turning day into night. The thick billowing smoke, its crimson underbelly exposed, rolled across the rooftops and rained down cinders and ash over the town.

Suddenly there was a thunderous explosion and an immense fireball roared up into the sky. 'Watch out,' somebody yelled, 'it's the paint store on the docks.'

The crowd screamed and ran back as debris cascaded out of the sky. A wave of noise and pressure from the blast rolled outwards like thunder, nearly knocking Pavel from his horse. Paint cans shot skywards, then fell to earth, bursting into an explosion of flame.

Pavel's horse shied and took flight in a frenzied gallop. The crowd scattered on all sides as the horse bolted along the riverbank. Pavel leaned back in the stirrups and reined in the animal as hard as he could. The horse finally slowed to a walk. When he finally brought the horse to a halt, Pavel dismounted, and led the horse to a nearby stand of trees where he tied it to a low branch in the shade.

He ran back towards the wharf. 'Why isn't anybody doing anything?' he yelled at the group of people huddled down the embankment for protection.

'We're waiting for the Fire Brigade.' came a shouted response, 'What's taking them so long?'

'I sent someone to find out,' answered Pavel, 'but we can't wait, we need to start fighting the fire now.'

'What do you want me to do?' shouted Alexei over the roar of the flames.

'Ride to my store and get the staff to send down every bucket and empty sack they can lay their hands on. Then go around the other merchants. We'll need all the buckets we can get.'

'What about the Fire Brigade?'

Pavel gave Alexei a shake of his head, 'I haven't got time to explain.'

Alexei spurred his horse and set off in the direction of the Moskovsky Street store just as Dmitry rode up. He was panting with exertion and carried a set of large bolt cutters in one hand.

'What's taking so long?'

'I've come from the Fire Station. There's nobody there and the front doors are chained and padlocked. I got these from the shop and I'm heading back there now.'

'We need the fire tenders down here urgently,' said Pavel. 'Do you need someone to go with you?'

'No,' shouted Dmitry, as he made to ride off. 'There are already people up there helping. We broke into the fire station through a side door. I just need to cut the chain on the main doors so we can get the tenders out and we'll be here as soon as we can.'

Thousands of people crowded the riverbank with more arriving every minute. Most had run from their houses clutching hastily bundled possessions. Many crouched below the lip of the embankment to shield themselves from the heat, while others pushed their way onto the boat station wharf and the other piers.

Pavel spoke to those around him. 'I need someone to organize a line down to the river. We have buckets on the way and the fire tenders are going to be here soon.' He looked to a group of men, 'I need a volunteer.'

A burly man stepped forward and nodded and immediately started shouting at people nearby to form a line. The shortest route to the water, from the top of the embankment, was over fifty meters. A path to the water's edge was cleared, and every able-bodied man was coerced and pushed into line.

Trolley-loads of sacks were first to arrive. They were handed down the line, dunked in the river, and manhandled back up the embankment where they were used to beat out grass spot fires.

The buckets arrived and were hastily filled, then passed up for throwing on the burning walls of the houses closest to the river. It was a fearsome job for the water throwers; heads swathed in damp cloths, they ran forward as close as they dared, before casting the meager contents of their bucket at the flames. But it quickly became clear their efforts were futile and Pavel was forced to intervene. 'Let those houses burn,' he yelled, 'we can't save them now. Throw your water on the walls of the surrounding houses.'

Finally, a fire tender came into sight, hauled down the street by a group of men heaving on empty traces while others pushed from behind. The ancient fire tender consisted of a large iron tank on a bullock cart and a man-operated seesaw pump handle at one end that pumped water into an accumulator.

Dmitry rode up to Pavel. 'We couldn't get any horses, but these prisoners were on their way back to camp from the farms. The officer allowed us to use them. They're either German or Austro-Hungarian I think, but one of them seems to know what he's doing.'

Pavel looked at the men, POWs clad in an odd assortment of German uniforms. The accompanying guards had shouldered their rifles and were also helping move the cart.

A tall Russian officer with a large moustache was riding alongside the tender. He stood up in his stirrups and looked around, 'Who's in charge here?'

Pavel ran up to him, 'Thank God. We need to get the tender into operation urgently. I hope we can get it to work.'

The officer looked around. 'Schultz,' he shouted.

One man stepped forward. He was short and stout with a shaven head, an immense walrus moustache, and wearing grey German army trousers held up with braces.

'His name's Werner Schultz,' said the officer. 'He said he was a fireman in Hamburg before the war.'

The officer spoke rapidly to Werner in German, and then turned to Pavel, 'He's all yours, and the rest of them too.'

'But what about guarding them?' asked Pavel, 'I don't want to be responsible if they try to escape.'

'The guards will look after them. We're in the middle of Siberia and there's nowhere to run. Most don't want to go back to the fighting anyway.'

The officer touched the peak of his cap with his riding crop. 'I'll ride back now and send more POWs to help.'

Pavel shouted across to Dmitry, 'Is the other tender on its way?'

Dmitry shook his head, 'No, this is the only one that works. They've been taking parts off the other one to keep this one working.'

Pavel cursed. 'My father donated these and they've damn well allowed this to happen!'

The prisoners, under Werner's direction, pushed the tender into position, rolled out the hoses and connected the nozzle. Pavel rapped on the wall of the tank.

'It's only about half full. Get them to stop throwing water on the houses,' he instructed, 'and fill the tank instead.'

Four men manned the pump handles and started the seesaw action. Werner kept an eye on the pressure gauge then shouted a warning to the men holding the hose nozzle. He turned a handle, the flat hose bulged and bucked as the water snaked through it, and the hose finally emitted a jet of water.

Werner ignored the buildings that were well alight, instead directing the water onto charring walls threatening to burst into flames. Their objective was to stop the westward spread of the fire into the main part of the town but, with the wind pushing the fire front forwards at a frightening pace, this was proving increasingly difficult. The fire was already cutting a wide swathe of destruction from the riverbank through the town.

The width of Moskovsky Prospekt was proving a formidable firebreak, but the small side streets running off the avenue were little impediment to the fire's advance. Repeatedly the fire fighters, trying to make a stand in one of the side streets, had the fire leapfrog over their heads.

Supplying water to the tender was a laborious task. As the fire fighters moved further into the town and away from the river, they had switched to bringing in water by small tank carts from the nearby railway station, but the tank was drained faster than it could be filled. Many times they had to wait frustrating minutes for fresh supplies.

The fire fighters were becoming exhausted and gaps started to appear as men staggered away and collapsed. The pump-handlers stripped off their shirts and wound them around their hands to relieve the blistering. It was strenuous, backbreaking work pushing the heavy handles up and down and, every few minutes, other men had to step in to relieve them.

Pavel spotted Dmitry at the fire tender and ran over to him. 'What about your mother and the girls?'

'They're still at the house but they aren't in any danger.'

'That can change in an instant,' yelled Pavel over the roar of the fire. 'Tell them I insist they go down to the river and get them to take Uncle Vasily with them.'

The officer, true to his word, had collected more POWs from the camp to assist. They finally started making headway by letting the east part of town burn itself out while working to limit the western spread of the fire. But frustratingly, just when they had started making progress, the tender ran dry and the fire fighters were forced to watch helplessly as the fire regained momentum.

'We need more water and more people,' Pavel shouted at Werner. 'I'll run down there and see what's happening.' Werner was unsure of what Pavel said until he indicated an empty bucket and pointed to the river and then to the tender.

'*Ja*,' agreed Werner.

Pavel found both bucket lines still operating, but they were agonizingly slow, as men and women arduously passed their load from hand to hand. Full buckets were accumulating on the top of the embankment but there were only a few able-bodied people available to carry the laden buckets up into the town.

Pavel spotted Alexei in one of the lines.

'Can someone find handcarts? The tender keeps running out of water.'

'How come we're organizing all this?' asked Alexei, 'Where's the bloody Zemstvo when you need them?'

'They're in Tomsk for a meeting but the news must have got through to them on the telegraph by now.'

'And the Fire Department?' asked Alexei.

'I think I know where they may be, but let's not discuss this now. You and I are about the only ones who can keep us from a total disaster. I just want you to get me more water for the tender.'

Alexei didn't reply. He just nodded and ran off towards the market.

The buildings along the waterfront were now just smoking heaps of blackened timber and smoldering embers. Brick chimneys stood sentinel over the collapsed ruins of houses. Some of the larger brick buildings looked outwardly unscathed, but many of the interiors had burnt and their roofs had fallen in. Every space on the wharves and piers was filled with evacuees jostling for space amongst the mountains of possessions rescued from their houses. Most were reluctant to move far from their home, vainly hoping their presence might save the property. Some people would sprint back into the inferno to salvage some precious possession. Others tried to stop them, but many who ran back into their burning houses never returned.

Men staggered back from the fire front, gasping for breath, red-eyed, blackened and exhausted from the heat. Women ripped up petticoats, soaked them in the river, and bathed their faces, while others ladled out water to slake their thirst.

Pavel found Dmitry at the riverbank returning with Maria and Galina, Mara and Iya.

'You can stay here or go to the dacha,' Pavel told them. 'But whatever you do, stay together.'

'No, I'll stay and help,' said Galina and turned to Mara. 'Come on, let's get to work.'

Galina ran to the top of the embankment, slid on her bottom down the muddy bank, and took her place in one of the lines while Mara and Iya joined those handing out drinking water.

'I need to get back to help,' Pavel told Maria. 'You must look out for the girls, and when it's over, we'll meet back at the house.'

Abruptly the wind shifted, and a cloud of dense smoke, imbedded with glowing embers, rolled back over the crowded embankment. It was thick, acidic smoke that burnt people's skin and fiercely stung their eyes. The crowd panicked, pushing and shoving down the slope to the river and away from the toxic cloud. People were trampled in the rush, and those nearest the water's edge were forced into the water.

The river became full of flailing arms and bobbing heads as more were pushed into the icy water, and in seconds, the strong flood current swept them away.

'Help them,' yelled Pavel. He pushed through the crowd until he reached the water's edge. The spring melt stopped his breath as he waded in chest deep. Others waded in too, linking arms to keep from being swept away, but many were already beyond reach and rapidly disappearing downstream in the turbulent current. Some tried to swim to the shore, fighting vainly against the cold and the channel current which dragged them further out into the wide river.

Galina had stripped down to her petticoat and had also waded in. A young boy screamed as he lost his grip on an old pier and was quickly sucked underwater. Galina splashed forward and dived headlong into the water. Somehow in the murky water she found an arm and a bunch of hair and hauled the boy spluttering to the surface.

Galina kicked her way back to shore and crawled back onto the bank where she lay, panting with exhaustion, her wet bodice and petticoat plastered to her body and her teeth chattering from the cold.

Rescuers could only stay in the water for a few minutes at a time. Pavel, after helping several people ashore, was numbed to the bone and forced to climb out. He crawled, on hands and knees, back to the top of the embankment. The wind had shifted and it was now clear of smoke.

Blankets and towels were being handed out to the rescuers and survivors. People stripped off their saturated clothes, without thought of modesty, and vigorously toweled their bodies to regain circulation.

An old lady helped Pavel take off his sodden shirt while another yanked off his boots and poured a stream of muddy water onto the ground. The old lady rubbed his chest and back with a rough towel until he yelped in pain. His teeth chattered so much it was difficult to speak.

Only after Pavel had been buttoned into a dry shirt did he finally manage to reduce his shivering. He pulled off his wet socks, threw them away, and managed to slide his half-frozen feet back into his boots.

Handcarts had appeared and were being loaded with full buckets and pushed up the street. Pavel managed to stand and set off after the carts. The radiant heat from burning houses was almost welcoming as it thawed and warmed his chilled body.

Smoke was everywhere, obliterating vision entirely and then, in an instant, clearing.

Pavel almost crashed into Dmitry running down the street through the smoke. 'Did you find Uncle Vasily?' he asked him.

'He refuses to budge so I left him there,' answered Dmitry. 'But our house is gone.'

'House, do you mean Tolstoy Street?'

'The fire jumped Moskovsky Prospekt. One minute there were no fires there, and then suddenly, it was across on the other side of the street. Nobody can understand how it could have happened.'

Pavel ran up the street towards their house. When he got there he was shocked and could not believe the pile of smoldering stumps was all that remained. All the houses on the west side of the avenue were untouched by the fire except theirs.

Pavel stood, shaking his head in disbelief. He walked over to the still smoldering ruins. There was a strange smell in the air. He crouched down, picked up a piece of timber and sniffed it, then handed it to Dmitry.

'Can you smell that?' asked Pavel.

'Smells like kerosene.'

Pavel slowly stood up and brushed off his hands. 'The bastards! They first looted, then they burnt.'

Pavel took Dmitry by the elbow. 'There's nothing to do here. Go back to the river and find your mother. Get her to take the girls to the dacha – tell her I insist.'

'What will you do?' asked Dmitry.

'I will stay here until I'm no longer needed, then I'll come out to the dacha.'

The clouds of black smoke rolling over the town and masking the sun made it impossible to discern when day became night. The blackened silhouettes of the fire fighters moved like jerking marionettes in Dante's Inferno against the glow of the dancing flames.

Nobody was sure when, but the wind suddenly shifted and light rain started to fall. At first the drizzle evaporated from the heat before it reached the ground, but the rain persisted, and gradually became heavier.

The burning timbers started to spit and sizzle. Isolated fires flickered for a while and then gradually died. The larger fires remained, but they were now mostly consuming themselves and had stopped spreading.

Leaving Werner in charge Pavel staggered down Moskovsky Prospekt and, by sheer chance, stumbled on to his store. The shop was somehow untouched by the flames and in relief he collapsed against the door, slid to the ground and fell asleep.

He awoke, shivering with cold, his clothes saturated from the rain. He was so tired and aching he could not move and lay on the pavement, his mouth open, savoring the raindrops falling onto his swollen tongue and parched lips. Finally he managed to lever himself upright and set off, hobbling his way towards the river.

It was now pitch black. Most of the familiar buildings had been obliterated and many streets were blocked by fallen timbers or collapsed brick walls. It was hard to find a path through.

Groups of people appeared, and then abruptly disappeared again into the murky darkness. People were scratching around in the remains of houses, or just walking dazed through the ruins. Some were calling out for lost loved ones. Panicking animals – horses and cattle – would gallop out of the darkness, frantically trying to find a way out of the terrible maze.

Pavel felt like a blind man stumbling through the darkness, hoping his path would somehow lead to the river. Then out of the darkness a figure emerged holding up a lantern and leading a horse. 'Father, is that you?'

Chapter 5

THE AFTERMATH

03 May 1917

THE COMPOUND HOUSING three Sukhov dachas lay a few versts south of the town close to a sweeping bend in the Ob River. After Pavel's father died the dachas were little used. When the business went bankrupt Vasily withdrew to his house and Pavel had bought the stud farm. The family now had little use for the compound and the buildings had remained closed for years. They had quickly fallen into disrepair and the vegetable garden overtaken by weeds.

When Dmitry finally got his father back to the compound Maria was waiting. She helped slide him off the horse and, between the two of them, carried Pavel into one of the dachas and laid him on a hessian bed.

The girls had already taken over one of the other buildings. It was Uncle Vasily's old dacha, filthy and full of spiders, but they set about cleaning it up and managed to make it somewhat habitable.

Dmitry went off to sleep in old Grandfather Sukhov's dacha that, long ago, had been converted into a garden implement storeroom. He managed to find some empty sacks to make a bed, spread out his coat, and quickly fell asleep.

Maria sat by Pavel for most of the night, bathing his face and eyes, and feeding him water and some light food. He quickly fell asleep but dozed fitfully, waking often with a dry racking cough and a raging thirst. Gradually the coughing subsided and he fell into a deep sleep.

In the morning Maria left him still sleeping in the care of Iya and Mara, and asked Dmitry to harness the horse to the trap, and drive her and Galina into town. Where the fire had first begun there were now just piles of black smoldering rubble and the overpowering stench of wet charcoal. With the smoke now cleared, they were shocked at the extent of the destruction. 'The main shop escaped the fire,' said Dmitry, 'do you want me to take you there?'

Maria shook her head. 'I want to go to the town house.'

'But there's nothing left, nothing to see.'

'Take me there, I insist.'

Maria sat silently in the trap and stared at the ruins of their house. Dmitry was used to his mother's stoicism; there were no tears, just a set jaw and a steely gaze. After a time, she stepped down from the trap and started poking around the ashes with a stick.

'There's nothing left,' said Maria finally, 'absolutely nothing.'

'We think looters set fire to the place,' said Dmitry.

Maria turned and looked back at Dmitry. 'What do you mean looters? You didn't tell me.'

'You can still get the whiff of kerosene.' replied Dmitry, 'It's faint now, but the smell was stronger yesterday.'

Maria bent over, scooped up a handful of grey ash, and let it trickle through her fingers. She shook her head, 'Ashes to ashes; dust to dust,' she whispered to herself. She carefully brushed off her hands, and climbed back into the trap alongside Galina.

'These looters,' she asked Dmitry, 'do we know who they were?'

'We guess they came from the camps since almost everybody else was down at the river,' answered Dmitry. 'The smoke was so thick up here nobody would have seen a thing and they burnt the place to cover their tracks.'

Maria made the sign of the Cross. 'God forgive me, but those Bolshevik deserters are godless creatures. How could they do this to people, is it just that we have something they don't have? Damn all Bolsheviks to hell, and their devil incarnate Lenin with them. He is to blame for this and, if he were dead, I would spit on his grave. Never ever mention the name of Lenin in my presence again. Never!'

'Mother!' exclaimed Galina.

Pavel was up and had washed himself in the outside trough by the time Maria, Dmitry and Galina arrived back.

'How are you feeling?' asked Maria.

'Like a train hit me, but I'll be fine.'

'I had Dmitry take me to the town house.'

'Then you've seen there's nothing left.'

Maria walked over to Pavel and touched his hand. 'We are alive and have a roof over our heads – that's more than you can say for a lot of the folk.' Maria looked around the compound. 'It's not that I mind staying here, but shouldn't we move back to the farm?'

'You know I worry about the danger there. You know yourself what the people from the camps are capable of.'

'But how safe is it here? After what they did to our house, is any-where safe?'

Mara came over to join them. 'Alexei Alexandrovich rode by this morning while you were in town and Papa was still asleep.'

'That's good,' said Pavel, 'at least we know he's all right.'

'He looked very tired,' said Mara, 'and wanted to leave to catch up to his men. He said he'd gather up some things at the stud farm and send them back. He talked about canvas to make tents.'

Pavel nodded, 'Alexei's a good man.'

Pavel pulled on an old coat he kept at the dacha.

'Where are you going?' Maria asked.

'To find my horse – hopefully it's still tethered where I left it. Then I'll go to check on my stubborn old brother, and after that I'll go to the shop and make sure it hasn't been looted.'

'What about us?' Maria asked. 'Do we wait here?'

'No, take the trap and go to the farm. Dmitry can make sure you're safe. He's got his rifle, and Galina should carry one too. I'll stay at the dacha tonight and come out tomorrow, and I'll try to bring Vasily with me.'

Pavel found the horse where he had left him, still tethered to the tree and munching on a small pile of oats someone had placed on the ground.

'I thought you'd be back sometime.' There was a cackle of laughter. Pavel looked up at the set of legs and dirty bare feet dangling from the branch above him. The man dropped to the ground. He was dirt-encrusted with the last vestiges of a greatcoat hanging off his scrawny frame.

'I've had to fight off plenty of people, all wanting to steal your pretty pony.' The man held out his hand, 'Got to be worth something. I even fed and watered him.'

'Thank you, I appreciate it.' Pavel felt in his pocket for some coins.

The man spat on the ground, "Got to be worth more than that.'

Pavel pulled a couple ruble notes out of his wallet and handed them over.

'That's all you're going to get.'

Pavel rode the short distance through the debris-strewn streets to Vasily's house. It was still standing; some of the brickwork had been singed black and the wooden shutters had burnt, but the basic structure was still intact.

Vasily was slow to answer the door. Pavel had to pound on it and shout, before it finally inched open. The pale, bloated face of Vasily peered suspiciously out of the dark interior. 'Who is it?' he growled.

'Your brother,' answered Pavel, roughly pushing open the door.

Vasily was dressed in pajama trousers, a threadbare cardigan and an old pair of carpet slippers. He smelled, as the whole house smelled, of vodka, stale sweat, urine and moldy food. Open food cans, empty bottles and old newspapers were piled in every corner.

'Get yourself washed and dressed,' instructed Pavel, 'you're coming with me. Maria, Dmitry and the girls are about to leave for the farm and you can go with them. You can't stay here like this and anyway, with all the homeless people, it's going to get dangerous in town.'

'No, I won't,' answered Vasily, 'and you can't make me.'

'Look outside, half the town's burnt down and there's no electricity or water, let alone food to go around. I'm told there's more than twenty thousand homeless and they're going to come looking for somewhere to shelter. It's impossible to stay holed up in this house by yourself. If you come with us out to the farm we can look after you.'

'I'll keep the doors bolted.' Vasily picked up the twelve-gauge shotgun leaning against the wall. 'If anyone tries to get in, they'll have this to contend with.'

He shuffled across the room and opened the pantry. There were rows of tinned food crammed onto the shelves and cases of vodka stacked in the corner.

'I can last for months.'

'But this house – it's putrid. You're living like a dirty old hermit.'

Vasily shrugged his shoulders. 'It suits me. Now go away and leave me alone.'

Pavel stood outside Vasily's house and shook his head. He didn't have the time or energy to fight his brother, not today anyway, and there were more urgent matters needing his attention.

He walked his horse up the street and tethered it outside the Moskovsky shop. A long queue of people had formed in front of the store and there were shouts of 'Open up, open up.' A defiant-looking Katrina stood, arms crossed, barring the door.

'What's going on?' asked Pavel.

'They're trying to strip the shelves clean. There'll be nothing left for anyone else.'

Pavel edged past her and looked around the store. Many of the shelves were already empty and the warehouse behind, usually stacked high with rows of bags of flour and grain, was just half full.

Two shop assistants who had made it to work were standing behind the counter, looking terrified. They had pulled down the blinds over the front windows in the hope it would shield them from attack.

'Unlock the rifle cabinets and get out some rifles plus boxes of ammunition,' Pavel instructed one of the staff members. 'Then get two men from the warehouse, one to guard the front door, and one the warehouse. Give them a rifle each, and I'll take one too.'

Pavel opened the front door and walked out on to the street carrying his rifle in the crook of his arm. Katrina was still there, blocking people from entering the store. 'Go back inside,' he told her, 'and get the staff ready. We're going to ration four cans of food for each person, half a kilo of flour and the same for salt and sugar. And tell them to raise the blinds. I want this to be fair and open.'

'What about the pricing?' asked Katrina?

'Normal prices', answered Pavel, 'but cash only and no credit without my authority. We'll only allow in six at a time. Deal with them quickly, and then admit another six.'

Pavel walked slowly down the line of people and explained the rationing process. The shouting and abuse died down and there were nods of agreement. An old woman grabbed hold of Pavel's arm.

'I've shopped at your store for years, why should I have to wait in line with everyone else?'

'Because the other stores have burnt down and we can't just look after our customers, we have to try to look after everyone.'

The first customers had filed past the guard and Pavel went back into the store and took Katrina aside. 'Do we know if the telegraph is working? We need more stock urgently.'

'I've already sent the clerk up to the Railway Station to check and we're preparing an order now. But the bank is closed so I'm not sure how we can transfer money to the suppliers.'

'Leave that to me,' replied Pavel.

Pavel spent the next few hours sorting out the re-ordering and then rode up to the telegraph office at the railway station. He found the telegraph line through to Novonikolayevsk was still working but the station was crowded with people, spilling out of the waiting rooms and onto the roadway. Refugees, desperate to flee the big cities just months before, were now clamoring to get back on trains and away from the burnt-out town.

Pavel had to elbow his way into the station building to get to the telegraph office. The ticker-tape machine was busy clattering away as news of the disaster went out over the wire and pledges of assistance trickled in from other towns in the region. The Government and the big cities in the west were not so forthcoming, but their Siberian compatriots on this side of the Urals were scraping together whatever meager support they could muster. Shipments of clothing, canvas and other aid from Novonikolayevsk, Irkutsk and the Regional Government in Tomsk were being arranged, and the Barnaul Zemstvo members were urgently trying to make it back from Tomsk.

Pavel had to wait an hour before he finally managed get his order out, but only after slipping the clerk a few rubles. He could only hope his suppliers were able to get it onto a train.

He left the station and rode through what was left of the town. The magnitude of the catastrophe was staggering. Block after block of houses, shops and warehouses had been razed. Pavel estimated nearly one-third of the town was in ruins.

People who had lost their houses crowded into whatever structures still remained intact – halls, churches, old warehouses, and the few homes that had escaped the devastation. Groups of people were scratching through the still-warm ruins, scavenging any materials they could get. Shantytowns made of roofing-iron, pieces of canvas, charred timber, and cardboard were being hastily erected.

The aid shipments, if they did arrive, would barely touch the issue of food and shelter. With the war and the scarcity of funds, there would be little money available to rebuild the town, let alone feed it. Pavel doubted the Zemstvo Council and Tsaplin's Bolsheviks would want to work together. The tussle for control between the landowner-dominated Zemstvo and the people's Soviet could only make matters worse, and Pavel feared that, without an effective police force or army to maintain control, security in the town could easily degenerate into armed conflict.

When Pavel finally made it back to the store at dusk, a "closed" sign had been hung on the door and the blinds pulled down. Katrina let Pavel in and showed him around. The shelves were all empty and the warehouse only contained a few sacks of flour, potatoes, and pumpkins.

'We kept them for the soup kitchens,' she explained.

'That won't go far,' replied Pavel, 'but at least I managed to get an order through. Let's pray it gets here quickly.'

Pavel wearily climbed the steps to the office and slumped into his chair. From the bottom drawer of his desk he pulled out a bottle of vodka and two shot glasses.

'Here,' he said to Katrina, 'have one of these. It's been a long day for both of us.'

Just as they tipped their glasses, there came the sound of banging on the front door and shouts of men's voices calling, 'Open up.'

'Don't they realize we've got nothing left to sell. I'll go,' volunteered Katrina.

'No, it's too dangerous,' said Pavel, levering himself out of his chair and picking up his rifle. 'You stay here.'

The front door handle was being twisted and the knocking was insistent.

'Go away, we're closed,' shouted Pavel through the door.

'It's Matvei Tsaplin, and I demand you let us in.'

'You don't demand anything at this time of night,' answered Pavel.

'I'm representing the Barnaul Soviet,' came the reply. 'We need to talk.'

Pavel unlocked the door, opened it slightly, and pointed his rifle through the gap. He could make out Tsaplin with three large men standing alongside him.

'There's no need for that,' said Tsaplin, taking a step back.

'I'm here alone, save for my manageress. If you want to talk, then come in alone, or not at all.'

Tsaplin looked around at his companions and nodded. He took a step towards the door. 'All right.'

Pavel relocked the door behind Tsaplin and kept his rifle ready. The Bolshevik looked disheveled, not his usual dapper self, and seemed agitated.

'What can I do for you, Mr. Tsaplin. It's already late, and we're closed.'

'I'm here on behalf of the People's Soviet of Barnaul.' Tsaplin said, drawing himself up, and then pausing, as though waiting for the weight of his words to take effect. 'The Soviet is very concerned.'

'We all are,' answered Pavel, 'but what's this got to do with me? Shouldn't you be talking to the Zemstvo about this?'

'The Zemstvo only represents the landowners and merchants, and they'll always look after their own. It has no legitimacy in our view; only the Soviet looks after the interests of the ordinary person.'

Pavel shook his head. 'I'm sure they'll do their best in very trying circumstances, but I'm no longer on the council, so why are you telling me this?'

'Profiteering,' Tsaplin spat the word out, 'You merchants are taking advantage of the situation.'

Pavel flushed with anger. 'Look around you Mr. Tsaplin. See the empty shelves. Ordinary town folk lined up this morning and bought everything we had. We had to ration to prevent hoarding, and we distributed it as evenly as we could, and at normal prices. Do you call that profiteering? Don't ever accuse me of that.'

'There's a far more serious accusation,' said Tsaplin, ignoring Pavel's response. 'They say you funded the Fire Chief's hunting expedition, which is why the whole department was away when the town burnt.'

'The Fire Department works for the Zemstvo, not for me,' bristled Pavel. 'I'm in no position to authorize any of their actions. You need to ask the Fire Chief, not me. Their absence is unacceptable, as was the pitiful state of the fire equipment.'

Tsaplin held up his hands, 'I suggest these are very serious allegations and we will be forming a committee to look into these matters. I'm just giving you the courtesy of letting you know.'

'Under whose authority?' Pavel bristled. 'The Zemstvo Council is the only one I will answer to, so let people with these false allegations go to them. Meanwhile, I would suggest that, rather than searching for scapegoats, the Barnaul Soviet should work with the Zemstvo to help these poor ordinary people who are now hungry and homeless. It's what the rest of us are doing. Now, if you don't mind, you need to excuse me.'

'We'll leave it at that for tonight, but I warn you Sukhov, you have questions to answer before the people'.

Pavel made it back to the dacha well after dark. He had first walked with Katrina to see her safely home. It was still dangerous with the electric streetlights out and the streets strewn with debris. Even in the dark, groups of men and women were still about, holding lanterns and picking over the ruins.

Once at the dacha he fumbled for matches and managed to get the hurricane lamp going. Maria had left some sausage and bread out on the table for him. Though he had hardly eaten all day, he had lost his appetite for food. He found a bottle of beer and was sitting at the table nursing it, still thinking about his encounter with Tsaplin, when there was tapping on the window.

Pavel grabbed his rifle and stood by the door. 'Who is it?' he demanded.

'It's me,' came the whispered reply, 'quick, let me in.'

Pavel recognized the voice and unlatched the door. The Fire Chief, dragging a venison hindquarter, staggered through the door and hefted the leg, still dripping with blood, onto the table.

'What the hell are you doing here?' hissed Pavel.

The Fire Chief, panting with exertion, collapsed into a chair.

'We got here as quickly as we could. We saw the smoke, but the flood kept sweeping us downstream. We've only just managed to get back.'

'It probably would be better if you'd never made it.'

'Is it as bad as that?' asked the Fire Chief.

'Worse,' answered Pavel. 'Most of the town is burnt to the stumps, hundreds of people are dead, and those surviving have nothing left. You bloody lied to me and took all your men away, you probably never asked permission from the Zemstvo, and your equipment was in an appalling state. The Soviet, if not the Zemstvo, is going to be after your head. You need to realize that if you ever show your face in town you're a dead man.'

The Fire Chief held his head in his hands.

'It's not my fault; it's the Zemstvo who pushed me to do this. They never paid us.'

Pavel sat back in his chair and drummed his fingers on the table while the Fire Chief sobbed. He looked a pathetic figure.

'I should be turning you in, but I'll give you this one chance. And it's not just because you've implicated me in this horrible mess.'

'How could that be?' the Fire Chief asked.

'Because they've found out I supplied your expedition and could easily string me up as well. The Bolsheviks will have little mercy for the likes of you.'

'So, what do you suggest?' asked the Fire Chief.

'You need to get the hell out of town tonight. Get as far away from here as you can, somewhere where they don't know you.'

'But, my wife, my house?'

'I don't care, stay here and die then. She will make a fine widow.'

'And my men?'

'The same with all of them,' answered Pavel, 'If they're caught, they'll be strung up.'

'What will you do?' the Fire Chief asked.

'I'll stay and defend myself before God and the Zemstvo. The Bolsheviks don't care for the rule of law, however, I'll take my chances. But for you, your position is indefensible, I'm afraid.'

The Fire Chief slowly levered himself out of the chair and walked towards the door.

'And there's one more thing,' said Pavel. 'This discussion tonight never took place. If you're caught, I expect your silence – it's the very least you owe me. Now, get the hell out of here and take that damned meat with you.'

Chapter 6

THE GUILD MEETING

June 1917

PAVEL SWITCHED OFF the lights, stepped out of the side entrance of his Moskovsky store, and quietly locked the door behind him. He stood still for a moment in the dark shadows of the side alley to check if anyone had seen him. There was nobody in the narrow alley, just some over-flowing rubbish bins stacked against the brick wall, and the stench of rotting vegetables and cat urine. He was convinced the few people hurrying past the top of the alley under the electric streetlights of the main street would not be able to see him.

The evening was fine, with clear skies and a waxing moon. The town was deathly quiet, with most of the inhabitants preferring to be off the streets well before dark. Apart from the sound of receding footsteps on the cobblestoned street, all he could hear was drunken laughter coming from one of the camps down near the river.

Pavel turned up the collar of his old dark overcoat and pulled on his peaked workman's cap. He was dressed as a wharf laborer, in a pair of rough wool trousers with rolled-up cuffs and old scuffed boots.

He picked his way carefully past the rubbish to the end of the alley where a wooden slat fence blocked the way. He had removed most of the nails the day before and easily swung two of the planks aside.

Squeezing himself through the gap, he set off over a narrow stretch of vacant land, crossed a narrow cobble-stoned street, and ducked quickly into another alley leading down towards the canal through the burnt-out area of the town.

Already weeds were sprouting everywhere through the piles of charred timber and bricks. The light was fading quickly but he dared not use a torch, and had to pick his way through the rubble, one careful step at a time. The path through the wasteland avoided the main thoroughfares and the chance of being recognized. Nobody ventured into this section of town at night, except for roaming packs of dogs picking over the heaps of rubbish. Pavel kept a lookout for them, afraid their barking would bring unwanted attention.

Finally he reached the western edge of the wasteland where the fire had been halted and the riverbank warehouses remained intact. Here Pavel paused. New shantytowns had sprung up next to this fire-razed area, and there would be people moving about. This was a Bolshevik part of town and there would be armed Bolshevik militia roaming the streets. While having no official authority, they would often randomly stop people on the street and arrest anyone who they considered was not one of their own. Ordinary townsfolk, inadvertently straying into the wrong part of town, were often never seen again, or their bodies found dumped in the wasteland or floating down the river.

Pavel tugged his cap down over his eyes, took a deep breath, and stepped out along the street. He walked unhurriedly, and the people who passed gave him scarcely a second glance in his workman's clothes. Most of them avoided making eye contact and hurried on by.

He would cross the street and hug the shadows of the buildings to avoid the groups of people huddled around makeshift braziers. Warehouse men and barge loaders had finished for the day and makeshift bars serving vodka, beer and *samogon* moonshine were over-flowing with drunken revelers.

There were child beggars about and once, when he was passing an alley, a young girl whistled softly to him and opened her coat. Pavel glimpsed her naked, emaciated frame with a distended stomach and tiny, pubescent breasts. Disturbed by the sight, he quickly shook his head and hurried on. He thought for a moment about going back and giving her some rubles and telling her to go home, but he dared not.

Pavel cursed to himself about the meeting's location. It was a dangerous journey to cross into Bolshevik territory. A farmhouse location had been considered, but most were even more afraid of travelling through the countryside after dark. Bolshevik checkpoints were at all the main town entrances and bridges, so getting out of town was as hard as getting back in again.

Instead the Merchants' Guild had chosen the old silver smelting plant down on the Barnaulka Canal, some distance away from where it joined the Ob. The smelter's tall wire mesh fence and padlocked gates had kept out the squatters and would help provide security for the meeting. The smelter had closed in 1893 when the lode of silver ore in the nearby Altai Mountains was depleted. The large brick buildings, still technically the property of the Tsar, now stood empty and near derelict. An ancient caretaker, along with his two ferocious Rottweilers, lived on the site and scared off would-be intruders.

The Barnaulka Canal cut through a bend in the main river and formed an island. The only access to the smelter was via a narrow rusting iron bridge, and this was inside the fence.

Pavel measured out ten large steps to the left of the main padlocked gate. Here the wire mesh had been cut and bent back to leave a small gap. He was ten minutes early so he stood in the shadow of a nearby old oak tree and watched and waited. There was no sign of the dogs – he had been told they would be leashed and muzzled for the night. Pavel could smell the mud of the canal and hear lapping water sloshing around under the loading piers where the ore barges used to berth.

In the still evening air, he heard the sound of boots on cobblestones as a squad of militia came down the road just off to his right. He drew back into the deep shadow of the tree, but they kept on marching and gradually faded into the distance, heading south along the riverbank.

Pavel was just about to move when a lone, dark figure appeared hurrying down the lane towards the fence line. He wore a long black coat with his face hidden under a wide brimmed fedora hat. The man quickly pulled back the wire mesh and, holding onto his fedora, ducked through the gap and ran the short distance over the bridge to the factory door. He rapped quietly on the door. It was quickly swung open from the inside, and the man stepped through the opening.

Pavel made one last check in all directions and slid through the gap in the fence. He was careful crossing the bridge, mindful not to raise a clatter on the old iron structure, and hurried towards the door. After just one rap it was swung back and a hand extended out of the dark interior, urgently beckoning him inside.

'Quick, go straight ahead, down to the office at the far end.'

Pavel could not see the person who had spoken, but hurried straight on as directed. He picked his way through the gloom of the factory's central isle, past lines of rusting, disused machinery, towards the faint lights of the offices at the end. Armed men stood back in the shadows of the walls along the way.

The windows of the offices had been covered with newspapers so the occupants appeared as fuzzy silhouettes, and Pavel could only just make out the sound of muffled conversations.

A tall, broad-shouldered man in a grey suit blocked the entrance to the office. Holding a revolver in one hand, he stepped forward and used his free hand to frisk Pavel. He took the old service revolver from the pocket of Pavel's coat and placed it on a table already covered with an assortment of weapons.

'You can go in now, sir. Pick it up after the meeting.'

The old factory canteen, walls stained yellow by years of tobacco smoke and smelling of decades of sweat and boiled cabbage, was crammed with merchants and other businessmen. People were standing around in small groups at the back of the room, conversing in hushed tones and smoking. A veil of blue cigarette smoke hung suspended in the room.

Lines of chairs had been placed facing a wooden trestle table draped with the Russian Imperial flag and the flag of Siberia. Three men in grey suits sat behind the table, their chairs clustered together, as they huddled in conversation. Above them, slightly askew, was a framed photograph of the Tsar and Tsarina hanging from a nail in the wall.

One of the men behind the table looked up and acknowledged Pavel. He leaned over and tapped an empty glass with his pen.

'Gentlemen, I think we're all here now. Please take your seats so we can start.'

Pavel unbuttoned his coat, took a seat close to the door, and looked about the room. There were several faces he recognized – two fellow ex-Zemstvo members from past councils as well as a small number of landowners, but most of the attendees were members of the Merchant Guild whom he knew well. However he could not see any Jewish shop-owners from the *shtetl*, which both surprised and aggravated him. He did a quick mental count – probably about twenty people.

There was one man standing apart from the others who seemed oddly out of place. It was something about his clothes – a tweed jacket with one empty sleeve folded back and pinned. A livid red scar ran down his forehead and across the cheek of his rugged, chiseled face, his jet-black hair heavily oiled and combed straight back in the modern European style. He stood against one of the walls quietly surveying the room.

The chair behind Pavel scraped and a hand clamped on his shoulder. 'Pavel Dmitrievich, it's good to see you back at one of our meetings.'

Pavel looked around, grinned, and extended his hand back over his shoulder.

'It's good to see you again, Nikifor Trifonovich; I just wish it were in better circumstances. The Guild Committee put aside their rules and invited me, and others. This is not just about the Guild, these are strange times we live in.'

One of the men behind the table stood. 'Gentlemen, we need to get started, but first, the Royal toast. Please take a glass, and all stand.'

The grey-suited man from the door had been moving around the room with a large tray handing out shot glasses of vodka.

'Gentlemen', the Chairman turned towards the photograph, 'to the Tsar and Tsarina of All Russia, may Our Lord protect them and deliver them to safety.' There was a chorused 'Amen' and then a clatter of seats as everyone sat.

'A few points of order before we proceed,' said the Chairman, 'we need to keep this meeting orderly. There can be no raised voices or disruptive behavior since it may draw unwanted attention. Secondly, when it is time to leave, we need to do so in an orderly fashion. The guards outside will give you instructions.'

The Chairman coughed into his fist and continued. 'And finally, we welcome some guests to our Guild Meeting tonight.' He nodded towards the man seated at the table on his right. 'We have a friend and member from our fellow Petrograd Guild who brings us news from Petrograd and the front.' The Chairman waited for the murmuring to die down. 'And we welcome some of our local land-owners who have made the trip into town, and many of you know that Pavel Dmitrievich Sukhov, while no longer a Guild member, has been invited by the Committee. We hope all our guests will contribute to this important discussion.' There was an audible rumble of, 'Hear, hear.'

'And, last but not least, we are honored to have a military observer from our trusted British ally, Captain Spencer. I'm not sure if it's his real name but, I warn you, he speaks fluent Russian, so mind what you say.'

There was a smattering of laughter, and the scar-faced man with one arm smiled and gave a small bow.

'And where is the Zemstvo Council?' asked someone from the back of the room. 'I see past members, but no-one from the current council.'

'The Zemstvo has sent their apology,' answered the Chairman. 'They are all under close surveillance by the Bolsheviks. Their attendance would have jeopardized the safety of this meeting, and we all have taken enough risks to get here.'

The Chairman waited a moment for the conversation to die down, and then introduced the man from Petrograd. There was muted applause as he rose to speak. He was a small balding man, with a puffed-out chest, full of self-importance, and tending towards the melodramatic. He waved a sheaf of papers in the air. 'Guild Merchants of Barnaul, I bring great news.' He paused to look around the room. 'Two days ago, the offensive by our army, ably led by our Commander-in-Chief Aleksei Brusilov, began. Preceded by an enormous artillery bombardment, he launched two attacks – one in the south in Galicia against the Austro-Hungarians, and one in the north against the Germans. The defection of some Czech units fighting for the enemy created a huge gap in their line and the Russian Army has stormed through. They've captured thousands of prisoners and many guns, plus we have gained a significant amount of territory. As I speak, the enemy is being pushed back on all fronts. Complete victory is in sight!'

Those present had risen from their seats almost as one. Some were backslapping and embracing each other, and a few were wiping tears from their eyes. One man, shaking a victorious fist in the air, shouted out, 'Go and tell that to Lenin and his comrades who want us to capitulate to the Germans.'

The Chairman jumped to his feet and held up his arms, 'Gentlemen, please keep your celebrations subdued.'

Pavel had risen too, but quietly declined to join in the excesses of the celebration. Neither, he noticed, had the British observer who remained nonchalantly leaning against the wall and quietly observing the meeting's reaction.

The Chairman had trouble calling the meeting back to order.

'Gentlemen, there's nothing further that we can add to this piece of momentous news, so we should quickly move on. We have many important issues to discuss tonight.'

One of the landowners, a large rotund man with tufts of hair protruding from his ears, stood and looked around the room. He nodded to the Chairman. "If I may?'

The Chairman waved him to go on.

'Thank you for allowing non-Guild members to attend, and it is truly splendid to hear such momentous news, but it's our own security we are most concerned about, and that will not go away with what's happening on the front. Our families and our properties are under threat out in the country, as you are in the town. In fact, you could argue we are in more danger because of our isolation. Many of us have experienced attacks on our properties, our persons, as well as the theft and killing of our livestock. We ask what has happened to law and order, and who is responsible? We have no functioning police force, the Army is away fighting in the West, the Zemstvo seem impotent, and the only visible force are the self-appointed Bolshevik militias which seem to be aiding and abetting this anarchy. What are we to do?'

There was audible support from the other landowners in the room.

The Chairman rose to his feet. 'We have a proposal from Mr. Sukhov,' he waved his hand towards Pavel, 'to form a civilian militia for this very purpose.'

'But that would be like a declaration of war against the Bolsheviks. It could only make the situation worse.'

Pavel swiveled around. He recognized a merchant from the east side of town, a small thin-faced man with a shaven head. 'We would have two opposing armed groups patrolling our streets and that can only lead to bloodshed. Besides, their militia is largely made up of deserters, and that means they are trained soldiers. What hope would an untrained civilian militia have?'

'What hope do we have if we do nothing?' someone else asked.

'You heard our friend from Petrograd', continued the merchant, 'we are on the threshold of a great victory. The people will renounce the Bolshevik call to withdraw from the war. They'll lose support and their cause will collapse. We only have to wait.'

'What if we don't win this victory,' asked Pavel, 'or it takes much longer to achieve? Do we sit back and wait, while every day our lives are threatened?'

'And what about those of us in the country?' asked the landowner spokesman. 'What's a town militia going to do to protect us?'

The debate proceeded back and forth between those wanting to do nothing and wait, and those wanting to form a militia. The vexed question about the countryside seemed to get lost as the arguments ebbed and flowed. An exasperated landowner shrugged and raised his hands in the air. 'It looks like we're being left to fend for ourselves.'

But even within the two opposing groups there was dissension about the best path forward.

'That is the problem with these sorts of meetings,' Pavel said out of the side of his mouth to Nikifor, 'the easiest decision will always be no decision.'

The meeting turned even more acrimonious when Pavel suggested they should involve the Jewish merchants.

'We're facing one of the greatest threats to our survival,' he said to the meeting, 'and here we are, bickering amongst ourselves. We all need to work together, and that includes the Jewish shop-owners.'

'The Jews are all Bolsheviks,' came a retort from the back of the room. 'You just have to look at their leaders.'

'We've only heard rumors about Lenin, though we understand Trotsky is a Jew. But I ask you, does that make all Jews Bolshevik, or all Bolsheviks Jews?'

Nikifor stood and raised his hand to gain notice of the Chairman.

'Gentlemen,' he said, addressing the meeting, 'it seems we are get-ting nowhere. Perhaps we should ask our *anglais* observer what we should do?'

Captain Spencer straightened himself and looked at the Chairman. He gave the Chairman an almost imperceptible shake of the head. He was clearly hesitant, but finally felt compelled to speak.

'I am here as a guest of this meeting,' he said, 'not as a military adviser and my government has no wish to take sides in local politics. That aside, we are delighted to hear of the Russian Army's offensive against our common enemy and commend you all to continue your support of Mr. Kerensky's government and your armed forces.'

'Then what happens if the offensive fails and Kerensky's Government collapses, whose side will you be on then?' someone asked.

'I cannot answer hypothetical questions.'

'Will you help arm and train us?' asked Nikifor. 'After all, it is the Bolsheviks who want to pull Russia out of the war and leave the Allies fighting alone. We would have thought to have a strong opposition to the Bolsheviks would be in your best interests.'

Captain Spencer shook his head. 'I am sorry, I have no authority in this matter.'

There was a degree of exasperation among the audience, and many threw up their hands in disgust.

'But at least,' suggested Pavel, 'you may take our request to your superiors.'

The captain looked at Pavel. 'That I will.'

The big man in the grey suit had come back into the room and was whispering something to the Chairman.

'Gentlemen, gentlemen,' the Chairman shouted for order, 'it seems our meeting has brought unwelcome attention. There is a group of armed men at the gate demanding access. The caretaker is holding them off with the dogs, but we all must leave immediately.'

The room fell silent, and there was a rush of people grabbing coats and making for the door. Outside the big man in the grey suit was handing back weapons. 'You may need this', he told Pavel.

Pavel hurried back down the central factory isle. Just before he reached the outside door someone grabbed him by the elbow.

'We need to talk, but let's get out of here first.'

Pavel spun around. He had not noticed Captain Spencer follow him out of the meeting room.

'It's too dangerous to go out through the fence,' whispered the captain. 'Quick, this way.'

Captain Spencer led him to the far end of the island.

'Down here, we have a boat.'

Pavel slid, feet first, down the embankment. A pair of strong hands grabbed him out of the darkness and unceremoniously lifted him over the gunwale into the wooden cutter. There were muffled curses in English as British soldiers appeared out of the darkness and crammed onto the cutter.

'Are we all here?' asked the captain.

Oars pushed the cutter away from the bank. It slid silently out of the canal and into the current of the Ob River.

'We'll drop you off down river once it is safe,' Captain Spencer whispered to Pavel.

They did not start the cutter's engine, just letting the current take them, and the helmsman intuitively steered them into the blackness as the flow took them into mid-stream and away from the bank.

The distant sounds of shouting and barking dogs reached them, then a burst of rifle fire, and then silence.

Captain Spencer leaned over to Pavel. "I don't think things will have ended well back there, and I wanted to talk to you anyway. It's a pity the meeting turned out the way it did, but I'm not surprised. There are too many factions and too many agendas. You should find a few like-minded people you can trust and just work with them. A small, close-knit cell is much more effective, and secure. There's something I would like you to do for me. It's not a lot, but it's important.'

Pavel nodded and Captain Spencer continued.

'I would like to get reports about things that are happening in the town and the region. Not just about what the Bolsheviks are up to, but the other political factions too. How the town is faring, what folk are thinking, you know the sort of thing, rumor and gossip, no matter how trivial — any information to help us know what's happening around here. Will you do this for me?'

'Of course,' replied Pavel, 'but how will I get these reports to you?'

'We will give you instructions, but please understand, it's not without its risks.'

Captain Spencer whispered to the helmsman. 'Head to the bank over there before we get too close to the rail bridge.'

The cutter nudged silently into the reeds. The oarsmen held the cutter steady while Pavel jumped onto the bank as Captain Spencer raised a hand in silent farewell.

Chapter 7

THE SOUTH
WESTERN FRONT

July 1917

SERGEI VINOKUROV HAD learned from his father Alexei to be resourceful at the stud farm, and rather than buy new, always look to use what was around them. He had found a couple of old chairs and a dilapidated table in the shelled-out house and dragged them out into what remained of the courtyard.

It was still hot even though the sun was well past its zenith. He draped his khaki jacket over the back of the chair, took off his forage cap, and ran a dirty hand through his swept-back blond hair.

Mikhail Mehenov pulled up the other chair and sat facing Sergei across the table. In contrast to Sergei, he had a dark, swarthy complexion with lank, black hair and several days' growth of beard. His eyes were hooded with heavy bags, a consequence of the lack of sleep over many weeks of the campaign. While Sergei was short and lean,

Mikhail was tall and robust with large forearms and hands. Both were in their late twenties, but the war and the weight of command had aged Mikhail more than Sergei, who still retained traces of buoyant youth.

Sergei unwrapped the chess pieces from the oily rag he kept in his jacket pocket. Mikhail touched one of Sergei's clenched fists, took the white queen, and busied himself with setting up his side on the chessboard.

'Lucky bastard,' Sergei sighed, 'that's three in a row.'

'Luck's got nothing to do with it. Mathematical probability gives you the same chance as me.'

Mikhail leaned forward and pushed the white king's pawn forward two places.

'The King's Gambit – is that the only opening you know?' asked Sergei.

Mikhail smiled as he sat back. 'And of course you're going to do something different.'

'Have you heard from your family lately?' asked Sergei, as he mirrored the move with his own king's pawn.

He knew Mikhail had picked up a wad of mail when the weekly delivery came up to the front yesterday. Mikhail pulled a sheaf of folded paper out of his blouse top pocket. 'The usual wife stuff,' he said.

'Iya must write every day,' said Sergei, 'and I get nothing.'

'Not true,' responded Mikhail, 'your father writes to you, and even Galina does occasionally. Iya has always been the writer in the family. You just have to accept her sister is different.'

'So, are they all out on the farm?' asked Sergei.

'Everyone except for Pavel Dmitrievich; the stubborn old bugger refused to close the shop after the fire and stays at the dacha during the week. Iya says her mother is worried sick they'll do something to him. Apparently the shop's window had bricks thrown through it so many times he's had to board it up.'

'It makes you question what we're doing fighting the Germans when all this crap is going on at home,' commented Sergei.

Mikhail moved his knight forward. 'You'd be hard pressed to find anyone who doesn't want to get out of this bloody war. Most of the regiment would prefer to be at home bringing in the harvest.'

'So is Galina all right?' asked Sergei.

'Iya says all the family is fine, so I guess so. Maybe you should write to her yourself one day. If you scribble something out I'll send it with my next letter.'

'Have you finished the inspection?' asked Sergei, as he moved his black queen's pawn two places forward. 'It was your turn tonight.'

'Yes, it's done. They're all tired and hungry with the usual grumblings. But we're down to four cartridges per man for those who have rifles, and that's maybe just two-thirds of the battalion. Still, they can pick up a rifle when a man goes down. They all know the drill by now.'

'What's happened with the re-supply?' asked Sergei. 'We started out well equipped, and now we're trying to defend with our bare hands.'

Mikhail shrugged as he moved out his white knight.

'They're trying to blame it on over-extended supply lines, but I can't see how, since we've been pushed back almost to where we started.'

'And I always thought Vasily Alekseyev was a damned good Chief of Staff and worked hard to look after the men.'

'I heard from a *Stavka* officer Kerensky pushed him aside for Brusilov so he could have an Army Commander who wouldn't argue against him about this disaster of an offensive.'

'Don't talk to me about the *Stavka*,' laughed Sergei, referring to the General Staff Headquarters at Mogilev, 'overflowing with St. Petersburg nobility who worry more about whether they are having caviar for lunch or if the Chablis is sufficiently chilled.'

Mikhail snorted. 'They say Brusilov is so preoccupied with appeasing all the various political factions he doesn't have time to run a war. He's trying to walk a fine line between what the Tsar wants, what Kerensky is telling him to do, and the demands of the Officer's Union, besides debating with all these soldier Soviets. Even the Bolsheviks get his ear; he's trying to be all things to all people and, in the meantime, the Germans are kicking us to death.'

'Now Kerensky's last roll of the dice has failed,' asked Sergei, 'what do you reckon is going to happen to his Provisional Government?'

'Kerensky must be in a very vulnerable political position. The failure of the offensive can only increase support for the Bolsheviks' demand for a peace settlement. Lenin only has to give the government one small shove and the whole house of cards could tumble down.'

Mikhail paused, and then quickly moved another piece. 'We should get on with this before the light fades.'

The sound of a rifle shot came from over on their left, and then other rifle shots were heard up and down the line. Most were distant, but a few were disconcertingly close.

Mikhail listened intently, trying to work out the location and intensity of the fighting. 'It sounds like their patrols are out probing our lines. I hope our men aren't wasting ammo.'

'I'll go and check,' said Sergei, reaching for his forage cap.

'Sit down and make a move. The sergeant will come and tell us if we're in any trouble. If it's still the Austro-Hungarians then I'm not worried, but they've been shifting German reserve divisions back from France to shore up this front. We shove the Austrians back, they bring in German shock troops, and then it's our turn to get pounded and pushed back.'

'How many times have we fought over this pile of rubble?' asked Sergei.

Mikhail looked around at the fallen bricks and debris of what was left of Ternopol – everything was in ruins.

'By my count I think it's the third time we've won it back. At least someone's finally buried the stack of rotting corpses in the town square. Probably the Germans, last time they overran the place; they're good at that sort of thing. Now, it's your move again.'

Sergei pondered for a time over the board, then moved a knight forward. 'One, two, and one across; there you go, counter that.'

He sat back and pulled a tobacco tin from his pocket as Mikhail contemplated his move. 'Want one?'

Mikhail waved the tin away. 'Don't try to distract me.'

A sudden loud fusillade of rifle shots came from just a few houses away. Mikhail and Sergei both involuntarily ducked, but the shots were not directed towards them.

'Bloody hell, that was close,' said Sergei. 'We should go and find out what's happening.'

He quickly scooped the chess pieces into the rag and stuffed them in his pocket.

'I reckon I'd have won anyway.'

Before Mikhail could respond, the familiar figure of the regiment's Master Sergeant came into view, making his way carefully through the shelled-out buildings towards them.

'Come forward, *Podpraporshchik*.' Mikhail waved a hand in his direction. 'We heard the rifle fire. Is there trouble?'

The Master Sergeant, ever mindful of snipers, moved in a crouching run, never standing tall and never running in a straight line. He held his rifle at trail and was dragging a stuffed sack with his free hand.

He pulled up short of them by several metres and cautiously raised himself upright. The Master Sergeant was a mountain of a man, standing over six feet tall with a huge nicotine-stained walrus moustache. Years of endless military campaigns weighed heavily on his face, giving him a perpetual look of weariness.

'Permission to speak, your honor.'

'Just stand-easy and tell us what's the problem.'

The Master Sergeant hesitated and shifted nervously from foot to foot. 'It's the men, sir. Up and down the line our troops are pulling back and they want to pull back too. They've asked me to come and talk to you.'

'Look, Master Sergeant,' said Mikhail, 'we've been assigned this sector to hold, and we'll bloody well hold the place until told otherwise. Has any message come through from Mogilev to say we should abandon Ternopol?'

The Master Sergeant shook his head.

'What the other units are doing, I've no idea,' continued Mikhail. 'We should contact Mogilev and find out. But until we're ordered to withdraw then we'll stay and defend this piece of shit. Is that understood?'

'The soldiers' committee has had a meeting and they've decided we should pull out,' said the Master Sergeant.

'I don't give a fuck what the soldiers' committee wants,' shouted Mikhail. 'Go and get the men assembled in the square over by the smashed clock tower but leave the forward sentries out. Let's get this sorted out, now!'

The Master Sergeant hesitated.

'Master Sergeant,' snapped Mikhail, 'I said now! Move, or I'll have you up on court martial.'

The Master Sergeant did not budge. He stood there looking anxious and breathing heavily.

'The men have already started pulling back sir,' he said. 'There's nothing you can do to stop them.'

'I bloody can, and I bloody will.'

Mikhail looked across at Sergei. 'Go and get Lieutenant Herzen and the other officers and non-comms. This is desertion we're dealing with.'

Mikhail turned back to the Master Sergeant.

'Don't the stupid bastards know that the death penalty has been reinstated for disobeying orders and deserting your post? The idiots are heading straight towards a firing squad.'

Sergei pulled his jacket off the back of the chair and grabbed his cap. The Master Sergeant quickly brought his rifle up.

'You won't be going anywhere, sir.'

Mikhail and Sergei both reached for their Mauser pistols.

'Stop! Keep your hands where I can see them, or I'll shoot,' commanded the Master Sergeant.

'Master Sergeant,' said Mikhail quietly, 'put down that gun and don't do anything stupid.'

'Neither should you, sir,' answered the Master Sergeant. 'You just stay right there and everything will be fine. I volunteered to be the one to tell you. If others had come instead, you'd be dead by now.'

Mikhail and Sergei glanced at each other, and then back at the Master Sergeant.

'So, where the hell are Lieutenant Herzen and the others?' demanded Mikhail.

'They're all dead, sir.'

Sergei made a lunge for the Master Sergeant, but Mikhail grabbed him and hauled him back.

'Steady on, Lieutenant, first let's get out of this alive, and then we can sort it out.'

Mikhail let go of Sergei's arm and drew himself upright. 'So, we're now adding murder to the charges of deserting your post and disobeying orders. Is that right Master Sergeant?'

The Master Sergeant ignored the question. 'We all go back a long way. You're both different from the other officers. I've always respected what you tried to do for the men. It's why I came myself, and why I brought these.' He nudged the sack forward with one foot.

'So, what's in the sack?' demanded Sergei.

'Ordinary soldiers' uniforms; you won't get one *verst* in what you're wearing. The troops are shooting any officers they come across.'

'Where's the telephone operator?' asked Mikhail, 'I want to talk to Mogilev. The *Stavka* need to know what's happening up here.'

'Don't even bother trying,' responded the Master Sergeant, 'the wire's been cut and the telephone's destroyed.'

They stood in silence for a while, edgy and nervous, not knowing what would come next, until Mikhail broke the impasse and spoke. 'Very well Master Sergeant, how's this mess going to end?'

'Unbutton your holsters slowly with your left hand and take out your Mausers with your thumb and forefinger – one of you at a time. Then throw them in the corner over there. Once you have done this, I'll leave.'

'And after that,' asked Mikhail, 'what do you suggest?'

'Wait here for thirty minutes at least,' said the Master Sergeant. 'If you try to follow too quickly, the men will kill you.'

'I suppose you expect us to thank you?' barked Sergei. His face was flushed red and he stood, clenching and unclenching his fists.

'Let's just get on with it.' The Master Sergeant waved his rifle towards Sergei. 'You go first.'

'Lieutenant,' instructed Mikhail, 'just do as he asks, and do it slowly. We don't want any silly accidents.'

Mikhail's Mauser followed Sergei's into the brick dust in the corner of the building.

'Thank you, gentlemen,' said the Master Sergeant, with visible relief. He was still pointing his rifle at them. 'Understand this was hard for me to do.'

'So, this is farewell then?' asked Mikhail.

The Master Sergeant took a step forward as though to embrace them, but then thought better about it. There were tears in his eyes.

'I'm going home,' he said, 'and you should think about it too. The war is as good as over. We have our farms and our loved ones to care for now.'

'You may say the war is over,' answered Mikhail, 'but tell me, who's going to defend the motherland when you and your comrades all bugger off?'

The Master Sergeant did not respond. He gave a quick shrug of his shoulders, turned on his heels, and jumped the low brick wall. Sergei and Mikhail remained where they were, staring at his retreating figure until they lost sight of him in the ruins.

They found Lieutenant Herzen two houses down the street. He was in the front room of a shelled-out house lying face down in a pool of black congealed blood. His throat had been slit from ear to ear and there were several bayonet wounds in his torso.

Sergei crouched down and turned him over. A look of surprise was frozen on the Lieutenant's boyish face. His subaltern, a lad of less than seventeen, lay next to him, curled into a foetal position. He had been bayoneted to death. The telephone operator had been cornered in the back yard of the house. His face had been pulverised into a mash of blood and bone by a blunt instrument. His telegraphic equipment was next to him, smashed to pieces. Big lazy black flies buzzed everywhere, crawling over the faces of the dead men.

Mikhail and Sergei stood and starred at the corpses. Neither felt any revulsion – they had seen too many mutilated bodies.

Mikhail slowly shook his head. 'Isn't it pitiful it has finally come to this; what the hell's happening to the army? The regiment, the camaraderie, the loyalty – all gone to hell.'

'Shall we bury them?' Sergei finally asked.

'You have to assume we don't have any sentries out any more. The enemy patrols must already be pushing into the outskirts and finding nobody's there. I don't think we have much time.'

'What about those uniforms the Master Sergeant gave us?' asked Sergei. 'It doesn't seem right trying to slink away in a private's uniform.'

'Let's take them with us, we can decide later.'

Chapter 8

THE VOLINSKY LIFE-GUARDS

July 1917

MIKHAIL CRAWLED OVER the rubble of what was left of a shelled house. He took off his cap, cautiously raised his head above the broken windowsill, and scanned the broken ground to his front. He thought he glimpsed a movement, perhaps the dark green of a German *jaeger* light infantryman, but could not be sure. Just then there was a flurry of shots over to the far right, followed by the crash of a returning volley and the short, sharp stutter of a light machine gun. Then another brief silence, before single shots started punctuating the air. Mikhail ducked back under the windowsill and looked at Sergei.

'I'm sure there are German *jaegers* out in front of us, and by the sound of it, they've run into opposition.' he whispered.

'That means we still have troops in the area,' said Sergei.

'Exactly, and the fighting is somewhere over there,' answered

Mikhail, pointing to his right. 'Let's work our way back and then make our way in the direction of that fight. If they're our troops, we should try to join up with them.'

Mikhail and Sergei, crouching as low as they could, scrambled back through the ruins. They had their Mauser pistols out and swept each new piece of ground they crossed for sign of any troops – whether German, Austrian or Russian. All were potential threats since, in the confused fighting going on, they would tend to shoot first and identify later.

Their progress was slow. They were leapfrogging from house to house through the ruined town, never certain what or who they would find in any building. There were also snipers about, skilfully camouflaged and hiding amongst the town's ruins. A bullet could come from any direction.

Mikhail and Sergei had gone through officer training school together, had fought together, and had learned their street-fighting skills over the campaign. They had a well-practiced routine. Mikhail would generally lead, carefully surveying each patch of ground to their front and off to each side before leaping the wall and running to the shelter of the next wall or building. Sergei stayed back to provide cover. When Mikhail had reached his destination, Sergei would tumble over the wall and sprint in a weaving pattern across the space to join him.

'Do you want me to go first this time?' panted Sergei.

'First or second doesn't matter,' replied Mikhail. 'Sometimes it's more dangerous to go second since they'll have had time to target the space.'

Sergei laughed. 'Why do you think I want to go first?'

The sound of the skirmish was becoming progressively louder as they moved through the town. The Mosin-Nagant rifle issued to the Russian infantry had a distinct sound when fired and they now had a rough idea where the Russian defenders had taken up position.

A continuous salvo of rifle fire was coming from a line of houses just off to their right and, again, there was the intermittent stutter of a light calibre machine gun firing from one of the house's lower windows. Mikhail could just make out the muzzle flashes. The lone machine gun was spraying the derelict buildings on the other side of the narrow street, filling the air with brick dust as bullets slammed into the buildings.

'Jesus,' said Sergei, 'they're almost on top of each other, just the street separating them. They're forcing the Germans to keep their heads down.'

'A bloody waste of ammunition, if you ask me,' replied Mikhail. 'They'd be better to conserve machine gun ammunition for an attack. But then, while all the racket is going on, and the Germans are ducking for cover, it could be an ideal time to try to make it across that wasteland to those houses.'

'As long as those Russian troops don't open fire on us as well. How the hell will they know we're not part of a German attack?'

'We need to get close as possible and see if we can signal them.'

Mikhail and Sergei crawled forward on their hands and knees. They had managed to skirt around the fighting so they were approaching the rear of houses at an angle. Mikhail raised his head over the low brick wall of a laneway and quickly pulled back. He signalled to Sergei to stay where he was and crawled over to him.

'There's a *jaeger* sniper and his spotter just on the other side of the wall,' he whispered. 'They've been trying to work their way around the Russian position.'

'What do you want to do?' asked Sergei.

'They've taken up position in the laneway just on the other side of this wall. They've got their backs to us and are searching for targets in the houses. We can take them from behind, but we'll need to jump them together.'

Mikhail and Sergei slowly inched their way back over the rubble towards the wall. Every footfall and handhold carefully placed so as not to disturb anything that could create a sound. It was painstakingly slow, but both knew what they were doing and were well practiced. They crouched below the top of the wall, gripping their Mauser butts in both hands. On Mikhail's signal they raised themselves up and slid their Mausers over the top.

The splayed figures of the sniper and his spotter were just a few metres below them. Intent on scanning the houses in front of them, they remained unaware of the threat behind. The sniper was concentrating on adjusting the telescopic sight, while the spotter had removed some bricks in the lane wall and was peering through the small gap with his compact tripod-mounted telescope. Both had taken off their helmets and had laid them on the ground beside them.

Mikhail gave a hand signal to Sergei to take the one on the right. 'Now,' he hissed.

Both their Mausers fired in unison. The two green-jacketed bodies jerked as the bullets slammed into them. Mikhail's shot hit the sniper at the base of the skull and blew away part of his face. He lay face down in a pool of own blood, with his limbs still twitching.

Sergei's bullet had hit the torso of the spotter. There was a large black stain quickly spreading over the back of his tunic. He lay still for a second, and then started to scream and flail his arms around in the dust. Sergei sprang over the wall and placed his Mauser against the man's skull.

'Don't waste ammunition,' yelled Mikhail. He jumped the wall, grabbed a loose brick and crashed it into the back of the spotter's skull. There was an audible crunch of breaking bone, and the man went limp.

'Was that necessary?' asked Sergei.

'He had a gut wound,' answered Mikhail. 'He would've been lying here in agony for hours before he died.'

'Yes, but a bloody brick?'

Mikhail shrugged and grinned as he wiped his hands on the sniper's tunic. "I keep telling you you're too sensitive.'

There was an audible curse in Russian from somewhere on the other side of the lane wall, and then a barked order. It came from just a few metres away.

'We're Russian,' shouted Mikhail. 'We've just taken out a couple of German snipers who were trying to outflank you. Can we come in?'

'How many of you?'

'Just two of us,' shouted back Mikhail, 'officers from the 11th

Division. We were holding the line over to your left. All our men are gone. Hurry, we can't stay out here forever.'

They could hear a muffled discussion being conducted in Russian.

'I hope they're okay we're officers,' whispered Sergei. 'I'd hate to think we are just about to jump out of the frying pan into the fire.'

'Come over the wall in front of you,' finally came the reply, 'and run like hell towards the back of the house. We'll try to cover but expect to take enemy fire when you're crossing the gap. Tell us when you're ready.'

'I'm not going to drag this bloody sack with me,' said Sergei.

'Leave it behind; we shouldn't need it now. But let's take the sniper's rifle and any ammunition they have.'

Mikhail stripped the ammunition bandoliers off the two Germans and looped it across one shoulder, while Sergei pulled the rifle out from under the sniper's body and wiped the blood off it.

Mikhail glanced over at Sergei. 'Whatever happens, just keep on going. No stopping to help. Good luck.'

'We're coming in now,' shouted Mikhail.

They tumbled over the wall and dropped onto rough ground. Scrambling to their feet, they sprinted and weaved across the broken rubble of the wasteland towards the house.

A fusillade of shots erupted. Bullets whipped past them with an angry whine, splattering into brickwork and kicking up dust around their feet. They crashed into each other trying to squeeze through the narrow door at the back of the house, tripped over, and fell through the door onto the rough wooden floor. They lay there for a moment, gasping for breath.

'Are you okay?' asked Sergei.

'I think so,' laughed Mikhail, 'I can't feel pain anywhere.'

A young, baby-faced Russian officer stood over them with his revolver drawn and pointing at them.

'Where the hell have you come from?' he demanded.

'Lieutenant Sergei Vinokurov of the 11th', Sergei panted, 'and this is Kapitan Mikhail Mehenov also of the 11th. We held the left sector of the town over there, but our troops mutinied and deserted.'

'Sadly, an all too familiar story,' said the officer. 'Are there only the two of you?'

'I'm afraid so,' answered Mikhail. 'All the other officers are dead, killed by our own men. We weren't at the command post when it happened, so I guess we're lucky. We heard the fighting over here, so we thought there was still one active unit in the area and we decided to try and join up with you.'

The officer lowered his revolver and holstered it. Mikhail and Sergei both levered themselves upright and started to dust themselves down.

'Well, you're lucky you found us, but we're not out of this yet,' said the young officer. 'There's a big danger of us being cut off. We're probably going to have to fight our way out.'

'How many men do you have?' asked Mikhail.

'We've three companies spread out along this street, but the bastards have already worked their way into the houses on the other side of the street, and now they're making their way around to our rear – as you've just found out. It seems they're mostly skirmishers, so it's unlikely they'll rush us until reinforcements come up.'

'Ammunition?' asked Mikhail.

The young officer shrugged and laughed. 'We've just a few rounds per man. We're also low on rations and almost out of water. All the wells are poisoned.'

'So, who are you?' asked Mikhail.

'The Volinsky Life-Guard Regiment, at your service, sir.' The young officer gave a mock bow.

'And your men,' asked Mikhail, 'are they still willing to fight?'

'We took some troublemakers and executed them this morning,' answered the young officer. 'It seems to have put some resolve into the rest. We're one of the few regiments holding what's left of the town – there's us, the Izmailovsky's, the Moscow and the Grenadier Regiments. But we're scattered about, so there's no cohesive line, and most of our communications have been knocked out.'

'Are you in touch with headquarters?' asked Mikhail.

The young officer shook his head. 'It seems every line has been cut.'

He looked at Mikhail's epaulettes. 'It is Kapitan, isn't it?'

'Yes, and who is in command here?'

'The Major and our Kapitan are both dead, Sir. A mortar round took out the command post a few hours ago.'

'So, Lieutenant, does that leave you the most senior officer left?' asked Mikhail.

'Yes, but there's another lieutenant and some sergeants to help. But now you're here, sir, I would be pleased if you took command. I don't have much experience at this sort of thing.'

'All right,' answered Mikhail, 'but remember, they're your troops, not mine. You could start by showing us your position, and please allocate Lieutenant Vinokurov here a company to command.'

They were about to follow the lieutenant when Mikhail stopped him. 'Forgive me, I didn't ask your name.'

The young lieutenant drew himself up and saluted. 'Lieutenant Alexander Gorokhov, at your service, sir.'

'Well, Lieutenant Gorokhov,' said Mikhail, 'I think we can assume they'll have brought more troops up by now and will try to rush us at dusk. By the look of the sky, that's not too far off. We need to get our position prepared and set up firing zones. We also need to secure a line of retreat; it's going to be impossible to hold this position for long.'

'There's another line of houses about 50 metres behind us,' replied Lieutenant Gorokhov, 'I've already put some men in there in case we have to pull back.'

'That's a good start,' responded Mikhail, 'and your wounded?'

'A dozen or so,' answered the lieutenant. 'We've got them in a room out the back.'

'Get any of them who can walk or crawl to make it back to the rear as soon as it's dark, and the rest can stay here. Don't allow anyone to help them. We need every able man to be at his post or we'll be overrun. Do you understand?'

'Yes sir,' answered the Lieutenant.

'And while you're at it,' continued Mikhail, 'issue instructions that nobody is to open fire until they're almost on top of us. We don't have enough ammunition for indiscriminate fire, and we want them to get close enough for us to be able to drag their bodies in and strip them. Getting their rifles, ammunition and water are as much a priority as defending this position.'

'Yes, sir, I'll send the message around immediately.'

'And stop that bloody machine gunner of yours spraying the houses across the street. We'll need every bit of ammunition when they attack, and he needs to keep his barrel cool or it will jam just when we need it. Now let's look at your current positions, we haven't much time.'

The attack came sooner than expected. Dusk had just started to settle over the town when there was a loud *pop* above them. The sky above the town, and all the buildings, was instantly bathed in a stark phosphorous white light.

'They're sending up flares,' yelled Mikhail. 'An attack's coming in. Everyone to your posts, now!'

Chapter 9
THE STRANGER

Barnaul August 1917

PAVEL SAT AT his desk in the upstairs office of the Moskovsky Street store. He had been staring at the month's accounts without really taking in the meticulous hand-written figures in the ledger. He knew the figures didn't contain good news – another profitless month and few signs of improvement.

He looked down into his store. The shelves had been restocked but, after the panic buying following the fire, customers had dropped away. The people who had lost everything were starving and forced to forage for food in the forest. Many of the townsfolk had little money to buy even essentials. The pawnbrokers were running a thriving trade, and bartering had become the most common form of transaction.

Many of the town's citizens had fled westward, unaware the big cities in European Russia were often in an even more perilous state than fire-ravaged Barnaul, where there was food to buy if you had the means. If you didn't, there was always stealing, which had now become so prevalent civilian guards were posted to protect the stock.

Pavel had reduced staff and stock levels, but customers were declining at a faster rate than he could cut costs. The combined effects of the war, the fire and successions of failed harvests, along with the growing fear and despondency of the townsfolk, were all continuing to weigh heavily. Barnaul felt like a town under siege.

He snapped shut the large green leather-bound ledger and handed it back to his Chief Accountant. 'I'll look at it later, I need to go out.'

He took his frockcoat and hat off the stand and hurried down the stairs. 'I'll be over at Nikifor Trifonovich's store if anyone's looking for me,' he told Katrina, as he hurried out the door.

Two armed guards, sitting in chairs in the street outside the main door, jumped to their feet when Pavel emerged. 'One of you stay here and guard the store,' Pavel told them, 'I only need one to come with me.'

Pavel glanced at the boarded front window of his store. Someone had thrown a rock through the window a few days ago. Pavel had finally given up replacing the glass, and timber planks would now have to suffice. A "Business as Usual" sign pinned to the planks was flapping in the breeze. Pavel paused to re-pin it while he checked the street for danger. Apart from the usual collection of beggars and deserters, there were few people brave enough to be out, apart from a small barefoot boy busily pasting a notice on a nearby lamppost.

'What's this?' asked Pavel, 'Can I see the poster?'

The boy put down his glue bucket and brush and took one from the roll tucked under his arm. 'Give it back when you've read it, mister.'

It was the notice for a public meeting that evening in the Town Hall calling for the establishment of a Barnaul Soviet and the election of a Soviet Committee. Everyone welcome, it said.

Pavel couldn't help smiling to himself. *As though I would be welcome.* He folded the poster and put it in his pocket.

'Hey mister, that's mine.'

The guard stepped between them. 'Get out of here you little grub before I box your ears, you've got plenty of posters left.'

'Leave him be,' said Pavel as he tossed the boy a coin. 'There, I've paid for it.'

Pavel cut through Tolstoy Street to Svobody Place. The urchin had been busy. There were signs for the meeting plastered about the place and they were attracting attention from those out on the street. Word would spread quickly.

He walked into Nikifor Trifonovich's store. 'Please stay outside with the other guards,' he instructed. 'I'll be fine.'

A shop assistant nodded and pointed to the back office. Nikifor was sitting behind his desk nervously fiddling with a pen. The blinds had been pulled down and a single desk lamp cast a small pool of light over the desk, leaving the rest of the office in deep shadow.

Pavel sensed something wrong, something out of character with his friend, and regretted leaving his guard out on the street. He pushed his unease aside and extended his hand.

'Nikifor Trifonovich, what's this about, why did you ask me to come over?'

Nikifor, without standing or offering a return greeting, briefly grasped his hand across the desk and indicated one of the visitor's chairs. Pavel remained standing while he felt in his coat pocket.

'Have you seen this?' he asked, unfolding the poster and handing it to Nikifor.

'Of course, they're all over town.'

'So, the politics of Petrograd and Moscow are finally coming to Barnaul,' said Pavel. 'Our own Soviet, I wouldn't have thought we'd be that important.'

'I think we both know who is behind this.'

'Not Matvei Tsaplin by any chance?'

'Who else?' A man's voice came from behind him. Pavel spun around and peered into the shadowed recesses of the office. He could just make out the dark outline of a man in a black fedora hat and a long coat with the collar turned up.

'That weasel,' continued the man, 'has been working to consolidate his power ever since the fire, as you should know, Pavel Dmitrievich Sukhov.'

'Who the hell are you and how do you know my name?' demanded Pavel. 'Come forward into the light.'

The man stepped forward and extended his hand. 'I'm glad we can finally meet. I've been an admirer of yours for a while.'

He spoke in a quiet, confident manner with the cultured, slight French accent of the Russian elite.

Pavel, without taking his eyes off the man, glanced over at Nikifor. 'What in damnation is going on here?'

Nikifor shifted uncomfortably in his chair. 'They asked me not to tell you and I agreed. Rest assured, we're in no danger.'

'You look somewhat familiar; do I know you?' asked Pavel.

He could now make out the man in the half-light – tall with a thin, pasty-coloured face, rimless glasses, and a pencil-line moustache.

'I was at the last Guild meeting, the one down at the old silver smelter. We all had to leave quickly so we missed the opportunity to meet.'

Pavel now recalled the man in the black fedora who brushed past him as he was standing under the tree before the meeting.

'And your name?' asked Pavel.

'Names can be dangerous these days but you can call me Grigory. I hope you will forgive Nikifor Vasilovich for arranging this meeting. These are dangerous times, and secrecy is necessary.'

'So what's this about?' demanded Pavel.

The man indicated the chairs in front of the desk. 'Perhaps we should all sit down and discuss this.'

He unbuttoned his coat, removed his hat, and placed it on Nikifor's desk.

'Please,' he waved towards one of the chairs.

The man's head was shaved bald. There were beads of sweat glistening on his skull and his eyes were sunk in deep sockets giving him a sinister skeletal look in the faint lamplight.

Pavel remained standing. There was something about this man, the way he was assuming an authority over everyone in the room, which put Pavel on edge. 'If I don't get answers soon, I'm leaving. You're right, Mr. Grigory, or whoever you are, these are dangerous times.'

The man calling himself Grigory sighed. 'If I tell you my name, it could bring you harm. I withhold it for your benefit, not mine. We are all on the same side and, besides, you have your man outside. I mean no threat; I'm simply here to ask your help.'

'On whose behalf?'

Grigory waved his hand as if to push the question aside and continued. 'I think you would agree the three of us would call ourselves "Greater Russians". The blood of Mother Russia, that is European Russia, still flows through our veins even if we live far from Saint Petersburg or Moscow. We're not Ukrainians, Serbs, Mongols, Jews or the like, and we've all grown up under the Tsars and distrust those wishing to harm our institutions and destroy the Russian way of life.'

Grigory indicated the vacant chair again. 'Mr. Sukhov, would you please sit and give me the courtesy of hearing me out?'

Reluctantly, Pavel reached for the chair and dragged it towards him. He positioned it carefully, deliberately leaving as much space as possible between him and Grigory, while allowing himself to keep an eye on the door. 'Please go ahead, I'm listening.'

Grigory pulled off his leather kid gloves, folded them, and placed them neatly beside his hat. He leaned forward and spoke in a hushed whisper.

'I want to talk about the Tsar and the Royal family. None of us can be happy with their circumstances.'

Pavel tugged nervously at the collar of his shirt. He didn't like the way Grigory had leaned close to him. Besides, he didn't quite understand the question. 'You mean the abdication? He may have been pressured, who knows, but it must have been his decision. By all accounts he seems happy enough in Tsarskoe Selo.'

Grigory gave a short, contemptuous laugh. 'Tsarskoe Selo; a summer palace or a summer prison?'

'I've no idea of their circumstances,' resumed Pavel, 'other than what I read in the newspapers and, let's be clear, our family has always supported the Royal family. Anyone who moved east to settle Siberia owed them a lot, but that was two generations and two tsars ago. However, 1905 changed my view on the Tsar, and the views of many Russians. I didn't support the revolt at the time, but Nicholas agreed to a new Duma and then didn't allow it to work. He foolishly tried to cling to his old powers, and now he's been forced to abdicate.'

Grigory slapped his hand on the desk. 'The Duma,' he contemptuously spat out the words, 'is just a stinking cesspit of debaters, revolutionaries, academics and lawyers! All talk and no action. What good is the Duma, other than a platform for the political extremists to shout out their treasonous filth and stir up trouble? Russia always needs a strong guiding hand, and the Tsars have always been there for their people. Inherited yes, but don't they have that divine right? Do you doubt it?'

'Divine right or not, there doesn't seem to be any inclination, by the Duma, Kerensky, or the Army, to bring him back. Obviously the Monarchist Party would, but they are few in number. Even his brother, Grand Duke Michael, doesn't want to step into his shoes and is prepared to leave the throne vacant. Besides, it's common knowledge Nicholas wants to take his family to Britain – hardly the plan for a Romanov to remain at the helm.'

'You may not know, but the British have flatly rejected the idea,' answered Grigory, emphatically. 'That Marxist Prime Minister of theirs, the man with a strange name.'

'That would be Lloyd George?' suggested Pavel.

Grigory raised an eyebrow. 'Yes, I believe you are right. He's too worried what the English workers' unions might do about a cousin of their king being allowed into the country. This commoner, a Welsh coalminer would you believe, is filling King George's head with threats and poisonous lies.'

'I've got no idea what this Lloyd George would be telling his king,' said Pavel, 'however it's open knowledge the Bolshevik Party is calling for world revolution and for the workers of Germany, France and

England to rise in support of their Russian comrades. Perhaps he has a point?'

By now Grigory was getting agitated, and leaned forward again, bringing his face uncomfortably close to Pavel's. 'So, to appease the workers,' he hissed, 'he's prepared to sacrifice his own cousin. What sort of English weakling is that?'

Grigory slumped back in his chair and held up both hands. 'I apologise, you see I can get quite emotional about this.'

'You talk of the Tsar being sacrificed,' asked Nikifor, 'what do you mean by this?'

'Don't believe everything you read in the newspapers,' answered Grigory. 'Tsarskoe Selo is a place of imprisonment for the Royal family. They may have taken residence there after the abdication, but do you think they're allowed to leave? Kerensky will never admit it, but they're actually under a form of house arrest and we have deep fears for their safety.'

'Surely nobody in their right mind, even Kerensky, would touch a hair on their head,' said Pavel. 'The Romanovs, no matter what you think of them, are sacred to the Russian people. Kerensky couldn't be that stupid.'

'It's not Kerensky you have to worry about,' said Grigory, 'it's the Bolsheviks. You see what's going on in Barnaul with the new Soviet, and it's happening all over the country. They're stirring up as much trouble as they can – strikes and marches every day in the cities and getting the soldiers to mutiny. They've little regard for the Duma and treat it with contempt, and they don't have any intention of getting a plebiscite. Their plan is to sieze power at the first opportunity, and despite all the fancy rhetoric from Kerensky, he must know his days in government are numbered.'

'So, you think the Bolsheviks will harm the Tsar?' asked Pavel. 'If they want power, then they need to keep the people on their side.'

Grigory barked a laugh. 'Do you think the likes of Lenin and his cohorts worry for a minute what the people think? Just read their manifesto. The Mensheviks want a gradual progression, through education of the masses, towards a socialist state. The Bolsheviks say damn to all that, we won't wait for generations to educate the people to our way, we demand it now, and we will seize power first and worry about the consequences later.'

Pavel felt himself becoming agitated. 'I asked whether you think the Bolsheviks would harm the Tsar, I didn't ask for a political treatise. If they want a deal with the Germans, then why risk upsetting them? There's the Tsarina, a German princess, and the Germans helped Lenin get back to Russia. The children, especially little Alexander – surely not!'

'Don't believe that for a moment,' answered Grigory. 'The Germans are more interested in getting Russia out of the war against them and will turn a blind eye to anything the Bolsheviks do. And you can't imagine the Bolsheviks want a live Tsar becoming the rallying point for all those who oppose them, and believe me, there are many of us.'

Pavel shifted uncomfortably in his chair. 'You seem convinced we're going to have another revolution, but just look where the last one got us. Anyway, we're four thousand *versts* from Petrograd and the Tsarskoe Selo, so what's this got to do with us? We're all busy people, Mr. Grigory, so why don't you get to the point?'

Grigory had got out of his chair and was pacing the room. Pavel waved to him to sit back down. 'You're making me nervous, so what's this about?'

Grigory sat and wiped his brow with a handkerchief. 'Can I trust the two of you to keep a secret? What I'm about to tell you, only very few people know.'

'Trust,' answered Pavel, 'is a rare commodity these days. It's safer to mistrust than to trust. You have the benefit, Mr. Grigory, of knowing who I am, and possibly the values I represent. I know nothing of you, and secrets come with a responsibility and the real possibility of danger in these times.'

'I have weighed these considerations but, if I'm to get your support, you at least have the right to know, otherwise how can you make a decision?'

Pavel and Nikifor looked at each other and nodded.

'If it finally explains why you're here,' said Pavel, 'then, let's get on with it, shall we?'

Chapter 10

THE HANGING TREE

Barnaul, August 1917

'KERENSKY AND HIS government's days are numbered.' Grigory had gone over to check the office door, and then returned to his seat. He was leaning forward and almost whispering. 'But his fall won't be as you'd expect. Not sacking by the Duma, no realignment of political factions, no fall-out from the failed offensive, just a coup – a straight ruthless grab for power.'

'By whom?' asked Pavel. 'We hear rumours like that every day. One day the Bolsheviks, one day the Kadets, one day the Monarchists, even one day the Army may get off the political fence.'

'But this time it's serious,' continued Grigory, 'Lenin is back in Petrograd. A few days ago he managed to cross the border from Finland. The Germans allowed him to transit across Germany from Switzerland since it's in their interests to get him back into the country. His anti-war stance will only aid the German war effort against the Allies.'

'How can you be certain of this?' asked Nikifor.

'That he's back?' shrugged Grigory. 'We've old friends who watch the borders for us. They know who comes and goes, and they don't miss much, even if people are in disguise.'

'Old friends?' asked Pavel.

'I can't really say,' answered Grigory, 'except they've a good network and we can trust the information.'

Pavel shifted uncomfortably in his chair. 'You're talking about the *Okhrana*, aren't you? Kerensky may have officially disbanded the Tsar's Secret Police, but we both know that doesn't make them go away, it just hides them from view.'

'Exactly,' said Grigory, 'but let's just put the *Okhrana* aside for a minute.'

'No, don't just put them aside,' said Pavel. 'The *Okhrana* are still probably the most hated bastards in all of Russia, and you say they're old friends? How many people disappeared, were tortured, or murdered under their watch? You couldn't even start to count.'

'But they have their uses.'

'So, they've found out Lenin is back in the country and the Bolsheviks are hatching a plot to throw out Kerensky. Hardly surprising news.'

'Please let me continue,' said Grigory. 'They've also people working undercover at Tsarskoe Selo. The government is nervous about continuing to hold the family there. The Germans are getting perilously close to Petrograd, and the old palace is on the outskirts of the city. Nobody would want the Tsar captured by the Germans; imagine how they would use him as a bargaining chip, even if the Bolsheviks were in power. The nub is Kerensky is secretly moving the Tsar and the family away from Petrograd this month.'

'Understandably,' said Nikifor.

Grigory held up his hand to silence Nikifor. 'But it's where they're moving them to which is important; they're planning to bring them across the Urals. The old Governor-General's mansion in Tobolsk is being readied as we speak.'

'Tobolsk!' exclaimed Nikifor. 'It might be this side of the Urals and in Siberia, but it's still fifteen hundred versts from here. Anyway, why is this so important?'

Grigory jabbed his finger at Nikifor. 'Just think about it - the Tsar is currently under a form of "soft" house arrest by Kerensky and guarded by Government troops, but who knows where their loyalty lies. You have the Petrograd Garrison and you have the Bolsheviks en masse in the city's streets. It would be very hard to free the Tsar while he is in Petrograd and, the minute a Bolshevik coup is successful the guards will be replaced by their own, and it would be impossible to free them. Now we have this one opportunity.'

'I'm sure the Tobolsk mansion will still be heavily guarded,' pointed out Pavel, 'so what's the difference? Whether they're Kerensky's guards or Red guards, they're hardly going to stand aside and let you take away the Tsar.'

'We are confident we can free the Tsar, that's not the problem. We have a large organization and people already in place in Tobolsk, and importantly, we have sympathisers within the unit guarding the Royal family who will act on our instructions. I don't underestimate the difficulties, but we can succeed. However, the timing is critical; we must move as soon as they reach Tobolsk, before there is a Bolshevik coup and the guards replaced. The bigger problem is what happens after we free them.'

'Would you have him resume the throne?' asked Pavel. 'He's not exactly the most popular of figures.'

'It's what Nicholas represents that's important. We see him as largely symbolic – someone who can rally the anti-Bolshevik forces under one banner. It is when, not if, the Bolsheviks stage a coup. Kerensky is weak and powerless to stop them. The Bolsheviks may have some control in the major cities, but elsewhere they have little support. The problem for those of us who oppose the Bolsheviks is that, while we may be larger in number, we are split. While there are many organizations that oppose the Bolsheviks, we are too disparate. We need a leader to unite us as one, and the Tsar can be that figurehead for us.'

'Do you think the Army is going to stand on the sidelines while all this is happening?' asked Pavel. 'They've just replaced Brusilov with Kornilov, will that make a difference?'

'Brusilov was Kerensky's man and more inclined to stay away from politics, but Kornilov is different, who knows what he will do? But, in the end, we can't just rely on the army commanders, they've got their hands full with mass mutiny and desertion. There's no guarantee the soldiers will obey their orders.'

'What you are saying,' said Pavel, 'is the Bolsheviks will take over and both Kerensky and the generals will be powerless to stop them. Meanwhile, the Tsar is being moved to Tobolsk where you plan to free him. What happens next?'

'Immediately we free the Tsar, we'll need troops to protect him and the family. The local Bolshevik Soviet will do their best to stop us for sure, but we have strength of numbers. We already have the Cossack Ataman of the Tobolsk region on side, and his Cossack Host is prepared to assist, but they're desperately short of horses; the Army has requisitioned too many of them. We need as many as we can get, we need them urgently, and we're prepared to pay whatever it costs.'

'But you must know my Don horse stud; it's quite small, hardly enough to make a significant contribution.'

'But we know you've a friend with a large stud.'

Finally, thought Pavel to himself, *finally it's out on the table. They want Alexei's horses.*

Pavel sat back in his chair and took a deep breath. There was silence between the two men, and Pavel could see Grigory straining for an answer.

'Why ask me?' said Pavel, finally breaking the silence. 'Why not ask him yourself?'

'All we're asking for is your assistance.'

Pavel quietly slid one hand down into the outside pocket of his coat and felt for the reassuring touch of his old service revolver.

'Mr. Grigory,' Pavel spoke quietly and slowly, 'you've come to me with no name, you work for a mysterious organization which has links to the *Okhrana,* you have hatched a plan that requires horses, and you want me to act on your behalf to speak to a friend, because I guess, you are afraid to ask him yourself. I ask myself, why is this so?'

Grigory went to interrupt, but Pavel held up his hand. 'Let me finish.'

Pavel continued. 'I've sat here for the last hour in my friend's office listening to you and wondering why you didn't approach me directly and ask for a meeting, It is probably because I would have asked too many questions and then would have said "no". Would I be correct?'

Grigory shifted uncomfortably in his chair. 'How could I answer that when I don't know the questions?'

'Then, here's a question for you. Are you armed?' Pavel leaned forward towards Grigory.

'Isn't everybody these days? It's in my coat pocket.'

Pavel took his own revolver out and laid it on the desk with the muzzle pointing away from Grigory. 'Don't worry,' he said, 'I've no intention of shooting you, just keep your hands where I can see them.'

Nikifor went to leap to his feet, but Pavel waved him back down. 'Nikifor, please sit down, it's okay.'

'You see,' continued Pavel, 'my friend with the horse stud had a wife, but she's now dead, God bless her soul. But you knew that, didn't you Mr. Grigory? The thing about his past wife was that she was Jewish and, even though my friend is not, because Jewish lineage is passed down on the woman's side, their only son is also classified as a Jew, isn't that right Mr. Grigory?'

Grigory shifted uncomfortably in his chair. There were beads of sweat on his forehead.

'We're talking about the Black Hundred,' said Pavel, 'and that is why you avoid making direct contact with him.'

'Would it help if I denied they weren't involved? But we're representing all the anti-Bolshevik coalition, not just one faction.'

'But you,' said Pavel, pointing a finger at Grigory, 'you are from that organization, are you not? I'm not sure whom I despise most, the *Okhrana* or your bunch of thugs who go about burning synagogues and murdering Jews in the name of Russian Nationalism. You would have even worked your damnedest to stop his "Jewish" son entering officers' school, wouldn't you? And please don't give me your old, tired world Jewish conspiracy theory – I don't believe it.'

'You're going to push aside,' said Grigory, 'our only chance to bring Russians together to fight the Bolsheviks?'

'But what you're asking for is a pact with the devil,' answered Pavel. 'Do I want a Russia run by the Bolsheviks, or a Russia run by a puppet Tsar whose real masters are the disbanded remnants of our hated Secret Police and a banned collection of ultra-nationalist Jew-murderers? God help me, what sort of nightmarish choice is that?'

'Is that your final word then?' demanded Grigory, as he rose to his feet and reached for his coat.

'Yes, it is and, apart from everything I've said,' Pavel also stood and picked up his revolver, 'I'm not inclined to ride for days out to my friend's place, knowing full well what his answer will be. And I would not lie to him about who is involved. Yes, that is my final answer.'

Grigory slowly pulled on his coat and reached for his hat and gloves.

'We will remember this, Pavel Sukhov. We gave you an opportunity to serve your Tsar and country, and you threw it back in our face.'

Pavel spent the next morning at the dacha writing a report of the meeting. He spent hours agonising over the report, writing several drafts before deciding on the final wording. He remained unequivocal in his opposition to the Black Hundred, however he was worried whether the English captain would have a different view and see this as a missed opportunity. But what had been done and said was now over, and he decided to write it as it was, without explaining or excusing his actions.

After burning the discarded drafts and locking up the dacha, he rode out to the site of a derelict factory on the south of town. He checked carefully that nobody was watching before removing the loose brick in the wall and placing the envelope in the cavity. Next, he tied a strip of rag to a nearby thorn bush.

Pavel then stopped by the railway station where he telegraphed an order to a supplier in Irkutsk for a specific item. The recipient of the message would inform their contact in the British mission something was waiting for collection.

Every few days Pavel passed the site to check if the rag strip had been removed so he would know if the report had been picked up. On the fourth day the rag strip had been untied and left under the thorn bush. The report had gone but, upon checking, there had been no message left.

The empty "Dead Letter Drop" was something of a relief. Pavel always fretted while one of his communications sat there uncollected. Inadvertent discovery by someone was unlikely, but he was painfully aware of the dangers of being followed and being seen leaving something in the hiding place.

Pavel didn't consider himself a spy *per se*, as he kept reminding Maria Ivanova, more a chronicler of local events, comings and goings, and the changing mood and allegiances in the town; more like a newspaper columnist recording both the important and the trivial. I'm not exactly stealing state secrets, he had told her more than once, but Maria remained concerned, knowing full well any inference her husband was passing information to the British could have serious consequences.

Nobody had given him any formal training; however, he was always careful, following the captain's advice about varying his route, doubling back, and checking reflections in windows to ascertain whether he was being followed.

Now that the report was gone, and the rag marker had moved, Pavel was confident it could only be one of the captain's men. A weight had been lifted off his shoulders and he decided to reward himself with a few days' break from the store and ride out to the farm to see the family.

The next afternoon Pavel, accompanied by a guard, left the store and the town and headed out towards the farm. Careful to avoid the camps on the outskirts, they took a detour away from the main road. The narrow track wound through tall grasses and copses of birch. Above them, the hot summer sun shone remorselessly in a cloudless sky but, under the canopy of the trees, it was refreshingly cool.

The guard had been this way before and led the way.

'What's causing that noise over there?' Pavel asked the guard at one point along the track. 'Over to our right, something has excited those ravens.'

The guard pulled up his mount and listened to the loud screeching. He nodded knowingly. 'That would be what they call the hanging tree. The ravens are telling us there's human carrion to be had, it's best we avoid it.'

'The hanging tree, I've never heard of it.'

'It's where the comrades string up people they don't like,' said the guard, 'out of sight of the town.'

The large oak tree stood in the middle of a small clearing about eighty meters off the side of the track. Suspended from its limbs were several thick rope nooses. From two of the nooses hung the dark shapes of bodies gently swinging with the afternoon breeze.

The guard hung back, reluctant to ride into the clearing, but Pavel kneed his horse forward for a closer look. The ravens, pecking away at the bodies, rose screeching into the air and flew off to perch in nearby trees.

Grigory's boots had been removed, his ankles tied together, and his hands roughly tied behind his back. His bloated face, with its eyes pecked out, lay twisted sideways by the knot of the noose that had snapped his neck, and a blackened swollen tongue lolled out from between his lips. Pavel felt his stomach heave.

'That's the man who was at Mr Trifonovich's store,' stated the guard, who had ridden up behind Pavel. 'And by the look of it they tortured him before stringing him up.'

'How do you know that?'

'Just look at his hands,' said the guard prodding at the body with his rifle to twist it around, 'they've ripped out his fingernails, and look at his chest.'

As the body swung around, Pavel glimpsed multiple burn marks on his chest and the tip of every finger was a mash of congealed blood.

'We should leave quickly,' said the guard. He was impatient to get far from the clearing. 'Somebody could come.'

Pavel sat and stared at Grigory for a moment, then turned to the guard. 'I need to get back to town urgently, forget the farm.'

Pavel burst into Nikifor's shop. 'Where is he?' he demanded of the shop assistant.

He tracked down Nikifor counting stock out in the back store-room. He was alone. 'I thought you'd ridden out to the farm?' asked a surprised Nikifor.

'They've caught Grigory and have hung him. We happened upon his body by chance, on our way out to the farm. But, to make matters worse, it is clear he was tortured first.'

Nikifor sat himself down on a sack of flour and stared at the floor. When he looked up, his face was ashen with fear. 'You don't think . . . do you?'

'He would have been forced to give them our names; he would hardly bother protecting us after the other day. What else he told them, who the hell knows?'

'Dear Mother of God,' he breathed, 'what do we do?'

'Even vague links to the Black Hundred is absolute anathema to them. They're bound to come looking for us and we'll end up swinging like Grigory. Tortured too, probably.'

'So, what do we do now?' asked Nikifor.

'What we don't do is sit and wait for them to walk through that door. We both need to get the hell out of town as quickly as we can. We'll just have to close our stores, or leave others to run them. There's no time to lose.'

'Where will you go?' asked Nikifor.

'I'll go out to the farm and stay there until I think it's safe, if it ever will be again. You can come too, if you want.'

Nikifor despondently shook his head. 'I think we should go our separate ways. If we're both out at your farm, it will just prove to them we're in this together. My brother has a hunting cabin in the Altai Krai, deep in the forest. They'll never find me there.'

Nikifor looked up at Pavel. 'I suppose you blame me for all this?'

Pavel shook his head. 'You weren't to know, however there's no time for recriminations. Here,' said Pavel extending his hand, 'let us depart as good friends. Who knows if we will ever see each other again?'

Chapter 11
MOGILEV

September 1917

THE TRAIN CARRIAGE rocked violently as it clattered over a switching point and started to slow. Lieutenant Gorokhov worked his way along the train corridor, pushing through the mass of soldiers who were crammed into every space. He slid open the compartment door at the end of the carriage and put his head inside.

'We're starting to come into Mogilev, sir. Are you sure you want to leave us here?'

'Christ,' said Sergei, waking with a start, 'are we there already?'

Sergei used his sleeve to wipe away the condensation from the window and peered out into the night. A few blurry images of house lights had started to appear, but he could see little else.

Mikhail and Sergei had been playing two-handed whist to while away the time, but soon got bored with the endless hands. Sergei managed to doze, while Mikhail forced himself to scribble a note to Iya for the first time for weeks. He knew no letters meant she would be expecting the worst, but writing had been impossible during the retreat. He expected there would be a reliable post office in the headquarters town and wanted to take the first opportunity to send it off.

Mikhail and Sergei were both dog-tired, as were all the surviving members of the Volinsky Regiment on the train, but the constant rocking and jolting of the train and the cramped conditions in the carriages made meaningful sleep almost impossible. The officers and non-commissioned officers were fortunate to get seats in a compartment but, even then, there were ten of them crammed together on hard bench seats, with some sitting on the floor. The rank and file filled the corridors, many trying to sleep on their feet or waiting their turn to squeeze into a spot on the floor. The walking wounded took up the few spaces in the remaining compartments, while stretcher cases were laid out in tiers in freight wagons to the rear of the train.

The rearguard action through the ruins of Ternopol had been relentless and frightening. Just trying to keep the regiment intact had taken all of Mikhail's efforts. For days he had gone without sleep apart from snatching an occasional nap; it was the combination of hunger, thirst, fear and adrenalin that kept him going.

The regiment had suffered severe losses, but it could have been a lot worse. The Germans harried them every step of the way but, perhaps knowing the Russian Army was already in flight, held back from staging a full-out assault. Still, there was little respite. It was Jaeger light infantry, and more particularly the snipers, who caused most problems. Every day, Mikhail's unit suffered a relentless trickle of casualties from hidden snipers who had infiltrated the ruins of the town.

It was the wounded, not the dead, that became the major headache for Mikhail. The dead they simply left but, not having the manpower to stretcher wounded, they were also forced to leave those badly wounded behind. It was usually clear who would and would not survive. Wounded who could walk or crawl were urged to the rear, but the rest were abandoned to their fate. All Mikhail could wish them was either a speedy death, or the forlorn hope they would be treated humanely by their German captors.

Ternopol and Southern Galicia were now in the past. The regiment had somehow made it back, finally crossing through a new Russian defensive line established from remnants of fleeing units.

'It's somewhat ironical,' Sergei had pointed out to Mikhail as they crossed over the mounds of freshly dug earth from the new trenches, 'that this new line is further back than when we started this bloody spring offensive.'

Mikhail just gave a nonchalant shrug of his shoulders. 'I told you this would happen.'

If the Volinskys had expected to be welcomed as saviors, what happened next came as a rude shock. Without explanation they had been force-marched to a nearby railhead and unceremoniously bundled onto trains, the baton-wielding military police herding them on like cattle.

'We're being pulled back to recover and rebuild our numbers,' was the general explanation amongst the soldiers, but Mikhail was not so sure. The mood of the military police at the railhead suggested something very different.

Mikhail stood and stretched, 'The Lieutenant and I really don't have a choice,' he said to Gorokhov. 'You know we're assigned to a regiment that no longer exists, except maybe on paper. We have no option but to report to GHQ.'

'Don't forget us, will you?' asked Gorokhov. 'You could always ask for a posting to the Volinskys.'

Mikhail laughed. 'You're suggesting the Army might do something sensible for a change. Good luck back at the Petrograd Garrison, or wherever they're taking you, and don't take any notice what the press is saying about you giving up Ternopol too easily. Easy for them to say, but they're overlooking the fact you lost over half the men in the process.'

Mikhail clapped a despondent-looking Gorokhov on the back.

'Look, in the city people are panicking about the German advance. The press and the politicians are feeding off this rot about the retreat, and they're looking for scapegoats. It's the way things have always been, but never forget you were one of the few who staged an orderly retreat, and you bought time for the rest of the army.'

Their train was routed to an empty platform far from the station building, and it was made clear they would only be stopping for a short time to take on water and extra coal. A solid line of military police stood along the platform, preventing the men from disembarking. After the hours of cramped conditions, the soldiers were exasperated, but stoically accepted their condition; to the men, Russian command decisions had always been a source of contemptuous derision.

A group of peasant women, bundled up in heavy coats with their heads wrapped in scarves, crossed over from the other platforms and tried to sell food, cigarettes and vodka to the men. The military police threatened to beat them back with batons, but there was little point, since very few soldiers had money to buy anything; the Volinskys hadn't been paid for months.

Mikhail and Sergei wearily climbed down to the platform. After the fug of the carriage, the fresh, cool air of the night was enough to shock them awake.

'What the hell's going on here?' Mikhail demanded of the nearest military policeman. The man's face remained impassive, and he stood, blocking their path.

'Orders, Sir, and I suggest you get back on the train.'

'The Lieutenant and I are not from the Volinsky Regiment, we are part of the 11th.'

'Then why aren't you with them?'

'Because they mutinied and ran,' spat back Mikhail, 'unlike the Volinskys.'

The policeman stared at their regimental shoulder flashes and then held out his hand. 'Papers,' he demanded.

All Mikhail and Sergei had was their pay books, and they handed them over. The policeman flicked through the pages and then walked back to speak to an officer. There was a short, muted discussion before the officer came over. 'Where's your kit?' he asked.

'Left behind somewhere in Ternopol,' replied Mikhail tersely. He outranked the army lieuteant, and his impatience was starting to show. 'The only gear we've got is what we've been wearing for the last two weeks. Now, if you don't mind, we need to find ourselves a billet, a change of clothes, and something to eat.'

The officer snapped to attention and saluted. 'There's a billeting desk in the main station building,' he said, as he stood aside, 'but you'll find the station very crowded, and be careful, the mood of the rank and file is not good.'

'What's been going on?'

'There was a meeting yesterday at the Opera House. Kornilov is trying to wrest back control of the army, and the Soldier Committee representatives are not very happy.'

'Kornilov?' asked Sergei.

'He's your new Commander-in-Chief. Kerensky fired Brusilov for the failure of the offensive.'

'But it was all Kerensky's idea,' said Mikhail, shaking his head.

The officer just shrugged. 'Look, I know we may have seemed heavy-handed tonight, it's hard to know where loyalties lie these days.'

'But the Volinskys?' asked Mikhail.

'We've been ordered to keep them away from the other men and see them quickly on their way, that's all I can tell you, sir.'

Mikhail and Sergei turned to wave farewell just as the water hose was swung back to the tower. The train gave a single short blast of its whistle, and with a crash of couplings, the train gradually pulled away from the platform. They stood and waited while the final carriages slid by and watched the red lamp of the last carriage recede into the night.

Sergei shook his head, 'Maybe we should've stayed with them, and to hell with Mogilev. They're some of the bravest men I've ever known.'

All the stairs and overhead walkways connecting to the main station building were jammed with long lines of sullen soldiers shuffling forward to get out to the platforms where trains, waiting for their carriages and wagons to be filled with occupants before moving off and being replaced by another. Mountains of kit bags were being loaded into boxcars and stacked pyramids of rifles took up all the remaining available platform space. Even more Military Police, with red armbands and whistles, were bellowing out commands and pushing soldiers with their batons to move them towards the waiting trains.

'Jesus,' said Sergei, 'we're not going to be able to make our way through that lot, let's go back to the end of the platform and find a place where we can cross the tracks.'

They had to walk a distance back into the rail yards before they could find a way to get to the station building. Even here there was frenetic activity. Rows upon rows of boxcars stood in near darkness, while lines of cavalry horses waited in turn to be led up the lowered ramps.

'That looks like a whole cavalry division,' commented Sergei. 'I haven't seen this much activity since before the last offensive.'

'There's something odd going on here,' said Mikhail, pulling Sergei up. 'It's not just the way they treated the Volinskys, or that Brusilov has been sacked. Just look at the direction the trains are heading. The front and the bloody Germans are that way,' Mikhail turned and pointed back down the track, 'but the loaded trains are all heading out in the other direction, and that's towards Petrograd. I think we're being led a merry dance here.'

'But there seems nothing too merry about what's going on here,' said Sergei, scratching his head.

Mikhail clamped a hand on Sergei's shoulder and laughed. 'You're right of course, but this is Russia after all. We've spent our whole fucking history staggering from disaster to disaster. Now, let's go and find ourselves a bed.'

'And food,' said Sergei, 'and not forgetting a bath.'

'And vodka, bucket loads of the bloody stuff.'

Mikhail and Sergei pushed open the large wooden swing doors leading into the cavernous waiting room. The stench, a combination of body odor and damp clothes, was overpowering. The room was crowded with soldiers, mostly lower ranks, jammed together shoulder to shoulder. A blue haze hung suspended above the crowd – almost everyone had a cigarette clutched in their hand.

'Private,' Mikhail had to shout at the man to try to make himself heard above the din of voices in the hall, 'will you let us through?'

The man turned, looked them up and down, but did not budge. 'Fucking officers,' he sneered to his companions, and spat on the floor. The wall of soldiers showed no inclination to let them pass.

Mikhail was weighing up the option of attempting to barge through the crowd when two burly military policemen entered through the doors behind them. They carried un-holstered revolvers and held heavy wooden batons.

'We're trying to get to the Billet Office,' Mikhail explained, 'but these soldiers are refusing to let us through.'

'Stay close behind and follow us,' said one of the policemen as he jabbed his baton hard into the back of the nearest soldier and shouted, 'Move aside.'

Led by the policemen, they pushed and bludgeoned a path across the room amid a chorus of shouts and curses from those soldiers being pushed aside.

The solid oak door was blocked by more armed military police, but they stepped aside to let Mikhail and Sergei through. The Billet Office was a large, wood-paneled room, mostly devoid of people save for a young bespectacled corporal who sat at a desk and one officer leaning back in a chair and warming himself next to a single stove.

Mikhail thanked the policemen. 'We wouldn't have made it without you. There seems to be a lot of angry men out there. What's their problem, is it about Kornilov?'

'You're right, they're not happy,' said the more senior policeman. 'It's not just they're being shipped out, it's more about where they're being sent to and why.'

'We noticed the trains are heading out towards Petrograd,' said Mikhail.

The policeman glanced around to check nobody was listening. 'There are rumors that Kornilov is planning to make a move against Petrograd.'

Mikhail shook his head. 'There are always rumors.'

'All these infantry here, along with a division of cavalry, are being positioned close to Petrograd. Officially the men are being told they're to protect the capital in the event of a German break-through, but the soldiers think they're being used as pawns, and the intent of the Stavka is something different.'

'Like what?' asked Mikhail. 'Considering the proximity of the Germans it seems logical. Do the soldiers' committees now think they can make strategic decisions?'

'However, if there's trouble in the city, the Army could step in to keep the peace.'

'What sort of trouble?' asked Sergei.

'You know, from all those protests and strikes.'

'No wonder the soldiers' committees are so edgy,' said Sergei. 'The Army may step in to stop the Bolsheviks from taking over?'

'Look,' interrupted Mikhail, 'we don't want to stand here talking politics, we've just arrived and need a billet for the night. Is there someone here who can help us?'

The policeman pointed to the corporal at the desk. 'There's your man.'

Mikhail patiently waited in front of the desk while the corporal scribbled down some detail into a large leather register. Mikhail coughed politely, but the corporal had his head down and kept writing. Finally, Mikhail rapped the desk. The corporal slowly looked up. With an unconcealed look of disdain, he held out his hand.

'Your orders and billet requisitions.' He added a reluctant "sir", after a pause.

'We don't have any,' answered Mikhail. 'We've come here for re-assignment since losing our regiment at Ternopol. All we need is a billet for the night. We'll get new orders when we visit GHQ tomorrow.'

'We've only billets reserved for those with orders. The town is already full. I can't give you what I haven't got.'

The officer warming himself at the stove looked over. 'Ternopol, that damned hell hole,' he said, as he levered himself out of the chair and walked over to the desk. 'The corporal is right; the town's overflowing with displaced officers looking for a bed.'

The officer reached over and tore off a piece of paper from the corporal's pad. He borrowed the corporal's pencil and scribbled something down.

'You can try this place – it's the best I can offer. But no guarantees they'll have anything.'

He handed the piece of paper to Mikhail. It just listed an address – No 13, Pereulok Vladmirova.

'How do we find this place?' asked Mikhail. 'We've never been to Mogilev before.'

'There are *droshkys* outside the station. They'll know this place well, but you could easily walk there. Hrysyna Street is directly opposite here. Pereulok Vladmirova is down Hrysyna, third on your right.'

The corporal, with a smirk on his face, leaned sideways and looked past him.

'Next please.'

Mikhail looked around. Another couple of officers had managed to get through the door into the office.

'Is this where we can find a billet?' asked one of them.

'Good luck,' answered Mikhail.

Chapter 12

PEREULOK VLADMIROVA STREET

Mogilev September 1917

A LIGHT DRIZZLE WAS falling. They stood for a moment under the station portico while they buttoned up their greatcoats and turned up their collars.

'Apparently it's not far,' said Mikhail, 'but since it's dark and raining let's take a carriage.'

A line of *droshkys* stood waiting across the street from the station, bone-thin horses standing morosely in their harnesses, munching away in their nosebags, while the drivers huddled around a nearby brazier. Mikhail walked over and handed one of the drivers the piece of paper. He held it to the light of the brazier, grinned, and indicated towards his *droshky*.

'Jump in, Sir.'

They turned off the main street in front of the station and drove down a narrow side street lined with a collection of cheap hotels, small, noisy bars bursting with soldiers and tottering drunks. Near the far end of the street the driver turned right into a laneway and halted the carriage.

'That will be five rubles sir.'

'We've hardly gone a hundred meters.'

The driver just shrugged and held out his hand. 'Then next time, with due respect, sir, you should walk.'

A collection of waiting *droshky* carriages crowded the narrow laneway, their drivers in groups, impatiently stamping their feet and blowing into their hands.

The light from the gas lamps spilled out into the darkness, reflecting off the damp, black cobblestones. Through the lace-curtained front windows came the sound of raucous laughter. A throng of officers stood drinking in the front drawing room, with more leaning out of the open windows on the second floor. From somewhere upstairs a piano was accompanying a group of loud, off-key male voices singing a bawdy ditty.

'This isn't a bloody billet,' exclaimed Sergei, shaking his head in disbelief, 'it's a bloody brothel, admittedly an officers' brothel!'

'Maybe we should go back and insist on something else,' growled Mikhail.

'To hell with tramping back to the station in this rain,' said Sergei. 'I'm tired, hungry and thirsty, so what do we have to lose?'

They walked up the front steps. The solid looking front door was closed but appeared unlocked. They pulled at the doorbell lanyard and waited.

'Nobody's going to hear us with that bedlam going on,' said Sergei. 'Let's just go in.'

They had to lean on the door to push it open. Somebody was lying just inside the door. It was a cavalry officer of indistinguishable rank in jodhpurs, riding boots and spurs with a white shirt unbuttoned to his waist. He lay spread-eagled across the hallway clutching a bottle of brandy in one hand.

'Steady on old fellow' he shouted, as Sergei stepped over him into the hall, 'watch the brandy!'

A matronly woman, with a large bust and graying hair pulled back into a tight bun, blocked the hallway.

'Sorry,' she said, rather curtly, 'all the ladies are currently occupied. You'll have to come back tomorrow.'

'Actually, we're just after a couple of beds for the night,' said Mikhail. 'They've told us all the officer billets are taken and this was the only option.'

'Well, all our beds are occupied too,' the madam waved her hand towards a party of revelers, 'but some of these fine gentlemen will be going home to their wives soon. So, if you're prepared to wait, you can sit out the back in the kitchen. Is it just a bed, or will you want company too?'

Mikhail shook his head, but Sergei laughed. 'He's married, but for me, let's see how the night unfolds.'

The madam smiled and pointed down the hall. 'Straight ahead and take the last door on the left. One of the staff will be able to get you something to eat and drink. I'll be down in a minute – since you're not regulars it's strictly cash in advance or no bed, no food or drink, and no lady either for that matter.'

The kitchen was warm and cozy. A scrubbed wooden kitchen table almost filled the room, with bentwood chairs jammed in between the table and the walls.

An ancient cast-iron stove, tucked away in an alcove, creaked and groaned from the heat of the fire. A large pot sat on the stovetop emitting a mouth-watering aroma, and a battered samovar gently hissed away in the corner.

'God, that smells good,' said Mikhail. 'I've got stomach cramps just thinking about it.'

Two women, of indeterminate age with heavily painted faces, sat around the table re-applying make-up and pushing loose strands of hair back into place. A tall officer with a handsome chiseled face, jet-black hair, greased and combed straight back, sat slouched in one of the chairs. Perched on his knee, a petite redhead, holding a bowl, was spooning soup into his mouth.

The women all wore similar clothing – loose-fitting linen bodices trimmed with lace, pantaloons tied under their knees, and pink satin slippers on their feet.

'If you want some soup,' said one of them, pointing to the pot on the stove, 'help yourself. The bowls are on the dresser and there are spoons in the drawer. If you want a drink, there's vodka and glasses in the cabinet.'

She tugged at the other woman, 'Come on, we've got to get back to work.'

The tall officer emitted a loud burp, wiped his mouth with a napkin, and smacked the redhead on her bottom.

'That's enough for me, I don't want to spoil my dinner,' he said, as he gently levered her off his knee and pushed her onto one of the vacated chairs.

'The borscht is delicious. You should try some, it's actually got real meat in it for a change.'

'Thanks,' answered Sergei, rubbing his stomach, 'if it tastes as good as it smells, it'll be wonderful. We haven't had a proper meal for days.'

'You gentlemen just arrived?' asked the officer.

'We've just got in from Ternopol', answered Mikhail. 'They couldn't find us anywhere to billet so they sent us here. We didn't really expect this.'

The officer leaned back and gave out a deep, sonorous laugh. 'You could've done a damned lot worse than this place. I reckon they've done you a favor. Ternopol, eh, what's your regiment?'

'We're originally with the 11th but the bastards mutinied,' said Mikhail. 'We just managed to escape with our lives; the other officers weren't so lucky.'

'That appears to be a common tale,' said the officer, 'but please go on.'

'We managed to attach ourselves to the Volinsky Regiment,' continued Mikhail. 'They had lost a lot of their officers during the retreat so they were keen to have us aboard. We fought a rearguard action back through Ternopol until they established a new line.'

The officer leaned forward. He appeared genuinely interested. 'Then you would have done a lot of house-to-house fighting, close combat, that sort of thing?'

Sergei pulled a face. 'Unfortunately, bloody experts at it, if you'll excuse the expression.'

'So, what are you doing here? Why aren't you with the Volinsky Regiment?'

'Their train was routed through Mogilev on the way back to their barracks in Petrograd. We thought it best to get off here and get officially re-assigned. It was all a bit strange how the Volinskys were being treated, as though they were being blamed for the retreat. They weren't even allowed to disembark at the station to stretch their legs.'

'Understandable,' said the officer. 'They're one of the few units that haven't been politicized by the Bolshies. Best to keep them away from everyone and get them back to their barracks. They may be more use to us back in Petrograd.'

Mikhail nodded as he spooned more soup into his mouth. 'I think I understand now.'

'You'll find the town's full of strays like you. Things are a bit chaotic at the front – parts of units and officers scattered all over the place – but we're gradually getting it sorted out.' The officer reflected for a moment. 'Speaking of Petrograd, do either of you know the city?'

Mikhail and Sergei looked at each other.

'We were both students there before the war,' answered Sergei.

'Does that mean you know your way around the city?'

Mikhail pointed over to Sergei. 'This one knows every bar and back alley in the place. He could get us around blindfold.'

The officer turned to his redhead companion. 'Can you get me a piece of paper and something to write with?'

The girl pouted, reluctantly rose to her feet, and started scrabbling through the kitchen drawers until she found a pencil and an old notebook. The officer ripped out a page.

'My name is Major Listnitsky and you can find me in the main building of the General Staff Headquarters. Room 117, second floor.'

He tore out another blank page and handed it to Mikhail.

'Both of you write down your name, rank and number so I can pull your files from registry. I might have a job for you. Be there at nine tomorrow.'

'Who do we report to when we get there?' asked Mikhail.

'Just come straight up to my office. I'll sort out the details.'

Major Listnitsky stood and brushed himself down. 'Must go – my wife is having a dinner party tonight. I'm expected.'

He gave the redhead's shapely bottom one last squeeze and smiled. 'She's a lively one and comes highly recommended.'

She flashed a dimpled smile at Sergei and leaned over to give him a better view down her bodice.

Sergei flushed bright red at the glimpse of her firm, milky-white breasts and pink nipples. He leaned over and furtively whispered to Mikhail, 'How much money do you have on you?'

Major Listnitsky chuckled. 'A bit short, are we?' He peered down the hallway and bellowed. 'Olga, are you there?'

There were footsteps in the hall and the house Madam appeared at the kitchen door.

'My dearest Olga, treat these gentlemen as my guests, their bill can go on my account.' Listnitsky grinned at Mikhail and Sergei. 'Spend wisely; it's the Army's money. We call it recruitment expenses. Until tomorrow then.'

'How can we ever repay you?' asked Sergei.

Listnitsky clapped a friendly hand on Sergei's shoulder. 'Don't worry, you're about to.'

'My name is Tanya,' she cooed as she slid into Sergei's lap and ran her fingers through his tousled mop of blond hair. She suddenly wrinkled her nose.

'When's the last time you bathed?'

'Well, there was the retreat, and then the train. I guess . . .' Tanya slid from his lap. 'Stay here a moment; I'll go and run a bath.'

'I wouldn't mind one too,' Mikhail called after her.

Tanya popped her head back around the door and smiled. 'It only fits two. You'll have to wait.'

'And what about Galina?' Mikhail asked Sergei after Tanya had left them.

'We're just pen pals,' laughed Sergei, 'so I'm still a free man and this is one of life's simple pleasures. You know celibacy is bad for the soul.'

'And so is the pox,' said Mikhail, wagging his finger at Sergei.

Chapter 13

THE STAVKA HEADQUARTERS

Mogilev September 1917

THE GENERAL STAFF Headquarters was a bewildering assortment of decaying Romanesque buildings near the town center, laid out over a large area of parkland, intersected by wide gravel roads and lines of ancient oak trees, and surrounded by a tall wrought iron fence.

Like an army of worker ants, clerical staff could be seen scurrying between buildings laden with mountains of files.

'If victory was measured in paperwork,' commented Sergei, 'we would have won the war years ago.'

A steady flow of gleaming black staff cars, carrying high-ranking officers, entered and left through the heavily guarded gates.

Mikhail and Sergei stood at the gate while their papers were inspected. The sky was a pale blue with streaks of thin high cloud. An unseasonably northerly wind felt like it was straight off the arctic and had them shivering from the cold.

They were finally let in through a side gate where a sentry directed them to a small office. At least it was out of the wind, and they were happy to wait while an adjutant checked their papers again and questioned them on their business. Mikhail showed him the piece of paper with Major Listnitsky's name and room number. The Adjutant gave them a knowing look and left the room to speak to someone on the telephone. After a few minutes he returned and pointed towards a large pastel yellow wooden building on the far left of the compound.

'Go across there, through the main doors, and go direct to Room 117. It's upstairs on the first floor,' he told them. 'I'll detail a man to escort you.'

'I think we can find our way,' said Mikhail.

'That's not the point,' answered the Adjutant brusquely, 'this is *Stavka*, we can't just have people wandering about by themselves.'

Mikhail and Sergei, accompanied by a guard, crunched their way across the long gravel pathways. The old Alexander Palace was the largest building within the compound and stood well apart from the rest. Two stories high, it had tall windows with French doors opening out onto a surrounding terrace. Smoke from a dozen chimneys rose up into the air where it was whisked away by the stiff breeze.

Guards opened the main doors and their escort led Mikhail and Sergei into a large hall with polished parquet floors and high ceilings with old crystal chandeliers. The hall was bustling with staff, hurrying in and out of adjoining rooms and running up and down the sweeping marble staircase. Everybody seemed to be moving at a frenetic pace, as though a sense of urgency and importance governed every action.

The staccato clatter of typewriters filled the hall. Female secretaries, neatly dressed in army khaki uniform, were seated at desks in a long line against one wall.

'I'll leave you here,' said their escort, 'go straight up the stairs. You will find the offices numbered. Room 117 should be towards the end of the corridor.'

'I need to post a letter first,' asked Mikhail, 'do you have a mail-room?'

'Go down that corridor over there, on the right, three doors down. Hand it in at the censor's desk. They'll need to pass it first.'

Just as their escort turned to go, there was a crunch of tires on the gravel driveway in the forecourt of the building. A long motorcade of staff cars came to an abrupt halt outside the main steps.

A barked command echoed through the hall. 'Attention! Commander-in-Chief entering the building.'

Everyone in the hall froze on the spot and stood rigidly to attention. Even the typewriters fell silent as the secretaries hastily pushed back their chairs and stood up behind their desks, arms at their sides.

Their escort glanced sideways at Mikhail and Sergei. 'Stand to attention,' he whispered out of the side of his mouth, 'and don't move, it's General Kornilov.'

The main doors swung open and a line of fierce-looking armed bodyguards marched at double-time into the hall. Between the lines of guards strutted a short, wiry man with exceptionally dark Mongolian-like features accentuated by a jet-black moustache and manicured goatee beard. He and his entourage strode, without a sideways glance, across the large hall towards the set of large double doors of a conference room.

Apart from the sound of marching boots on the parquet floor there was absolute silence in the room until suddenly, from somewhere across on the far side of the hall, a handclap was heard. Spontaneously, the clapping was taken up by others and quickly spread until soon everyone in the room was applauding. There were shouts of "Kornilov! Kornilov!" and one of the secretaries came out from behind her desk, curtsied, and offered the general a large bouquet of flowers.

Kornilov graciously accepted the flowers, took off his cap, smiled, and bowed to the people in the room. Then just as quickly he was gone, the doors of the conference room slamming shut behind him, as four of his bodyguards took up position to guard the doors.

'How extraordinary,' Mikhail said to their escort, 'is it always like this?'

'The man who is going to save Russia from itself,' replied their escort. 'If Kerensky could see this, he would shit his pants.'

'And probably Lenin too,' quipped Sergei.

The order, "Stand easy!", echoed through the hall and people started returning to their work. The secretaries took their seats, and the noise from the typewriters resumed, with even more intensity than before.

'Would you look at those bodyguards,' said Sergei. 'I've heard they're Tekintsy warriors.'

Kornilov's bodyguards wore pink-colored jackets and large shaggy white hats. They could have been characters from a comic opera, except for their narrow-slit eyes and ferocious looks, and a formidable armory of weaponry.

'They're from the time the general spent in Turkestan,' answered Mikhail. 'I've heard nobody would dare cross them they're so fiercely loyal to him.'

Mikhail pointed to a clock on the wall. 'Look at the time. Let's hand in this letter and get upstairs. Wouldn't pay to be late for the major.'

They climbed the ancient marble staircase, the steps worn concave by countless feet, and found themselves in a dimly lit corridor running the full length of the building with offices leading off on both sides. They counted down the polished brass room numbers until they found Room 117, right at the far end of the corridor. The solid oak door was closed, however they could hear the sound typewriters coming from the other side.

Mikhail knocked and heard a female voice call "come in". The anteroom housed two secretaries at desks and a line of chairs along one wall, occupied by nearly a dozen officers of varying ranks in an assortment of regimental uniforms. There were also two men in civilian clothes.

'We're here to see Major Listnitsky,' Mikhail said to the younger of the secretaries, a pretty girl with blond plaits curled and pinned up in traditional Russian style.

She gave them a smile. 'You all are here to see the Major. Your names please?'

She ran her finger down the sheet of paper, ticked off two names towards the bottom of the page, and pointed towards some vacant chairs. 'There are a few in front of you, I'm afraid.'

Mikhail and Sergei sat and waited. Sergei tried to strike up a conversation with a captain of artillery sitting next to him, but the elder of the secretaries glowered at Sergei and put a finger to her lips.

They waited more than two hours, watching those before them being called, one by one, into the rear office. The numbers gradually dwindled until Mikhail and Sergei were the only ones left. Finally, the young secretary waved Mikhail up to the desk. He indicated Sergei. 'No, no, we're together,' he told her. 'Major Listnitsky told us both to come.'

The secretary frowned, picked up the phone, and had a brief, muffled conversation behind her hand. She put down the phone and picked up the two remaining files. 'You may both go in.'

Major Listnitsky sat, nonchalantly leaning back in an office chair, with his boots resting on the desk. He was leafing through a file and pulled his reading glasses down his nose when they came in. 'Ah good, you did come after all. Sorry for the wait, it's been a busy day.'

He waved at two chairs in front of his desk. 'Take a seat – no need for the usual formalities.'

The room was bare, save for a single large desk piled high with manila folders, the visitors' chairs, and a large street map of Petrograd pinned to the wall. French doors opened out onto a small balcony overlooking the front courtyard, allowing a faint stream of sunlight into the room. Flecks of dust hung in the sunlight and the room had that musty smell of old damp paper.

The major swung his legs off the desk, walked over to the French doors, and stared down at the courtyard. 'I guess you may have encountered our new Commander-in-Chief downstairs,' he said, looking out the window with his back turned. 'He's a formidable character, and quite different from Brusilov. Things are a bit hectic around here, as you may have seen, and the general expects everyone to operate at the same pace as he does.'

'We were down there when he arrived', said Mikhail. 'Those guards of his . . .'

'Yes, and he can even speak their language which is a real problem for the rest of us, but that aside, let's get to the point why you're here.'

The major turned away from the window and faced them. 'I've been tasked to urgently put together several missions. The other officers you saw out there,' he indicated towards the anteroom, 'are also being sent into Petrograd, but there is one job in particular that is sensitive and requires special skills. I think you two could be just the men for the job. I'm taking a bit of a gamble, but frankly, I don't have the time and I need to take you on face value. I hope you won't disappoint.'

'Mission?' asked Mikhail.

'You're not being re-assigned to a unit, not at this moment anyway. You are about to go on paid leave from the Army, and you will be taking that leave in Petrograd.'

Sergei looked sideways at Mikhail and grinned. 'Petrograd!'

'Don't get too excited, young man,' said the major, 'this isn't any holiday, far from it.'

The young secretary had left their folders on the major's desk. He picked up one, opened it, and cleared his throat. 'Kapitan Mikhail Mehenov, late of the 11th. A graduate from the Pavlovsk Military College in Saint Petersburg.'

'We both are, sir,' confirmed Mikhail.

'Fellow students eh, and you say you know your way around the capital?'

'Unless it's changed since we were there – it's been a few years.'

'I can assure you it hasn't,' replied the major, waving towards the street map on the wall. 'But, in my mind, that's not the main credential. What sparked my interest in the two of you was your experience in urban street fighting. The retreat in Ternopol must have been horrendous, and you somehow managed to get the Volinsky Regiment out of the mess and still maintained a coherent fighting structure.'

'I would like to think so,' said Mikhail.

'Don't be so bashful, Kapitan,' said the major. 'Now tell me about your parents, especially the political leaning of the family.'

'My parents are both dead, sir. I'm married to one of the Sukhov girls; they're really my family now. Mr. Sukhov is the main merchant in Barnaul, and he also has some factories and a small horse stud.'

'And the politics?'

'They're not Bolsheviks, if that's what you mean, probably more democrat than anything. My father-in-law had been a tsarist over the years but, since the February Revolution, you could call him disillusioned with the old regime. I do admit, though, my wife does hold some rather socialist views on things, and there's always a lively debate around the dining table.'

The major smiled. 'Show me a dining table in Russia where there isn't.'

He picked up the other file, opened it, and frowned. 'Lieutenant Sergei Vinokurov.'

Sergei straightened in the chair. 'Is there a problem, sir?'

'I'll be blunt: your file says you're Jewish.'

Sergei flushed bright red.

'It wasn't noted on your original file,' continued the major, 'but somebody has stamped it since then. I assume it was done after you went through military college, or you wouldn't have got in.'

'But I'm not really Jewish,' protested Sergei. 'My mother was, but she passed away years ago.'

'I'm afraid the nuances of racial lineage get lost on people, and some of the people you will have to deal with may not appreciate you aren't a practicing Jew. But the bigger question is whether you can keep your mouth shut and not rise to the bait.'

'Rise to the bait, I don't understand?'

'These people can be very forthright. They may say things you vehemently object to and you may be deeply insulted. I cannot risk you losing your temper and saying or doing something that would jeopardize the mission.'

'Religion's not the sort of thing I talk about,' answered Sergei, 'I guess I'm not really that religious at all. If the mission is that important, and I'm considered a risk, why not just send Captain Mehenov?'

'Because lieutenant,' said the major, taking off his glasses and polishing them on his tie, 'this mission is bigger than just one person alone. You two, in the limited time we have talked together, have described how you acted as a team in close combat in an urban setting. Don't let that go to your head; you're all I've got with those credentials.'

'Then', said Sergei, shifting uncomfortably in his chair, 'I'll guarantee I'll keep my head down and mouth shut.'

'Well then, let us keep it like that, shall we? And your father?'

'He owns the Tyumentsevsky Horse Stud in the Pavlosk region. Mikhail's father-in-law and he are good friends. Our families are close, which is why we went away to military college together.'

'Am I to assume a similar political persuasion?'

'The stud is quite isolated, and father does his best to keep politics away from the workers. He says it can only cause trouble.'

'Good luck with that,' said the major, as he walked across to the map and jabbed at it with his finger. 'The officers I'm sending into Petrograd will all be going in "undercover". You will be in civilian clothes, and even though you are officially on leave from the Army, if you get apprehended, the Army will disavow all knowledge of you.'

'Who would apprehend us?' asked Mikhail.

'All sorts of people – the Bolshevik mob will pounce on anyone remotely looking like officer class. Kerensky is also deeply suspicious of the Army's motives and jumps at every shadow, and everyone thinks there's a German spy down every alley. Put all that together, and you are about to walk into a snake pit of suspicion. Besides, rumors of coups abound everywhere. It's the only thing people are talking about;

in their mind it's just a question of who jumps first. Will it be the Bolsheviks or the Army? Why is the 3rd Cavalry Corps being positioned so close to Petrograd? Will the Government run or stay? Everyone seems to have forgotten the Germans are just up the road in Riga and could attack at any time.'

'So why are we, and all the other officers, being sent into Petrograd?' asked Mikhail. 'Won't that just reinforce the fears of an army coup?'

'It's a precaution,' answered the major, perching himself on the edge of his desk. 'There's no denying it may look suspicious to some, but we need to be prepared for any eventuality.' The major jabbed a finger. 'The one certainty is the Bolsheviks will make a move, and probably soon.'

The major picked up a pamphlet from his desk and waved it at them. 'You just have to read this – Lenin's "What is to be Done" – it's all here in black and white. They intend to grab power rather than endure more failures at the ballot box. The Army owes it to Russia to prevent this. It's not a case of Kornilov, or the Army, wanting to take over.'

'So, what's our role in all of this?' asked Mikhail.

'We've been told there are many organizations in the city prepared to come out on the streets to resist a Bolshevik coup, but they are asking for support. They may be enthusiastic and willing but, without doubt, they will lack weapons, training, organization and leadership. That's where you come in. Let me be clear, gentlemen, your job is to organize and plan, not start a revolution. But if the 3rd Corp is activated and needs to enter the city to restore order, then your actions will be crucial to the success of this operation.'

'And how will we know the time to act?'

'The people you will be working with will know. The situation in Petrograd is very fluid and very dangerous, and changes by the day, but you will know when the time is right. We may not be in contact every day, but there is a secret line of communication we can use.'

'And the other officers?' asked Sergei.

'They have their own missions, separate and different to yours. The two of you will be acting independently of them. We don't expect you will have contact with any of these officers once you are in the city, in fact we actively discourage it.'

The major walked over to the door and opened it. 'Sophie, can you come in here for a minute, and bring the paperwork.' He turned back to Mikhail and Sergei. 'You will need to sign for your leave, and then this young lady will take you down to the Quartermaster to have you kitted out in civilian clothes. Then, she will take you over to the Training Section – we call it "tradecraft" – basic skills to keep you in communication, and hopefully keep you alive. After you have completed your course, we will give you a detailed briefing. Is all that clear?'

'With due respect, major, are we being asked to volunteer for this mission?'

The major looked at them and shook his head. 'While I can't order you, "no" is not an acceptable option. Now, please go with the young lady.'

Sergei grinned. 'That will be a pleasure, sir.'

'Lieutenant,' the major quickly retorted, 'before you get ideas above your station, this young lady is my wife's niece.'

Chapter 14

THE STALKERS

Barnaul September 1917

PAVEL'S TROIKA REACHED the top of the crest where the rutted dirt track started its descent into the shallow valley. At the bottom of the valley, a line of willows marked the watercourse of a small stream, close to where the homestead stood. In the late afternoon light, the house lay in shadows; however, Pavel could easily pick it out and was pleased – someone in the family had the foresight to light the house lanterns for the approaching dusk.

They must be expecting me, or someone?

The crest had always been a boundary for Pavel – the journey's end was finally in sight, and he was now entering his land. At one time he had thought of this as a haven, an island of serenity far from the despondency and danger of the town. But ever since the deserters butchered one of his horses, the isolation of the farm and leaving the family alone out here brought new concerns.

The torture and hanging of Grigory had troubled, even frightened, him. He hadn't liked the man or his politics, but was horrified at the terrible treatment people could inflict on another human being - the red, raw burn marks all over Grigory's body a testament to the pain he must have endured. Perhaps, surmised Pavel, the hangman's noose had come as a welcome release.

He and Nikifor had departed town on their separate ways, Nikifor to the safety of his brother's cabin in the forest, and Pavel to the comparative safety of the farm. He had moved quickly, instructing his driver to harness the horses while he hastily packed. Fortunately they made it out of town without encountering trouble. He was aware of the location of Bolshevik militia checkpoints at the main exits of the town and, with local knowledge, knew paths that could take them around these.

Once out of the town, the track leading to the farm wound for several *versts* through thick forest. It did not quite have the tangled denseness of the *taiga*, but enough to easily hide a person from view. That worked for Pavel's escape, but it would also work for anyone else moving through the forest, or lying in wait along the track.

Pavel couldn't quite put his finger on what alerted him first, but there was something or somebody behind him on the track. Not close, but not too far way. Occasionally there were faint, unusual sounds not normally associated with the forest and, another time, a flock of ravens were disturbed and rose, screeching into the sky.

Pavel had instructed the driver to halt the troika twice, and they sat motionless, in tense silence, straining to listen.

Was that the faint sound of hooves on the track behind them, or was it his imagination? Was the almost imperceptible swish of something moving through the undergrowth just the light breeze rustling the leaves in the canopy? It was difficult, almost impossible, to discern.

Whoever was back there did not want to be seen, and neither did they appear to want to catch up to him. The sounds Pavel heard seemed to remain a similar distance behind them and, whenever he had the troika stop, the forest quickly lapsed into a disquieting silence.

After a time, the dark, tangled forest gradually thinned out into clusters of silver birch and dappled sunlight, and the track emerged onto a stretch of open grassland. Several hundred meters ahead, across the open space, the track mounted a low crest before dropping out of sight where it wound down into the hidden valley.

Pavel glanced back over his shoulder and urged the driver on. 'Make the crest as quickly as you can,' he told the driver, 'and pull up once we're on the other side.'

The driver flicked the reins and the three horses pulled at the traces and broke into a fast canter. As the troika bumped over the rutted track, Pavel kept looking back, fearful of the vulnerability of being out in the open and half expecting to hear the report of a rifle. But mercifully no bullets came, and the troika managed to pass over the crest without incident.

The driver pulled hard on the brake and reined back the horses as Pavel slid his rifle out of its leather holster and pulled out the binoculars from under the seat. 'Stay with the horses,' he instructed the driver as he stepped down from the stationary carriage.

Bending low, he carefully worked his way over to a rocky outcrop off to one side of the track. He crawled over the last piece of ground and slowly raised his head above the rock.

From his vantage point he gazed back over the open, undulating grassland to the edge of the birch trees in the distance. Carefully shielding the binocular lenses from reflecting the low sun, he adjusted the focus and slowly swept along the forest edge, concentrating on where the track emerged from the forest.

At first Pavel thought they were just a couple of blackened tree stumps among a copse of mottled silver birch. He ignored them until one of the stumps moved, and then the other moved as well.

Two riders slowly emerged from the forest and halted their horses at the edge of the forest. They appeared not to want to move into the open, electing to stay close together in the shadows of the trees. One of them pointed up the track in Pavel's direction, and then over his shoulder, towards the forest behind.

In the fading light it was difficult for Pavel to bring the riders into clear focus, and they were too distant to distinguish facial features. He noted the crossed ammunition bandoliers and the way they carried their rifles slung over their backs with the muzzle pointing down. Their horses had the dusty brown shaggy coat and heavy set of working farm horses, and each horse carried large double saddlebags.

I don't know who you are, but I know what you are.

Pavel rolled on his side, worked the bolt of his rifle, and pushed a round into the chamber. He adjusted the rear sights up to maximum and then carefully slid the rifle forward, resting it on top of a low rock.

Steadying the rifle, he took a deep breath and held it while he drew a bead on one of the men. It would be a long shot, possibly too long, and he couldn't afford to miss. He needed to take one of them down and hope the other would flee.

Come on you bastards, just another hundred meters.

But they did not move. They just sat talking to each other and then, as suddenly as they had appeared, wheeled their horses and rode back into the forest.

Pavel waited until they were gone, then slid back down the slope until well below the crest. He then carefully rose into a crouch and ran back to the troika. The driver looked at him quizzically. 'Is everything all right, sire?'

'They've gone, I think.'

'Who were they?' asked the driver.

'We'll never know,' answered Pavel, with a shrug. He didn't want to alarm the driver. 'Maybe hunters, or just travelers – perhaps they were lost. We don't get too many people who come out to these parts.'

He climbed up into the carriage and sheathed his rifle. It was only then he noticed his hands were shaking.

A thin veil of mist had formed along the stream at the bottom of the valley as the troika bumped its way down the rough dirt track. The valley air was heavy with the fragrance of wood smoke; cooking would be underway in the homestead kitchen and the workers' cooking hut, and several fireplaces would be alight, warming the big house as the evening temperature quickly dropped.

The driver eased the troika to a halt in the holding yards, a large area of trampled earth bordered by gable-roofed stables. A young bare-foot peasant boy ran out to grab hold of the bridles and steady the horses.

Several wagons and carriages took up one corner of the yard, and a group of shrieking children were using them to stage a mock battle. A saddle and tackle room, a yard office, and a blacksmith's workshop completed the compound, the rough-sawn timbers of the buildings painted with black creosote.

Behind the stables stood the peasants' quarters, an enclave of six small huts for the married workers, and one long dormitory building for the single men. The farm had fewer workers these days, with so many being away at the war; it was mostly the laughter and chatter of womenfolk that drifted on the stillness of the evening shadows.

Pavel picked up his rifle and valise and stepped down from the troika. 'Can you find the foreman and ask him to come up to the house?' Pavel instructed the driver.

He walked over the footbridge to the picket gate at the bottom of the homestead's garden. As he swung the gate open, Berkut and Sokoi, a pair of angular Borzois with studded leather collars, loped down through the wet autumn leaves, wagging their tails and barking joyfully. The dogs nuzzled cold wet noses into Pavel's outstretched hand. He leaned down and scratched the soft curly coat between their ears, and then pushed them away as they leapt up at him in excitement. The dogs were tall and could easily knock him over in their exuberance. Pavel growled, 'Away', and pointed up towards the verandah. The dogs immediately obeyed and bounded off ahead of him up the grassy slope.

The rambling two-story homestead stood on the far slope, above the stream, its timber walls and the roof's wood shingles bleached silver-grey by the elements. Windows, edged with pastel blue shutters, were latched back to catch the last of the evening sun. A wide verandah flanked all sides of the house, and an old wisteria vine wove through the verandah latticework; its purple flowers, now shed, lay scattered across the lawn already damp with evening dew.

Maria Ivanova had come out on to the verandah, a shawl wrapped around her shoulders. She had a frown on her face, but relaxed when she recognized Pavel. Dmitry was with her, a rifle cradled in his arms like a soldier standing guard.

'An unexpected pleasure,' said Maria, descending the steps and giving him a peck on the cheek. 'We didn't expect you until Friday.'

'Trouble in town,' replied Pavel. 'It's better I'm out here until it calms down a bit.'

'Have you closed the shops?'

'No, Katrina will keep them running.'

Maria's smile faded. 'I'm sure she will,' she said curtly, then stood back and gave him an appraising look. 'Been crawling around in the grass have you? There's mud all over the front of your suit.'

'A couple of men were following us on the track. I went back to have a look, they've gone now.' Pavel wanted to change the subject. 'The house lanterns?' he asked. 'You said you weren't expecting me.'

'The neighbor rode over a few days ago to warn us. He says there's a band of partisans been seen in the area. The other day a farmhouse over near the Pavlovsk Trakt was ransacked and burnt. People were murdered. We've taken to lighting the lanterns as a precaution.'

'I'm not sure it would stop anyone, but I guess it can't do any harm.'

A maid had come out on to the veranda with Pavel's slippers. She shooed the dogs away and knelt to help Pavel take off his riding boots. The dogs came back to sit, one on either side of Pavel, their heads tilted, watching quizzically as the maid tugged away at the boots.

Iya joined them on the verandah, her frizzy hastily pulled-back hair looking a bit unkempt. There were red rings under her eyes and her cheeks were flushed.

'Mikhail.' It was more of a question than a statement.

Pavel gave a slight shake of his head. 'I'm sorry, there's still nothing.'

Iya clapped a hand across her mouth, turned and ran back inside the house. Pavel could hear her running down the hall and up the stairs, and then the loud slam of her bedroom door.

Maria shook her head, pushed one of the dogs aside, and pulled up a cane chair next to Pavel. 'How many weeks is it now?'

'We visit the Post Office every day, and I drop by the Town Hall regularly to check the casualty lists. No mention of Mikhail, or Sergei for that matter, but what's strange is there's no casualties listed from the 11th Division at all. Perhaps they've been pulled out of the line.'

Maria frowned, 'Isn't no casualties good news?'

'The papers say thousands of our men have been taken prisoner, perhaps Mikhail may have been captured, but the whole 11th?'

Maria gripped Pavel's forearm. 'What about that man, you know the *anglais* you send reports to? He may have contacts at Mogilev; perhaps he can make enquires?'

Pavel shook his head. 'If I thought it would do any good – but I've only met him once and don't know where he is or even if I know his actual name. I think he just calls himself Captain Spencer.'

Maria sat in silence for a while, smoothing out the pinafore on her lap. When she finally spoke, she said, 'Iya's convinced some harm has come to him. You can see what she's like, a bundle of nerves, apart from when she's sipping laudanum.'

'Can't you stop her?'

'I'm not sure I want to try. You should see the state she gets in when she runs out.'

'And Galina?'

'Galina just keeps being Galina,' answered Maria. 'Doesn't show anything on the outside, but I know she's worried.'

'About Mikhail?'

Maria playfully punched Pavel's arm. 'You silly man, it's all about Sergei, not that she hears much from him anyway.'

'I'm doing the best I can,' said Pavel with a sigh. 'Many families are in a lot worse position than us – they've already lost sons to the war and all we're worrying about is a letter not arriving for a couple of weeks. With the state of the war it's a miracle any mail gets through at all. We shouldn't try to read into it any more than that.'

The maid returned and set down a tray holding a shot glass, an ice-cold bottle of vodka, and a silver bowl of caviar on a nearby table.

'Don't let the dogs knock it over,' said Maria, as she stood up to leave. 'I need to go and give the cook a hand. She's all in a fluster with you turning up unexpectedly, as you did.'

Pavel shook his head as he reached for the bottle. 'Don't worry, they won't have a chance.'

Maria wagged a finger at him. 'Don't be long, and don't drink too much of that stuff.'

Pavel could see the foreman coming through the garden gate and heading up towards the house. 'I asked the foreman to come and see me,' said Pavel, 'it won't take more than a few minutes.'

Pavel stood and started unbuttoning his frockcoat as Maria walked back into the house. 'And make sure Iya joins us for supper,' Pavel called after her retreating figure. 'She knows family rules.'

Pavel leaned against a verandah post in his shirtsleeves and lit a cheroot. The foreman, dutifully standing off until Maria had gone, coughed politely to announce his presence. The dogs gave him a perfunctory bark, then settled down again.

'Good evening, Ivan Nikolayevich.'

The foreman removed his cap and held it in front of him, scrunched up in his fists. He was an old man and continual exposure to the elements had left his face tanned and hardened to the color and consistency of saddle leather. Two tufts of white hair above his ears punctuated his glistening scalp, giving him the comic look of a circus clown.

'I believe you wish to see me, sire.'

'Come up onto the verandah, I want a quiet word.'

The foreman hesitated, accustomed only to the servants' entrance, but Pavel insisted, indicating the cane chair next to him.

Pavel opened his cheroot tin. 'Here, take one.'

Pavel struck a match on the stone step and cupped the match in his hand as the foreman leaned forward.

'The driver probably told you we were followed tonight,' Pavel said. 'Two horsemen tracked us all the way from town. They stopped just after leaving the forest.'

The foreman just nodded, intently studying the end of his glowing cheroot.

'Have you had reports of any sightings recently?' asked Pavel. 'Anything unusual happened?'

The foreman stared out into the distance and blew a thin stream of smoke into the damp evening air. 'They come and go, sire. Sometimes I see them, or sometimes hear that they've been, but mostly I don't get told.'

'Do you know who they are and what they're doing out here?'

He shook his head.

'I don't exactly know, all I know it's about politics. They bring pamphlets for those who can read, but they mostly just talk to our people, sneaking into their quarters under cover of night. Same as other farms in the area I hear.'

'Bolsheviks?' asked Pavel.

'Aye sire, I believe it's mostly them.'

'What are they trying to do, stir up trouble?'

'Putting temptation in our people's way, sire, like the Devil himself. Tell them they can have things not rightly theirs, and if you ask me, things they'll probably never have. These are godless people doing the devil's work. I don't trust them, that's what I say.'

'What do they tell them, these Bolshevik people?'

'They'll take your land and give it to them, there'll be peace and the men will come home from the war, and there'll be bread on every table.'

'What of our people – what do they think?'

'I've worked for your family for years, including your father, sire.'

'I don't doubt your loyalty, Ivan Nikolayevich, but what about the others?'

'It's the women who are the trouble, sire.' Ivan looked down at his feet and shook his head. 'With the men away, there's only old men like me who've heard it all before, or young boys with chaff between their ears. But the women listen; they want their men home, and the idea of taking the rich people's land, it's a temptation. I catch them whispering about it to each other all the time, but none of them understand there'll be a price to pay. Nothing good comes for free.'

'But we've given them allotments and they've food on the table; nobody ever goes hungry here.'

'But there's still the war and the men away, and then,' the foreman looked around at the house, 'they see this and want the same for themselves.'

'Then you think there'll be trouble?'

The foreman shrugged as he flicked the stub of his cheroot away into the darkness of the evening. 'Depends.'

'On what?'

'Depends what happens in town and on the other farms, and our people just believe what they're told.'

'And that,' said Pavel, 'is only what the Bolsheviks want them to hear.'

'Seems to be that way, sire.'

'Thank you, Ivan Nikolayevich, that will be all for now. But I want you to tell me the moment you think there'll be trouble. If I'm not here, you tell Maria Ivanova, I'm relying on you for this.'

The foreman stood, put his cap back on, and had started walking down the steps when he turned and looked back at Pavel.

'Sire, you also need to know our people are frightened – these are bad men who come to see them. They use threats against anyone who does not agree with their politics.'

"What sort of threats?'

'They tell them they need to choose between your way and their way,' replied the foreman, 'but tell them there's only one choice.'

Chapter 15

THE DINNER AT THE FARM

Early September 1917

THE FAMILY ASSEMBLED that evening in the dining room. At six sharp Maria banged the dinner gong, sending it reverberating through the large house; just one loud *gong* was enough to bring the family hurrying lest they incur their mother's wrath.

Pavel was allowed to be a little late, especially since he had just ridden out from town, but this gave the family time to assemble and wait for his entrance, for the meal could not start until he was seated. He was mindful of this, and careful not to abuse this patriarchal privilege.

The long dining room was towards the back of the house, next to the kitchen area for convenience of serving. An ancient Persian rug, purchased decades ago by old Grandfather Sukhov from a passing caravan, covered most of the oiled timber floor. The walls were lined with dark varnished timber and heavy red velvet curtains hung over the windows to keep in the heat.

The room was warm and inviting. The crackling open fireplace at one end and the row of ornate kerosene lanterns suspended above the table bathed the walls in a soft, flickering light. The Sukhovs' town house had its own supply of electricity, but out here in the countryside, the lighting and heating came from traditional sources.

The walls were adorned with large portraits of previous heads of the family – the stern, heavily-bearded glowering faces and rigid postures of Pavel's father, his grandfather and his great-grandfather. However, recently Maria had had their wedding photograph reframed, reshuffled the traditional order, and positioned it in pride of place above Pavel's chair at the end of the table. Pavel was a bit startled when he first saw the addition, but silently acquiesced to preserve marital harmony.

A long, heavy sideboard ran down one wall, laden with covered silver serving dishes, each with small kerosene warmers. Two young maids wearing dark skirts with lace aprons and caps stood silently at either end of the sideboard, with downcast eyes and hands clasped before them, waiting to serve the meal.

Pavel had changed for dinner into a soft, collarless peasant shirt, loose Cossack-style breeches, and slippers. An unashamed devotee of Tolstoy, he was always reading his books. In particular, he was fond of "The Cossacks", the tale of Olenin, a young officer who turned his back on Moscow society and travelled to Chechnya where he became infatuated with the simple Cossack way of life, though his experience was unfortunately marred by heartbreak, his unrequited love for a beautiful Cossack girl. Pavel had read and re-read the story several times and it celebrated, in his mind, the simple yet satisfying existence of life in the countryside, driven by the pure forces of nature, far removed from the industrial grubbiness of the Russian cities to the West.

A long, polished mahogany dining table, purchased and imported at great expense from a salon in Paris, was covered with an intricate white lace tablecloth that Maria had made by hand. The table separated Pavel and Maria, sitting at each end like two bookends, with the four children taking up positions along either side. There was an unspoken order: Galina, the eldest, always sat next to her mother to assist with serving the meal if required. The position opposite her was reserved for the next eldest, Iya, while the two younger members of the family in order, Mara and Dmitry, were always at Pavel's end of the table, hoping distance would protect them from their mother's ire should they inadvertently commit any breach of dining etiquette.

And of course, Berkut and Sokoi always managed to slip unnoticed into the room and, like silent sentinels, took up position in the dark recesses under the table, as close as they could get to Pavel's legs. There, they waited patiently for his hand to slide morsels surreptitiously to their eager mouths below.

Mara and Galina sat quietly conversing in French while waiting for the others to arrive, until Maria came into the room and glared at them. Effortlessly and without halting their conversation, they switched to Russian just as their father entered the room with Dmitry. Pavel didn't mind them speaking French; they had learned the language throughout their school years and were totally fluent, but the aristocracy and aspiring middle classes who often refused to speak their mother tongue annoyed Pavel and he had steadfastly refused to learn French. For the girls in the family, it was like a secret code, but Maria likened it to talking behind someone's back, and forbade French in Pavel's presence.

Iya was last to arrive, entering the room slightly puffy-eyed, but calm in a melancholy sort of way. She took her allotted place at the table where she sat quietly, head down and kneading a damp handkerchief in her lap.

Despite Iya's pervading air of despondency and the nagging threat of the horsemen and the night visitors, Pavel was in a surprisingly buoyant mood. Perhaps it was one too many glasses of vodka, or the relief of getting out of the town and finding the family still safe. The farm had always felt like a cocoon – isolated, impregnable and shielded from the realities of the outside world. Not even those who had stalked him, nor the knowledge of secret visitations, could dent his intrinsic belief in the security of home. While seeds of doubt had been sown, and his belief partially shaken, Pavel was determined to remain resolute.

'Welcome home, Papa.' It was Galina with her broad smile, and a bobbed, short haircut. She was wearing her tweed riding jacket and a suede split-riding skirt. 'I'm sorry; I haven't had time to change. We've a new foal down at the stables.'

'Great to hear, everything's okay I hope?'

'Don't worry, he's absolutely gorgeous and suckling well, and his mother's doing just fine.'

Pavel laughed. 'Then we have something to drink to.' He got up to go to the sideboard, but Maria coughed politely and waved him to sit down.

'Perhaps we should say grace first?'

'Forgive me, Maria Ivanova.'

Pavel extended his arms and the family reached out, joined hands, and bowed their heads. Pavel quickly went through the recitation, the words tumbling out in a rush, as though he was in a race to get to the end. While the rest of the family crossed themselves, Pavel reached over to the sideboard for the decanter of red wine and filled his own glass.

'Is this the Romanian?' he asked, holding his glass up to the light and admiring its deep, rich color.

'You're down to the last few cases,' said Maria, in a disapproving tone. 'You should make it last.'

'Damn those Germans cutting off the Crimea,' said Pavel, waving the decanter around, 'so hard to get anything decent these days – ladies?'

Maria mouthed "*no thank you*", but Galina and Mara pushed their glasses forward. Iya declined with a shake of her head. 'I'll just have water.'

Pavel winked at Dmitry who grinned and surreptitiously slid his glass over towards his father.

'Pavel Dmitrievich!' exclaimed Maria.

'It's all right *mushka*,' responded Pavel, 'he's nearly seventeen. In my book if he's old enough to go to war, then he's old enough to drink. I'll only give him half and he can add water.'

Maria just shook her head and gestured to the maids to start bringing the dishes to the table.

'Great,' said Pavel, rubbing his hands together, 'I'm starving.'

'Can't you find someone to feed you in town?' asked Maria. It was a loaded question that Pavel decided to ignore.

'I left in so much of a hurry, I didn't have time to have any lunch.'

'Was there trouble in town?' asked Galina. 'Is that why you left early?'

Pavel looked down the table to Maria and gave a small shake of his head. 'Nothing that's out of the ordinary,' he answered, 'the same old stuff – deserters loitering about, the camps causing trouble, a lot of stealing, the Soviet trying to throw its weight around.'

Galina went to ask another question, but Maria clapped her hands. 'You heard your father. He hasn't eaten all day so we can discuss this later.'

One of the maids carried over a large silver bowl, placed it carefully in front of Maria, and took off the lid. At once the room was filled with a wonderful, rich aroma.

'I'm afraid it's only borscht,' said Maria apologetically, 'but we've cuts of cold venison, with hot mashed potato, the last of the summer's green beans, and gravy to follow. We just didn't expect you out so soon.'

'Sounds wonderful,' said Pavel, unfolding a large white napkin and tucking it into the front collar of his shirt. 'Anything beats cold sausage on a slab of stale black bread.'

'Undoubtedly washed down with a bottle of beer,' laughed Mara.

'Or two,' added Galina, 'and don't forget the cheroot.'

'Girls,' said Maria sharply, 'stop making fun of your father and pass the bowls down.'

Maria ladled out the soup, ensuring each bowl received a large piece of succulent meat swimming in rich brown gravy, a spoonful of caramelized onions, and small, tender pieces of beetroot. 'I'm afraid it has only been on the stove for three days, not the normal five,' said Maria, 'so I can't vouch for the tenderness of the meat.'

'I'm sure it will be wonderful,' said Pavel. 'Borscht, the staple of the people and the land; Lev Nikolayevich Tolstoy would be proud.'

'The dear Count,' said Iya, picking up the bowl of sour cream and emphatically spooning a large dollop into the center of her bowl, 'may have dressed like them, talked of his love for them, but I'm sure he never had to eat like them. Father, this is not peasant food – they can only dream of borscht like this.'

'I think we should be careful what we say,' said Pavel, glancing towards the maids. 'We should wish for every Russian to eat as well.'

'And how is that going to happen?' asked Iya, who looked over at Mara and indicated with a flip of her hand. 'Go on, show Mother and Father what you found.'

Mara blushed and fumbled in the pocket of her pinafore. She pulled out a crumpled piece of paper and smoothed it out on the table. 'One of the boys in the class had this.'

Iya put her spoon down. 'It's somewhat ironical, but Mara and I are teaching the children to read and write, as you have requested us to do.' She leaned over, tapping the piece of paper for emphasis. 'So, now they can read Bolshevik pamphlets to their parents. This is how they're going to get their borscht – *Peace, Land & Bread*. What they don't have they'll take, and they plan to take from us.'

Iya took the pamphlet and pushed it towards Pavel. 'You should read what it says.'

'I don't need to,' answered Pavel, 'they're all over town.'

'And did you know about our workers?' asked Iya.

'The foreman just told me this evening.'

Maria arched her eyebrows, and then shook her head. 'We shouldn't be talking about this in front of the staff.'

The maids gave each other a surreptitious glance, and then resumed their rigid stance with their eyes fixed to a spot on the floor in front of them.

'Mother,' said Iya, 'there's nothing that's said, or goes on in this house, the staff doesn't know about. Besides, they don't just hate us for what we are; they hate us for what they are.'

'We should get on with the meal,' said Maria, indicating to the maids to clear the bowls and bring the next course. Once the dishes had been placed on the table, she dismissed them from the room with a wave of her hand.

Pavel stood over the venison wielding a fork and a razor-sharp carving knife. The dogs caught the scent of the freshly cut meat and stirred under the table, nuzzling into his leg. He sliced thick portions then passed the plates down for Maria to serve the mashed potato, while Iya served up the beans. As the gravy boat was being handed around, Galina asked, 'Then what are we going to do, stay here and wait for something to happen, or leave like everyone else?'

'It would be good,' said Mara, carving off a tiny portion of meat and delicately piercing it with her fork, 'if Father could stay out here with us more often, or do you plan to go back into town?'

'Monday,' answered Pavel. 'We've a business to run, and something,' he waved his knife around the room, 'has to pay for all of this.'

'How long do you think we can keep the shops open for? You're always complaining about the lack of customers these days, so why do you persist?'

'There's Father's reports for the *anglais,* I guess 'interjected Iya.

Maria gave her a sharp look. 'You know never to speak about that.'

'Besides,' said Pavel, 'if I was out here all the time, we wouldn't know what on earth is going on. Lenin could have taken over Russia and we'd be none the wiser.'

'Do you think a newspaper that is two weeks old keeps us up to date with current events?' asked Iya. 'Does that offset the danger we are in?'

'There's always the telegraph,' retorted Pavel, defensively.

Iya smiled. 'Papa, only when the partisans haven't cut the wire again.'

'I am,' said Dmitry, taking a sip of his wine, 'teaching Iya and Mara how to shoot, if that helps.'

Galina laughed. 'I think we'll all be in danger of our own lives if that happens.'

'Dearest sister,' said Iya, putting down her knife and fork and folding her hands into her lap, 'I don't care much for Dmitry's silly little cans on the fence, I just want to learn how to load a rifle and pull the trigger. If it comes to a decision between being raped then murdered, and placing a rifle muzzle in my mouth, then I'll know what to do.'

'Iya,' Maria slapped her hand angrily on the table, 'talking about taking one's life is sacrilegious.'

'Then Mama, what would you suggest we do?'

'We should eat the food God has graciously placed on our table.'

The family lapsed into silence as everyone concentrated on devouring the meal, all except Iya, who prodded aimlessly at the food on her plate.

'What do you think is going to happen, Papa?' asked Galina. 'The newspapers you bring home aren't just old, they're confusing.'

Pavel sat back and took a sip of his wine. 'Kerensky, it's hard to see how he can hang on. The Mensheviks, the Bolsheviks, and Kornilov all vying for power – the whole thing's a mess, and that's beside the fact that we are supposed to be fighting the Germans.'

'Perhaps,' proffered Maria, 'it would be better if General Kornilov and the Army take over the reins and stabilize the situation, even just for a short period of time.'

'But Mother,' said Iya, her hands clenched into a fist, 'that would inflame the situation further. The workers would be enraged. They'll see it for what it is, supporting the old regime and resisting change. Then just try to get the Army to step back once they've tasted power. Instead of the Duma, we'll have the generals running the country. What sort of progress is that?'

Galina pushed her plate away. 'Do you think your Menshevik friends will do a better job?'

Iya glared at her. 'They're not my friends,' she retorted sharply, 'but Russia needs to change, or change will be thrust upon it. At least the Mensheviks offer a planned and peaceful path forward, even if it leads us towards a Marxist socialist state. They're better than the Bolsheviks who just want to grab power.'

'They wouldn't dare,' said Mara, 'I've read they don't have enough support.'

'That's never worried the Bolsheviks,' said Pavel. 'Lenin is so convinced he's right he can't be bothered to wait for public opinion to catch on to his theories. He'll just drag Russia along with him.'

'I don't understand,' asked Maria, 'how can they just overthrow the government?'

'Mother,' said Iya, 'it's called a revolution – a violent minority seizes power while the rest of the nation mutely stands by and watches.'

'But we'd fight them,' said Dmitry, indignantly – his face flushed bright red.

Pavel laid a restraining hand on his arm. 'And that, my son, is called a civil war, and nobody would ever want that.'

'Russians fighting Russians,' said Maria emphatically. 'God forbid, it's inconceivable.'

'Hardly inconceivable,' said Iya, 'remember Americans fighting fellow Americans in their civil war.'

'But that was all about slavery,' responded Maria, tersely.

'And so, Mama, is this.'

Iya abruptly stood and pushed her chair back. 'If you will excuse me, I'll go upstairs and write to Mikhail so Papa can post it on Monday or, dare I say, send it into that black void which is known as the Russian Army postal system.'

'I'm sure some of the mail does get through,' suggested Pavel, without too much conviction.

'When you don't get any response,' answered Iya, 'you wonder whether it's all worth it, but I feel duty bound to at least try. It's hard when the person you're writing to may not be alive. And what do I tell him? If he is alive and ever makes it home, we may not be here. We might have been forced to disappear off into our own dark void. In the vastness of Russia, how will we ever find each other again? Leave a note pinned to the front door?'

'You should try to be positive,' said Pavel. 'The Army doesn't get a lot right, but it is good at posting casualty lists, and I haven't seen his name appear.'

'You should tell him about the new foal,' suggested Galina brightly, 'that's some good news.'

Iya threw her arms into the air in exasperation.

'Here we are, teetering on the brink of revolution and civil war and you suggest I write about a foal. Perhaps, on a lighter note, I should also include a bit about shooting holes in tin cans.'

'First of all,' said Dmitry, with a smirk, 'you need to hit one of the tin cans.'

Chapter 16

TRAIN TO PETROGRAD

Mid September 1917

THE VIEW THROUGH the grimy carriage window was flat and mostly featureless as the train chugged its way slowly northward towards Petrograd from Mogilev. It was traveling parallel to the Gulf of Finland, but well inland. Only an occasional reed-banked river and series of small lakes or swamps broke the monotony of the otherwise bleak landscape. Spots of rain flecked the windows and distorted the view, leaving the autumn leaves of the birches, larches and oaks just a blurred palette of mixed color moving in slow motion across the window.

Mikhail had taken the seat next to the window. For a while he kept wiping it with his sleeve as the moist heat of the carriage condensed against the cold glass, but he soon gave up trying to look out, and squeezed himself back into his space on the uncomfortable wooden bench seat. He had tried to sleep, but the cramped conditions, together with the overpowering stench of sweat and damp clothing, and the jolting of the carriage, kept him awake.

He glanced at Sergei next to him. He was in a deep sleep, with his head thrown back and his mouth open. Mikhail smiled. Sergei and the ever-energetic Tanya had spent one last boisterous night together. Over the last few days they had become noticeably fond of each other, although Tanya always maintained a professional detachment, and steadfastly refused to give up other customers unless Sergei paid for the privilege. Fortunately, Major Listnitsky had not made a return visit that may have posed something of a dilemma for both Sergei and Tanya.

Mikhail wasn't devoid of yearnings and even a touch of jealousy, as he observed the developing relationship between Sergei and the diminutive redhead. It had made him acutely aware of his self-imposed celibacy, and his mind kept drifting back to Iya and their own sexual relationship, back to their student days when they had shared the joy of discovering the pleasures of each other's young bodies. Now he worried whether it would be possible to rediscover and reignite past passion, or even if the desire was still there.

A life without women had not been an issue for Mikhail at the front. The ever-present threat of death, the physical exhaustion of long military campaigns, and the constant demands of command pushed any sexual desire far into the background. The companionship of a woman had long since been replaced by the camaraderie of the Officers' Mess, and the sense of shared danger with his men in the trenches. The latter had been true until the mutiny, which had shaken, if not destroyed, his feeling of kinship with the ordinary soldier. He now looked upon any of the rank and file with a significant level of distrust and a deeply troubling uncertainty as to whether his relationship with his men could ever be the same again.

Lodging in the Mogilev brothel, surrounded constantly by women in various states of undress, had rekindled some of his sexual desires – for the first time in years. He contemplated taking one of them upstairs, but thoughts of returning home with a dose of the pox blunted his enthusiasm. Besides, the sight of the ladies in the morning light, with frazzled hair and without makeup as they slouched around the kitchen table smoking and drinking coffee, was singularly unattractive.

Mikhail reached into his greatcoat pocket, pulled a dog-eared, faded photograph of Iya out of his wallet, and smoothed it out on his trouser leg. It was an image of her head and shoulders. She was staring straight into the camera with a small sideways tilt to her head, her lips slightly parted in a partial smile, and an inquisitive look in her eyes. She wore a plain linen sailor's top and no jewelry, save for a pair of small, plain earrings. Mikhail stared at the photograph, then closed his eyes and tried to recall an image of her as a whole person, not just a truncated one of her head and shoulders.

'Your girl?'

Mikhail looked up at the officer sitting opposite him. He was in a crisp, clean uniform with creases like knife-edges, and carried a brief-case on his lap with a chain around the handle padlocked to one wrist.

'*Stavka*', Mikhail thought to himself.

Mikhail blushed and slid the photograph back into his wallet. 'It is actually my wife, but the photograph was taken in our student days, back in Saint Petersburg as it was known then.'

'You're going on home leave?'

Mikhail shook his head. 'She's moved back to be with her family in Barnaul while the war is on. The lieutenant and I,' Mikhail nodded towards the sleeping Sergei, 'have been given a few days' leave in Petrograd. He was also a student when I was there. Neither of us has been back to the old town for years.'

The officer then became serious. 'If you think you'll be welcomed as a returning hero, then think again. And, if you were considering revisiting some of your old student haunts, then I would recommend against it. The reception could turn quite ugly, even if you are in civilian clothes. They only need to get a sniff you're an officer, and somebody will pick a fight with you. Better to stay off the streets if you can.'

'We're staying with friends,' lied Mikhail, then turned his head to look out the window, preferring to end the conversation before the officer asked too many questions.

Mikhail and Sergei had boarded the scheduled civilian train at Mogilev but, since it was a headquarters town, the train was mostly crammed with army personnel. A few suited businessmen occupied seats, probably army contractors or suppliers, Mikhail surmised. Most of them looked decidedly uncomfortable being surrounded by men in uniform. It was as though they carried a hidden guilt that fate had provided them with an escape from military service and, in turn, that had given them an opportunity to enrich themselves from the army's insatiable needs and bulging purse.

Mikhail and Sergei sat jammed together with three other officers on a bench seat designed for four. There had been no reserved seating – just a scramble to get on the train and find the first empty space. Most of the lower ranks reluctantly deferred to their superiors, and stood in the corridors, but not without much loud, and undisguised, grumbling.

'Welcome to our new egalitarian society,' suggested one of their fellow officers. 'We all better get used to it.'

'How can you tell who the enemy is these days?' The officer had leaned forward and whispered, mindful that the soldiers outside their compartment might overhear their conversation. 'Even some of our colleagues are now openly siding with the Reds. I've heard Brusilov may be now backing them; who would believe that?'

'I would say that's all about self-preservation,' commented another officer. 'If you're Brusilov, and you've just been sacked by Kerensky, you'll have revenge on your mind.'

'To be fair to Brusilov,' said another, 'he always had Russia's interests at heart. He was never a politician.'

'And that was his problem,' said another. 'He sat back and allowed Kerensky, a damned politician, to meddle. Either you have a command structure running the army, or you have the politicians and the soldiers' committees, but you can't have all of them.'

Mikhail leaned back with his eyes half closed, trying to ignore the discussion going on around him. The same tired lines were being repeated over and over in countless conversations throughout Russia but, in a crowded carriage, there was no escape from them.

The talk turned to the recent fall of Riga.

Not damned Riga again, Mikhail thought to himself.

The pain of failure was felt throughout the army. It surpassed even the ignominy of the failed Kerensky offensive.

A German force had, without warning, swept in from the sea and captured the coastal city. The politicians and civilian population in Petrograd had fallen immediately into a state of panic – Riga was within striking distance of the capital. The Germans just needed to advance a few hundred *versts* and they could lay siege to Petrograd – just another military disaster to be placed at the feet of the Army, and this time they had nobody else to blame.

'After our offensive failed,' a young lieutenant remarked bitterly, 'the Germans were supposed to go back to fighting those damned English and French on the Western Front and leave us alone. But someone forgot to tell their High Command.'

'Riga is a dagger pointed at the heart of Russia,' opined a large, almost obese, colonel lounging in the corner of the carriage where he took up an inordinate amount of room and had hardly spoken a word for the entire trip. 'We're all doomed,' he continued. 'It's the last nail in the country's coffin. We're caught between an irresistible German force pushing out of Riga, and their agents provocateurs, Lenin and his Bolsheviks, who are undermining our rear.'

'We might not like the Bolsheviks,' suggested one officer, 'but I don't think we can label them German agents.'

The fat Colonel lunged forward and pointed an accusatory finger at the officer. 'So, what would you call them, eh? The Germans take this man Lenin, stick him in a sealed train in Zurich and allow him to transit halfway across Europe, and then sneak him into the country through Finland. This bastard is now secreted in Petrograd issuing orders to his Bolshevik comrades to do everything to undermine the

Government, the Army and the war effort. And I'll tell you something else you might not know – those damned Germans are secretly funding the publishing of *Pravda* and *Izvestiya*. Lenin and his Bolsheviks might not be German agents by name, but they damn well are by deed.'

The officer sat back in his seat, affronted by the forceful comments of the Colonel. He was about to respond when the Colonel leapt to his feet. 'Gentlemen, please excuse me. I need to attend to an urgent call of nature.'

He stepped over their legs and pushed himself out into the crowded corridor. They could hear the oaths of the men as he maneuvered his large frame through the tangle of bodies as he headed towards the back of the train.

The commotion in the compartment had woken up Sergei. 'Our Colonel', he commented with a yawn, 'seems a bit of a firebrand.'

'I bet he's never been anywhere near the front,' said the affronted officer. 'The bastard would struggle to get himself out of the door of the officers' mess.'

The other officers in the compartment looked away and remained silent, uncomfortable about criticizing a senior colonel, especially in front of the soldiers in the corridor.

'The colonel is right,' said the *Stavka* staff officer. 'Kerensky doesn't seem to know who we should be fighting - is it the Germans, the Bolsheviks, or the Army and General Kornilov? And the *Izvestiya* our Colonel friend was talking about is claiming the fall of Riga was a deliberate plot by us officers to undermine the Government and give Kornilov an excuse to seize power. This is the rot the papers are feeding the public. Little wonder we are *personae non gratae* in Petrograd.'

'Don't they see the Bolsheviks are trying to turn the people against the Army?' asked Mikhail.

'Everyone seems to be swallowing it, including Kerensky. The man is convinced we're about to stage a coup.'

'What do you expect,' laughed the Colonel, who had suddenly reappeared and was squeezing his way back into the compartment. 'He's just a damned lawyer – full of piss and wind.'

Just then the train jolted as it passed over some points and started to slow. They were moving into the suburbs of a nondescript town; rough wooden dwellings, sad-looking unkempt back yards, and damp washing pegged out on lines slid past the window. The train slowed further and gradually pulled to a halt alongside a platform.

Mikhail wiped the window and peered out into the gloom, looking for a station name.

'It's Novosokolniki,' said the *Stavka* officer. 'We're about halfway. I suggest you all get off and stretch your legs. I'll stay here and mind our seats.'

It was cold and miserable outside with a light, misty rain falling, but it was a relief to get some fresh air. The wooden bench seat had become intolerably uncomfortable and a walk to get the circulation flowing was worth braving the weather.

A group of peasant women appeared, scampering across the tracks, each clutching a basket of wares to sell. Sergei bought some steamed dumplings with an indistinguishable filling, which he and Mikhail agreed was probably cabbage mixed with some sort of meat. The plump, white buns had been wrapped up in a tea towel and had retained their warmth. Both Mikhail and Sergei agreed they were surprisingly delicious.

'Look up there toward the front of the train,' pointed out Sergei, as they strolled the platform, eating and smoking. 'What do you think is going on?'

The driver and fireman had climbed down from the locomotive and were surrounded by what looked like the Stationmaster and a group of senior army officers. There was a lot of shouting and gesticulating going on.

'Looks like our fat colonel friend in the middle of that fracas,' said Sergei. 'Do you think we should go over and find out what's going on?'

'Remember what Listnitsky told us,' said Mikhail. 'Don't get involved in anything that's not our business. Besides, our friend the colonel seems to be holding his own.'

Just as Mikhail spoke, the colonel pushed his way out from the group, jumped down onto the tracks, and ran across over to the main platform and entered the Stationmaster's office.

Sergei laughed. 'Did you see that? For a big man he can certainly move quickly when he wants.'

The light was on in the office and Mikhail and Sergei could make him out through the window. He was standing at the Stationmaster's desk with one hand cupped over his mouth, talking rapidly into the telephone.

'If you ask me, there's trouble up ahead,' said Mikhail.

'What if we can't get through to Petrograd today?' asked Sergei.

'Listnitsky said there'll be someone on the train who will contact us if something goes wrong. We'll just have to wait and see what happens.'

'All this fucking cloak and dagger stuff,' huffed Sergei, 'I think I'd rather be back in the trenches. Come on, let's get back on the train, I'm starting to get wet.'

They pushed their way back into the carriage. The *Stavka* officer had kept his word and had fended off soldiers trying to take their seats.

The colonel appeared at the compartment door, panting with exhaustion, and managed to squeeze himself back into his place in the corner.

They heard the conductor's whistle blow, the couplings crashed, and the train jerked slowly into motion. The carriage swayed violently as it rattled over a series of points and then started to pick up speed.

Mikhail looked out at the low, early winter sun, just visible through the misty rain. 'It looks like we're turning west.'

'Very perceptive, my dear Kapitan,' said the colonel, giving Mikhail a mischievous grin. 'They are re-routing us through Luga, and then on to Gatchina. The direct line to Petrograd is closed – a large section of the track seems to have mysteriously disappeared.' He gave a small, shrill laugh, then slumped back into his seat, his hands clasped over his bulging stomach.

'Disappeared?' asked an officer. 'How could that happen?'

'You would need to ask the railway workers,' replied the colonel, with a dismissive shrug of his shoulders.

'What about the line to Gatchina?' asked Mikhail.

'It's where the 3ʳᵈ Cavalry Corps is stationed, but, after that, who knows.'

The train stopped at Luga to take on water and coal, allowing sufficient time for a quick stroll and a cigarette. It wasn't raining but there was a cold, inhospitable wind blowing.

When Mikhail and Sergei stepped down onto the platform, they hadn't been prepared for the crowds of military personnel and mountains of material. It was like the preparation for a campaign.

On either side of the tracks the bivouacs, like a large, tented city, extended far into the distance. Lines of tethered cavalry horses were strung out in long, ordered rows and the artillery parks were packed full of ordnance.

One group of soldiers stood out from the rest. They wore khaki Cossack-style cavalry coats that reached past the tops of their high riding boots, stiletto daggers jammed through their belts, and woolly astrakhan hats perched jauntily on their heads, giving them a look of devil-may-care insolence. But it was their faces that were most striking – weathered, evil-looking faces, with waxed moustaches and cruel, steely eyes.

'Jesus,' exclaimed Sergei, 'I thought Kornilov's Tekinstzy warriors looked scary enough, but these bastards take the prize!'

'They're the Savage Division.'

Mikhail and Sergei spun around. It was the fat colonel who had walked up, undetected, behind them. He grinned. 'Savage by name, savage by nature – they're the backbone of Kymov's 3ʳᵈ Cavalry Corps, so note them well. You two may be involved in opening the gates of Petrograd for them.'

'I don't understand,' said Mikhail, trying to keep a straight face.

'Let's drop the pretence,' said the colonel, 'we both know why you're here. The one redeeming quality of those gentlemen over there is that they're Muslim tribesmen from the Caucasus and distrustful of everyone except their own kind. The Bolshevik cadres have yet to make any inroads among them, so they are one of the few units we can trust. If the Army enters the city they will be at the forefront of the advance.'

'Mothers of Petrograd,' exclaimed Sergei, 'hide your daughters!'

The colonel ignored Sergei's comment. 'Listen carefully, we haven't much time,' he said, lowering his voice to a whisper. 'There's a change of plan. The train will be forced to stop at Gatchina – the railway workers have ripped up the lines past there as well, and it's still a hundred *versts* short of Petrograd. There are also barricades erected, and trenches dug, at all the entrances to the city and, they've cut the telephone lines to Mogilev.' The colonel looked around to make sure nobody was within earshot. 'When we stop at Gatchina, stay in the compartment until everyone has disembarked. Once the carriage is empty leave quickly, but not onto the platform. The door on the other side will be unlocked; I've borrowed a spare key from the *provodnitsa* carriage attendant. Once you are down on the tracks, move quickly towards the rear of the train. There'll be ten of you in total. A man dressed in the clothes of a railway worker and carrying a red signal lantern will meet you. Follow his instructions exactly. He will get you out of the rail yards. We have lorries waiting to get you to the outskirts of Petrograd. People will meet you there who can get you past the barricades and into the city. Any questions?'

'Have any other instructions changed?' asked Mikhail.

'No, your mission in Petrograd remains the same. You may be a day or two late for your rendezvous, but they've been told to expect that.' The colonel gripped Mikhail by the arm. 'You need to get out of uniform and into civilian clothes before you enter the city. The situation is extremely volatile and, I'm afraid, the dangers have just got worse.'

'Will you be coming in with us, sir?' asked Mikhail.

The colonel shook his head. 'No, there are other groups that need shepherding into the city. You'll probably never see me again, but that reminds me; do not, under any circumstances, exchange names or details of your mission with the other officers. Treat them as though they don't exist. It wasn't meant to happen like this, but that can't be helped. The two of you have one of the more important jobs to do, so good luck. You'll need every bit of it.'

Chapter 17

MOIKA STREET, PETROGRAD

September 1917

'I'D FEEL SAFER sitting under a damned German artillery barrage.'

'Sergei, for God's sake relax,' said Mikhail, 'or at least try to look relaxed. You're making me nervous.'

They were sitting on a park bench in the *Letniy Sad* Summer Gardens overlooking the Moika canal that bisected the city, cutting a passage between the Fontanka and Neva rivers.

The autumn sun was filtering through the yellow leaves of the lines of tall linden trees, casting mottled shadows across the facades of the buildings running down the length of the canal towards the Winter Palace. The tall, three-storied buildings with their arched windows were painted in shades of light yellow or pale red ochre, complementing the imperial eggshell blue walls and white colonnades of the Winter Palace in the distance.

Normally the brown, slow-moving waters of the canal would be bustling with small craft – mostly bringing sightseers up the canal from the Neva to the gardens, but today there were few boats to be seen, and certainly no sign of anyone out for recreation.

'How can I not be nervous? We're sitting like ducks in a shooting gallery,' commented Sergei. 'Don't you think they could have nominated a less conspicuous spot?'

'I don't like it either,' answered Mikhail, as he sneaked a glance up and down the footpath bordering the canal, 'but we don't have an option, we just need to sit it out.'

'I'd feel a lot less conspicuous if there were more people around. There's hardly anybody out on the streets except us, apart from groups of militia. I thought Kerensky had banned the Red Guard. I mean, who are these people?'

'Whether they're Red Guard, or not, is academic if you ask me. Groups of deserters, factory unions, students, demonstrators; they band together and take over the streets. Any group faintly claiming to support the Bolsheviks can just put on a red armband and they think they own the place. It's not so much a case of them taking control, it's more that Kerensky has relinquished control. I ask you – how many police have you seen around the place?'

'Not one,' answered Sergei. 'They've damn well disappeared.'

'I was told,' continued Mikhail, 'the police waded into the demonstrators with their usual brute force, but this time they were vastly outnumbered, and now they can't afford to show their face in public in case they're lynched by the mob.'

Some of the militia had started to build sandbag emplacements at major intersections, and truckloads of them could be seen moving to the outskirts to occupy freshly-dug trenches that now encircled the city.

'It's like they're preparing for a battle,' Mikhail commented, 'but it's obviously not against the Germans.'

The whole of Petrograd had an empty, almost eerie, feel to it, as though a violent storm was about to break over the city. At the Moscow Railway Station, and even down the normally bustling Nevsky Prospekt, there was hardly anyone to be seen, and those out on the street appeared in a hurry to be somewhere else. There did, however, remain lines outside the few food stores that were open, of those people hungry and resolute enough to take the risk.

The previous night their guide had managed to lead them, by a circuitous route, past the manned barricades and hastily-dug trenches. The defenses were still sparsely manned, especially away from the main entrances to the city. In the dark, drizzly night their guide easily slipped past the flimsy defenses by crossing unguarded fields, or by creeping through the back yards of suburban dwellings.

Once past the outskirts, the guide left them to make their own way. The group of officers who had left the train together now split up, with pairs of them heading off in different directions and on different missions.

Mikhail and Sergei had found a disused building in an outer industrial suburb that became their sleeping quarters, and in the morning, they ate at a local café frequented by factory workers. It was noisy and crowded, but Mikhail and Sergei were left alone to nurse their steaming mugs of tea near the window, leaving the other occupants preoccupied with wolfing down some food and a hot drink before starting their shifts.

The talk in the café was all about Kornilov and a possible army coup, with little discussion about the potential for a German attack. It was as though, as Mikhail later suggested to Sergei, they had already decided Russia was going to withdraw from the war; it seemed to be a *fait accompli* to the workers crammed into the café.

Mikhail and Sergei left the café and set off across the city. It was Sergei's almost encyclopedic memory of Petrograd's back streets and laneways that got them to the rendezvous point in the park without being stopped. It was a relief to have avoided testing either their false papers, or their rather flimsy alibi for being in the city – a couple of itinerant typewriter salesmen wandering the streets of Petrograd could easily be taken for officers disguised in civilian clothes.

Their trainers at Mogilev kept insisting the Red Guards and the militias were mostly illiterate workers, peasants who had come to the city to find work and escape the poverty of the rural villages. At best they might recognize some official-looking stamp, but the written word would mostly be incomprehensible to them. While in theory the reassurance sounded plausible, Mikhail and Sergei were happy to avoid putting it to the test.

⁂

The Summer Garden, bordering the lower section of the Moika canal, had been nominated as the place for the rendezvous.

'Wait there between eleven and midday each day,' Major Listnitsky had told them. 'Someone will approach you and ask you this question.' He had handed Mikhail a piece of paper. 'Learn it by heart, as well as your response, and then destroy it. If the phrase does not match *exactly*, get the hell out of there because it's probably a trap. If nothing happens within three days, try getting back through the lines and to Mogilev as best you can.'

⁂

'It only takes one militia group to spot us,' observed Sergei, sitting on the bench and nervously fiddling with his tie. 'We're exactly the type of people they're looking for.'

'I know it's already midday,' responded Mikhail, 'but let's just give it another few minutes.'

Mikhail took another surreptitious glance up and down the footpath, but he didn't have any idea who they were supposed to be looking for. Then, off in the distance, a lone figure appeared. 'Look,' Mikhail touched Sergei's arm and nodded in the direction, 'there's someone coming.'

'It's a woman,' responded Sergei, dismissively. 'We're supposed to be meeting a representative of the Union of Officers.'

'But what's she doing walking alone in the park? Damned risky if you ask me.'

They sat and watched her walking purposefully along the canal path. As she got closer, they could make out a handsome, slender young woman wearing a straw boater with her dark hair pulled back tight in a bun. Mikhail guessed she was about twenty-five. She carried herself well, with a touch of confidence, and wore a long dark blue dress, with matching gloves, and carried a folded umbrella in the crook of one arm.

Sergei grinned and nudged Mikhail. 'Now, there's a sight for sore eyes.'

The woman continued at a brisk pace without once looking in their direction, apparently intent on a destination further down towards the palace. As she neared their bench she glanced over, briefly hesitated, and then walked over.

'Can one of you gentlemen direct me to the Smolny Institute?' she asked, brightly.

Mikhail inwardly tensed. *Smolny* was the password. 'It is quite a way from here,' replied Mikhail, standing up. '*You must be new to St. Petersburg*,' he said, deliberately using the old name for Petrograd.

She smiled. 'I'm relieved you've finally turned up.' She looked around, checking there was nobody within earshot. 'We were afraid when you didn't show up yesterday that you may not have been able to get into the city.'

'We're sorry,' replied Mikhail, with an apologetic shrug, 'but the railway workers upset our plans; we lost a full day.'

'Yes, there are problems everywhere.'

Mikhail went to hold out his hand, but she waved it away. 'We should look like friends meeting in the park,' she explained, 'or it may raise suspicions. My name is Vera Lebedev, but please just call me Vera.'

'We were expecting someone else,' said Sergei, a bit hesitantly, 'we didn't think . . .'

'They would send a woman, is that what you mean? Frankly, it's easier for a woman to get around without being stopped. They're hunting for army officers infiltrating the city, and I clearly don't fit that category. Anyway, I'm here to take you to my brother. He's a senior officer, but don't use any military formalities in public. And please don't speak French – it's too dangerous.'

'Of course,' replied Mikhail, 'but please also call us by our Christian names. I am Mikhail, and this is Sergei.'

She nodded, but seemed distracted, and was looking over Sergei's shoulder. 'Don't look around, but a group of militia have just entered the park. I don't think they've seen us yet, but we'd better move quickly.'

Mikhail stole a quick look out of the corner of his eye. He could just make out four men who had entered through the wrought iron gates on the far side of the park. They were still some distance away, but Mikhail could see they wore distinctive red armbands and had side arms strapped to their belts.

For the moment, their immediate focus was a person just inside the park gate, and they had the unfortunate man pinned against the park fence while they scrutinized his papers.

'Follow me,' Vera said in a brusque, business-like manner. 'There's another exit further down. We need to get out of the park and across that bridge over there. The Russia Hotel on the other side of the canal and, once we are inside the hotel, we should be safe.'

Vera slipped her arm through Mikhail's and set off at a brisk pace.

'Pretend we are lovers. We'll look less suspicious this way, and maybe they won't stop us.'

Sergei quickly glanced back over his shoulder. They were still interrogating the man. There were raised voices, and one member of the militia was pushing the man about.

'Don't look at them,' she hissed out of the corner of her mouth, 'I feel sorry for him, but thank God it's not us.'

They were only a few meters from the park's exit when there was a shout from the direction of the militia. 'You, over there, stop!'

'Ignore them,' said Vera. 'Just keep walking, and don't look back.'

There was a sudden whip-like crack.

'Oh, Mother of Jesus,' gasped Vera, 'what was that?'

Sergei glanced back. Two of the militia had broken away from the group and were running after them. 'It was just a shot in the air, but I suggest we'd better make a run for it.'

Vera let go of Mikhail's arm, and the three of them ran for the exit. They were nearly to the bridge crossing the canal when a volley of shots rang out. Mikhail grabbed Vera's hand and was almost dragging her across the bridge. 'Crouch when you run,' he shouted at her. 'They've only got revolvers. They'd need to be lucky to hit anything from that range.'

There were horse carriages and tarpaulin-covered delivery vans parked all along the side of Moika Street. The three of them ducked behind a large truck and, for the moment, were lost from their pursuers' sight.

The sound of running feet on the gravel path over the other side of the canal slowed, and then stopped.

'Where did they fucking go?' they heard a man say.

'Stay behind the wheels of this truck,' whispered Mikhail, 'They don't know which direction we've taken.'

They heard a curse, and then a mumbled conversation. Finally, after a few anxious minutes, they could hear receding footsteps back along the gravel path.

'I think they've given up,' whispered Sergei. He moved to the back of the truck, knelt next to the rear wheels, and peered out from under the tray. 'They're walking back towards the others,' he whispered to Mikhail and Vera. 'Let's give it a few more minutes.'

'We are close to the hotel,' Vera whispered back. 'We just need to make it to those glass doors over there.'

The hotel doorman must have heard the gunfire and had stepped out onto the street. He was a huge man, wearing a peaked cap and a military-style uniform with a bright green sash. He stood, holding open one of the doors, and urgently beckoned them forward.

Sergei checked the retreating backs of the militia and hissed at Mikhail and Vera. 'Make a run for it, now!'

Vera clamped one hand on to her boater, hoisted up her skirts, and made a dash for the open door with Mikhail following hard on her heels. Sergei did one last check, then also sprinted for the door.

❧

The three of them stood in the foyer, panting for breath. The doorman bolted the door behind them. 'Don't worry, you're safe now,' he said, with a conspiratorial grin. 'Nobody gets through these doors without my say-so.' He then snapped to attention and touched the peak of his cap. 'Welcome back to the Russia Hotel, Countess. Prince Lebedev awaits you in the Tea Room.'

'Thank you,' responded Vera, taking several deep breaths and patting down her dress. She walked across to the foyer mirror, took off her boater, and made an adjustment to her hair. Outwardly she appeared calm, but Mikhail could see her hands were shaking.

Vera beckoned Mikhail and Sergei to follow. 'This way, gentlemen,' as she led them through a set of frosted glass swing doors off the main lobby.

It was as though they had stepped into the past, a Russia that most thought had ceased to exist, and a very different world from the one outside.

The Tea Room floor was decorated in classic black and white checkered tiles. Potted ferns separated sections of the large room into small, discreet nooks, and in each nook was a setting of white cane furniture with white linen tablecloths and brass table lamps. The room had that slightly dank, earthy smell of a country mansion conservatory.

A faint, almost indiscernible, murmur of polite conversation and the *chink* of fine china drifted through the room. There were just a few impeccably dressed civilians seated about the room – men in tailored frockcoats and cravats, and women in voluminous white lace dresses and large hats.

An ancient maître d' stood hovering at the reception stand. Vera gave him a familiar nod, then led them straight to the far corner, where a young, aristocratic-looking gentleman in frock coat and pin-striped trousers sat cross-legged, delicately nursing a cup and saucer. He had a closely shaven head in the Prussian style, and a chiseled handsome face with a pencil-line moustache.

'My brother,' Vera whispered to Mikhail, 'he's a Lieutenant Colonel, but no names or ranks, even here.'

Lieutenant Colonel Lebedev did not rise out of his chair, nor extend his hand in greeting. He leaned over to give Vera a brotherly peck on the cheek, and then indicated with a nod of his head that Mikhail and Sergei should take a seat. 'Gentlemen, I'm glad you could finally make it.'

'We are both pleased to meet you, sir,' answered Mikhail, ignoring the jibe.

Lebedev turned towards Vera. 'I was concerned when I heard the gunfire. Was everything all right out there?'

Vera placed her hands flat on the linen tablecloth to stop them shaking. 'Just some of those horrible militia people firing shots into the air but, fortunately they were pre-occupied with some other poor man in the park.'

Mikhail was impressed with Vera's outward calm, and the ease of her lie to allay the concerns of her brother.

'Damn,' she exclaimed, 'I think I may have dropped my umbrella somewhere in the park!' She smiled, 'Perhaps I'll go back for it later.'

'I doubt it will be still there, but never mind, I'm glad you weren't in any danger.' Lebedev waved over to the maître d'. 'I assumed you'll be having tea. I've already taken the liberty of ordering some for you.'

Mikhail wasn't quite sure if he was referring just to Vera or to all of them, but he replied with a polite 'thank you'.

Lebedev felt in the pocket of his waistcoat and pulled out a fob watch. 'Good grief, look at the time. We need to get going.'

He looked at Mikhail and Sergei. 'It doesn't need both of you. Who is the more senior?'

'I am,' answered Mikhail.

Lebedev put his cup down and leaned forward, dropping his voice to a whisper. 'There's a man who lives upstairs in this hotel – he is registered as Yevreinov, but his real name is Vladimir Purishkevich; you may have heard of him?'

Both Mikhail and Sergei stiffened in their chairs. Lebedev noticed the reaction and smiled. 'Yes, he does come with a certain reputation, but he is what he is. This man is difficult, and has a provocative nature, and he makes his sentiments very clear. But he is important to us. Purishkevich claims his organization, which he says is large, can assist us to get the 3rd Corps into Petrograd by creating a diversion. It would be very useful to have the Bolsheviks looking over their shoulder when we make a move, if you know what I mean?'

'Yes, I do,' answered Mikhail. 'It's been decided then – the Army will come in after all.'

'You've seen what's it like out there. Do you think Kerensky still has any control? Frankly, we don't have an option.'

Mikhail indicated Sergei, and then himself. 'And our role will be?'

'Take his people, train and organize them, and decide on an appropriate diversion. This will potentially be a street fight and I understand you are both well credentialed. Purishkevich is a notoriously tricky man, which is the reason I am here today. I'll deal with Purishkevich, the man and his politics, and I'll leave the operational side to the two of you. Understood?'

'And this organization of his?' asked Mikhail, although he half-suspected the answer.

'They call themselves the "Archangel Michael Union", but you may know them better by their former name – the Black Hundred.'

Chapter 18
PURISHKEVICH

The Same Day

MIKHAIL AND LEBEDEV climbed the three flights, using the staff stairs off the side of the kitchen.

'The lobby elevator and main stairs are watched,' Lebedev told Mikhail.

Lebedev had obviously used this route before; the staff just smiled and nodded as he led the way through the kitchen. He was a tall, athletic man and took the steps two at a time. They quickly got to the third floor; he pushed open the door, and they walked briskly down the carpeted corridor.

Purishkevich's suite was easy to spot. Two burly, shaven-headed men dressed in ill-fitting grey suits guarded the entrance. They knew Lebedev by sight and opened the door for him to enter, but Mikhail was stopped and roughly frisked for weapons.

'You're not armed?' Lebedev asked, when Mikhail joined him in the small anteroom. He sounded a bit surprised.

'We left our weapons in our valises at the Moscow station luggage deposit. If we'd been stopped, and they opened our cases, we would be in all sorts of trouble.'

One of the guards ushered them into a large lounge room overlooking the street and the canal. The room was filled with heavy, old-fashioned furniture and large Chinese vases potted with aspidistras. An immense glass chandelier hung from the ornate plaster ceiling, and large paintings of scenes of smoke-filled Napoleonic battles and portraits of generals mounted on rearing chargers covered the walls.

A trim man of medium height, with a shiny, bald head and high forehead, rimless glasses, and a manicured goatee beard stood in front of the blazing fire. 'You're late,' he barked. 'When is the damned army ever on time?'

'Apologies, Vladimir Mitrofanovich,' replied Lebedev, giving him a slight bow. 'It was difficult for the officers to get into the city, but they're here now, so we can start work.'

'Are you going to introduce me?' he snapped impatiently.

Lebedev hesitated. He hadn't bothered to ask for Mikhail's name when they were downstairs. There was an awkward silence before Mikhail quickly stepped forward and offered his hand.

'Kapitan Mikhail Mehenov, at your service, sir.'

Purishkevich grabbed his hand in a vice-like grip and pulled Mikhail towards him, so close their noses were almost touching. Mikhail smelt tobacco and brandy on the man's breath, and instinctively pulled back, but Purishkevich's grip held him close.

'So, my Kapitan, you are to teach us skills of modern warfare. May I ask, what are your credentials?'

Mikhail quickly glanced over towards Lebedev, mindful of his insistence he alone was to lead the discussion. Lebedev had little choice and nodded for him to continue.

'I have experience in house-to-house street fighting, sir, as well as hand-to-hand combat. I was told those skills may come in handy here in Petrograd.'

'And pray tell me, my good Kapitan, where did you learn these skills?'

'Ternopol, sir.'

Purishkevich barked a laugh. 'That bloody fiasco! You didn't run like all the other deserting scum?'

'No sir, we were with the rear guard – the Valinsky Regiment – and we fought our way out.'

Purishkevich released Mikhail's hand and started pacing the room, then stopped, and swiveled back towards Mikhail. 'Tell me, what do you think of this man Kerensky?'

'I don't get involved in politics, sir, I follow orders.'

'And these Bolshevik fellows, you must have had some in your regiment?'

'They murdered some of my fellow officers, sir.'

Purishkevich strode over and clapped him on both shoulders. 'Ah!' he shouted jubilantly, looking over towards Lebedev. 'This is what I like to hear – a man with a grudge to settle! Don't give me your damned political claptrap, give me a man with hate in his belly – there's a man I can trust!'

Purishkevich waved his glasses accusingly in Lebedev's face. 'And what about you and the Army – can you be trusted?'

Lebedev went to take a step backward, but then decided to hold his ground.

'Or has the officer corps been infiltrated by Jews and communists too?' continued Purishkevich. 'I've been saying this for years, but who in the Officers' Union or the *Stavka* bothered to listen to me. You all just left me pissing into the wind.'

Lebedev went to protest, but Purishkevich grabbed hold of his arm and dragged him over to one of the windows overlooking the street.

'Tell me, Lieutenant Colonel, what do we have out there?'

Lebedev, flushed with rage, started stammering a reply, but Purishkevich was clearly not interested in his response. 'I'll tell you what you see,' he continued to shout while still clutching Lebedev's jacket, 'you see Red Guards everywhere that Kerensky was supposed to ban, and do you see those army-issue Mosin-Nagant rifles they're carrying? That weakling Kerensky has unlocked the doors of the city arsenal since he's terrified of an army coup. The Bolsheviks are over at the Smolny Institute handing out weapons to every damned factory Soviet and fucking peasant who wanders by. Kerensky has opened Pandora's Box, and all this because the fucking Army can't get off its arse and march into the city. Four days ago, you could have walked into this place without firing a shot, and now look what you're facing.'

Lebedev finally managed to remove the grip on his jacket. 'You're over-stepping the mark, sir,' said Lebedev, lowering his voice, trying to instill some calm into the conversation. 'The Army is facing a difficult situation with the soldier Soviets, but we're doing our best. The 3rd Corps, as you know, is poised to enter the city.'

'Poised!' shouted Purishkevich, throwing both arms in the air. 'All I've heard for the past week is they're bloody *poised*. My definition of *poised* is someone sitting around doing nothing! Tell me, what was Kornilov thinking when he appointed that useless bastard, General Krymov, to lead the 3rd Corps?'

'He's a good officer, despite the stories you hear.'

'He made a total cock-up of the retreat in Romania.'

'General Kornilov has given him a chance to redeem his honor and dispel those malicious rumors. Like you said about the kapitan here, Krymov will have fire in his belly.'

Purishkevich stood in the center of the room with his thumbs tucked into his waistcoat pockets, tapping one foot in an agitated fashion. He looked up at the chandelier as if invoking the Lord.

'And why in hell's name,' he paused for dramatic effect, 'do you have that bunch of savages in the 3rd Corps? Any damned vestige of support for the Army is being pissed down the drain. Those crazy Moslems strike terror into the entire population!'

'The Native Division, or "Savage Division" as you call them, are the finest shock troops we have. They're ably led and, I can assure you, they'll be kept under control.'

'Ha!' mocked Purishkevich, pointing to the window. 'Go tell that to the good citizens of Petrograd.'

'They've been chosen because they're free of political contamination by the Bolsheviks. Unfortunately, we cannot say the same of many of the Russian divisions.'

'Then why aren't they marching on the capital? And do you think this Lenin person is sitting idly by waiting for them to turn up at the city gates? The man is as cunning as a sewer rat.'

'I can assure you, Vladimir Mitrofanovich, the Army will not let you down.'

'Then let there be no misunderstanding, my men will not lift a finger until the Army is at the gates. And I mean beating down the gates, not a hundred damned *versts* away. Then, and only then, will my Archangel Michael men move.'

'I can assure you, sir, the 3rd Corps advance is any day now.'

Purishkevich strode across the room, grabbed Lebedev by the crotch with one hand, while his other hand grabbed him behind his neck and pulled him towards him. Mikhail went to intervene, but Lebedev waved him away.

'Just remember one thing, my dear Lieutenant Colonel Lebedev,' Purishkevich hissed into his ear, 'don't ever leave me standing in Nevsky Prospekt holding my cock in my hand. If the Army leaves me here without support, with whatever little life is left in me, I'll hunt you down to the ends of the earth.'

Lebedev broke free. 'Sir, your behavior is totally unconscionable.' He stood, red-faced and stammering, 'I've told you the Army will not let you down and, as far as I'm concerned, that's my final word.'

'Kapitan Mehenov,' barked Purishkevich.

Mikhail clicked to attention. 'Yes, sir.'

'Be in the alley at the back of the hotel at dawn tomorrow.' He turned and waved one of his guards over. 'Fyodor here will take you to meet my men.'

Purishkevich did not wait for an acknowledgement. He abruptly turned on his heels and walked out of the room.

Mikhail and Lebedev made their way back down the staff stairs. Halfway down Lebedev suddenly stopped and swung around to face Mikhail. 'Don't utter a word about what went on in the meeting, not one word to your colleague, my sister, or anyone. Do you understand?'

Sergei and Vera were waiting for them in the lobby.

'I hope the meeting went well?' asked Vera.

Lebedev leaned forward, and quickly kissed her on both cheeks. 'My job here is done,' he said, somewhat dismissively. 'I need to get back to Mogilev urgently. I'll leave these two gentlemen with you. They're expected back here at first light tomorrow. I'll keep in touch with you through our usual channels.'

He turned to Mikhail and Sergei. 'I don't hold high expectations for Purishkevich's men, but see what you can do with them, and make sure they're ready.'

Without a nod or farewell, he swung around and strode off in the direction of the hotel kitchen.

'My brother always comes back in a foul mood after seeing that horrible man,' said Vera, with a dismissive shrug. 'I apologize if he seemed a bit curt. Let's give him a few minutes start, and then we'll also leave by the back entrance.'

'Where are we going?' asked Sergei.

'To the Admiralty buildings at the bottom of Nevsky Prospekt,' said Vera. 'From there we can catch a trolley car to the Moscow Station. That's if we still must go there.'

'I'm sorry,' answered Mikhail, 'but our valises contain our uniforms, our revolvers, and money we need to equip and train Purishkevich's men. It was just too risky carrying that stuff around with us.'

'But you don't need to come with us,' suggested Sergei. 'We know the way.'

Vera shook her head. 'I am afraid you're stuck with me. I'm your link to the Officers' Union, so we need to stay together. But let's not discuss this now, the quicker we get this done and off the streets the better.'

Without another word, Vera set off at a quick pace in the direction of the Admiralty.

Mikhail looked at Sergei and laughed. 'I guess we're expected to follow.'

The electric trolley car was packed with government office workers heading home for the day. Vera managed to squeeze into a seat, with Mikhail and Sergei standing, holding on to the leather straps, as the trolley car swayed and clattered its way up the broad avenue. They positioned themselves close to the open doors in case they needed a quick exit but were comforted by the anonymity of merging in with the crowd of passengers. The ticket conductor did not give them a second glance as she pushed through the car, rattling her cash tin and dispensing tickets.

Groups of Red Guard were at the main intersections along Nevsky Prospekt but, for now, they kept waving the trolley cars through.

Mikhail leaned over to Vera, and whispered, 'Where are we going after Moscow Station?'

'Our family home,' she whispered back, shaking her head. 'Let's not talk now.'

A plump matron, squashed into the seat next to Vera, had started giving them strange looks. Vera removed the glove from her left hand. There was a large diamond ring on her wedding finger.

'Don't you just love the ring?' Vera asked her, beaming proudly and splaying her hand. 'We've just got engaged, and our friend over there will be our best man. Isn't it exciting?'

The matron broke into a broad smile and reached for Vera's hand to get a better look. The two became immediately engrossed in a detailed conversation about wedding dresses.

Sergei took advantage of the distraction to lean outside the open door of the carriage to see further up the street, just as the trolley car slowed.

'They're stopping all the cars at the bridge over the Fontanka

Canal,' Sergei whispered into Mikhail's ear. 'We'd better get ready to bolt. Let Vera know.'

Mikhail caught her eye and gave a small jerk of his head.

'I think this is our stop,' Vera said to the matron. 'It was lovely to talk to you.'

Vera stood up and moved close to Mikhail, holding on to him to steady herself. 'What's wrong?'

'They're searching all the cars ahead. We need to make a run for it.'

In the row of halted trolley cars they were fourth in line. Red Guards had entered the first car, and were gradually working their way down the line, releasing them one at a time.

'Let's get off now', whispered Sergei. 'We can duck around the back of the car.'

From somewhere up ahead, a succession of shots rang out. Passengers in their car started screaming, and many cowered down between the seats. There were sounds of running footsteps, shouts, and more screams as pedestrians in the street scattered in all directions, running for shelter.

'Quick,' hissed Mikhail, 'it's our best chance. Let's get the hell out of here!'

The three of them clambered down from the trolley car. People were seeking any vestige of cover. Some crouched in doorways, while others had flattened themselves on the pavement.

'Stay together,' shouted Mikhail, as he sprinted across the boulevard towards a narrow alley. As they ran, Mikhail glanced up the street towards where the shots had been fired. He could see militia holding two struggling men, both bleeding profusely from gunshot wounds.

'Jesus Christ!' Sergei almost barreled into Mikhail, who had suddenly stopped in his tracks.

'They were in our group from the train,' shouted Mikhail.

Sergei briefly glanced up the street. 'Let's keep moving, there's nothing we can do.'

They pushed into the crowded alley and found some space at the far end where they leaned back against the brick wall, panting from exertion.

'Stay here,' Mikhail whispered, 'I'm going back to have a look.'

Sergei grabbed Mikhail's arm. 'They told us not to get involved.'

'Don't worry, I won't.'

He worked his way back to the entrance and cautiously peered around the corner. The two officers were down on their knees, each being held upright by militiamen. A man in a long black leather coat came up behind them with a revolver, placed it against the back of one of the men's head, and pulled the trigger. He then took a step sideways and executed the other officer in the same fashion.

Four men took hold of a leg and arm each and dragged the bodies across to the bridge railing. They lifted the bodies up and heaved them over the railing. There was a splash, and then silence.

The Red Guard in the leather coat was shouting instructions and waving the militia back to recommence searching the trolley cars.

Mikhail worked his way back down the alley to Sergei and Vera.

'God,' gasped Vera, her face pale with fright 'we heard more shots, what's happening now?'

'It's over,' he said, quietly, 'but we can't stay here. They're bound to start searching the surrounding streets as well, and they'll be on the lookout for officers in civilian clothes. We need to get out of here now.'

Mikhail looked about. The people crammed into the alley were all terrified, cowering down against the walls, and holding their hands over their heads. He felt conspicuous, the three of them standing there in good clothes surrounded by office and factory workers, as well as old people, women and children. 'But how?' Vera asked. 'This alley is a dead end. We can't go back out onto Nevsky, it'll be a death trap.'

Sergei jerked his head in the direction of the end of the alley. 'I've told you before, I know my way around here.'

He led them to an old blue, chipped door at the far end of the alley.

'God, it stinks,' said Vera, referring to the overpowering smell of urine and stale beer.

'It's the back delivery entrance of a student bar I know,' said Sergei.

Sergei thumped the door hard with his fist, waited, and knocked hard again. Finally there was the sound of someone shuffling across the yard.

'What do you want?' The muffled question was the croak of an old man.

'Anton, is that you?'

'Who's asking?' came the guarded response.

'It's Sergei Vinokurov, do you remember me? I've come to pay my bill.'

'Vinokurov,' said the old man, trying to recall the name. 'Vinokurov – I think I still have a chit somewhere. But why come to the back gate?'

'You would have heard the shots,' answered Sergei. 'The Reds are pulling people off the trams and shooting them. If you open the door, I'll give you the money, then we'll be gone.'

There was silence, then finally the sound of a bolt being slid back. The door creaked open, just a chink, enough for one bleary eye to peer out.

'Just pass me the money and bugger off.'

'How much, I can't exactly remember?'

'Twenty rubles should cover it, and that's without interest.'

A grubby hand was thrust through the gap of the door. 'Now pay me, or I'll call the Guards.'

Sergei grabbed the old man's wrist and yanked hard, while at the same time, hitting the door hard with the heel of his boot.

There was a splintering of wood followed by a loud groan, and the old man's wrist went limp. Sergei leaned against the door, pushed it open, and stepped over the prostrate body.

'Come on in,' he said to Mikhail and Vera, waving them forward, 'and try bolting the door behind you.'

Sergei dragged the old man out of the way and propped him against a wall. He had blood running down his face from a cut to the temple and was barely conscious.

'Sorry Anton,' said Sergei, giving him a pat on the shoulder, 'I told you it was urgent.'

Anton groaned, stirred, and opened one eye. He slowly raised a hand and wiped the blood away from his face. 'I should have known it was you – you drunken, whoring bag of scum.'

Sergei patted his pockets and looked at Vera. 'Can you lend me twenty rubles?'

Vera dug into her handbag. 'Men and their damned bar bills!' she said, stuffing the notes into Anton's jacket pocket. 'We can't leave him like this; we should get him some water and bandage his wound.'

'Don't worry about him,' laughed Sergei. 'He's a tough old nut. You should see him crack students' heads and throw them out on the street.'

Anton, by this stage, had managed to prop himself up better, and looked them up and down. 'My guess is you're in trouble with the Guards.'

'We were just trying to get to the station,' said Vera. 'Can you help us?'

Anton cocked his head and gave Vera a quizzical look. 'Why the station? The trains aren't running 'cause they've ripped up the tracks, or haven't you heard?'

'We've got bags at the luggage office, but they're stopping people crossing the canal.' Vera knelt down next to him and put her hand on his arm. 'Please,' she gently pleaded, 'will you help us?'

Anton gave Vera an appraising look, and cackled. 'So, what's a nice girl doing mixed up with a ratbag like this? If he thinks twenty rubles is going to get your bags back, then he's got another thing coming.'

'You know a way?' asked Vera, dabbing at his head wound with her handkerchief.

Anton grinned. 'There's always a way in Russia.'

Vera opened her handbag. 'We're prepared to pay.'

Anton looked at Sergei. 'You've got luggage chits?'

Sergei felt in his pocket. 'You'll get them for us?'

'You could try collecting them yourself, but my guess is you'll end up in the Neva too. And, for the trouble, it will be fifty rubles for me, and twenty for the luggage clerk – payment when I return with the bags.'

'But can we trust you?'

Anton sneered. 'That I won't return with the Guards? No, but what's your other option?'

Chapter 19

THE LETTER

October 1917

THE TROIKA EASED to a stop in the yard, the three horses snorting with exhaustion and lathered in sweat, despite the cold. The carriage was laden high with trunks and boxes. Pavel was squeezed in beside the driver, nursing a carton on his knees while, in the back seat, Katrina was wedged between a suitcase and a trunk. Another two fully laden tarpaulin-covered wagons, driven by men from the store, pulled into the yard and stopped alongside. 'Let's get this lot unloaded,' Pavel told the driver. 'Tell the foreman to put the stores in one of the barns, and have the trunks and suitcases brought up to the house.'

Pavel jumped to the ground, and took Katrina's hand to help her down.

'Are you sure this will be all right?' she asked. She was shivering, and her face pinched with cold, despite her large sable coat, hat and muff.

'Of course, now let's go up to the house and get you warm. Maria Ivanova will be waiting for us.'

The family, all except Iya, had come out onto the verandah. They stood huddling in coats and shawls, trying to shield themselves from the cold wind blowing from the northeast across the steppes. Maria left the others and strode down the lawn towards Pavel, took him by the arm, and pulled him aside.

'What's *that* woman doing here?' she hissed in his ear.

'It's Katrina from the store.'

'I know *who* she is, but what are you doing bringing her to the farm?'

Pavel turned and spoke to Katrina. 'Please go on ahead, we'll be there in a minute.'

Katrina started to say something, but stopped herself, and set off up the slope towards the verandah.

'Isn't it enough she has you to herself in town?'

Pavel gave Maria an angry look. 'You don't think that . . .'

Maria cut him off abruptly. 'Just tell me what's going on here?'

'I've closed both stores, and the tannery, and have paid off the staff. Tsaplin's thugs have now taken over the town, and it's just too danger-ous to keep the businesses running. They're snatching people off the street and taking them away to God knows where. I just couldn't leave her behind, she wouldn't have survived five minutes, so I insisted.'

'You could have asked me first,' said Maria, fighting back tears, "I *am* your wife, after all.'

'There was no time, and no warning. I don't know what's going on, but apparently the same is happening all over the country. We may still have an elected government, but it seems it's the Bolsheviks who are now in control.'

'I don't care about either Barnaul or Petrograd, it's just here I care about.'

'Look, we're both freezing to death. Let's get up to the house and out of this damned wind.'

Maria pulled her shawl tightly around her shoulders, clenched her mouth, and followed Pavel as he strode up the lawn. 'She can sleep in the spare maid's room by the kitchen.'

Pavel stopped and turned. 'Why not one of the guest rooms?'

'Because it's my house, and I decide who sleeps where.'

Pavel sat alone in his study in front of the fire and poured himself a liberal shot of vodka. He rolled the spirit around his tongue, savoring the taste, then he tilted his head back and allowed the mellow, viscous liquid to slide slowly down his throat, feeling the warm glow of the alcohol spread gradually through his body. He was reaching over to refill his glass when Maria walked in. She shooed the dogs out of the room and closed the door firmly behind her.

'We need to talk.'

Maria sat down in the chair opposite, kneading her hands. She took a deep breath. 'Look, I'm sorry about what I said before, but you've been in town alone for weeks, and I've been worried sick. So, tell me what happened.'

Pavel took another sip of his drink. 'They have arrested the Zemstvo members and have taken over the telegraph office. They've raided all the stores and confiscated goods by gunpoint – for "redistribution" they said. If anyone tried to stop them, they were arrested and shot. Fortunately we got wind of it. We quickly loaded up some wagons, and managed to get away before they arrived.'

'How did you get out of town without being stopped?'

'You should have seen the roads – it was chaotic. Every road was crammed with loaded vehicles and people, all desperate to get out. Tsaplin's men could only stand back and watch.'

'And did anyone try to stop them, the Bolsheviks I mean?'

Pavel shrugged. 'Who is there – the Zemstvo, the Army, the Police? They no longer exist in the town and, if I had tried, I'd be dead by now.'

'But, surely . . .'

Pavel took another sip, then offered the glass to Maria, and was surprised she accepted. She took hold of the glass gingerly, wrinkled her nose, and took a tentative sip.

'Our only hope now is Kornilov,' sighed Pavel, and held up his hands, 'but he's thousands of *versts* away on the other side of the Urals. We'll have to deal with this ourselves.'

'And how do we do that?' she asked, handing the unfinished glass back to Pavel.

'We sit tight here at the farm, and hope somebody does something to end this madness. I'm going to ask the foreman to set a sentry on the track to give us some warning.' Pavel gave an exasperated sigh. 'What else can we do? Let's just give it a few days and see what happens.'

'But our workers?'

'We're just going to have to trust them,' answered Pavel. 'What option do we have? Maybe there's still some loyalty there.'

'And, Vasily, you haven't mentioned Vasily – where's your brother?'

Pavel put his glass down, stood up, and walked over to the fireplace. He remained there, hands thrust in pockets, staring for a long time into the fire. When he finally spoke, there was a tremor in his voice.

'He's dead.'

Maria gasped and put her hands over her mouth. 'It can't be true! What happened?'

'While the wagons were being loaded, I ran over to his place to get him. This time I wasn't going to take "no" for an answer, but I was too late. All his furniture had been thrown out into the street, and that bastard Tsaplin had taken Vasily's house over as the Barnaul Soviet's offices.'

'And your brother?'

Pavel turned to face Maria. He was struggling to hold back his tears. It took a moment before he could summon the words and, when he finally spoke, the words tumbled out in a rush. 'I found him lying in the gutter, in his pajamas and in bare feet, would you believe! They had thrown him out of the top window, along with the furniture. Animals, they're just a bunch of damned animals!'

Maria got up and walked over to Pavel. She buried her head in his chest and wrapped her arms around him. 'I'm so sorry.'

Galina climbed the stairs, hesitated a moment, and then knocked quietly on Iya's bedroom door. 'It's me.'

There was a faint 'Come in', so she entered and closed the door behind her.

Iya was sitting in a rocking chair next to the window with an open book in her lap. She had a shawl wrapped tightly around her shoulders and was rocking gently back and forth in the faint stream of wintry sunlight. It was cool in the room, but not cold. 'What's going on downstairs?' she asked. 'I was going to come down but heard Mother talking to Papa. She sounded angry.'

'He brought Katrina out here to stay with us.'

'He did what?' Iya stopped rocking and sat bolt upright. 'No wonder, I'd be furious.'

'But there's worse news. They're in the study, and at least they've stopped shouting at each other, but you can still hear every word. Papa has closed the stores because the Reds are running around looting the town, and then he went to get Uncle Vasily and found they had killed him and had taken over his house.'

Iya gasped and held her hands to her mouth. '*Mon Dieu.*'

Iya sat in silence for a moment. When she finally spoke, her voice sounded distant.

'I know he's Papa's brother, but I never really liked Uncle Vasily. He really became strange, the way he locked himself away like a hermit. I hate to say it, but it doesn't surprise me he's dead, and I'm not sure I ever felt anything for him. But I'm sad for Papa.'

Iya snapped the book shut on her lap. 'Shouldn't we go down?'

'I think it's better we leave them alone. At least Mama is in there and they've stopped shouting at each other.'

'And this Katrina woman,' asked Iya, 'what's she doing here?'

'I heard Papa say she would have been killed if he left her behind, but I know Mother thinks there's something more.'

Iya vigorously shook her head. 'Other men do that sort of thing, but surely not Papa. He's not like that.'

'But, I feel sad for Mama,' said Galina. 'You know what it must be like, the things that go through a wife's mind when her husband's away for a long time.' Galina flushed red. 'I'm – I'm sorry, I shouldn't have said that.'

Iya held up her hand. 'Don't worry, it's true.'

'Do you think Mikhail is like that too?'

'Every wife does – especially if their husband's a soldier. You know the type of women who follow the army around.' Iya turned in her chair and gave Galina a questioning look. 'Don't you ever wonder about Sergei?'

Galina blushed and didn't answer the question. Instead, she thrust her hand into the pocket of her pinafore and pulled out a crumpled envelope.

'Papa brought this home with him. He said it just arrived the other day. It's postmarked "Mogilev".'

Iya caught her breath. 'It's nothing official, is it?'

Galina laughed. 'No, it's addressed in Mikhail's handwriting. It's his appalling scribble for sure.'

Galina walked over to the door. 'I'll leave you to read the letter alone. Just let me know if he's mentions anything about Sergei.' She gave a little flip of her hand and smiled, 'Not that I'm really interested.'

'No, please stay,' pleaded Iya. 'Just in case it's bad news, please don't go.'

Galina sat down on the window seat, twining a strand of her hair as she waited for Iya to read the letter. It was a single sheet of paper with Mikhail's handwriting filling both sides. There were black marks all over the page where the censor's pen had blanked out words and, in one case, a whole sentence had been inked. Iya scanned one side, and then quickly turned it over.

'Oh, my God,' whispered Iya. She crumpled the letter in her fist and, with her other hand, wiped tears away from her eyes.

'Is anything wrong?' asked Galina.

Iya carefully smoothed the letter out on her dress. 'No, there's nothing wrong. He's alive and well.'

'So, why the tears?'

Iya shook her head. 'I'm sorry – it's just the relief of it all. Weeks without knowing, and always fearing the worst.'

Galina leaned over and held her sister in a hug. 'That's wonderful news. He didn't mention Sergei by any chance?'

'They've been in Mogilev together, but no mention of what they're doing there. There's something about re-assignment, but it's not clear. The censor blanked out the next sentence. Mikhail says he was rushing to get this in the post before they left, and just wanted to let me know he's safe and well.'

'Mogilev,' said Galina, 'at least that means they are away from the fighting.'

'It's probably just a short reprieve before they're re-assigned, and then it will be back to fighting again.'

'So now we have to wait for the next letter,' said Galina.

Iya wiped her eyes with her handkerchief, and then noisily blew her nose. 'It's the waiting I hate most, the terror of the unknown until the next letter arrives, praying that it won't be one of those horrible government telegrams.'

Iya looked Galina in the eye and patted her on the knee. 'Pray tell me, dearest sister, what are you going to do about that man of yours?'

'You mean Sergei? What's there to tell? He's not here.'

'You could start by writing to him more often, and then at least he may start writing back.'

'We're not letter writers like you and Mikhail, we are different.'

'What's different?' answered Iya. 'You are a man and a woman, aren't you? I mean, has he ever kissed you?'

Galina blushed and looked away. 'He held my hand, once.'

Iya burst into laughter. 'Oh my god, you are innocent, aren't you.'

She reached out and took Galina's two hands in hers. 'Now, look at me.' Iya put on her serious face. 'Has mother ever had a talk with you, you know, woman to woman?'

'Well, yes, once she did. I don't know who was more embarrassed, she or I.'

'So, my guess is you didn't learn anything.'

Galina shook her head. 'Just the monthly thing, and that I should save myself for my husband, the sanctity of marriage, that sort of thing.'

'I take it you don't know anything then. Babies don't come from the cabbage patch, you know.'

'I'm not that stupid,' retorted Galina angrily. 'I see the animals on the farm doing it all the time.'

Iya rocked back and laughed. 'Are you going to hoist your skirts and get down on all fours? Slightly unbecoming if you have a new lover.'

Galina wrenched her hands away and abruptly stood. 'Don't treat me like a child; I'm older than you. Just because you're married . . .'

'I'm sorry, I didn't mean . . .' Iya hesitated. 'Look, please sit down and let's talk – sister to sister.'

Galina reluctantly resumed her seat and pointedly looked out the window. 'What is it then?'

Iya leaned forward. 'You need to understand about men and s-e-x. It's really quite fundamental – if you don't have it with them, they'll find it elsewhere.'

'What has that got to do with me? We're not even married!'

'But that's exactly the point. Just look at Russia – years fighting the Japanese, and now the Germans and Austro-Hungarians, and who knows what's next? A whole generation of young men dead or maimed, and they're our generation, and Sergei is one of the few survivors. The country is full of unmarried girls with scant prospects, aside from the thousands of grieving war-widows desperate for any husband and someone to help put food on the table. And then, look at Sergei – young, single, handsome, a mop of blond hair and a cheeky grin that would make most women weak at the knees, and he's heir to a fortune. What's more, he's alive with all limbs intact!'

'But I'm not interested in the money!'

Iya gripped Galina's arm. 'I know you're not, but while you dilly-dally around, thousands of women out there would grab him with both hands. Do you think they'll be worrying about preserving their virginity, that's if they still have it? Do you really think they care about the sanctity of marriage?'

'So, what do you suggest I do? We're separated by thousands of *versts*, and who knows when we'll see each other again.'

'Then you pray,' insisted Iya. 'You pray to God the Bolsheviks do take over and pull us out of this god-awful war. You pray for peace and that our men will be sent home. You pray Sergei will come back and, if he does, you're the one who grabs him with both hands. Haul him up to your bedroom, lock the door, and get him to teach you everything mother never told you – I'm sure he's quite capable. And finally, don't let him out until he agrees to marry you and, if need be, fall pregnant!'

'Are you saying we should support the Bolsheviks?'

'What do you want,' asked Iya, 'to have the love of your life along-side you, or to keep hold of all these possessions? It seems clear to me we can no longer have both.'

Chapter 20

LEBEDEV HOUSE, PETROGRAD

Mid-October 1917

MIKHAIL SAT ALONE in the kitchen at the rear of Lebedev House sipping quietly on a glass of chilled vodka, while chewing absentmindedly on a piece of sausage. It wasn't that he was hungry, but the food mitigated the effect of the vodka and slowed down his drinking. He didn't want to wake up in the morning with a sore head.

Vera was still out somewhere in the city. It was dangerous moving around the city at the best of times, let alone at night, and Mikhail was worried and decided to wait up for her. Meanwhile, the household staff had gone to bed, as had Sergei.

It was already dark outside, and a cold wind was sweeping branches of trees in the back yard against the windowpanes. The twigs scratching against the glass had startled him several times and made him think someone was tapping at the back door, but he had become used to it, and finally relaxed.

Lebedev House was the seat of the old aristocratic family on a street named after them, the *Ulitsa* Lebedeva, near the Finland Station on the northern side of the Neva River. It was a rambling three-story colonnaded mansion with a grey stone facade much in need of repair. Set back from the street, it was shielded from view by ancient oak trees, and guarded by a high spiked fence.

Vera had avoided the main front entrance when they first arrived at the house on the previous night. 'It stays locked these days,' she advised Mikhail and Sergei. 'It's more private to use the rear entrance.'

She had led them down a narrow, cobblestoned alley bordered by tall, dilapidated timber fences, until they got to a gate that was partially obscured by ivy. 'I'll give you both a key, so just come and go as you please,' she had told them.

The interior was dark, cold and mostly unoccupied save for a wizened old butler, and his wife who acted as housekeeper and cook. To help them there was a flaxen-haired maidservant, a young attractive girl, with a ruddy face and an upturned nose.

'Since both our parents passed away, the house is hardly used,' Vera had explained. 'I prefer to stay with friends, but my brother often stays here when he comes up from Mogilev.'

Vera had led them through rooms of dark, brooding paintings, white dust covers hiding disused furniture, and up the curved mahogany staircase where she showed them their bedrooms on the second floor.

'I'll get the maid to make up your beds. Meals will be served in the kitchen since the stove is always kept lit there during the winter months. We don't bother trying to heat the rest of the house.' Vera laughed. 'Body warmth and piles of quilts help, but I can get the butler to light your fires, if you want.'

Mikhail grinned and shook his head. 'For two soldiers used to sleeping on the floor of a muddy trench, this will be just fine.'

❧

Mikhail and Sergei rose early the next morning, crept out of the house without waking anyone, and set off to the Russia Hotel. A cold wind moaned straight off the Gulf of Finland. The streetlamps were still on, but they cast only a narrow cone of light onto the damp, black cobblestones. They were thankful for this – it was relatively easy to move unseen through the streets and the only militias in evidence were huddled around braziers on street corners and easy to spot from a distance.

Fyodor was waiting for them in a darkened doorway at the back of the hotel. He just grunted when he saw Mikhail and Sergei and waved them to follow. For a large man he was agile and moved at a jog through a labyrinth of alleys, down towards the waterfront, and thence to the side entrance of a large, disused warehouse.

A large group of men had assembled in the warehouse – there were fifty-two when Sergei did a count. 'Not exactly the hundreds of men itching for a fight I thought Purishkevich had claimed,' said Sergei.

'Either a gross exaggeration,' answered Mikhail, 'or they just haven't shown up.'

They were of various ages, from lads of fifteen or sixteen through to old men well past their prime. They were an odd assortment. The younger ones, in rough clothes, had that mean, hardened look of street-fighting thugs or petty criminals. The older men were an odd mixture of tsarists, retired ex-army officers in bits of old uniforms, and zealots mostly wearing black, with some displaying various religious paraphernalia. While this older group seemed more politically motivated, Mikhail judged they would be less capable when it came to a fight.

'As the old saying goes,' said Sergei, with a shake of his head, 'this is going to be like weighing frogs.'

Mikhail and Sergei conducted an inspection of their weapons, and as they had expected, there was an odd assortment: a variety of shotguns, old hunting rifles, and service revolvers. Some even had ancient blunderbusses. A few of the younger group had handguns, but most carried daggers and coshes hidden in their clothing.

'I suspect,' said Mikhail, 'these are their usual weapons of choice in a street fight, but not much use for our operation.'

Sergei worked his way through the group, checking what ammunition they had and distributing money with instructions to buy more. 'We're going to need more rifles,' he told Mikhail, 'as well as more men if we can get them. The Red Guard has hardened veterans amongst them, and they're properly armed. It would be like leading lambs to the slaughter.'

'We'll talk to Vera tonight. Hopefully she can get a message through to her brother. In the meantime, I'll talk to Fyodor while you check the ex-officers and find out who is still capable of leading a unit, but I suspect the last time any of them fired a shot was probably the Crimean War.'

It quickly became apparent that Fyodor was not just Purishkevich's nominee, but also the natural leader of the group. Mikhail took him aside to discuss possible targets. Most of Fyodor's suggestions were ill conceived, too ambitious, or downright suicidal. He sensed the hand of Purishkevich in many of the ideas.

'It's not your boss who's putting his arse on the line,' Mikhail told Fyodor bluntly, 'it's us, and this group. We're here to create a diversion, not to start a war.'

However, when he was pressed for further options, one of Fyodor's suggestions did have merit. Somebody in Purishkevich's organization had discovered the secret location of the Bolshevik headquarters.

'It was quite easy to find,' advised Fyodor. 'One of our men followed a courier sent by a Red Guard unit. They've taken over the Kschessinska Mansion – it's on *Ulitsa* Kuybysheva. We think Lenin has his office on the second floor overlooking the street.'

'I've been told Lenin has gone into hiding somewhere in Finland,' said Mikhail. 'Are you sure he's here?'

Fyodor shrugged his shoulders. 'Does it matter? It's still their headquarters, and it's where their orders come from.'

'You're right, it doesn't matter,' agreed Mikhail. 'If a diversion is required, then disrupting their communications could be just perfect.'

A street map had been spread out on a table. Fyodor circled the mansion's location. There was a park over the road from the front of the house, and an alley at the rear.

'We could approach the building using the cover of the park. Is there a rear entrance from the alley?'

Fyodor laughed. 'Of course, it was the home of the Tsar's mistress. There's just one main street entrance, but there's, how would you say, a more discreet entrance at the back.'

'I never knew,' said Mikhail, with a look of disbelief.

'To be fair,' answered Fyodor, 'it was before he married the Tsarina. You can't exactly blame him. You should have seen her – the prima ballerina at the Mariinsky. What a beauty! And I've heard he wasn't the first Romanov she bedded.'

Mikhail and Fyodor left Sergei at the warehouse to continue the training while they headed off to reconnoitre the mansion. Since the Army's move into the city could happen any day, they couldn't afford to lose any time.

There were even fewer people on the streets than the day before. Residents needed compelling reasons to venture outdoors, and the city had an eerie, almost abandoned, feel to it. Piles of uncollected garbage had been left in the street for packs of dogs to rummage through. Rats, too, had come out of the canals and sewers, and could be seen crawling over the garbage in broad daylight.

'Lucky it isn't summer,' commented Mikhail. 'This place would smell like a cesspit.'

'It's the work of the Bolsheviks,' said Fyodor. 'They organized the City Hall workers to strike.'

Mikhail and Fyodor found they could watch the mansion, unde-tected, from the park across the street. The building was a two-storey structure with a modern art-deco façade and large decorative glass windows overlooking the street. The second floor, where Lenin was said to have his office, had tall French doors opening out onto a balcony.

'Ideal for delivering his victory speech to the Bolshevik masses,' joked Fyodor.

'Where are the guards?' asked Mikhail. 'Are you're sure this is their headquarters?'

Fyodor nodded. 'Just wait and see. The front entrance is locked, and they don't post any guards so they don't draw attention to the place. The couriers come and go by the back entrance down the alley.'

Mikhail and Fyodor walked across the park until they could get a better view of the alley. After a few minutes their patience was rewarded. Two men, who had been nonchalantly walking down the street in front of the mansion, suddenly veered around the corner and disappeared off down the alley making for the rear entrance. A few moments later, another man emerged from the alley and made his way towards a nearby tram stop. In a short time of waiting and watching, they saw several people entering and leaving the alley.

"I see what you mean,' Mikhail said to Fyodor. 'This is clearly their center of command. Let's go and have a better look at the park.'

The park had a line of large trees along the street frontage, and many shrubs and low bushes just inside its low, wrought iron fence.

'Ideal cover,' said Mikhail, pointing towards the shrubbery. 'If we approached at night, we could probably reach the edge of the park undetected. And the trees will provide excellent protection if they start shooting at us.'

'Are we going to storm the building?' asked Fyodor.

Mikhail shook his head. 'I'm not interested in killing or capturing Lenin, even if he is there, and I don't think your people have the skills to stage a successful assault. All we need to do is stay here in the park, shoot out the windows, and make them keep their heads down. If we cut the phone lines, as well as stop couriers, then we cut his communication to the outside.'

'How do we get up there to cut the telephone lines?' asked Fyodor, pointing to the wires high up on the building's wall.

'We need a grappling hook and a long rope,' answered Mikhail. 'Throw it over the wires and yank like hell. That should bring them down.'

Fyodor grinned and nodded. 'I think we can manage that, but how are we going to get to the park without being detected?'

'We march to the far side of the park from the warehouse.'

Fyodor looked perplexed.

'For a start,' continued Mikhail, 'we get everybody to dress like workmen, and we get some of their wives to sew red armbands for us all to wear. A bunch of us marching down the street will be indistinguishable from any other militia unit.'

'But they use passwords that they change daily. Without it we wouldn't get past the first checkpoint.'

'Again, that's easy,' replied Mikhail. 'You know those Red Guards who are posted near the warehouse up on the main street?'

Fyodor nodded. 'Yes, those two lads are there every day.'

'We need to assume they'll have been issued with the password, so when the day comes, we grab them and haul them back to the warehouse. A pair of pliers and five minutes is all I need. And some old rags to stuff in their mouths, so they don't shout the place down.'

'And the pliers?' asked Fyodor. 'What are they for?'

'People seem to have an aversion to having their fingernails pulled out. I find it works every time.'

Mikhail was just about to cork the bottle and go to bed when there was a sound at the back door, and then a key turning in the lock. Even though he expected it to be Vera, he reached for the Mauser beside him on the table, cocked the trigger, and aimed at the door.

'Don't shoot, it's only me,' came a female voice from the other side of the door.

Mikhail smiled to himself as he put on the safety catch and placed the gun back on the table.

'If that's vodka, then pour me a drink,' said Vera, as she walked into the kitchen with a grim look on her face and throwing her handbag on the table.

Mikhail poured her a glass and pushed it across the table. She grasped it with two hands, drank it in one gulp, and then slid it back to Mikhail.

'I'll have another, if you don't mind.'

Mikhail shrugged. 'Of course,' and refilled her glass.

As she scraped back a chair opposite and sat down, he noticed dried tear marks on her face, and a large bloodstain on her tunic.

'That blood on your clothes, is that yours? You're not wounded, are you?'

Vera looked down at her tunic. 'Don't worry, it's not mine, it's Krymov's.'

Mikhail was startled. 'Krymov, do you mean General Krymov of the 3rd Corps? What's his blood doing on your jacket?'

'The very one,' said Vera, with a deep intake of breath. 'It's a long story.'

Vera held her tunic out and looked at it with disgust, unbuttoned it, and tossed it in the corner. 'The damned thing's ruined, but it doesn't matter anyway.' She had a linen bodice under the tunic, which was also stained with blood.

'Sit down and tell me from the beginning,' said Mikhail, pouring them both another drink.

Vera sat down and ran her fingers through her hair. 'I had gone to Kapitan Zhuravsky's house to deliver a message. He's a friend of my brother, a member of the Union of Officers, and a conduit for messages to and from Mogilev. I was about to leave when a car pulled up in the driveway and, would you believe, out stepped General Krymov.'

'What the hell was he doing in Petrograd? If the army was moving, then we would have heard about it!'

'Exactly,' answered Vera. 'We were all surprised, but then Krymov told us his story. He'd been ordered by Kerensky to come into the city alone, and explain what the 3rd Corps was up to. Krymov told us he didn't want to show his hand yet, so he decided to obey Kerensky's order. He stuck with the official line that his troops are positioned to prevent a German attack from Riga, but Kerensky didn't believe a word of it, and demanded that he surrender his command.'

'How did Krymov get into the city?'

'Kerensky must have done a deal with the Bolsheviks to let him through the barricades, but that's now irrelevant.'

'Do we know what Krymov said to Kerensky? I hope he told him to go to hell. Kornilov's his boss, not Kerensky,' said Mikhail. He pointed to Vera's tunic on the floor. 'But that still doesn't explain the blood.'

'It's about the 3rd Corps,' said Vera. 'Krymov couldn't get them to move, which is part of the reason he agreed to come in for the meeting. They refuse to advance on the city.'

Mikhail slammed the palm of his hand on the table. 'What the hell has happened to the Savage Division? They were supposed to be our most reliable troops.'

'You've got to take your hat off to that bastard Lenin. He managed to turn them around by sending Muslim clerics through the lines to talk to them. The clerics are also from the Caucasus, and they happened to be in Petrograd for a Soviet congress. It seems they convinced them Kerensky is the legitimate government, and the Savage Division is duty bound to support the elected Duma.'

'Good God!' Mikhail exclaimed. 'How can any Bolshevik, Muslim clerics or not, try to convince anyone they support the Government – the very people they're trying to overthrow!'

'Say what you like,' answered Vera, 'but it worked. The Savage Division has now declared they'll remain neutral and categorically refuse to move, and there's nothing anyone can do to make them budge.'

'Then this whole damned operation has turned into a farce. What can stop the Bolsheviks now if we can't get the army in?'

'With all due credit to Krymov, he did refuse to surrender his command to Kerensky.'

Exasperated, Mikhail threw his hands in the air. 'Command of what, exactly?'

'The final bit in this horrible saga,' said Vera, wiping her eyes. 'Krymov asked to use Zhuravsky's study to write to Kornilov and explain what happened. A few minutes later we heard a gunshot. We rushed in and found him still alive. We did our best to stem the blood but, in the end, we couldn't save him.'

'Well, I guess,' sighed Mikhail, shaking his head 'the poor man finally succeeded at something.'

Mikhail went to pour himself another drink but pushed the bottle away. 'It's a damned shame,' he said. 'Just when we were making some headway with Purishkevich's men, and I really thought we could achieve something.'

Vera sighed. 'There's one thing I haven't told you. They've arrested Purishkevich on the basis he was conspiring with Kornilov, and now they are going after the rest of his organization, and any other Kornilovists as well. Kerensky's secret police – and I'm sure the Bolsheviks are helping – are rounding up all officers they can find in the city. Someone from Purishkevich's organization is bound to provide them with a description of the two of you, so you need to get out as quickly as possible.'

Mikhail stared at her. 'If they link Purishkevich to your brother, then they may well come banging on the door here. You should leave with us.'

Vera covered her face with her hands, and slowly shook her head. 'I can't. I'm one of the few of us who can get around the city relatively easily without being stopped, and I know where many of the officers are located. They've asked me to stay and help get as many out as possible.'

'And where are we supposed to go, is it still back to Mogilev?'

Vera threw her head back and gave an ironic laugh. 'You need to hear the final piece of this farce. Kerensky has ordered Kornilov to be placed under house arrest. But by whom, you may ask? So Kornilov has had the *Stavka* move into a monastery outside of Mogilev and has appointed his own warriors as prison guards. It's a joke.'

'Then should we go to Mogilev?'

'It's really up to you,' answered Vera. 'The army is splintering all over the place. The main discussion right now is with Anton Denikin and the Don Cossack *Host*. Kornilov is looking to take what forces he can to the Don, join up with the Cossacks, and fight the Bolsheviks from there.'

'Then we go there.'

'Not necessarily,' answered Vera. 'My brother is heading to Omsk where a separate army will be formed from volunteers. There's talk of a new Siberian government being based there, and there are rumors the British may be bringing in someone. There's also a huge stockpile of armaments in Vladivostok that the Allies shipped in for Russia's war effort. They don't want the Bolsheviks to get their hands on it, but I believe they will let our new Siberian Army have it. There's only one way we can get it out of Vladivostok, and that's on the Trans-Siberian. The Siberian force is going to be critical.'

'Well, both Sergei and I are Siberians, so we should go there.'

Vera laughed. 'You don't call yourself Russians?'

'Not after today, I don't.'

Mikhail leaned forward across the table. 'We're sitting here talking about civil war with the Bolsheviks, but technically Kerensky and the Duma are still running the country.'

'As someone explained to me, it's not that the Bolsheviks have seized control of the city, it's that Kerensky has relinquished control to them. Most of us expect it's just a matter of days, if not hours. I would expect Kerensky is planning to sneak away as we speak and, if he isn't, then he's a greater fool than I thought. The few Duma representatives remaining are holed up in the Winter Palace guarded by a Women's Battalion and a bunch of *Kadets*. Anyone could walk in and take the place at any time. If the Bolsheviks storm the place, it's more symbolic than anything. It just needs some contrived excuse, and it'll be all over in the blink of an eye.'

'So, poor old Russia staggers from one war straight into its own civil war.'

'Yes,' she said, pushing back her chair and standing up, 'and we both better get on with it. Where's Olga? I need her to do something urgently for me.'

'Your maid, she's gone to bed.'

'Well, I'll go and drag her out. This is important.'

Mikhail gave Vera a rueful smile. 'I'm not sure I would recommend that.'

Vera's face had a momentarily look of puzzlement. 'Oh God, don't tell me – Sergei!'

'She took a bit of a liking to him. Is there anything I can do to help?'

Vera disappeared into the bathroom. Mikhail could hear her rattling around in a cupboard, and then she reappeared, holding a towel and a small dark brown glass bottle.

'I hope that's not what I think it is,' said Mikhail.

Vera showed him the label. Mikhail could just make out the copperplate script – "*Hydrogen Peroxide*".

'I'm going to turn myself into a blonde. Don't just sit there. Get undressed down to your shorts and singlet. This stuff stains and I can't do it myself. I need you to wet my hair and then comb this stuff through it properly. You can't afford to miss any bits.'

Vera, stripped to her petticoat, draped the towel around her shoulders, and walked over to the kitchen sink. 'Let's get on with it. Stand behind me while I lean over the sink and comb it up from the roots.'

'Is it only your hair you want done?' asked Mikhail.

'There are, my dear Mikhail, some places a lady would prefer to do herself.'

Mikhail laughed. 'I was actually thinking of your eyebrows.'

Vera stood shivering as she wound the towel around her head. 'Hopefully I'll look like a new woman, and if I borrow some of Olga's clothes . . .'

Mikhail looked down at the front of his shorts, blushed, and quickly turned to retrieve his trousers.

'No need to be embarrassed,' said Vera, giving Mikhail an impish smile. 'It makes a woman feel good to know she's desired.'

Vera walked around the table and took hold of Mikhail's hand. 'I wouldn't bother with the trousers, not just yet anyway. I've just one last favour to ask of you before we both go off to war. Please.'

Chapter 21
THE BARNAUL FARM

November 1917

PAVEL SAT IN his study, nursing a glass of vodka in one hand and a cheroot in the other. Sokoi and Berkut lay stretched out at his feet, while spruce logs crackled away in the hearth, filling the room with a warm, smoky aroma.

Despite the late afternoon sun's rays trickling in through the window, it was already quite dark in the room. Pavel had asked the maid not to light the kerosene lanterns, preferring instead to sit quietly in the half-dark, basking in the soft glow of the fire and listening to the sounds of the house.

Since closing the shops, he had kept busy helping prepare the farm for winter. There was always an endless list of tasks to do, especially with the manpower shortage on the farm, and he spent days toiling alongside his workers, and found he appreciated the hard physical labor. It gave him a sense of quiet accomplishment, but more importantly, pushed the troubles of the town and its politics out of his mind.

Forage and horse feed had been stored away, the barns prepared, and the horses rounded up and brought into the yards. Mountains of firewood had been chopped and stacked on the house's verandah; animals were slaughtered and hung in the meat safes, while the larder and the cookhouses were filled with provisions and preserves.

The weather had just started to turn, the air having a crisp, sharp edge to it, and the sky losing its summer haze and turning a deep cobalt blue. The first of the morning frosts had arrived – freezing the grass into glistening brittle spikes and leaving the water troughs with thin gossamer-webs of surface ice. A light snowfall had come the previous night, but just a dusting, quickly melted by the rising sun.

The track into the town remained usable, however it was becoming increasingly muddy and rutted. Fortunately, there had been no unwelcome visitors and, with each new frost or snowfall, the farm would become gradually isolated from the town. Pavel had recently checked the track and asked his foreman to run one last trip into town before the first severe winter storm would cut them off completely.

He could not risk going into town himself, but was eager to find out what was happening. The notion there might be any shops open with anything on their shelves was perhaps a forlorn hope; however, a wagon had been loaded with surplus farm produce to barter, where possible, for scarce items.

But it was information Pavel craved. Since he had closed the shops and left town, they had received no news – they had no idea whether Tsaplin and his Bolsheviks were in control in the town, nor what was happening in the rest of the country. Their closest neighbors on surrounding farms were in a similar situation, all shunning the town, and being wary of any contact with travelers moving though the countryside.

Pavel had stood with the foreman on the verandah looking out over the steppe, towards the distant Altai Krai Mountains. Already there were dark, ponderous snow-bearing clouds forming over the mountain peaks.

'It's just a matter of days,' Pavel told him, 'and, then we might not be able to get through. Are you okay doing this? It could be dangerous.'

The foreman looked up at the sky and nodded. 'Better me than you, sire. They know your face, but I hardly ever go into town. To them I'll just be another old peasant with a cart.'

'If they try to confiscate your goods, don't stop them. We'll survive without them. But speak to a few people and, better still, buy some newspapers.'

Pavel knew the arrival of the next storm would bring almost complete isolation, with the track obliterated from sight and the farm becoming its own closed world. Even travel by sleigh would be difficult. This was both a blessing and a curse. When the blizzards came in and the temperatures plummeted, those in the town would be unwilling to venture outside its perimeter, and that would make unwelcome visitations even more unlikely.

But being isolated and somewhat protected brought a different set of concerns. As he had said to Maria that morning, this was little comfort when you didn't have any idea what dangers were just over the horizon, and what you would be facing when Spring finally arrived. Sooner or later they would have to face up to what was happening in the town.

'Perhaps the Tsar will come back,' suggested Maria, without any real conviction.

'There was talk of him going into exile, maybe to England, to his cousin, King George. But it's the Army we need. This General Kornilov could be the man to sort this out. Forget the Duma, you can't preserve democracy when you have the Bolsheviks tearing it down, and the Tsar never allowed the Duma to function properly anyway. So, let the Army stabilize the situation first, and then see what we can make work.'

For the family there was still a level of incredulity about what was happening, or how it could happen at all. But they were becoming weary of the futile debates speculating about possible outcomes, particularly when they didn't have any idea of what was going on outside the boundary of their property.

Pavel frequently pointed out to anyone who would listen that this was the downside of him leaving town but, as Iya had retorted, any attempt to obtain information wouldn't be a lot of use to the family if their father ended up swinging at the end of a rope.

The family dinners were now marked by lengthy lapses in conversation, once the usual daily topics had run their course. Maria did her best to keep cheerful, and occupied the talk with important household matters, such as how the preserving was going, or the dessert she planned for tomorrow's dinner. Katrina and Maria had reached a type of unspoken truce, but avoided each other as much as possible, with Katrina inclined to eat her meals with the cook in the kitchen.

The rest of the family kept busy as best they could. Iya withdrew for most of each day to her room, buried in her books and writing poetry, but did join them for meals where she, albeit with diminishing conviction, continued to spar with Pavel over politics. She had not given up the prospect of receiving further correspondence from Mikhail, but became increasingly insular and terse with the other family members as each day passed. As soon as she learned the foreman was making one last trip into town, she sought him out and pressed him to check the Post Office.

Mara felt most of all the absence social contact with her friends in town. However, she was reconciled to this loss by the knowledge that many of them had already left for Harbin, or elsewhere, along with their families. To fill the gap, she spent countless hours practicing the piano or using a reluctant Dmitry to learn the latest dance steps from the instruction book she had received from Moscow when the mail was still getting through.

Never being able to abide being trapped all day in the house, Galina occupied her days helping muck out the stables and looking after the horses, which had now been all moved in from the paddocks. There they would remain for the winter, except when being exercised in the yards on fine days. Both Galina and the horses relished this break from the routine and a chance for fresh air.

She tried her best not to think of Sergei, or where he might be. It was an unanswerable question, so she threw herself into her work, sometimes at a feverish pace to keep occupied and not leave a moment to think.

Dmitry continued with the rifle instruction he was giving to Iya and Mara. However, he was becoming increasingly frustrated with their lack of enthusiasm for learning even the basics. 'This may save your life one day,' he kept reminding them, but to no avail. The rifle practice had ground slowly and inevitably to a standstill. Mara was never particularly interested in learning how to defend herself, maintaining that her woman's guile would be far more effective if confronted by a belligerent male. And when Iya finally declared she was sufficiently competent to kill herself at close range, Dmitry had angrily thrown his hands into the air and stormed off. There the lessons had halted.

Pavel, despite the physical toil, had become a light sleeper. The slightest sound would awaken him instantly, and then he would lie awake for hours, with one hand resting on his rifle by the bed, listening to the sounds of the house and beyond. A door creaking in the wind, the neigh of a horse down at the stables, or the hoot of an owl in the oaks would make him instantly alert. And often, as he lay there, doubt would creep into his mind – were the windows all latched? Had the cook remembered to bolt the back door? He would get up in the middle of the night, prowl around the house checking every door and window and, by the first light of morning, finally fall asleep exhausted.

When his chores were finished for the day, Pavel would often take his rifle and the dogs, mount his horse, and ostensibly go off hunting. It was less about shooting stag or snaring hare, although he would take the opportunity if it were presented to him, than about patrolling the perimeter of the property to look for signs of intruders. A guard had been posted on the track leading up to the crest, but it was cold and isolated up there, and Pavel was unconvinced of their diligence in keeping a lookout over a long period.

It became his habit to check daily, if weather permitted. In particular, he went looking for signs of activity in the area where the track from the town left the forest. He regularly found the tracks of various animals, and closely studied their scat to help identify them. Bear, deer, hare and wolf were common, but not once a horse or human footprint – except for today.

On the very afternoon the foreman went to town, he came across tracks of horses' hooves in the mud. He knew it was not the foreman and his wagon, since he could identify the wagon's wheel tracks that had passed over the top of the hoof marks. This meant these horses had passed that way earlier in the day, before the foreman.

Initially he was annoyed the foreman hadn't come back to report the tracks before proceeding into town but, having left at first light, it was understandable he may have missed them. It also meant, Pavel surmised, that these prints were likely made before dawn. Strange, and very troubling, that someone would be riding out this way that early.

Pavel dismounted and closely studied the hoof prints. It was hard to discern the number of horses in this group since the hoof prints were all mashed together and intermingled in the mud of the narrow track, but it was clear there were more than just a couple of horses – it was a large group.

On closer inspection Pavel could identify several individual hoof prints and noted they were shod horses, not wild steppe horses. This meant they had to be broken in, and probably were being ridden. They had exited the forest in file and, rather than spreading out across the open steppe, they had veered left together and headed away from the farm, but their direction was clear. He followed their tracks until he came to where they had forded a stream and decided not to proceed further.

Even though they were heading away from the farm, and further up into the shallow valley, Pavel was concerned. There were other farms and other families up there who could be at risk, and it was still uncomfortably close to their own farm. It was unlikely a large group of horsemen moving through this area would be local farmers. Apart from a hunting party, and that was highly unlikely at this time of the year, there were two other possibilities; it was likely they were either a Bolshevik unit sent out from the town to commandeer property, or bandits roving the countryside taking advantage of the lack of law and order and the resultant anarchy that prevailed. Each scenario carried significant and real danger.

Pavel could hear footsteps, the unmistakable footfall of Maria, marching down the hall. He quickly threw the stub of his cheroot into the grate and waved the smoke away.

'What are those dogs doing in here?' She clapped her hands and shooed the dogs out of the door. Berkut and Sokoi slunk out of the study, tails between their legs, and then scampered down the hall in the direction of the kitchen.

'You've been smoking again.'

He thought briefly about arguing the inalienable territorial rights of his study, but decided against it.

'The foreman has come back from town,' continued Maria. 'He managed to get a few supplies, and he's in the kitchen asking to see you.'

'Ah,' said Pavel, 'ask him to come through.'

Maria raised an eyebrow. 'You mean here?'

'Yes, I would prefer we're not overheard by the staff.'

The foreman, who rarely ventured into the servants' quarters, and never into the master's study, appeared nervously at the door.

Pavel beckoned Ivan Nikolayevich in and quietly closed the door behind him. He bade the foreman take a seat while he remained standing with his back to the fire. 'So, tell me how was it in there?'

The foreman hesitated, and sat nervously on the edge of the chair, scrunching his cloth hat in his hands. 'The town has many more deserters than before, sire, and a lot of people have moved in from the camps. They've taken over the empty houses of those town folk who've left. There's looting and groups of people drinking in the street, and men brawling, and there's killing going on. I saw a couple of bodies lying on empty ground, and there were even some people who had been hung from lampposts.'

'Really,' said Pavel, 'then who is in control of the town?'

'It's still supposed to be those Bolshevik people. There are groups of them with red armbands standing around at almost every corner, but they're all just as drunk as everyone else, and it seems to have been going on for days.'

The foreman handed him a crumpled bunch of broadsheet newspapers. 'I found these blowing around the streets and just grabbed what I could. There was nobody out selling newspapers that I could see, and I didn't really like to ask anyone questions. I hope they're what you are after.'

'Was there any mail?'

The foreman shook his head. 'The Post Office was boarded up.'

Pavel thanked him and ushered him out. He picked up the sheets of newspapers, went into the dining room, and spread them out on the table. There were a few copies of the same front page and some second and third pages of the two-week old copy of *Izvestia*, but it was enough to piece together the major news items. It was dated 26th October. The front page was largely dominated by two photographs – one of a battleship called the "Aurora", and the other of the Winter Palace in Petrograd.

'Can you get the family together?' Pavel called down to the kitchen. 'There's news.'

'A Pallada-class cruiser,' said Dmitry, glancing at the photograph as he entered the room. Dmitry, an avid student of *affaires militaires*, expressed his opinion confidently. 'It was brought back from the Baltic for repairs months ago and has been moored in the Neva off Petrograd ever since.'

The banner headline, in oversized bold print, announced "Victory for the People's Revolution", and below it the secondary headline, "Kronstadt Sailors and the Red Guard Storm the Winter Palace".

By now the family had all collected in the dining room and were keenly peering over Pavel's shoulder.

'It says here,' said Pavel, pushing his glasses up his nose and tracing his finger along the first column of writing, 'The battleship fired the opening shots of the revolution over the roofs of Petrograd; the Winter Palace was "heroically" stormed by the Red Guard and the sailors; resistance by the *Kadets* and a Women's Battalion who were guarding the palace was ineffectual, and the building was quickly occupied. Those remaining in the palace, many of them "Kornilovist" plotters who have been planning a coup to seize power from the people, either ran or were arrested. The Provisional Government has collapsed, and Kerensky is reported to have fled the country, secreted on a foreign vessel.'

'That's like the pot calling the kettle black,' said Iya. 'The Bolsheviks claim to have staged their own coup against the Kerensky government to stop the Kornilovists staging a coup against the Kerensky government.'

'A coup is still a coup, in anyone's language,' Pavel pointed out, rather indignantly. 'Kerensky's provisional government may have been cobbled together with an odd coalition of parties, but who gave the Bolsheviks the right to overthrow them? And besides, how many people have ever voted for the Bolsheviks? They've only ever been a minority party.'

'What happens now?' Maria was standing next to Pavel, agitated and kneading her hands in her apron.

'Let's not panic. We need to be careful about reading too much into this,' answered Pavel, 'it is *Izvestia,* after all.'

'Propaganda or not,' said Iya, 'it's clear the Bolsheviks have now seized power in Petrograd, and technically, that means they're now running the country. Look what it says here.' Iya stabbed her finger at the open page. "A Military Revolutionary Committee has been appointed and has declared "Final Victory for the Russian People". I mean they're not just talking about controlling Petrograd, they're talking about the entire country.'

'But, what does this mean for us?' persisted Maria. There were tears welling in her eyes, and her voice was raised. 'I don't care about what happens in Petrograd, I just care about us as a family and what happens here.'

'Unfortunately,' said Pavel, after a long pause, 'I think we need to admit that any hope of getting rid of Tsaplin and his Bolsheviks from Barnaul has just become a lot harder. The foreman tells me it's like a lunatic asylum in there, and everybody has been drunk for days, probably on looted liquor.'

Galina leaned forward and slapped the flat of her hand on the newspapers. 'And I think we can see why. They've finally got something to celebrate. They think they've won, and they believe we've lost.'

The family lapsed into an awkward silence, all standing around the table and staring at the newspaper spread out before them with a mixture of disbelief and shock.

'So,' said Maria, in a trembling voice, 'will they come out and take our farm away, and then what will happen to us?'

'That's a good question, mother,' said Galina, looking around the table. 'Do we fight, or do we run? This is what we've all been avoiding for weeks, if not months.'

Pavel pointed to the date at the top of the newspaper. 'That's two weeks ago, and we haven't seen anybody yet.'

Pavel had not told anybody about the tracks he had just discovered, and the foreman hadn't mentioned them on his return. He didn't want to alarm the family needlessly, and decided for now to bide his time, but the images of the hoof marks weighed heavily on his mind and had turned his guts into a hard knot.

'So, we wait,' said Galina. 'We wait until a group of horsemen ride down that track out there. Then what do we do?'

Pavel carefully folded the newspaper and tucked it under his arm. 'The first thing is we don't mention a word of this to any of the staff. We don't want to create trouble where there's currently none.'

'But how long can we keep it quiet?' asked Galina. 'Remember the night visits by the Bolsheviks to our workers, and that was not long ago. But, what about the foreman?'

'He just saw what's going on in town,' answered Pavel, 'but he can't read, so he doesn't know what's in here.' He tapped the folded newspapers. 'If the snow comes soon, and we're cut off, then we should be able to sit it out here for the winter.'

'And in spring?' asked Maria.

'Anything might have happened by then. Perhaps Kornilov, perhaps the Army?'

'But how will we know? Won't we be in the same position as we are now? We have some news that is already two weeks old and, by spring, any news will be at least four months old, if not more. Besides, how do we get any news if we can't go into town anymore?'

'Was there a letter from Mikhail,' asked Iya, 'or have the Army and my husband just disappeared?'

Pavel shook his head. 'The foreman told me the Post Office is closed. I'm sorry, but we can't expect to get any more mail, not for some time anyway.'

Iya turned and walked out the door, climbed the staircase, and slammed her bedroom door shut behind her.

'I'm sorry if you're all upset,' Pavel looked around at the family, 'I know it's not good news, but we need to face up to reality. It's no use burying our heads in the sand anymore.'

Pavel walked out of the room into the hall and took his coat down from the stand.

'Where are you going?' Maria called after him.

'I'm doing the only thing we can do. We need to alert Joseph Antonovich to the news; he's nearest to us. Then he can help spread the word around our other neighbors. If we are going to survive through this, we need to share information and band together to protect each other. There's enough light left. Dmitry and I will ride over to Joseph's and be back before dark. Galina, can you stay and keep lookout?'

'A lookout for what?'

'A group of men riding over the crest on the track.'

'What do I do if I see something?'

'Fire two shots into the air, and we'll return as fast as we can.'

Chapter 22

JOSEPH'S FARM

The Same Evening

PAVEL AND DMITRY pushed their horses through the line of trees marking the boundary between their property and Joseph's. The trees gave way to rough ground covered with thick hay stubble, the remnants of the last harvest before winter. The land sloped away from them, and they could just make out Joseph's farmhouse and outbuildings in the distance.

Dusk was quickly approaching, making it a little difficult to see but, at first glance, everything seemed normal – there was smoke coming out of the chimneys and lights on in the house. But Pavel sensed something was not quite right. The barn doors had been left wide open, and there were articles – pieces of furniture, clothing and other objects strewn over the grass near the house.

Pavel held his hand out and stopped Dmitry. 'Wait here while I go down and have a look. Meanwhile, you stay here and keep an eye out for a group of horsemen. If you see a sign of anyone, then fire a shot into the air.'

He rode slowly down the slope, nervously checking carefully for any signs of people or movement. The place seemed deserted, eerily devoid of almost everything except for the items scattered over the paddock between the house and the barn. As he got closer he caught the sound of screeching coming from the barn. He glanced up into the sky and could see large black shapes of ravens swooping and circling.

About halfway between the house and the barn he came up to the misshapen bundle of clothes lying, like a large, cast-off children's rag doll, on the ground. But, as he got closer, he realized it was not a bundle of rags. Pavel got off his horse and slowly walked towards it with a growing sense of unease in the pit of his stomach.

The man's body lay face down in the stubble with a kitchen meat cleaver half buried in his back. A trail of dried blood marked the agonizing progress over the rough ground, as though the victim had been attempting to drag himself towards the barn.

'What is it, Father?' Dmitry shouted from back up the slope.

'Stay where you are, there's no need for you to see this.'

He knelt next to the body and turned it onto its side. *Joseph.* Death had not come easily; his facial features were frozen in a final agonized grimace.

Pavel left Joseph where he lay, walked his horse over to the nearest fence, and tied it to the railing. He pulled his rifle out of its saddle holster, walked over to the barn and pounded the outside of the wall with the butt of his rifle and waited, then instinctively ducked as dozens of ravens flew, screeching, out the door and headed for the nearby trees.

It took a few moments for his eyes to adjust to the dark interior. He found Joseph's wife and his daughter, and another he assumed was a housemaid, in one of the stalls. Their hands had been tied together over their heads, and they were roped to a hitching point on the wall of the stall. Their skirts were pulled up above their waists, leaving their loins naked and exposed.

Each of them had been badly beaten, with blackened eyes, and swollen, bloodied lips. There were open wounds and raw flesh around their eyes and faces where the ravens had begun pecking at the bodies.

A wave of nausea almost overcame him, and he had to steady himself against the wall of the stall while he cleared his head. He had to wait a few moments before he could summon the strength to crouch down and place the back of his hand against the exposed skin of the maid's neck. She felt slightly warm to the touch, and he guessed she had been dead for less than an hour. *Rigor mortis* had yet to fully set in.

When he took his hand away it was smeared with blood, and he was shocked to find the back of her hair was a mess of congealed blood. He turned her over to find a bullet hole just behind the left ear. The shot had been angled upwards and the exiting bullet had punched a gaping hole through the top right of her skull. He checked the other bodies – each one of them had met a similar fate.

Pavel, bile rising in his mouth and his head swimming, staggered towards the barn door. He felt the urgent need to run from the horror, and get outside for fresh air. When he made it out of the barn, he sat on his haunches, closed his eyes, and leaned with his back against the barn wall while sucking in deep breaths.

When he finally opened his eyes, he found himself confronted by Joseph's body, just a few meters away. Somehow the sight of it helped clear his mind, and he realized what he had to do. He sat for a moment, steeling himself for the task, and then got up and walked over to the body. Taking Joseph by the collar, he dragged him into the barn and laid him next to the women in the stall. Grabbing a nearby pitchfork, Pavel covered the bodies with layers of loose hay, then took some kerosene lanterns and liberally sprinkled the liquid over the hay.

He walked out of the barn, took a cheroot from his tin, and struck a match against the doorframe. Taking a couple of deep draws on the cheroot, he blew on the tip to ensure it was glowing, flicked it towards the mound of hay, then turned and ran. There was a loud *whoosh*, and he felt a blast of hot air against the back of his neck.

Pavel stood well back. He could hear the hay crackling as it burnt. The dry hay caught fire easily and quickly spread, and before long he could see flames starting to lick up the inside of the barn's walls. Finally, a plume of thick black smoke billowed out from the open doors as the fire took hold, and the radiant heat forced him to move away.

He retrieved his horse, pushed his rifle back into the holster, and swung himself up into his saddle. With one last look at the burning pyre and a touch to the peak of his cap, he wheeled his horse and rode back up the hill.

Dmitry was sitting with his back to a tree with his fists clenched into his eyes. He was shaking, and Pavel caught a faint whiff of vomit.

'It's over now,' Pavel dismounted, crouched down next to him, and put a hand gently on his shoulder. 'I'll get you some water. I've got a bottle in my saddlebag.'

Dmitry looked up. 'Was it who I think it is?'

'Yes, and the others were in the barn.'

'You mean, Svetena and her mother?'

'And one of the maids.'

They both turned and looked down at the barn. It was now fully engulfed with flames, the thick black smoke billowing up into the still evening sky.

'You're not going to check the house?' asked Dmitry, his voice tremulous.

'No need,' responded Pavel, with a grim face. 'I know they'll have looted the place, but I think they're all accounted for, at least Joseph and his family, God rest their souls.'

'Was it the Bolsheviks?'

Pavel shook his head. ' Does it matter whether they're Bolsheviks or bandits? There's a murderous gang out there, and my concern is who's next.'

Pavel hoisted himself up into his saddle and wheeled his horse around. 'So come on, let's get going.'

'Where to?' asked Dmitry.

'Home, and as fast as we can!'

Chapter 23
THE DEPARTURE

PAVEL LED THE way at a gallop through the trees, and then reined in when he reached the open paddocks of their farm. Down below him in the valley he could make out the lights of the homestead. To his relief there was nothing that seemed out of the ordinary. He waited for Dmitry to ride up alongside him.

'Listen to me. When we get to the yards, take my horse. Don't bother getting them to unsaddle it. Go and find the foreman and tell him to get the two big carriages ready and horses harnessed while I go up to the house.'

Pavel glanced at the sky and saw pewter-colored clouds, heavy with snow, and felt the temperature dropping. He held out his hand in time to catch a large, soft snowflake drifting down. 'We're in for a blizzard, and this isn't going to melt this time. Get the foreman to change the carriage wheels over to sleigh runners and, tell him to be as quick as he can. Then get him to bring the carriages up to the house.'

'We're going to leave now?' asked Dmitry. 'It's going to be night soon.'

'Then hopefully we'll use the cover of darkness to get a head start on them,' said Pavel, spurring his horse forward.

Pavel swung down from the saddle, handed the reins to Dmitry, and ran up towards the homestead. Maria and Galina were out on the veranda, both wrapped in shawls. Galina was carrying a rifle in the crook of her arm.

'We saw the smoke over at Joseph's,' said Maria. 'We were worried. Is everything all right?'

Pavel paused to catch his breath. 'Far from it – Joseph, and all the family,' he hesitated, 'they're all dead – murdered.'

Maria paled and gasped. 'My God.'

'Who would do such a thing?' asked Galina, shaking her head and gripping her shawl tight around her.

'Does it matter?' answered Pavel. 'All that matters is we get out of here as fast as we can before we're all dead too. These same men could arrive any minute, or tonight, or early tomorrow. They're probably working their way around the farms in the district, and we could be next.'

Maria had a startled look of panic on her face. 'You mean, we're to leave now?'

Pavel gripped her arm. 'You need to understand that staying here isn't an option anymore. I counted the tracks, I think there are about seven of them, and there's no way we can protect ourselves against that number.'

'But what about our workers?'

'Who have we got to help fight them? The men are still away at the front – we've only old men, women, and a bunch of children. Apart from Ivan, is there anyone who we can trust?'

Maria opened her mouth to ask another question, but Pavel stopped her.

'Look, we don't have time for this. Just trust me that we need to get out of here. Our lives are at stake. Dmitry is down at the yards helping organize the carriages now. We leave in two hours – just one suitcase each. Keep it as light as possible, every bit of additional weight will slow us down, and remember they'll be on horseback and can travel faster than us.'

'Do you think they'll try to follow us in this?' asked Galina, pointing to the falling snowflakes. It was now snowing more heavily than before, and already everything had a thin coating of white.

'We have to expect them to come after us,' answered Pavel. 'Looking at what they did to Joseph's place, they're not after our furniture, our house, or our land. It's our money and your jewelry they'll want more than anything, and they're not afraid to kill to get it. We need to make sure we get a head start, and hope the new snow covers our tracks.'

'Where will we go?' asked Maria, wiping tears from her eyes.

'We'll head across country until we pick up the Pavlovsk Trakt, and follow it until we get to Alexei's farm. Let's pray we are safe out there. But not one word to any of the staff where we're going.'

'How long will it take?' asked Maria.

'I think three days, maybe four, depending on the weather, so you need to prepare enough food to get us through, but pack a separate lot of food for Dmitry.'

'Why, isn't he coming?'

'Don't worry, he's going too' replied Pavel, 'but I have a plan.'

'So, who else beside the family?' asked Maria, looking about her and lowering her voice to a whisper. 'What about some of the staff?'

'We've only room for us, and Katrina of course. The workers are going to have to look out for themselves.'

'Berkut and Sokoi?'

'There'll be no room in the carriages, but the dogs will be okay following behind. Just make sure you pack enough meat for them. Now enough questions, let's get going before it's too late.'

Maria turned and ran back into the house, shouting for Mara and Iya to come downstairs quickly. Then she hurried to the kitchen where Pavel could hear her issuing instructions to the cook.

'Galina, listen to me.'

Galina had not moved. She remained standing on the veranda, white-knuckled, shivering with the cold, and gripping the rifle fiercely.

'What was it like over there?'

'Worse than you can imagine. These animals are thieves, killers, and worse. As soon as you've packed, I want you to collect all the rifles out of the cabinet and every bit of ammunition you can lay your hands on. At some stage I expect you and I are probably going to have to fight them off.'

'What about Dmitry?'

'I'm sending him on ahead. A lone horseman can travel twice the speed we can. If he can make it through, he can get Alexei to send help down the *trakt*. I think it's our only hope of survival.'

The family assembled in the hallway. They were all dressed in multiple layers of clothes since, as the blizzard strengthened outside, the temperature kept plummeting. Everyone wore an outer layer of fur – a heavy bearskin coat, fur-lined boots, and the women all had fur muffs for their hands and scarves wrapped around their heads under their fur hats.

The women's dresses were weighed down with jewelry sewn into the hems, and Pavel had several gold ingots secreted in the lining of his coat. He didn't think it would fool an experienced bandit for a moment, but it was worth a chance.

Pavel had stored a wooden box, heavy with Mexican silver dollars, under the seat of one of the carriages. Worth its weight in pure silver, the Mexican dollars had become the default currency in most parts of Russia, and Pavel had been secretly accumulating a stockpile for months in preparation for such a moment.

The carriages, now with sleigh runners fitted, were standing in front of the house, and were being loaded under the businesslike supervision of Katrina. The household staff, not involved with the loading, lined up along the hall. They stood there in silence, watching the final preparations for the unexpected departure. Each one of them looked petrified, and several were stifling sobs. Maria had given each some money, but this had done little to quell either their anguish or their fear of whatever fate was about to befall them.

'Where's Mara?' asked Pavel, tersely, 'I told her not to disappear.'

Pavel could hear the piano in the front room. He recognized the serene, but mournful tones, of Beethoven's Moonlight Sonata, one of Mara's favorites. As he walked into the room she stopped, firmly closed the lid over the keyboard, then lightly ran her fingers over the polished mahogany. 'Goodbye, my beautiful old friend.'

Mara abruptly stood, and without looking at Pavel, walked past him out into the hall where she sat herself down on the bench seat alongside Iya and grasped her hand tightly. 'Are you all right?' she asked Iya.

'Of course not, how could I be.' Iya was fighting back her tears. 'I've been dreading this moment for months, and here we are, about to disappear off into the godforsaken wilds of Siberia without a message to anyone where we're going.'

'But, Mikhail and Sergei may be together, so there's a chance.'

'Are they? How can any of us know that?'

The two of them sat in silence. Iya withdrew into herself, and sat, staring blankly at the wall in front of her.

Maria found Dmitry and led him into the dining room to the *krasni ugol* red corner, where she instructed him to lift down both the icons. She then carefully wrapped them in their red embroidered cloth and carried them out to the hall.

'Everyone be seated, ' she told the family. 'We are going to pray for a safe journey.'

Holding the two icons in the crook of each arm, she walked slowly past the family members, bidding each of them to touch their fingers to their lips and then press them against the embossed surface of the sacred paintings. When she got to Pavel, she glowered down at him. 'I don't care, they're coming with us, or don't you want the Lord's protection?'

Pavel thought about poor Joseph lying dead in the field with his family raped and murdered in the barn, and wondered for a moment where the Lord's protection was then, but decided not to protest. 'Of course, my dear,' he answered, as he leaned forward and dutifully kissed the icons.

Maria and Iya were in one carriage, while Mara and Katrina were in the other. Suitcases, cartons and baskets of food were piled high around each of them, and heavy horse blankets, already coated with fresh snow, were tucked over their knees.

They had no room for drivers, so Maria took the reins of one carriage, and Katrina the other. Maria was very nervous since she had not driven anything for years – worried about keeping control of the horses and the carriage in the snow, besides the poor visibility. Katrina, however, was used to running errands for the store, and could handle a carriage with confidence.

While the final loading was completed, the dogs bounded around the carriages, excitedly wagging their tails and sniffing at everything, as though they were about to embark on a new adventure.

Pavel, Dmitry and Galina were alongside the carriages, mounted on horseback, with each horse carrying saddlebags stuffed with extra food and ammunition. Pavel rode over to Dmitry. 'Are you okay doing this?'

Dmitry looked nervous, but when he answered there was a note of determination in his voice. 'Yes, papa.'

'And you remember the way?'

'As long as I can pick up the *trakt,* I'll be fine.'

'Stay with us until we're over the crest and out of sight, then ride on as fast, and for as long, as you can. Remember to take rests, and to eat, and to look after your horse, for without her you can't make it. But above all, stay safe, stay alert, and avoid anyone you come across. If you don't get through, then we're all in trouble. If they come in the morning and find we have left, then chances are they'll try to follow our tracks and could catch up with us sometime late tomorrow, or the next day. If they do, I'm not certain how long Galina and I can hold them off. God may help us, but the others aren't going to be much help, so you and Alexei may be our best hope.'

Only the foreman had come up to the house from the staff quarters; he was standing forlornly, holding the bridle of one of the horses harnessed to a sleigh. Pavel rode over to him, leaned down from his saddle, and offered his hand. 'Look after yourself, Ivan Nikolayevich. I'm sorry we are leaving you like this.'

'God speed, sire.'

'What will you do?'

'Most of us will go into the forest to hide. The killing can't go on forever. Who would be left?'

Pavel didn't waste time with an answer. He waved the sleighs forward. 'Let's get out of here.'

The foreman let go of the bridle and slapped the horse on the rump.

As the sleighs topped the crest Pavel turned in his saddle for one last look back down into the valley. Through the slanting snow he could make out the house. It emitted a warm, diffused light into the darkness of the night, standing out like a beacon for lost travelers, but tonight, it was as though it was signaling a sad farewell. Through the swirling snow he could make out the dark shapes of figures, a group of women from the worker's huts, skirts hoisted, running up the slope towards the house.

They couldn't wait for us to leave.

Maria sat in the sleigh, holding the reins, grim-faced and staring straight ahead into the dark void of the blizzard. 'I'm not going to look back.'

Chapter 24

THE PAVLOVSK TRAKT

DMITRY LEFT THEM soon after they had mounted the crest and was quickly lost from sight in the gloom of the night and the driving snow. He had seemed confident he knew the way, but Pavel remained anxious. The snow was accumulating quickly on the ground and in the dark it was difficult to pick out objects in the landscape. They knew, if they kept heading in a northerly direction, they must meet the Pavlovsk Trakt at some point. But if the snow continued to fall, there was a chance they could ride straight over it without realizing it was there. It would be similar for Dmitry, but he had a better chance of locating it, since he would get there before the snow depth increased too much.

Pavel instructed Galina to stay alongside the sleighs while he rode forward, picking his way across the steppe, and signaling back with his torch to indicate the path to follow. He was worried one of the sleighs could accidentally slide off into a roadside ditch and topple over on to its side. His concern wasn't so much the danger to the passengers, but the time lost in having to unload the sleigh to get it back on the road.

Pavel roughly knew the distance from the house to the *trakt* and kept looking about for known landmarks. After several false starts, he came across a double line of bare poplars that he recognized. He dismounted, scuffed his boot around in the snow, and found a series of frozen wheel ruts leading through the line of trees and heading due west. He was confident this was the *trakt*. He also found a set of recent hoof marks, only just starting to fill with snow. It was a single rider that he hoped was Dmitry.

They had been travelling over rough, open steppe along simple, narrow tracks, but now they were on a defined and well-made road, they could pick up some speed and distance.

'We need to keep going until just before daylight,' he told Maria, 'then we'll get off the road and find somewhere to shelter and rest. We can't risk being spotted out in the open. It's about forty *versts* from here to the village of Pavlovsk. I want to reconnoiter it in daylight so I can work out if we can find a way to skirt the place.'

'And Alexei's place?'

'About another eighty *versts* further on from Pavlovsk, but we need to cut off at some stage to the south.'

Galina had ridden back to the group, just as the first crack of dawn was appearing on the eastern horizon. Pavel had sent her on ahead to look for a place to hide. 'I've found a disused barn off the side of the *trakt*,' she told Pavel. 'There's not much of it left, but it will shelter us from the wind and keep us out of sight of the road.'

The snow had stopped during the night, and the day was dawning clear and bright. The dark grey clouds were now far off towards the west, leaving the sky above them a deep blue, and the freshly fallen snow sparkled brilliantly in the rising sun.

'It's so clear you can almost see forever,' Maria told Pavel, as she shielded her eyes from the glare and looked about.

'That's not good for us,' he replied, 'we're too easy to spot. Once we get the sleighs off the road and out of sight, we'll need to cut some branches and sweep the snow to obscure our tracks, and pray we're not found.'

The family ate, and then slept for most of the day. The horses were also fed and rested, while the dogs were tied up to stop them running around. Each of them took turns at watching the road. Now the storm had passed, there had been some occasional traffic, mostly local farmers with draught horses hauling carts loaded high with feed. They had all passed by without any indication they had noticed the carriages hidden behind the old barn. Better still, there had been no sign of any armed group of horsemen riding towards them from the Barnaul direction.

'Perhaps we're not being followed after all,' he speculated to Maria, without any real conviction.

'But what if one of those farmers spotted us hiding here? They might be too scared to stop and investigate, but they could easily tell someone.'

'How will we know,' answered Pavel, as he kept anxiously scanning the *trakt* for any sign of people.

Late in the afternoon, when the shadows had lengthened and the light was fading, Pavel decided to ride the last few *versts* to check the village. Pavlovsk was a collection of rough-hewn timber huts collected around a village square, with the road cutting straight through the middle. It was larger than many of the villages along the *trakt,* more like a small town. The entrance into the village was partially obscured by forest, and Pavel was able to ride close to the outskirts and remain hidden. From his vantage point he could not see any barriers or people guarding the road entrances, but there was movement within the town, and most of the chimneys were emitting smoke. Pavel managed to locate a narrow track, not much more than a wide path, to the northeast that skirted the town, and then rejoined the main *trakt* on the other side.

He rode back to tell the others. 'I think we should make a move now rather than stay and risk being overtaken. I've found a way past the town, but we need to take it while there's some daylight left. We probably risk being seen by somebody, but I think it's worth it. If we wait until dark, it'll be too hard to find our way.'

Pavel led the way with Galina following in the rear. The rough road around the town ran close to several log cabins. While nobody came out to challenge them, or to watch them pass, Pavel sensed their passage was being closely monitored every step of the way.

'The whole village will know we've passed this way before the sun goes down,' said Pavel, turning in his saddle and speaking to Maria.

'Why should that bother them?' answered Maria, 'There must be travelers on this road all the time.'

'This is close to Barnaul, and they must know what's going on. Besides, we probably look like *kulaks* trying to escape, and you can bet they'll inform the first Bolshevik that comes along. These people will be poor forestry workers; there'll be no love lost for the likes of us.'

The family made it past the town without incident and managed to get back to the main *trakt* without either of the sleighs sliding off the narrow path. Relieved, they decided to keep pushing ahead, even though dusk was falling rapidly. A new moon was rising, and with the clear sky, it was bathing the landscape in a faint bluish light that reflected off the snow and made it quite easy for them to see their way.

However, with the clear sky came plummeting temperatures, and after two hours they were forced to call a halt. Everyone's hands and feet were frozen, and the first signs of frostbite were appearing on the tips of noses and exposed cheeks, even though they all had scarves wrapped around their heads.

Despite the risk, Pavel agreed they should find a place to stop and light a fire. They were going to need its warmth for them to survive the night. He chose a spot off the road that was sheltered by a copse of trees and set about collecting kindling and wood. Using some of the dry horse fodder, they finally managed to get a small fire going, and everyone huddled around, as close to the flames as they dared. Even Berkut and Sokoi managed to squeeze themselves into a space to bask in the warmth.

Pavel caught the distinct smell of burning hair. 'Keep an eye on the dogs,' he said, as he pushed them away. 'Any closer, and they'll go up in flames.'

The family crouched around the small fire but, while the warmth was welcome, they were very aware the fire could give away their position. As the night closed in around them, and the flames burned brightly, none of them could see much beyond the immediate periphery of the fire. It was a frightening prospect; while sitting and basking in the warm glow around the fire, someone could be walking towards them with a loaded rifle.

Pavel was tired after the long nights and days in the saddle. The constant tension of checking for possible pursuers was also draining, and his body's desire to sleep was crushing. But he forced himself to stay awake, regularly leaving the fire to regain his night vision and check the road for signs of movement. The cold would always force him back to the fire, where he would sometimes doze off without realizing it, and then wake with a start. Then he would force himself upright, and stumble away from the fire into the cold and dark to check their surrounds. However, the same cold also must have forced everybody on the road to seek shelter, and Pavel was relieved to make it through the night without sighting any man or beast.

The morning dawned, with a weak, wintry sun rising into a cloudless sky and lifting the temperature slowly to a relatively comfortable level. It was still well below freezing, but there was little wind, and they could remain warm if they kept moving about. They couldn't keep the fire burning, since the smoke would be easily spotted and give away their position. Pavel decided it was best to strike camp and risk travelling the road in broad daylight.

Despite the risk, it was a relief to be on the move again, with the knowledge that each *verst* travelled would be taking them further away from the danger of any pursuers. The snow was dry and firm, and the sleighs picked up pace, with the only sounds the faint hiss of the runners gliding over the surface and the muffled clip-clop of the horse's hooves on the snow.

Every so often they would pass through small, isolated hamlets – usually just a collection of a few simple log huts fringing the road. They knew if the huts were inhabited because of the chimney smoke, but not once did anybody venture out to either greet or query them. Sometimes there was the glimpse of a face peeping out behind a lace curtain, but that was quickly dropped back into place when the people inside thought they might have been seen.

Once they passed a farmer with his loaded cart going in the opposite direction. Pavel touched his hat in acknowledgement and said "hello" as they passed, but the farmer, with his gaze fixed into the distance, drove straight on without a word. Pavel could sense the man's fear.

A dozen *versts* further on they came across a large walled estate with wrought iron gates that had been pulled off its hinges and left lying on the ground. Ancient oak trees lined the driveway leading up to the building in the distance – the only part left standing were the brick chimneys, while the rest of the building was a pile of blackened rubble.

'Whether it's the same group or some locals, I've no idea,' Pavel said to Maria. 'But it means there's someone going around this area raiding estates, and this looks like it happened quite recently.'

'What should we do?'

'We've no option but to keep heading to Alexei's. The quicker we can get to his place the better. Who knows where this group is now, they could either be ahead of us, or behind us.'

'Dmitry would have come this way. Do you think he's all right?'

Pavel didn't have an answer for her question. He was worried too, and each new sign of destruction along the way only increased his anxiety, but he refused to give up hope.

Pavel and Galina took turns riding forward to check if the way was clear.

On either side, the landscape stretched away to the horizon. It was mostly featureless – a vast, empty, white wilderness with occasional clusters of silver birch. But, while it appeared flat to the eye, there were often folds in the ground that could easily hide a group of horsemen. Pavel searched for signs, particularly of fresh hoofmarks, but the light, fresh snow was easily blown by the wind and quickly covered up any tracks.

They were approaching a turn in the road where the view past the bend was masked by trees and low shrubs. Pavel was always nervous in these situations. The cover provided an ideal ambush position. This time it was Galina's turn to ride forward to check, and Pavel stayed back alongside the carriages. He was carefully following her progress towards the bend, when he saw her pull up hard, wheel her horse, and gallop back towards them. She pulled up white-faced and panting.

'There's a group of horsemen ahead. They're straddling the road and moving in our direction. I'm not certain if they saw me.'

Pavel looked around. There was nowhere to hide except for the cluster of trees, and that would be scant protection. He pulled his rifle out of the saddle holster. 'How many of them?'

'I guess about six, but I didn't stay around to count them.'

'How far away are they? Do you think they saw you?'

'About half a *verst* away, I think. I'm not sure if I was spotted.'

'Stay with the sleighs,' he instructed, 'and get them off the road and behind those trees as quickly as possible. Get everybody to grab a rifle and hide in those low shrubs. I don't care if the girls can't hit anything, but if we all fire together it may be enough to scare them off.'

'What are you going to do?'

'I'm going up to see for myself what we're facing, then I'll come back to join you. Make sure none of them accidentally fires off a shot until I'm back. We're going to need to take them by surprise.'

Pavel spurred his horse towards the bend in the road and pulled up as close as he dared. He swung out of the saddle and sprinted towards the cluster of trees, making sure he kept the thin copse of trees between him and the approaching horsemen. On hands and knees, he worked his way forward, being careful not to knock one of the limbs and cause a telltale cascade of snow from the branches above.

He could now see the horsemen, line abreast, moving towards him at a steady canter. It was difficult to see because of the spray of snow their horses were kicking up, but it looked like there were seven of them.

Leading the group was a large, bearded brute of a man wearing a flowing sheepskin coat and a woolen Cossack hat pulled down low over his forehead. Ammunition bandoliers crossed his barrel-like chest, and he carried his rifle slung over his back. He rode a large, powerful chestnut stallion that was cantering through the snow with ease, and quickly closing the gap to where Pavel lay hidden.

He had seen enough and needed to get back to the others quickly. He would have to rely on Galina hitting at least one target. His job would be to get the lead man, and then hope that between them, they could hold off the rest.

Pavel squirmed himself back away from the edge of the copse and then raised himself into a crouch ready to run back to the others. He took one last look over his shoulder at the horsemen. They were closer now – he gauged they would be at the bend in another five minutes, perhaps sooner.

But just then, something caught his eye. All the horsemen could now be seen quite distinctly, and there was something oddly familiar about the riding style of one of them. One of the riders, out to one side of the group, was a thinner, younger figure. He rode in the saddle easily, as though the horse and he were one. He held his reins in one hand, while his other rested casually on his thigh.

Pavel cursed himself that he had left his binoculars in the saddlebag of his horse. He cupped his hands around his eyes to shield the glare and singled out the rider again. He stared until he was certain, and then switched his gaze back to the leader of the group. He ran forward from the copse, out onto the open steppe, and waved and yelled as though his lungs would burst.

'Dmitry! Alexei!'

Chapter 25
THE YARD OFFICE TYUMENTSEVSKY STUD

December 1917

PAVEL AND ALEXEI waded through the snow towards the yard office. Alexei led since he was taller and heavier and could easily cut a swathe through the knee-deep snow. Pavel followed, carefully placing his feet in each of Alexei's footsteps, to minimize the effort required. Even then, he found himself panting from the exertion.

'I hope this is worth it,' he complained, as he struggled to keep up with Alexei.

Alexei turned in his tracks, looked back at Pavel, and laughed. 'You tell me another place where a man can have a smoke and a drink in peace. Anyway, I needed to get out of the house for a while – I haven't had so many damned women around for years, and the incessant chatter is starting to drive me crazy.'

'Shouldn't we have told them where we've gone?'

'They wouldn't believe for a minute that we're going to sort the horse tackle.' He waved an arm at Pavel. 'Come on, we're nearly there.'

Pavel looked up. It was bitterly cold, and the sky was clear and blue. A light breeze sent a fine, white powder scudding across the snow's surface, filling their footprints behind them. The low, weak wintry sun reflected off ice particles suspended in the air, creating a myriad of sparkling diamonds that danced all around them, and forced them to hold a hand up to their faces to shield their eyes from the glare.

Alexei had to push hard on the door with his shoulder to get it open. 'The damn door always swells and jams tight during the winter. I should get around to fixing it one of these days.'

The yard office was small, with a wooden desk, a couple of dilapidated chairs, and a rusting potbelly stove in one corner. Along its walls dozens of leather harnesses hung suspended from pegs. The room had an overpowering smell from years of accumulated dust, old hessian sacks, and harness grease. Two small, grimy windows let in a weak, diffused light.

'God', exclaimed Pavel, 'this place has all the home comforts of an ice box.'

Alexei grinned and pointed to the stove. 'That's your job.' He then went in search of a kerosene lantern while Pavel busied himself getting a fire going in the potbelly.

He found a pile of old newspapers, a box of tree twigs for kindling, and some chopped wood. Soon the fire was ablaze, and the old iron stove was creaking and pinging as it heated up and expanded.

'You'd be surprised how quickly that old thing heats up the place,' said Alexei, returning with a lantern in hand. He shook the lantern to check it held kerosene, placed it on the desk, and started pumping up the pressure.

'While I'm getting this going, check the lower right-hand drawer in the desk. I'm sure I left a bottle in there, and there should be a couple of glasses lying around somewhere.'

The unlabeled bottle, with a blackened cork jammed in the neck, was full of a clear viscous liquid with tiny particles in suspension. Pavel held it up to the light. 'What the hell is this stuff?'

'*Samogon,* the local brew. My workers have their own still and make it themselves. All sorts of leftover vegetable scraps go into it – mostly anything with starch or sugar. They sometimes even use beetroot. There's never one batch the same.'

'And the "floaty" bits?' asked Pavel, shaking the bottle so that they danced around in the liquid.

'Tarragon or rosemary usually,' answered Alexei, with a grin. 'Anything that helps kill the smell and the taste.'

'And you really drink this stuff? You know it could kill you.'

'They've had a few scares, but I don't think anyone's died – yet. They've become good at topping and tailing the stuff, so the poisons are left out. Come on, where's your courage? After a few sips you'll love it.'

Pavel located two glasses and went outside to clean them. He took a handful of snow, scrubbed the coating of oily grime out of the glasses, and filled them with fresh snow.

'I think we should water that stuff down,' he suggested when he returned.

'You're probably right,' laughed Alexei. 'That wife of yours is a bit of a demon when it comes to us having a quiet tipple.'

Alexei pulled out the cork with his teeth and poured a healthy quantity into each glass, the slightly bluish liquid turning a milky-white color in the snow-filled glasses.

Alexei pushed one of the glasses across the desk to Pavel, took his own glass and banged it on the table. 'We should have a toast,' he announced rather formally. He raised his glass. '*Na zdorovye!*' and then swallowed the shot in one gulp.

'To your health' responded Pavel, taking a tentative sip before he too swallowed the shot. He could feel the raw liquor trickling its way down his throat, and then a delicious warm sensation quickly spreading throughout his belly.

'Not bad,' he said, wiping the back of his hand across his mouth, 'not bad at all. I could easily have another one.'

'Let's pull up some chairs first,' said Alexei, 'and get that tin of cheroots out. Haven't had one for days and, besides, there's something I want to talk to you about.'

Pavel gave Alexei a quizzical look as he placed the cheroot tin on the desk between them and picked up the empty glasses. 'Help yourself while I refill these with snow.'

When he returned Alexei was tilted back in his chair, blowing a thin blue stream of smoke up into the ceiling.

'So, what's this about?' asked Pavel, as he leaned over to get a cheroot.

'First,' answered Alexei, pouring another shot into each glass, 'another toast.' He held his glass high, '*Za Zhen-shsheen* – to women!'

'Well,' said Pavel, laughing 'I can certainly drink to that; I've a whole damned menagerie of them.'

They clinked glasses and downed their drinks in one gulp. Alexei placed his empty glass firmly on the desk and sighed. 'That's enough for me. We can't afford to turn up for lunch in front of the ladies stinking of *samogon* and cheroots.'

Pavel laughed. 'A bit unlike you to worry about pleasing the womenfolk.'

'You know, that's a damned fine son you have. What he did, riding through that storm by himself to get help, it takes courage – and a lot of it.'

'You're avoiding the subject.'

'What subject?'

'Your new consideration for the fairer sex – it's not exactly the tough old horse breeder from the wilds of Tyumentsevsky.'

Alexei leaned back in his chair and poked his finger into his stomach. 'Do you see this? Those women are fattening me up for the slaughter. That borscht Maria Ivanova makes, I've needed to take my belt out another notch.' He tugged at the collar of his shirt. 'And look at this, not just washed, but damned ironed too!'

Pavel grinned. 'Almost presentable.'

Alexei leaned forward and slapped his hand on the table. 'And then, to add insult to injury, they all complained I smelled like the muck out of my own stables!' He threw his hands in the air. 'What do they expect? It's a damned horse stud, not a Moscow beauty salon. That Katrina woman made me have a bath the other day, and that's in the middle of fucking winter! The floor is so clean you could eat your dinner off it. I can't just flick ash anywhere I want, and just try walking into the house with your boots on – you won't make it alive across the doorstep!'

Pavel was laughing so hard he had to wipe tears from his eyes. 'Alexei my friend, you've lived far too long on your own. Look at me, I'm used to having women around – they do me good. If it wasn't for them, I would probably be lying drunk in a gutter somewhere.'

'Don't get me wrong, Pavel Dmitrevich,' said Alexei, suddenly turning serious, 'I'm not complaining, in fact the opposite. I love having them here, and not just the womenfolk, I'm happy to have every damned one of you.'

'Then what's your problem?'

Alexei looked around the empty yard office as though someone might be listening, then leaned forward across the desk and dropped his voice to a conspiratorial whisper. 'I agree, it has been far too long. Sergei's mother passed on years ago and, living alone while Sergei is away at the war, and being stuck out here, *versts* from anywhere, I admit I've let myself go. It's been your womenfolk that have made me realize that, and it's exactly like you said.'

'Realize what exactly?' asked Pavel.

'That a man needs a wife. They can be a real bother sometimes but, overall, I think they can be good for you.'

'So why tell me? Why not go down to the village and get yourself one? You're the richest man in these parts and, with all the men away at war, I'm sure there'll be a dozen young damsels, or even quite a few widows, who would jump at the chance.'

'Don't you think I've looked? I've even tried out a few, but either they're too young and silly, or too old and ugly. I'm afraid there's not a great selection out here in this part of the woods.'

Pavel gave Alexei a puzzled look. 'You don't mean . . . '

'No, no, don't get me wrong,' interjected Alexei. 'I'm not asking for the hand of one of your daughters – nothing against them, they're beautiful and smart, but a man needs someone mature, someone closer to his age. You know what I mean?'

'Like Katrina,' said Pavel, looking Alexei squarely in the eye. 'But what has that got to do with me? She's not my kin, so it's between you and her.'

Alexei's face blushed bright red. 'Look, we're both men of the world, and you and Katrina go back a long way, if you know what I mean. Barnaul is a small town and, when I come down for the horse market, I hear stories, gossip, that sort of thing.' He raised his hands in defense. 'Not that I believed all of it.'

'You shouldn't believe every bit of gossip you hear.' Pavel sat, fiddling with his empty glass and staring down at the desk. It was a while before he spoke, and then it was in measured tones. 'Look, you and Katrina, that is if she agrees to wed you, should just get on with it. You don't need my permission, and I'd be very happy for both of you. And there's one other person, and I'll not mention names, who will also be very pleased.'

'You mean, Sergei?'

'No, not Sergei, and you know exactly who I'm talking about.'

Alexei sat back. 'I have noticed things have been a bit tense between two certain ladies, but, in regards to Sergei, I do worry about what he might think. He was very close to his mother.'

'Alexei, you need to get on with your own life. Sergei's not here and, I hate to admit it, may never return. I'm not being cruel, but we think about Mikhail in the same way. All any of us can hope is that they're both somewhere out there.'

Alexei grinned. 'You're right of course. I should just get on with it. I think this requires another drink, a bit of liquid courage.'

'And the lady in question,' asked Pavel, 'do you know if she'll agree?'

'Oh yes, she'll share the marital bed, just as long as I bathe regularly.'

Pavel rocked back and laughed. 'And now I know why you took to bathing, you old devil. With women, there's always a damned catch. Now, this does call for a toast. Pass me your glass and I'll get some more snow.' He stood and wagged his finger. 'And this, Alexei Alexandrovich, is the last one.'

Pavel pulled open the door, stepped outside, and dug the glasses into the snow. As he straightened, he glanced up, and took a sharp inward breath. It was difficult to see in the glare of the reflected sun off the snow but, on the far side of the long snow-covered paddock, a group of horsemen was advancing, line abreast, directly towards them.

Pavel wasn't sure whether he had been seen. He dropped the glasses in the snow and quickly retreated into the yard office.

'What is it?' asked Alexei, when he saw the look of horror on Pavel's face.

'It's them, they've finally come.'

Alexei looked puzzled. 'Who are, "them"?'

'It must be. Who else could they be? We're in the middle of nowhere, and they've found us!'

Alexei pushed his chair back and rushed to the window. Using his sleeve, he wiped away the grime and peered out. 'Holy Mother of Christ!' He wiped the glass again to get a better view. 'I count six of them.'

Pavel looked over Alexei's shoulder. The horsemen were much closer now – close enough for Pavel to see the steam rising from the nostrils of the horses. The men were roughly dressed, wrapped in sheepskins with crossed bandoliers, wearing astrakhan hats with the distinctive red star badge. All had rifles slung over their backs. Their faces were dark, and their features indistinguishable, with encrusted icicles clinging to their eyebrows and beards.

'Both our rifles are back at the house,' Pavel urgently whispered. 'Should we make a run for it?'

'We wouldn't make it alive, but I've got rifles stored out the back in a gun locker.'

'Where are the keys?' asked Pavel.

'They're back at the fucking house, aren't they? But, get that poker. Quickly!'

Alexei grabbed the poker and rushed out of the room. Pavel heard the splintering of wood, and moments later Alexei was back, thrusting a hunting rifle and a box of cartridges into his hands. He also had a rifle. 'We need to take out at least one each to even up the odds. Pray the shots will alert Dmitry and Galina up at the house.'

They both crouched at the open door, and then crawled on their hands and knees out into the snow. Alexei led the way, following the track they had made from the house to the office, and pushing a deeper path through the snow, trying to keep out of sight. After a few meters Alexei stopped and looked back at Pavel. 'They don't know it,' he whispered, 'but they're heading straight towards a buried fence. When their horses blunder into it, they'll be forced to halt. It's our best chance, we'll both fire then.'

Pavel nodded, rolled on his side, and took off his mittens to cock the rifle and take off the safety. He had already loaded a cartridge into the breech. He lay as still as he could, blowing warm air onto his fingers to try to keep them working. From where he lay he could hear the horses snorting with exertion as they pushed their way through the snow.

'I reckon they're nearly there,' hissed Alexei. 'Keep your head down until I tell you, and then shoot the first one you see. I'll concentrate on the center, and you hit anyone on the right.'

Pavel's fingers were starting to freeze and stiffen up. He was wiggling them to keep the circulation going and was worrying how he could reload without fumbling.

'Just another meter,' whispered Alexei. 'Come on you bastards.'

Pavel lifted his head slightly to peer over the parapet of snow and ducked back again. The line of riders had halted. The lead rider had dismounted and was trudging through the snow, leading his horse forward by the bridle.

Alexei looked back at Pavel and gave an urgent shake to his head. They were now so close that Pavel could hear the crunching of the man's boots through the snow. Then, a dull "thud" as the toe of his boot met a buried wooden rail, followed by a grunt of satisfaction.

Pavel looked towards Alexei and saw him lying on his back in the shallow snow trench with a puzzled look on his face and his rifle laid across his chest. He waved an urgent hand at Pavel to stay as he was. 'Don't shoot.'

'Who goes there?' Alexei bellowed out.

There was silence, just the snorting of the horses. A few moments lapsed, and then finally came a reply.

'Is that you, father?'

'We were just about to damned shoot you.'

'That would have been some homecoming for a returning son.'

'Who are those people with you?'

'Fellow officers, friends.'

'And those red stars you're wearing on your hats? You haven't turned Bolshevik, have you?'

Sergei laughed. 'A badge of convenience, it's a long story.'

Alexei heaved himself slowly upright out of the shallow snow-trench and waded through the snow towards the line of horsemen. He stopped and took a long stare.

'Is that really you?'

Chapter 26
REUNION
THE STUD FARM

December 1917

MIKHAIL AND PAVEL reclined in a pair of comfortable old lounge chairs in the front drawing room of Alexei's house, both nursing a mug of steaming honey-infused tea. The fire was ablaze and Sokoi and Berkut lay stretched out on the rug in front of the hearth.

Mikhail was in ill-fitting, borrowed clothes. Sergei's were too small, so he had to make do with some of Alexei's that were at least a couple of sizes too large. He had shaved off the three weeks of beard, leaving him looking pale and haggard, with sunken cheeks and red-rimmed eyes.

Katrina had insisted they all shaved their heads, and all the hair from the other parts of their bodies as well. 'Lice,' she had pointed out. 'Look at you – you're all crawling with vermin, and lice carry typhus.'

She had made all six of them strip in the barn, and stood there supervising them while they completely shaved their bodies and scrubbed themselves, almost raw, with carbolic soap. Then she had their uniforms, shirts and underwear boiled for hours in the copper, and got them to dress in an assortment of clothes she had found by rummaging through every wardrobe in the house.

'If it wasn't that they're your only uniforms,' Katrina had told them, 'I would have happily burnt the lot.'

Pavel swirled his mug and took a careful sip of the hot liquid. 'So, tell me your story from the beginning, from when you left Petrograd, to how you found us here.'

Mikhail leaned forward, nursing the hot mug in both hands. 'Getting out of Petrograd after the coup was no more difficult than getting in. But, once out of the city, we were sort of stuck, with nowhere to go. It wasn't any use heading back to Mogilev since Kornilov and the *Stavka* had all walked out of house arrest there and were heading to the Don. And we didn't want to go there anyway, we wanted to get back here to join up.'

'I'm out of touch,' said Pavel. 'Is a Siberian Army being formed?'

'When we were in Petrograd, we were billeted at the Lebedevs' house. They told us about a separate Siberian army group being formed, and supplied from the Allies' stockpile of weapons in Vladivostok. The problem was how to get here – it's a damned long way, even on horseback.'

'And they would be still searching for officers,' suggested Pavel.

'That's the incredible irony,' said Mikhail. 'They're searching for officers, but not in the way you think. The Bolsheviks are scrambling to put their own army together from all the deserters and other communist supporters.'

'There's enough of them about, they are all over Barnaul.'

'Anyway,' continued Mikhail, 'Lenin has put one of his senior colleagues, a Jew called Trotsky, in charge of forming what they're calling the Red Army. But without officers they're just a disorganised rabble, and Trotsky is smart enough to know this. He can promote some

NCOs, but that ends up undermining the whole command structure, and you can't run an army without structure and discipline.'

'Then what's the solution?' asked Pavel. 'Not that we want them to get organized.'

Pavel noticed Iya had come into the room and had quietly sat down in the chair in the corner to listen to her husband's story. 'Please go on,' she asked, 'I'm desperate to hear how you escaped.'

Mikhail smiled, as he swirled his tea in his mug. 'I'm not sure if "escape" is the right term. The reality is the officers are not all staunch monarchists, or whatever you like to call them; there are many who are democrats at heart, or even socialists, and lots of officers sympathized with the causes of their soldiers. Of course, the mutinies changed this view for many, but there do remain officers who would be prepared to sign up to the Reds. Remember, for many of our professional officers, this is their only vocation. Even Brusilov, our previous Commander-in-Chief, has said he would be prepared to put politics aside if Russia could have one cohesive national army.'

'Are the Reds actually recruiting officers?' Pavel asked incredulously.

'They're doing so reluctantly, with a lot of opposition from within their own party, but Trotsky apparently is a man not to be trifled with. They do remain highly suspicious, and carefully screen any applicant, but their need seems to be overriding caution. That's where Anton and Kolya came in.'

'Is Anton the tall skinny one?' asked Iya. 'And Kolya the big, fat one with the beard?'

Mikhail laughed. 'An apt description perhaps, but you should speak kindly of them, they saved our lives.'

Iya had tucked her legs up under her and gripped her arms tightly around her knees. 'Tell me more.'

'We literally blundered into Anton and Kolya in a village outside of Petrograd. We just saw them as fellow officers, and hadn't realised they'd been recruited, so we approached them. They, on the other hand, had been sent out to locate officers who might be sympathetic to the cause. At first things were a bit awkward between us until they discovered we were from Barnaul and Tyumentsevsky. They admitted that they were from Novonikolayevsk, and it was then we realised all of us were just trying to make it home. They had only signed up to get a transport pass and a posting to Omsk where a Red Army group is being established.'

'So how did they save you?' asked Iya.

'Anton and Kolya schooled us on what to say, then took us back to the recruiting station. The Bolshevik recruiters trusted Kolya in particular. The man even looks and sounds like a damned Bolshevik thug, and he vouched for us, so here we are.'

'Omsk,' pointed out Pavel, 'is still a long way from Tyumentsevsky.'

'We finally got to Omsk by train where we were supposed to report for duty but, we didn't. Instead we stole horses from the cavalry lines there, and managed to get out of town before we were discovered.'

'I think you're making it sound a lot easier than it was,' suggested Iya.

'The train trip was the worst part since it was full of Red Army recruits who hated anybody who looked like an officer. If it wasn't for Kolya coming between us and them, we wouldn't be here today.'

'But you're safely here,' said Iya, brightly, 'and that's what counts.'

'Although I'm not sure we counted on being ambushed by your father and Alexei,' said Mikhail, with a mischievous grin.

Pavel grinned. 'You can't blame us for mistaking you for a Bolshevik raiding party with those hats you were wearing, but why did you decide to head for the stud; why not Barnaul, or Novonikolayevsk for that matter?'

'Omsk is firmly in Bolshevik hands, and we believe Novonikolayevsk is as well. We didn't know about Barnaul, but we thought this place would be safe, and we could use it as a base until we got in contact somehow with the new Siberian Army, wherever it's being formed. Anton and Kolya have contacts in Novonikolayevsk, and I would have checked out Barnaul. It was just luck you were here.'

'So now you don't have to go anywhere,' said Iya, happily. 'We can tell you for certain that Comrade Tsaplin and his Bolsheviks are in charge, so there's no need to ride all that way. Why else would we be here?'

'Then where is this new army?' said Mikhail, putting down his mug and scratching the prickly stubble on his head. 'It's bound to be along the Trans-Siberian somewhere, probably Irkutsk but, we aren't certain about that either. Anton reckons his contacts will know, so we're planning to somehow get him into Novonikolayevsk to find out.'

Iya frowned. 'Who exactly are "we"?'

'You can't expect him to ride all that way by himself, can you?'

'There's Kolya, and the others.'

Mikhail looked down, and took a deep breath. 'We're all in this together. You can't expect us to sit on our hands, can you?'

Iya abruptly stood. 'Three years away, and now this!'

She slammed the door behind her as she stormed out of the room.

Startled, the dogs yelped and leapt to their feet, looked around at the door, and then lay back down as though nothing had happened. A log shifted in the fire and Pavel got up, stepped over the dogs, and took hold of the poker to prod at the wood.

'Women!' he sighed.

He nudged the dogs with his foot. 'Come on you lazy hounds, time for a walk.'

'Maybe I could take them,' offered Mikhail, rather unenthusiastically.

Pavel looked around at him. 'Maybe you should go upstairs and talk to that wife of yours. There's enough warfare going on around this sad country of ours without having it in this house as well.'

The door opened. It was Sergei. 'What was the noise?' he asked.

Pavel gave him a wry smile. 'The wind banged the door shut.'

'What wind?' asked a bemused Sergei.

Pavel chortled. 'The wrath of a woman! Now if you will excuse us, we were just about to leave, weren't we Mikhail?'

'I was actually looking for Galina,' said Sergei. 'There are some new foals I want her to have a look at.'

'She's helping Maria Ivanova and Katrina make bread in the kitchen. I'm sure she'll appreciate any excuse to get out of that.'

Maria walked out of the kitchen into the hall. She was wiping her hands on her apron and had a smear of flour on one cheek. 'Dmitry,' she shouted. 'Are you there?'

'He's across in the tackle room helping Alexei,' Mikhail informed her, as he walked into the hall and started climbing the stairs.

'Mara, where are you?'

From the drawing room at the front of the house, the melodic strains of a Tchaikovsky piano sonata came to an abrupt halt. 'What is it, mother?'

'Galina and Sergei are going over to the stables, and Dmitry is out somewhere helping Mr Vinokurov, so I want you to accompany them.'

'But it's freezing outside.'

'The walk and the fresh air will do you good.'

There was a moment's silence before the clunk of the lid as it was firmly closed. 'I guess Pyotr Tchaikovsky is just going to have to wait,' Mara huffed, as she pushed back the piano stool.

The three of them, wrapped up in layers of clothes against the cold, trudged through the snow towards the stables. Sergei and Galina led the way with Mara walking several paces behind.

Sergei looked back. 'It'll be fine once we get there. They keep braziers lit so the horses don't freeze to death. You'll be as warm as toast.'

'Thanks a lot for getting me dragged out in the cold,' Mara replied tersely.

Galina looked around at her sister and smiled. 'You'll be just fine. I hope you brought a book to read.'

Sergei had trouble with the stable doors. He had to kick a mound of snowdrift away before he finally managed to lever one open. The inside of the stables was stuffy. There was an overpowering stench, a mixture of horse dung and hay, but it was warm and dry. Smoke from the line of burning braziers down the centre of the long stable rose lazily into the high ceiling to escape through vents to the outside.

The fires were being tended by a young peasant boy who quickly disappeared somewhere into the confines of the stable as soon as they arrived.

Mara wrinkled her nose. 'The place smells revolting. Does anyone ever clean it out?'

'Every day,' answered Sergei, 'but, don't worry, you'll get used to it soon enough.'

'I don't mind it at all,' said Galina, who had walked on ahead, moving down the long row of stalls. She glanced back over her shoulder.

'Come on, Sergei, show me the new colts.'

'You go, I'll stay here by the fire,' said Mara, who had found herself a stool and was pulling it up close to a brazier. 'I've seen enough horses to last a lifetime.'

Galina moved down the central isle of the stables, standing on tiptoe, to look over each of the stall doors. She stopped at one and unbolted the door.

'Here's one.'

'Careful,' Sergei quietly called out, 'they can be frightened of strangers.'

'I think I know how to deal with horses,' she answered back, a little more tersely than she meant.

The chestnut colt backed away, snorted, and struck one of its hooves on the earthen floor. Galina slowly held out her hand and gently stroked its forehead before sliding her other hand down to its forequarter. She spoke in low, soft tones until she could feel the colt's trembling gradually subside.

'You've always had a way with horses.' Sergei had entered the stall behind her, being careful to move slowly so as not to frighten the colt.

'They just need to know you're not a threat,' she spoke quietly, without turning to look at Sergei. 'As soon as you gain their trust, everything's fine.'

Galina allowed the horse to gently nuzzle into her as she stroked its neck. 'There you are, my strong, handsome man,' she cooed. 'You like me, don't you?'

'I assume you're referring to the colt?'

Galina looked at Sergei. He flushed red. 'I, I was only joking,' he stammered.

Galina dropped her hand from the colt's neck and took a step towards Sergei. 'You can kiss me if you want.'

She lifted her chin, parted her lips, and reached up for him.

Sergei, momentarily shocked, took a step back. 'But Mara is here.'

'Mara can't see us,' she whispered furtively, 'and anyway, sisters have an understanding. It is only Mother who insists we have chaperones. Are you saying you don't want to kiss me?'

'Yes, of course I do, but it's just,' Sergei hesitated. 'You know, it's about your parents, a sort of trust thing.'

'But they aren't here, are they?'

Sergei went to say something, but Galina cut him off and prodded him in the ribs with her finger. "And if you don't, I'll never talk to you again.'

Sergei smiled and reached for her. 'Well, we can't have that, can we?'

Mikhail found Iya in the bedroom, lying on the bed with her back to him, fully dressed. He closed the door, lay down beside her, and reached over. She shuddered at his touch and pushed his hand away. 'Leave me alone. Why don't you go away with the others – isn't that what you want to do?'

'I'm sorry about what I said downstairs. It didn't mean it to come out like that.'

Iya stifled a sob. 'What was I expected to think? All those years away, you turn up out of nowhere, just to tell me you're going away again.'

Mikhail propped himself up on one elbow, leaned over her, and gently kissed the nape of her neck. 'Darling, we have this one chance to right these wrongs, but we must do it quickly. It's as much about your father's stores and the farm as it is about me. I'd give everything to forget the whole damned civil war and just stay here, but that would be wrong, for you as well as the whole family. You're hiding here because the Bolsheviks stole everything you owned and threatened your life. They may have control right now, but they're disorganised and vulnerable. If we move quickly, then we have a chance. Every day we lose, is a day they gain.'

Iya lay in silence for a while, her sobs gradually subsiding. 'But killing each other, Russian murdering Russian, is this really the only solution anyone can come up with?'

'I wasn't the one who took the Duma by force and threw out our elected government. They've created the situation, not us. We either give in to them, or push back, and the quicker we do that the fewer lives will be lost.'

'So why does it have to be you?' There was still bitterness in Iya's voice. 'There's six of you, and you, the only married one. Why can't the rest of them go, and you stay here and help protect the family.'

Mikhail lay back and looked up at the ceiling. He reached out and could feel her trembling, and knew she was crying again. 'Novonikolayevsk is two days' ride, and I'll be back before you know it. I said I'd go because I'm the senior officer in the group. We need to establish contact with the Officers' Union in the town, and I was the one who worked with them in Petrograd. I've also met Count Lebedev who will be organising the new Siberian Army. It's only right that I'm there when we first make contact.'

'And then what?' Iya pushed herself upright, turned, and glared at Mikhail.

Mikhail sighed. 'They're a house of cards – one sharp prod and they'll come tumbling down.'

'And what about me, your wife?' Iya noisily blew her nose. 'You've been home for two days and haven't as much as pecked me on the cheek.'

She swung her feet to the floor and started tugging at the buttons on her tunic. 'Take your clothes off,' she demanded.

Mikhail looked surprised, and started to say something, but Iya cut him off. 'If it's good enough for you to go away again, then it's good enough for me to change my mind.'

'I don't understand.'

'We had an agreement when you went off to the fighting that we wouldn't bring a child into the world while the German war was going on. But that's now ended, and this is a new war, and a new agreement.'

Mikhail lay stretched out, naked on the bed, a thin sheen of sweat covering his torso. Iya lay on her side with her head resting on his shoulder and her arms around him. She had her bodice open, breasts pressed into his side, and her legs entwined with his.

'We weren't very careful,' whispered Mikhail, pulling her in tight and running his fingers gently through her hair.

'I don't care. I told you I've changed my mind.' Iya leaned over him. 'What is it to be then – a boy or a girl?'

'Either would be nice.'

'If it's a boy I would like us to call him Vasily – after Uncle Vasily. Papa would like that.'

'And if it's a girl?'

'Since I've chosen the boy's name, you can choose the girl's name.'

Mikhail lay still and thought for a moment. 'What about Vera?'

Iya stiffened. 'Where did that name come from?'

Mikhail turned his face away slightly. 'Nobody really, I just think it's a pretty name for a girl.'

Chapter 27

THE MEETING IN THE BARN

MIKHAIL PUSHED HIS horse through the snow to the top of the embankment. He halted and looked down through the bare birch and spruce trees to the broad stretch of the frozen river, its ice sheet buried under a mantle of snow.

Mikhail smiled with satisfaction. The snow on the ice did not look deep, and the flat surface of the frozen river would make for much easier going. He shielded his eyes from the glare of sun on the snow and thought he could just see the far bank. It was hard to know where the river ended and the riverbank began, but he guessed the line of bare tree trunks that stretched in both directions delineated the bank. His eyes followed the river north where it rounded a bend and was lost to sight, and then he turned to look upstream. There were no dwellings or people to be seen in either direction.

Mikhail twisted in his saddle and gave a low whistle. The tall angular figure of Anton joined him at the top of the embankment, followed quickly by the other three riders, each of them carefully maneuvering their horses up through the gaps in the trees.

'It's the Ob,' he said to Anton.

Mikhail spoke quietly. There was a trailing wind, and sound could travel far across a flat expanse of ice.

Anton nodded and looked around. 'I think we're getting close, but it's hard to tell with all this fresh snow.'

Mikhail glanced up at the sky. It was mostly clear, but there were long thin streams of wispy high clouds. He touched Anton on the shoulder and pointed skywards.

'Those "horses' tails" up there mean there are strong winds aloft, and a storm not too far behind. We need to hurry so we're not caught out in the open when the storm hits, and the quickest path will be over the ice.'

Anton remained silent for a moment, studying the landscape in both directions. 'It's risky,' he finally said. 'We'll be easy to spot if someone's out there.'

'If we cut across and stick close to those trees on the far bank,' replied Mikhail, 'we'll have some cover, just until we get to that bend in the river.'

Anton touched his cap with his riding crop. 'Okay, you're the kap-itan.'

'Kolya,' Mikhail said to the biggest of the men in the group, 'can you go down and check the ice?' Mikhail gave him a cheeky grin. 'If it takes your weight, we'll all be okay. Give me your reins and I'll hold your horse.'

Kolya, wearing a dirty woolen Cossack hat and a heavy coat, swung out of his saddle and pushed his way down through the snow to the river's edge. He swept the snow away with his foot to reveal the pale blue translucent ice, placed one foot gingerly onto the ice, and leaned forward. There was just the faintest cracking sound of the thinnest ice at the river's edge. Stooping over, he peered intently at the sheet ice and then jumped up and down on the spot a few times.

'Solid as a rock,' he called up to them.

Mikhail led the group forward across the frozen river to the far bank, and then turned downstream, towards the far bend in the river. At first the horses were nervous on the ice but, as soon as they sensed it was solid underfoot, they gained in confidence and speed.

When they neared the river bend, Mikhail sent Leonid forward to reconnoiter alone. A single horseman would be less visible and arouse less suspicion. Leonid, a wiry, agile man, was the only NCO in the group. He had gained experience as a forward scout and was good at using cover. While Leonid rode on ahead, the remainder of them sheltered under cover of the drooping riverbank willows. They watched as Leonid reached the bend where he left the ice, mounted the bank, and cut through the trees. Once in the trees he was quickly lost from sight.

The group waited. 'Something must have happened to him,' said Kolya, after they had been waiting for some time.

'Leonid's experienced at this sort of thing,' answered Mikhail, 'let's give him a few more minutes.'

But even Mikhail was getting nervous. They hadn't heard any gunshots from up ahead, and they began to debate again whether to follow Leonid's trail when he suddenly re-emerged. He was on foot, walking his horse back towards them, and raised an arm to wave them forward.

'Let's go,' Mikhail told the group, as he spurred his horse forward.

'Sorry to take so long, but I found some fresh foot tracks leading down the river.' Leonid was panting from the exertion of walking through the deep snow and negotiating the hidden debris on the forest floor. 'There's a damned ice fisherman out on the river, but he seems to be alone.'

'Can we get past without being seen?' asked Mikhail.

Leonid shook his head. 'There's a big bluff that will push us onto the ice, and in full view of him, unless we make a serious detour inland. And that could lose us hours.'

Menacing storm clouds were now clearly forming on the eastern horizon and moving inexorably in their direction. 'If it's just one ice fisherman alone, then we'll take the risk.'

The old man sat on a low wooden stool next to the hole he had cut in the ice. He was swathed in a hooded coat, with rags wrapped around his feet. Hunched over the hole, he was entirely focused on the hand line that dangled down into the black, icy water.

He must have heard their horses since he looked up sharply as they approached. Without taking his eyes off them, he slowly reached down with one hand to feel for his hunting knife on the ice beside him.

'I wouldn't do that if I was you.' It was Kolya who spoke. He had pulled his rifle out of its saddle holster, taken off the safety, and was casually resting the weapon on the pommel of his saddle. While the rifle wasn't pointed directly at the man, the intent of the threat was obvious.

The man's eyes narrowed as he studied Kolya, then he turned and spat on the ice.

'You're going to kill me, are you?' he asked. He displayed no discernible fear; it was almost as though he was goading them.

'Why would we do that?' Mikhail had pushed his horse forward through the group and pulled up between Kolya and the man.

'It seems that's what folks do these days,' he answered. 'Even if it's just to pinch your catch.'

'What do you hope to catch?' asked Mikhail. 'The fish aren't usually active at this time of year.'

The man shrugged. 'Maybe I could hook a perch. But, what choice do I have? A wife and starving kids back at the cabin, and nothing to put on the table.'

Mikhail felt in his saddlebag, pulled out a piece of dried beef, and tossed it to him.

'What's this for?' he asked, as he picked up the piece of beef and eyed it suspiciously.

'How far is Novonikolayevsk from here?' asked Mikhail.

'Around that far bend,' the man nodded downstream.

Mikhail could see another sweeping bend about a *verst* away.

He rode closer and bent low over his saddle. 'How do I know you're not lying?'

The man shrugged. 'Because, if I've lied, then you'll come back and kill me.'

'How do you know I'll do that?'

The man looked past Mikhail towards Kolya and nodded in his direction. 'If you don't, then he will.'

'And when we get to that bend, what's on the other side?'

'There's the rail bridge across into Novonikolayevsk. They've posted guards on the bridge, so you'll need to cut inland once you get past that embankment down there.'

'Why should we want to avoid guards?'

The man cackled to himself. 'Because, if I'm not wrong, those are officer's riding boots you've got on.'

'The insolent old bastard will inform on us without blinking an eye,' Kolya hissed to Mikhail. 'Tell me why I shouldn't shoot him?'

The man's head snapped around and he glared at Kolya. 'Because one single rifle shot will bring every Red Guard in these parts down around your ears.'

Kolya looked at him with disdain. 'Then why don't I get down off my horse, and quietly slit your miserable throat?'

Mikhail put a restraining arm out. 'Kolya, leave him be. He's alone and on foot. We'll be long gone before he can get to tell anyone, if he ever does.'

They found shelter in an old barn just before the storm came in. The barn's wooden walls leaned over at an alarming angle, and it creaked as it moved in the strengthening wind that moaned through the cracks and lashed snow against the wooden walls.

Anton left them to ride into the town alone, suggesting it was safer that way. 'A group of us would draw unwelcome attention,' he told Mikhail. 'I stand a better chance of getting in by myself, and I know where to go. Once I've established contact with the Officers' Union, we can work out what to do next.'

It was several hours before Anton finally returned. His face was pinched with the cold, and he stood close to the small fire they had lit in the center of the barn, flapping his arms and stamping his feet to restore circulation.

'Thank God for the storm,' he said after he had brushed himself clean of snow. 'Nobody, not even the Red Guard, was out in this weather.'

'You managed to make contact?' asked Mikhail.

'The address you gave me was correct. They were suspicious at first and wouldn't let me through the door, but I just had to mention Lieutenant-Colonel Lebedev's name and I was let inside. Then a retired colonel interviewed me. He wanted to know who we were, what units we had been with, and where we've been hiding. I gave as little detail as possible, but I had to give him something to prove we were *bona fide*.'

'Did he believe you?' asked Mikhail.

'When I told him we've been camping out at a friend's horse stud in the area, he suddenly became very interested. I didn't mention any names or locations, just that it was large and in an isolated area somewhere around here. He told me to wait while he sent out a message for some other people to come and meet me.'

'I hope that won't put Alexei in trouble.'

Anton shook his head. 'He understood the need for secrecy but, anyway, after about half an hour a couple of men showed up. One was the local Cossack Ataman, who I'd seen before, and the other, would you believe, was an Englishman.'

'An Englishman, in Novonikolayevsk! Why the hell is he here?'

'Seemed like one of those foreign military observers that used to be stationed with us at the front. Speaks excellent Russian.'

'It's a damned long way from the front,' observed Mikhail. 'More likely he's a spy.'

'He's looking for horses for the Ataman's regiment. The Bolsheviks have been confiscating them for their own use. The Cossacks have got men who want to fight, but not enough horses, and he seems to be prepared to fund the purchase.'

'He, meaning the Englishman?'

Anton nodded. 'They want to meet you.'

'It's not my stud, it's Alexei's, and for that matter, Sergei's too. But, neither of them are currently here.'

'You're the senior officer, and a friend of the family. They want you to act as an intermediary.'

Just then Leonid ran back into the barn. He had stationed himself down the hill in a thicket of trees to act as sentry. 'Horsemen coming in,' he panted. 'There are three of them.'

Anton looked surprised. 'I hadn't expected them so soon.'

'You told them our position?' Mikhail was angry.

'It was either we tried to get into town, or they came out to us. As I said, I know the Ataman, and I think we can trust the old colonel and the *angliiskii.*'

Mikhail shrugged. 'It's too late now anyway.' He turned to Leonid. 'Go back and keep lookout for us. Let the three of them through but let me know if you spot any other movement out there.'

The retired colonel was a tall, rigid man with a neatly trimmed grey moustache and thin, gold-rimmed glasses. He was wearing civilian clothes under his long riding coat. Riding alongside him was a man in a full-length oilskin coat with one of the arms empty and the sleeve folded back and pinned to his coat. He had a livid scar on one cheek and raised his riding crop in acknowledgement when Mikhail walked out of the barn to meet them.

The Ataman, a short, squat man with piercing black eyes and a dark complexion, was the only one in uniform – high cavalry boots, jodhpurs, a woolen Cossack hat and a gold-braided military jacket covered by a thick cape. He kept himself separate and ignored Mikhail's gesture of welcome. There was something about his demeanor Mikhail didn't like.

Mikhail stood to attention and saluted the colonel.

'Kapitan Mehenov, at your service, sir.'

The colonel gave a curt nod and gestured towards the Ataman. 'This is Ataman Krasilnikov of the Siberian Cossack *Host*.'

Mikhail gave the Ataman a shallow bow, 'I am honored, sir.'

The Ataman didn't return the salute; instead he turned to face the colonel. 'Ask him about the horses,' he said in a high-pitched, demanding voice.

The colonel looked at Mikhail and, was almost apologetic. 'The Ataman would like to know how many horses you can supply.'

'They're not my horses to supply,' answered Mikhail. 'They are the property of friends who have given us, and my family, shelter.'

'This man's useless,' spat the Ataman. 'We should go out there and get what we want.'

'My dear Ataman.' It was the Englishman who had ridden forward. He spoke in perfect, if slightly clipped, formal Russian. 'I think we agreed that we would ask the captain here to act on our behalf.' He turned to Mikhail. 'We are not common horse thieves. We need good, reliable suppliers of horses and are prepared to pay a fair price.'

Mikhail looked up at the Englishman and raised both hands. 'I can only ask.'

'And that is all we expect.' The Englishman brushed snow off his shoulder with his one good hand. 'Is it possible for us to carry on this conversation inside the barn? The snow is getting heavier, I believe.'

Mikhail looked down and shuffled his feet.

'I can understand your nervousness,' continued the Englishman. 'Word has it that there is a group of officers hiding out somewhere around the town. A fisherman has reported seeing you, and the Reds have patrols out searching the area.'

Mikhail heard Kolya give a *huff* and mumble something.

'Then,' said Mikhail, 'the quicker we finish this discussion, and all of us get out of here, the better.'

The Englishman, the colonel and the Ataman were already dismounting, tying up their horses, and making for the open barn door. Mikhail and the others followed them inside, where they congregated in a rough circle around the fire.

'We need to post more sentries,' said Mikhail, looking at Kolya. 'Will you go and help Leonid?'

As Kolya walked past Mikhail towards the door, he muttered out of the side of his mouth, 'You should have let me kill him.'

Mikhail let the comment pass and turned his attention back to their visitors. 'There's no guarantee I can persuade the owner of the stud. He's very much his own man.'

'Is he a supporter of the cause?' asked the colonel.

Mikhail hesitated. 'I think so, but he prefers to keep away from politics. But, in saying that, he has regularly supplied the Army in the past.'

'Then he should supply us,' shrilled the Ataman, who was clearly losing his patience.

The colonel intervened. 'I was told by your colleague you are a close friend of the family. Is that correct?'

Mikhail was guarded in his response. 'His son and I served together, and my father-in-law is a close friend of his father. He used to bring his horses into the Barnaul market every month.'

'Barnaul,' said the Englishman, showing a sudden interest. 'Are you from there?'

Mikhail was reluctant to answer. 'Perhaps in the past, but we've all been away at the front for years.'

'There was that big merchant store in town,' continued the Englishman in a breezy fashion. 'D.N. Sukhov & Sons – is it still there?'

'I believe you'll find it's now closed. As you will know, the Bolsheviks now run the town.'

'And the owner?' The Englishman gave a slight smile.

'My apologies, but I'd prefer not to comment.'

The Englishman turned, and walked back over to his tethered horse. He opened the flap of a saddlebag, withdrew a bulging calico bag, and hefted it in his hand. 'A deposit, and a signal of our good faith,' he said, handing the bag to Mikhail. 'Mexican silver dollars, you can count it later.'

'You trust these men?' barked the Ataman. 'We haven't seen one damned horse yet.'

'I trust the captain here will deliver us the first batch of horses by this month's end to a place that you, my dear Ataman, may nominate.'

'And if they don't turn up?'

'Then it is I, not you, who will take responsibility, but I am confident that won't eventuate.'

The Englishman led Mikhail aside and lowered his voice to a whisper. 'I would appreciate it if you would let Pavel Dmitrievich know that Captain Spencer sends his compliments and looks forward to making his acquaintance again soon. I feel assured he will do his utmost to persuade his friend to sell us the horses, as I believe your father-in-law will appreciate the importance of this.'

'How do you know this Pavel Dmitrievich, as you call him, is known to me?'

The Englishman just gave Mikhail a knowing smile and turned back to the group. 'We should all make haste in case we encounter a Red patrol, but first we need to decide on where and when.'

'If you're confident they'll not steal your money,' said the Ataman, 'get them to bring the horses to the *stanitsa* on the last day of this month.'

'Do you know where that is?' the colonel asked Mikhail.

'He doesn't, but I know the Cossack village well,' chimed in Anton.

Mikhail gave an ironic laugh. 'We came to join up with the Siberian Army, but it seems you've turned us into horse traders.'

'Only for the moment,' said the colonel, as he untied his horse and prepared to mount. 'I'm sure we'll find good use for you. But first things first, we need the Cossacks to help win this war, and the Bolsheviks have played right into our hands. How to make an avowed enemy of a Cossack? You take his horse away from him,' said the colonel with a smile, 'it's worse than stealing his wife.'

Chapter 28

THE STANITSA

March 1918

THE HORSES WERE corralled in two large yards surrounded by tall, strong wooden fences. They had been separated, the geldings in one yard, and the mares in the other. The horses had all been fed and watered before being yarded overnight but, as the day dawned, they were becoming anxious and frisky.

'What do you make the count?' Alexei asked, riding up alongside Pavel.

'One hundred exactly, and I've counted them twice.'

This was the third lot of horses to be delivered to the Cossacks' village at Krutikha. The first two groups, of just thirty horses each, had been delivered some months before. The Cossacks were pleased with the quality, and a fair rate was settled and paid.

The Ataman was keen to take delivery of more, but severe winter storms had intervened and made the journey impossible. It was frustrating for everyone, but it had been agreed they should wait for the first signs of spring before attempting to drive another group of horses over to the *stanitsa*.

'It can't be helped,' Alexei had said. 'If we get caught in a blizzard we die, and the horses die, and then nobody benefits. It's not worth the risk.'

Fortunately, the wild weather had also brought a halt to most outside activities, including nearly all the hostilities between the Whites and the Reds. So, while they lost time not being able to deliver the horses, the Cossacks were not being seriously disadvantaged. The Civil War, which had hardly begun before the snow arrived, now entered a period of enforced hiatus, with both sides using the time to prepare as best they could for the forthcoming spring campaign.

Pavel had accompanied the first two deliveries, hoping to meet up with the *anglais kapitan*, but both times he had been absent.

'Urgent business,' advised the colonel, who had taken over as the Englishman's delegate. 'He sends his apologies. There's a lot of politics going on, and he is helping organise the White Siberian Army.'

Pavel was uncertain what the colonel meant by "politics" but decided not to ask.

'Who will lead our army in Siberia?' Pavel instead asked. But the old colonel just gave him a wry smile, a shrug, and an evasive, 'Time will tell.'

Alexei nodded to Pavel and looked up at the sky. He was anxious to get going from the stud with the final consignment of horses. 'At least we've a fine day for it. We should get this mob moving. Where are the others?'

'Mikhail and Sergei are down at the front yard. They're ready to lead out. We've Anton and Kolya bringing up the rear. That just leaves the two of us as outriders.'

Alexei laughed. 'Six of us and a hundred damned horses who'll probably want to run off in all directions, but we'll manage somehow. Just as long as we keep that stallion pointed in the right direction, the rest should follow.'

'A few extra men would have been useful.'

'You know my view on that.' Alexei had remained adamant that he didn't want his workers exposed to outside politics. 'We've managed to survive thus far.'

'It's now spring, and you can't hide them away forever,' replied Pavel, but he was unwilling to press the point much further. 'They must realize by now something unusual is happening out there.'

Alexei stood in his stirrups and waved a farewell in the direction of the house. Pavel could see Maria, Katrina, Mara and Dmitry standing together on the veranda. The pregnant figure of Iya ran out of the front door, gave a quick wave, and then disappeared back inside.

'They'll be fine,' said Alexei. 'Dmitry and Galina, and my workers, are more than capable of looking after the place.'

Pavel couldn't see Galina in the group, but assumed she must be down at the stables. He raised his own hand in salute, tugged at the reins, and turned his horse towards the middle yard.

Alexei put two fingers to his lips and gave a loud whistle. Sergei leaned over his saddle and swung the yard gate open. He backed his horse away and cracked a whip high above the lead horses.

The first stallion moved through the gate, and then several mares followed. Soon all the horses from the first yard were cantering up the track leading towards the forest, their hooves churning up a fine spray of snow that hung suspended and glinting in the rising sun.

'Steady on,' yelled Alexei, 'we don't want to create a stampede.'

The horses, released from the confines of their winter stables, were keen to stretch their legs, and set off at a brisk pace.

Sergei and Mikhail, in charge of controlling the lead group, struggled to restrain some of the horses from cantering too far ahead.

However, after the initial show of exuberance, the lead horses slowed their pace.

They were mostly well behaved as the track was clearly defined, but, every so often and for no apparent reason, several horses would break away and head off in a different direction. It was the role of Pavel and Alexei to chase the breakaways down and urge them back to the main group. The work was exhausting, for man and horse, pushing through the drifts of snow, shouting and cracking whips until the errant horses, finally understanding the futility of their actions, gave up and returned.

'At this pace,' said Alexei, riding up alongside Pavel, 'we'll be at first camp by mid-afternoon, with time enough to corral and feed them before dark.' The first camp had already been established some days before, with a load of forage sent forward by wagon. It would be a welcome sight after a day in the saddle.

The long line of horses fell into a quiet, serene rhythm as they moved along the trail through the forest – the silence barely broken by the faint clip-clop of their hooves muffled by snow, the swish of their tails, and an occasional snort or neigh.

But the horses were now getting warm, both from exertion and the sun filtering through the tree canopy. Their condensed breaths hung in the still air, and their coats glistened with a thin layer of sweat. In the enclosed forest trail, the smell of the large group of horses was sharp and distinctive.

Alexei seemed nervous and kept looking about him. Not content with keeping his station, he kept spurring his horse up and down the line.

'What's the matter?' Pavel had asked him.

'I don't like the silence. It's too damned quiet for my liking. I reckon something's out there.'

As if it was a premonition, away in the distance came the faint, baleful howl of a lone wolf. It was followed by a brief silence, and then came several returning howls. Far off to one side, and hidden deep in the forest, a wolf pack was being called together by their leader.

Alexei reined in his horse. 'Damn! I just knew it.'

The horses had heard the wolf's howl as well. The whole line shied, and then came to an abrupt halt, all of them bunching together in a natural clearing in the forest. They froze to the spot, their eyes wide with fear and their ears pricked high. The older horses formed a tight circle and faced outwards, and a few of the stallions started snorting, whinnying, and striking their hooves on the frozen ground.

'It's been a long winter and the pack's hungry,' Alexei yelled across to Pavel. 'The wolf calls came from downwind, so they'll have the horses' scent.'

Alexei wiped a hand over his face and shook his head, as though resigned to whatever fate the wolves would bring. 'It's no use trying to outrun them, they can move through the forest a lot quicker than us.'

'So, what do we do, just sit here and wait?'

'I've seen wolves do this before. Without warning a couple of wolves will launch an attack from a direction you don't expect. They'll aim to panic just one or two horses into breaking away. As soon as they can isolate a horse, the whole pack attacks it. The poor, damned animal won't stand a chance. Sometimes it's best just to sacrifice one, and hope the pack stops their hunting to feed and satisfy their hunger.'

'We just let them take a horse?'

Alexei shook his head. 'Damned if I'm going to make it easy for them, so let's all keep circling the bunch and keep them together. When the attack comes, it will be quick as a flash, and probably from somewhere in the downwind direction. Keep your eyes on the stallions. They'll probably sense the attack before we do. Have your rifle ready but, if you spot something, make sure you have a clear shot and don't just blaze away. The last thing we need is to create a stampede.'

After the initial wolf calls, the forest had fallen back into an eerie silence. A wolf pack in this area would almost certainly be grey wolves. With thick, light-grey fur with white tips, they would be almost impossible to spot as they stealthily moved through the dim light among the snow-blanketed trees.

Then the wolf howls started up again. They were much closer now. Some came from downwind, but there were also isolated calls from both flanks, as though some of the wolves were trying to get ahead in a circling movement. Pavel tried to count the number of wolves from their separate howls. He thought he could identify six or seven individuals but, as they kept shifting position in the forest, it was impossible to determine the exact number.

At every wolf howl the horses shied, but kept their position, nervously bunching together into an ever-tighter group. Meanwhile the six riders continued circling them, rifles cocked and at the ready, and scanning the surrounding forest for any sign of movement among the trees and undergrowth. Several times Pavel thought he caught a glimpse of a dark shadow moving through the mottled black and white trunks of the birch forest but, just like a wraith, it was gone and he was left wondering whether he had seen anything at all.

Every time there was a small puff of wind a branch moved, a tree trunk creaked, or snow suddenly cascaded off a tree. Immediately everyone tensed, expecting this to be the precursor of an attack.

As if by a signal, the wolves' calls to each other abruptly stopped. A silence descended over the forest glade, and even the horses stopped their snorting and the nervous stamping of their hooves. It was as though the whole forest, and everything in it, was holding its breath, waiting and listening.

Then, in an instant, the silence was ripped apart. A single shot rang out, close by, and then another in quick succession. Pavel heard the yelp of a wounded wolf followed by an anguished howl. More shots, followed by a sudden flurry of disturbed snow amongst the trees off to one side and then, the sound of a large animal crashing through the undergrowth.

'Jesus bloody Christ,' shouted Alexei. 'What the hell was that? Who fired those shots?'

Pavel stood up in his stirrups and looked around to the other horsemen. He could make out all of them and counted them off: Alexei, Anton, Kolya, Sergei and Mikhail. Every man was shaking his head, bewildered – it wasn't any of them. Who was out there? It had to be someone else hidden amongst the trees.

The riders held their position, each man using his own horse to push at the mob, and keep the horses bunched.

There were no more shots, and the forest fell silent again, apart from the sound of whimpering and scrabbling from a wounded wolf trying to drag its maimed body away to cover.

'There's someone or something out there,' yelled Mikhail.

'A "something" doesn't fire a rifle,' Alexei yelled back. 'Keep your eyes peeled, but don't shoot. Whoever is out there has just saved our skin.'

The wolf howls had started up again, but they were lone calls coming from different parts of the forest. The howls were gradually moving further away as the survivors of the pack were calling each other and moving back into the depths of the forest to regroup.

'I can see a rider out there,' shouted Kolya, and pointed. 'Over there, through the trees.'

A lone rider gradually came into view, slowly weaving their horse through the snow and the tangled branches of the birch trees. There was something about the effortless, almost nonchalant riding style, which caught Pavel's attention. 'Don't worry,' Pavel shouted over to Alexei, 'I think I know who it is.'

Pavel spurred his horse forward and rode out to meet the incoming rider. 'What the hell are you doing here? You're supposed to be back helping to protect the homestead.'

Galina was wearing her split leather riding skirt, a heavy sheepskin jacket, and a fleece hat crammed on her head. She gave Pavel an innocent smile. 'I was downwind and they didn't pick up my scent. I managed to shoot the lead male and winged one of the older bitches, and maybe got another.'

Pavel took off his hat and wiped his gloved hand across his face. 'Your mother's going to murder me when we get back.'

Galina just smiled as she sheathed her rifle. 'I left a message telling her where I was going. I thought you might need some help.'

The next day they rode into the *stanitsa,* pushing the horses in front of them down the muddy lane that divided the village, a scattered collection of about twenty rough-hewn log houses with low thatched roofs located close to the western bank of the Ob. The roofs still had a thick coating of snow, and a cloying smell, a combination of wood smoke and animal manure pervading the air.

The horses were being pushed towards a temporary corral that had been built from tree branches at the far end of the village. Twenty or so burly Cossacks in rough farm clothes were sitting talking and smoking in the small square in the centre of the village. When they saw the horses coming down the lane, they got up and started sauntering down towards the corral.

Women and children stood in the open doors of their cabins to watch the newcomers ride through the village. The women wore colourful aprons and bright kerchiefs, with many balancing a young infant on their hip. The women neither smiled nor waved but stood gazing at the riders with dark stares – a quiet, unstated malevolence.

They've come to take our men away to war.

One little girl in a dirty pinafore came out as Galina rode by and gave her a curtsey, then reached up to touch the hem of Galina's riding skirt. The mother, standing in the doorway, shouted at her, and the girl ran back and hid from view behind her mother.

'Royalty,' said Sergei, as he rode up alongside Galina. 'She probably thinks you're the Tsarina.'

'I can't get over the number of children,' said Galina, looking around, 'considering the length of time the men are away fighting.'

Sergei grinned. 'A Cossack has a certain reputation. One child for each time they come back from war. Home, and straight to the bedroom.'

'Lucky them,' laughed Galina.

Pavel, Mikhail and Alexei pushed through to get ahead of the horses. Mikhail pointed towards two men on horseback who were off to one side of the corral.

'That's the Ataman over there,' said Mikhail, 'and the other one is the Englishman who says he knows you.'

Pavel nodded. 'That's him.'

Captain Spencer spurred his horse forward. He smiled broadly as he leaned over his pommel to grip Pavel's hand. 'It's good to see you again, Pavel Dmitrievich, even in these unusual circumstances.'

'We just hope this small contribution can help turn the tide.' Pavel turned and gestured towards Alexei. 'I should introduce you to my good friend Alexei Alexandrovich, they are his horses after all.'

'They're all fine horses,' answered the captain, shaking Alexei's hand. 'Even the Ataman is impressed, and that's no mean feat.'

'And this is my son-in-law, who I believe you've already met.'

The captain smiled at Mikhail and touched his riding crop to the peak of his cap. 'We shouldn't leave the Ataman waiting for too long, he's not good at that. Let's get the horses corralled, counted and inspected, and then we can conclude our business.'

'You'll find one hundred of the region's finest,' said Alexei. 'The wolves tried to take down a few, but we beat them off, thanks to Pavel's daughter.'

The captain raised an eyebrow and looked at Pavel. 'Your daughter?'

Pavel laughed. 'I'm blessed with three of them, but this one's different from the rest. Rides like a man, and shoots like one too. She wasn't meant to come, but she's not good at obeying her father's orders either.'

The captain grinned. 'I'd like to meet this daughter of yours but, let's get these horses into the corral first.'

Alexei and Mikhail rode off to help the others muster the horses towards the corral where the Cossack men waited. Some of them had climbed up onto the fence near the open gate and were counting the horses as they entered. Other Cossacks were moving among them in the corral, checking hooves and teeth.

The Ataman, meanwhile, had ridden over to talk to the captain. He did not bother to acknowledge Pavel. 'Captain Spencer,' the Ataman said curtly, 'my men have their orders. I'll leave you to deal with these horse traders.'

The Ataman then wheeled his horse and, without a word of farewell, rode back into the village.

'I apologize,' confided Captain Spencer. 'He's a difficult man at the best of times, but he's rather angry at the moment. I just had to intervene to stop him launching an attack on Novonikolayevsk.'

'But now you have these additional horses?' asked Pavel.

The captain shook his head. 'It's not about the number of horses; there are bigger things at stake. We are trying to get the Czech-Slovaks out, and an attack on the rail junction at Novonikolayevsk would likely see the Bolsheviks blow the rail bridge and leave them stranded.'

Pavel looked surprised. 'The Czech-Slovaks?'

Captain Spencer nodded. 'It's a long story, but there's about forty thousand of them, all seasoned fighters, strung out along the Trans-Siberian.'

'But I thought they were fighting for the Germans?'

'They were mostly fighting as part of the Austro-Hungarian Army – a lot of them became POWs, deserters who walked across the line. The Czech-Slovaks have been under the yoke of the Hapsburgs for centuries. They might have been fighting for them, but they hate them, and want to take this opportunity to gain independence. Now the Bolsheviks are pulling out of the war, we want them out of Russia and back on the Western Front, and on our side this time.'

'And the Bolsheviks and the Germans will allow this?'

'It's part of the Brest-Litovsk Treaty, in exchange for the repatriation of German and Austro-Hungarian prisoners.'

Pavel shook his head in disbelief. 'Strange times indeed.' Pavel then noticed Galina was riding over to join them.

'Father,' she said, as she rode up 'the Ataman's men have finished the count and are close to completing the inspection. We should be finished quite soon.'

The captain smiled and gave a slight bow from his waist. '*Mademoiselle* Sukhov, I believe.'

'You should just call me Galina Pavlona. And, your name, if I may ask?'

'This is Captain Spencer,' intervened Pavel, with a polite cough into his fist. 'I apologize sir, my daughter is rather more forthright than you are probably used to in London society.'

The captain smiled. 'Oh, I don't know about that. Galina should come to London and meet some of our modern city girls. I think she would be more than a match for them.'

'And tell me,' asked Galina, 'is Captain Spencer your real name?'

'Galina!' admonished Pavel.

The captain gave her a broad smile. 'You probably think I'm a spy. Please think of me merely as a military observer.'

'Then, if you don't mind me asking, exactly what are you supposed to be observing?'

'Hopefully,' answered the captain, with a wry smile, 'a White victory over the Bolshevik Reds. And we think you can do it.'

'With or without English intervention?'

Captain Spencer waved his arm towards the horses in the corral. 'It's this sort of support we can give. Let us not forget English troops are still fighting for their lives on the Western Front, a conflict made even more difficult by the Bolsheviks pulling Russia out of the war.'

'So, the English do not like communists?'

'We have a Westminster politician, a man called Churchill, who says this political *enfant terrible* would be best strangled at birth. It is why we are here.'

The captain leaned back and opened one of his saddlebags. 'It has been a pleasure meeting you, *mademoiselle*, and I would love to continue our discussion, but we should pay your father's friend for his horses and allow you to get back to the stud farm. I am sure your family will be anxious for your return. There are dangers everywhere.'

Captain Spencer started to ride over to pay Alexei, but suddenly wheeled his horse around. 'Before I forget,' he called to Pavel, 'will you ask your son-in-law and the other officers to join me with their full kit at the Cossack camp as soon as they can? It's going to be located somewhere between Novonikolayevsk and Omsk. I have a job for them. It's time for them to start soldiering again, I'm afraid.'

'How will they find the camp, it's quite a distance between those two cities.'

'Get them to ask here, at the *stanitsa,* on the way through. They will know where their men are located.'

Chapter 29
THE IRTYSH RAIL BRIDGE

Omsk, Mid May 1918

MIKHAIL SAT ON a grassy knoll overlooking the city from the east. He was resting his elbows on his knees in order to steady the binoculars. Sergei lay on his back alongside him. He had his hands behind his head and the peak of his cap covering his eyes, soaking in the warmth of the spring sunshine. Both of them had spread their coats out on the ground that was still cold and damp from the recent thaw.

From his vantage point Mikhail could see slabs of ice being carried down the river on the current. The ice made a rumbling sound as the edges of broken slabs bumped and ground past each other.

'Let me know when you want me to take over,' Sergei offered, rather unenthusiastically. 'Is there anything happening down there?'

'There's a bit of activity at the railway station,' Mikhail answered, 'and there's a group of railway workers down by the rail bridge over the Irtysh, but still no sign of any Czech-Slovak trains.'

Sergei rolled over onto his stomach and peered down at the town. He could easily make out the high, distinctive golden dome of the Dormition Cathedral, visible well above the other lower-lying buildings in the town. Even without binoculars he could follow the line of wooden merchant houses running along the main street down to the old fortress near the confluence of the Om and Irtysh rivers. On the eastern bank, close to the town center, stood the distinctive railway station designed in typical Russian neo-classical style and painted a pale blue with white colonnades.

'It looks like a wedding cake,' Sergei observed, with a laugh. 'The same architect who designed the Winter Palace must have got the commission for every damned railway station in Russia.'

'And, in comparison, the rest of Omsk looks just like any other grubby old Siberian town,' Mikhail commented, with a wry smile. 'Freezing in winter, a mud-hole in spring, and a dust bowl in summer. Give me the countryside any time.'

Without the binoculars Sergei could just make out the group of workers on the eastern bank of the railway bridge where the line, as it exited the bridge, swung north along the riverbank, towards the town and the station.

'What do you think they're doing?' he asked Mikhail.

'I guess they're a line maintenance crew. Even with binoculars it's hard to make out but, whatever they're up to, it must be urgent. I've never seen a railway crew work so hard; they're usually standing around smoking and leaning on their shovels.'

Mikhail slowly swung the binoculars further up the riverbank. Close to the railway workers were the horse lines of the Red cavalry. Soldiers could be seen moving among the horses, grooming, watering and feeding the animals. Mikhail pointed the lines out to Sergei. 'That's where we stole those horses, remember that?'

Sergei laughed. 'How could I forget? Crawling around on my hands and knees in the dark in mud and horseshit.'

'You would think,' Mikhail mused, 'they'd have worked out by now they're being watched.'

'You would think,' responded Sergei, 'they'd have sent out more patrols by now. Maybe they're afraid of what they might find.'

The Reds had kept mostly to the confines of the city, behind the makeshift barriers that had been erected, and had only sent out a few cavalry patrols that never ventured far from the cordon. The Ataman had deliberately kept his Cossack camp well away, hidden in the folds of distant hills and out of sight to all but the most venturesome. If a wandering cattle-herder or a hunter inadvertently stumbled upon the camp, they were dealt with quickly and brutally.

Sergei rolled over on his back again and occupied himself by staring up into the sky at a distant flock of black ravens lazily wheeling in the air currents. 'This is getting damned boring. And why send us? Even the guy who cleans the latrines is capable of watching for trains.'

'You don't think it's because our English captain doesn't trust the Cossacks?'

Sergei didn't bother answering the obvious. 'What really amazes me about the captain,' Sergei continued, 'is how he's kept the Ataman from attacking every town between Novonikolayevsk and here. I don't know how he does it.'

Mikhail chuckled. 'He must have a very compromising photograph of the Ataman, or something. But the English are very clear, they want the Czech-Slovaks out, and everything takes second place to that.'

'But how long are we expected to wait? The Czech-Slovak troop trains were reported passing Chelyabinsk ages ago, and there's still no sign of them.'

'Remember Chelyabinsk is nearly nine hundred *versts* up the line,' pointed out Mikhail.

'According to my calculation, answered Sergei, 'that should have taken them twenty hours at the most. And how long have we been sitting up here? The trains should have passed through hours ago as long as some petty Bolshevik *apparatchik* hasn't been stuffing them around.'

Mikhail pointed to the sky. 'Stop complaining – the sun is shining, the birds are singing, we're warm and dry, and nobody is shooting at us. All we have to do is watch the Czech trains through Omsk and then we can ride back to the camp and report.'

Mikhail raised the binoculars again and scanned up the line as far as he could see. 'The line's obviously open since there's been a number of POW trains heading through. My bet is the Bolsheviks are giving the Austro-Hungarians the up-track priority and keep shunting the Czechs off onto sidings.'

Sergei laughed. 'That's one way to really annoy the Czech-Slovaks.'

Both men lapsed into silence. Apart from the squawks of the distant ravens, the faint *chink* of sledgehammers on steel from the railway crew, and the occasional neigh from the cavalry lines, all was quiet.

Suddenly Sergei sat bolt upright. 'Did you hear that?' He quickly got to his feet and reached for his rifle. 'There's someone moving up behind us.'

Sergei ran across the small clearing, crouched down behind some underbrush, and peered through the trees down the hill. Mikhail dropped the binoculars and ran after Sergei, pulling his revolver from its holster and clicking off the safety.

Amongst the trees they could just make out a lone rider working his way carefully up the hill. He stopped and checked Mikhail and Sergei's horses where they had tethered them, well below the crest, and then cautiously continued his progress in their direction.

'It's all right.' Sergei gave an "okay" hand signal across to Mikhail. 'He's one of ours.'

The Cossack reached the top of the knoll and rode into the clearing. It was evident his horse had been ridden hard; it was breathing heavily and lathered in sweat. The young rider, with the single stripe of a corporal, did not dismount, but touched one finger to his woolen cap.

'The Englishman's compliments, sir,' he said. 'He wants you both to return immediately. We are striking camp. The attack on Omsk commences in two hours.'

'But the Czech trains aren't through yet,' pointed out Mikhail, 'and there's still no sign of them.'

The corporal just shrugged, nonchalantly. 'My orders were to deliver the message urgently and accompany you back to the camp.'

Captain Spencer met them at the camp's entrance. He had changed out of his civilian clothes into jodhpurs, a military khaki jacket, with a Sam Brown belt and holstered revolver. He wore a battered officer's peaked cap without insignia.

'I know what you're going to ask, but things have changed,' he said. 'We've received word from the Officers' Union in Omsk. They've been tapping into the telegraph line and inform us there's been a major blow-up between the Czechs and the Bolsheviks up the line at Chelyabinsk station. A fight started between the Czechs and a trainload of Austro-Hungarian prisoners going in the other direction. But then the local Bolsheviks got themselves in the middle of it and arrested some of the Czechs, and now fighting has broken out between the Czechs and the Bolsheviks.'

'But what has that got to do with launching an attack on Omsk now?' asked Mikhail. 'I thought we wanted to keep the line open across the Irtysh so the Czech trains from Chelyabinsk could get through? If it's just a brawl between the Czechs, the POWs, and the local Reds, then I'm sure the Czechs will easily prevail and get underway again.'

'I think,' continued the captain, 'the fighting is a lot more serious than that. The local Bolshevik commanders have been delaying the Czechs to prevent their three separate army groups from joining up. The Czechs have run out of patience and we think they are going to try to take control over their own destiny. Chelyabinsk might seem like just a local brawl, but I believe it could be the catalyst. I'm certain they'll fight the Bolsheviks every step of the way until they get their entire force out of Russia.'

'You seem pleased,' observed Mikhail.

'It's what I've been predicting for a while. With the Austro-Hungarians heading westwards, and the Czechs heading east, it was bound to happen sooner or later. Chelyabinsk may have just delivered you a new ally and, better still,' continued the captain, 'if the Czechs take control from the local Bolshevik commanders along the Trans-Siberian, it allows us to start moving up all those armaments stuck on Vladivostok's wharves.'

'But why attack Omsk now?' Mikhail asked, with a perplexed look on his face. 'Isn't there a danger they'll just blow the bridge over the Irtysh, and then we can't get their trains through?'

'We've also heard on the telegraph the Chelyabinsk Soviet asking the railway workers in Omsk to rip up a section of line to stop the Czechs getting through. They're trying to bottle them up.'

Mikhail and Sergei looked at each other and nodded.

'We think we know where they're removing the track,' said Mikhail. 'We could see a bunch of railway workers from our lookout, but couldn't work out what they were doing. It's down where the rail bridge crosses the river to the east bank. That means the Czechs would be stuck on the other side. It mightn't be blowing up the bridge, but it's just as effective.'

'And that's exactly why we've decided to go in now,' said Captain Spencer. 'At two o'clock the Officers' Union will create some sort of diversion in the center of Omsk and, at that moment, we'll launch an attack on the outskirts.'

'What do you want us to do?' asked Mikhail. 'Go in with the Cossack attack?'

The captain shook his head. 'It's a tall order, but your job is to keep the Cossacks under control. You know what they're like – one scent of blood and they'll forget the objective and go on a killing spree. We need to secure the post office and railway station as quickly as possible and make sure we stop the Bolsheviks sabotaging the communication and switching equipment. More importantly, we need to stop them ripping up the track, and get them to urgently repair whatever damage they've already done. And that's where you two come in.'

'We're hardly experienced railway maintenance workers,' commented Sergei.

'Your task is to capture the railway maintenance crews and, above all, keep them alive. Since railway workers are Bolshevik to a man, the Cossacks will want to kill them all. You have to stop them doing this.'

'Just two of us?' Mikhail asked.

'You'll be assigned to a troop of Cossacks who are designated for the task. They'll have been told what they have to do. You'll ride with them and make sure they follow orders.'

'And where will you be, sir?' asked Mikhail.

The captain grinned. 'Keeping a very close eye on our friend, the Ataman.'

The line of Cossack cavalry stood quietly below the crest of the hill, out of sight of the town. The front row carried lances, held upright with the butt of the lance resting in a leather stirrup cup. The tip of the lance carried a small red pendant and the horsemen all displayed the red shoulder epaulets of the 1st Siberian Cossack Regiment. Behind the front line of lancers were two more lines of horsemen carrying short cavalry carbines and razor-sharp sabers. There was a quiet air of nervous anticipation as the lines of cavalry stood waiting for the order to advance.

Captain Spencer, accompanied by a Cossack sergeant, rode up to Mikhail and Sergei. 'The Ataman has allocated you this sergeant's troop on the far left of the line to attack the bridge. Stick close to them. Once we've cleared the entry into the town, they'll be all yours. Do not allow yourselves to get involved in the main melee. The Czech-Slovak trains are already on their way and we need that track replaced.'

Mikhail saluted. 'Understood, sir.'

Mikhail looked over at the sergeant, a mean-looking man with a mouthful of yellow teeth and a large, ugly scar on his face.

'Have you been told about our task, Sergeant?' asked Mikhail.

The sergeant just nodded, and did not look at all pleased.

'He'd rather be killing Bolsheviks than capturing bridges,' said Captain Spencer. 'Go carefully, gentlemen.'

There was the faint crackle of distant rifle fire coming from the direction of the town. Captain Spencer checked his watch and nodded affirmatively. 'That'll be the Officers' Union starting their diversion. You need to hurry. The attack starts in two minutes.'

A whistle blew from somewhere up towards the center of the Cossack cavalry lines followed by a shouted command, 'Forward, Cossacks!' The lancers immediately led off, followed by the rest of the cavalry, walking their horses in line up towards the crest of the hill.

Mikhail and Sergei had joined the sergeant's troop just as the order to advance had been given. The troop stayed out to one side of the main Cossack line to avoid being splattered by the mud kicked up by the lead horses.

At the top of the crest the long line of horsemen halted and stood, looking down into the town. A gentle slope ran down for about four hundred meters towards the houses on the outskirts. The north-facing slope still had some patches of snow but it was mostly a muddy, barren stretch of open farmland with few obstacles to halt a cavalry charge.

One narrow dirt track, near the center of the line, led into the town. There was only a low log fence surrounding the town, and no gate of any substance. Bolshevik soldiers could be seen frantically trying to manhandle carts across the track to block the entry, but that left many other gaps to attack through. The defenses were meager, and the defending force seemed ill prepared for a full-scale cavalry assault by massed horsemen.

'It's a little too late for that,' commented Sergei, pointing towards the men shifting the carts. 'I think they're going to rue the day they didn't send out more patrols.'

The distinctive sound of bugles drifted up from the Red cavalry lines near the river as their troops were called to assemble. They could be seen scrambling to saddle their mounts and to form up.

'I'm amazed,' commented Mikhail. 'We seem to have caught them completely by surprise.'

'What are we waiting for?' asked Sergei. There was a tinge of nervous excitement in his voice. 'We should be attacking now, before they get their cavalry organized.'

'The Cossack commanders know what they're doing. They'll be

trying to keep us massed so we all hit their line together, rather than let troopers charge off ahead.'

The line of Cossacks started moving off the crest and down the slope at a slow, measured walking pace. Up and down the line there were shouted commands, 'Steady! Steady! Keep the line!'

Officers had their sabers drawn and were holding them out sideways to maintain formation and stop individuals or squadrons getting too far ahead. The ranks were silent except for the jingle of their cavalry harnesses and the sound of hooves striking the ground, like distant rolling thunder.

Mikhail and Sergei had both acquired Cossack sabers. They now unsheathed them and had them dangling down by their sides as they rode forward. They also unbuttoned the flaps of their revolver holsters, ensuring their Mausers were ready for use.

Sergei looked across to Mikhail and gave him a boyish grin. 'At last some action in this damned war. I've always wanted to be in a cavalry charge. Something to tell the grandchildren about.'

'Forget any romantic Tolstoy notions. This is for real, and people are about to die. Just don't lose your head – and remember our orders. It's all about the railway line.'

Rifle fire opened up from the barricades and bullets started thudding into the advancing line of cavalry. Every few moments a man would scream and then drop back, disappearing from sight, as he was swallowed up by the following lines of horses. Then, without warning, a horse would suddenly stop in its tracks and buckle as a bullet crashed into its chest. It would usually go down on its forequarters, sending the rider catapulting over its head, face forward into the mud.

'Close up! Close up!' came the constant cry from the officers. 'Fill the gaps and keep the line!'

Then, like the sound of a piece of calico being ripped apart, a light machine gun opened up against the far right flank of the Cossack line. Now they were under fire from machine guns, there was no holding the horsemen back. Immediately the lead officer yelled out. 'Level lances! Cossacks charge!'

Bugles sounded up and down the line, and a blood-curdling Cossack howl erupted. En masse they spurred their horses into a gallop. Sergei shouted out an exuberant *hurrah* and spurred his horse forward to keep up with the leading men in the troop. Mikhail instead pulled off to one side so he could keep a clear view, and see in which direction the troop went, as the charge quickly became a chaotic mass of horses galloping down the muddy slope.

It was about two hundred meters to the barricades on the edge of town, and the leading lancers crossed the gap in less than a minute. The thin line of Red infantry manning the hastily constructed barricades presented no match for the force of the charge. There was an audible *crunch* as the first of the horsemen hit the barricades, some managing to leap the lower obstacles, and others sweeping around through the gaps.

The Reds attempted in vain to ward off the long, stabbing lances with their bayonets. They died quickly, often huddled in groups, as lancers circled and plunged the bloodied tips of their lances into those still standing, again and again. There was no quarter given.

The first of the Cossacks were quickly past the barricades and poured between the gaps of the houses, crashing through gardens and fences as their momentum carried them towards the center of town.

The surviving Red infantry dropped their rifles and ran for their lives, heading back into the town, but they were quickly overtaken by the mounted Cossacks, who leaned forward in their saddles to better reach down with their slashing sabers. The Red cavalry didn't try to put up any resistance, and those who had managed to mount their horses used them to flee in the face of the attack.

Then, as quickly as the charge had begun, it was over. A strange stillness descended over the battleground. The crack of rifles gradually subsided to just an occasional shot, and the machine guns had fallen silent as they were overrun. The only remaining sound was the moaning and cries of the wounded strewn across the muddy, churned-up field.

Lone Cossacks were starting to pick over the ground, pausing occasionally to plunge a lance into a moving body, shoot a wounded horse, or search through the pockets and rucksacks of the dead.

Further off in the distance there was the receding sound of shouting and gunfire as the main force of the cavalry swept on through the streets of the town, in pursuit of fleeing Reds.

Mikhail had stayed in contact with his troop, as best he could. They had veered around the barricades on the far left of the town. He was pleased to see that they had remained a reasonably cohesive unit, and when they reached the outskirts, the sergeant had pulled them up and started to regroup the men. Mikhail spurred his horse forward through the group of troopers and grabbed the Sergeant by the arm. 'Let's get down to the bridge!' he yelled into the sergeant's ear, and pointed towards the far left of the town. 'Follow me!'

Mikhail led the way at a gallop, following a maintenance track that ran beside the railway embankment. Ahead he could see a group of men in blue overalls running across a muddy field close to the track. They were frantically trying to reach the edge of the forest, just two hundred meters away.

'Over there!' Mikhail shouted at the sergeant. 'Get your men to head them off before they reach the trees. And remember, we're to take them alive.'

The sergeant shouted out a command and a group of troopers veered away, spurring their horses forward in an encircling movement.

The men looked back at the horsemen bearing down on them. Some tried to run faster, but they were struggling to make any pace as they scrambled across the muddy field. Finally realizing they were not going to make the tree line, the railway workers stopped and clustered into a tight group. They stood, panting with exertion and looking terrified. Some of them fell to their knees in the mud, clasped their hands together, and started praying.

Mikhail pushed his way through the circle of Cossacks towards the workers. There were about fifteen of them, all wearing the distinctive rough blue overalls, jackets and cloth hats of track crew.

'Who's in charge here?' Mikhail demanded.

There was silence for several seconds until one man finally stepped forward. He had the rough, pugnacious face of a fighter, and immense hairy hands. He stood, with clenched fists, looking up at Mikhail.

'I guess that's me.' The man shrugged, almost nonchalantly.

'I want you to get your men back to the bridge and replace the track you've ripped up.'

The big man studied Mikhail for a second, and then turned his head sideways, and spat on the ground.

'You're going to kill us anyway,' he growled, 'so go and fucking do it yourself.'

'You,' barked the sergeant, 'do not talk to a *kapitan* like that!'

Mikhail put a hand out to caution restraint, but before he could speak, the sergeant leveled his carbine and pulled the trigger. The big man jerked as his chest exploded. He toppled backwards, thudding into the ground.

'Sergeant!' yelled Mikhail. 'What did I tell you?'

The sergeant ignored him and rode over to the railway workers. He looked down at the fallen man for a moment and then stared, one by one, at each man. Almost all of the railway workers were now crouching on their knees in the mud, with averted eyes and cowered heads.

'Is anyone still refusing to work, or do you all want to join your comrade here?'

The railway workers looked at each other and collectively nodded.

'Good,' said the sergeant, 'well, let's fucking get on with it, shall we?'

Chapter 30

THE EVE OF DEPARTURE

Tyumentsevsky, End of May 1918

AFTER THE COSSACKS had taken Omsk, and the Czech-Slovaks had made it safely across the Irtysh, Mikhail and Sergei had requested leave from the English captain to return to the stud. Mikhail was sensitive about spending too much time away from a heavily pregnant Iya, and Sergei wished to say a proper farewell to his father. There was also the dilemma he had about Galina. They had kept their new level of relationship secret; however he was uncertain about where it was going, or where he wanted to take it. But it was one of those loose ends that he felt obliged to tie up before he went away again.

The two men had seen enough of war to understand that campaigns of this nature are usually long, drawn-out affairs, and this might be the last time they would see the family for months, if not years. There was also the prospect at the back of everybody's minds that they'd never return or, worse, would come back maimed for life, but nobody ever talked about this.

Captain Spencer was hardly in a position to refuse their request – he wasn't exactly their commander – but he still thanked them for their contribution, and wished them a speedy and safe journey. Mikhail and Sergei had explained that this would be a brief home visit before they joined up with one of the new Volunteer White regiments being hastily formed in the "liberated" towns along the Trans-Siberian.

The action of the Czech-Slovaks at Chelyabinsk had given impetus to the White forces, not just the Cossacks, to organize and join them in fighting the Bolsheviks. The previously secretive Officers' Union now came out into the open, and became the kernel of the new volunteer regiments being formed in Omsk and nearby Tomsk. Surprisingly Tomsk, a city not on the main Trans-Siberian, was becoming a new centre for White resistance.

Anton and Kolya had stayed on with the Cossacks for a few more weeks, helping mop up the last remaining vestiges of Red units around Omsk. It was difficult and frustrating work, since it was relatively easy for any Bolshevik to hide their weapons and merge back into the general population of the city, or to disappear off into the surrounding forested countryside. Only through informers, or relentless hunting by small cavalry units, could they be winkled out.

The Czech-Slovaks were less interested in this, and continued their focus on securing the Trans-Siberian line and its immediate vicinity for as far along the track as they were able. Saboteurs were their immediate concern, as well as linking up with their fellow comrades spread both up and down the line. First, they wanted to get through to them, and then bring them all together into a cohesive army group under one command. Only then could they make a concerted push towards Vladivostok and the ships that would take them either back to the Western Front or, better still, to a newly formed nation separate from the Hapsburg Empire. This would be easier said than done; their troops were spread over such vast distances, and there were Bolshevik "warlords" still controlling large sections of the line, but the Czech-Slovaks were determined, and prepared to fight anyone who stood in their way.

After Omsk, it was the city of Novonikolayevsk that became their focus, since it was the next major Trans-Siberian hub towards the east. It was here the rail line crossed the wide Ob River, and the Czech-Slovaks needed to capture the bridge before someone blew it up. Novonikolayevsk was also the rail junction for the Altai-Turkestan line that ran south through Barnaul, and that was something that sparked the interest, not only of Pavel, but the whole family.

Outwardly, Pavel refrained from investing too much hope of a freed Barnaul. 'You only have to look at the map,' he kept telling everyone in the house. 'They've got Chelyabinsk and Omsk, so we've secured this side of the Urals. Now the next one must be Novonikolayevsk, and then Irkutsk and the Lake Baikal tunnels before somebody blows them up and sticks the cork firmly back in the bottle.'

'What about Moscow?' asked Maria Ivanova. 'Surely, if we're ever going to snuff out this revolution, we need to attack the source of the evil. We can't leave them hiding behind the walls of the Kremlin and think the revolution will just go away.'

Pavel kept pointing to his map that had become a semi-permanent fixture spread out over one end of the kitchen table. 'Just look at the distances; how could we advance that far over the Urals and manage to keep our army supplied? Look what happened to Napoleon. I say, let's free Siberia, and then worry about Western Russia later.'

Mikhail and Sergei had been back at the stud for a few weeks when Anton and Kolya returned, bringing news they had all been hoping for: the Czech-Slovak Legion had finally broken through, after heavy fighting, and had taken Novonikolayevsk. Step-by-step the Trans-Siberian was being wrested from the Bolsheviks. For the first time, the Czech-Slovaks were now in control of a large tract of the line, and could finally start uniting their three army groups.

'They're already starting to form a Novonikolayevsk Volunteer Regiment,' Anton proudly announced to Mikhail and Sergei. ' Kolya and I have already joined up. You two should join us.'

Mikhail grinned. 'That's okay for both of you – you're from there. I was rather hoping for a Barnaul regiment.'

'Well, that's unlikely to happen any time soon, so why not join? There's a couple of hundred of us, along with other ex-soldiers and civilians. It's surprising how many White supporters are now coming out to join up.'

Mikhail gave a cynical laugh. 'And they'll probably disappear just as quickly back into the woodwork as soon as the Reds reappear. Russians are notoriously fickle when it comes to standing up for their politics. But don't worry, we'll both join you, won't we Sergei?'

Sergei looked at his feet, and then after a moment, 'I guess so.'

The talk in the house was always about the indivisible subjects of the new politics, and winning the war, although none of them seemed to have a clear view about either, and this, in itself, created endless debates.

'You have to ask yourself,' Mikhail queried, 'what exactly are the Whites' objectives? We can't kill every Bolshevik in the country, and they can never kill all of us. The Czech-Slovaks have a clear objective; they want to control the Trans Siberian so they can get out. But what are ours? Is it territorial, or is it political?'

Pavel contemplated the question for a while, and was hesitant in his answer. 'I think,' he finally said, 'civil wars are less about territory won or lost, and more about winning the hearts and minds of the people.'

'Exactly my point,' exclaimed Mikhail, with a wave of his arms. 'How can you win over the common man if you stand for virtually nothing, except a vague notion about returning to the old ways, whatever they were. You mightn't agree with their politics, but at least the Bolsheviks are offering some sort of vision for the future and a better life, even if it is a lie.'

Pavel laughed. 'You're starting to sound just like your wife. Are you sure you're not fighting for the wrong side?'

Mikhail gave a shrug. 'If it wasn't for the fact the Bolsheviks sacked the Duma, and confiscated people's property . . .'

'Ah!' said Pavel, poking his finger into Mikhail's chest, 'so there *are* reasons why we have to fight them after all – an illegal coup, illegal confiscation of property, and to win back the democracy they stole from us. What better reasons can you have?'

'What about the Tsar,' asked Sergei? He was slouched in a lounge chair closest to the fireplace in the study where the men were relaxing after their farewell dinner. They were all nursing a glass of cognac, and Pavel had lit a cheroot. 'Does anyone really want him back? He was just as much an obstacle to democracy as the damned Bolsheviks. Does a return to the "old ways" mean he's to be reinstated on the throne?'

'If he's still alive,' scoffed Mikhail.

'That's what we all hope,' said Pavel, picking his words carefully. "Whatever you think of him, putting our monarch up against a wall is unacceptable. I can't believe even the Bolsheviks would contemplate doing such a thing.'

The subject of the Tsar and the royal family was a vexed issue in the household, and one generally avoided. Besides, nobody was certain where the Royal family was or what had happened to them. Along with many other things in Russia, there remained an information void, filled mostly with wild speculation.

'So, what do you think is next after Novonikolayevsk?' asked Pavel, deftly changing the subject to one of the safer topics of conversation. 'Do you think they'll send a force to clear out Tsaplin and his comrades from Barnaul?'

'I think,' said Mikhail, 'if you believe what Anton told us about what the Czech-Slovak artillery did to Novonikolayevsk, you wouldn't want them attacking Barnaul. We wouldn't have much of a town left. Novonikolayevsk is a ruin apparently.'

Mikhail swilled the cognac in his glass and took a sip. 'Anyway,' he continued, 'Barnaul would just be a sideshow. If the Czech-Slovaks are now dictating strategy, they will be concentrating on clearing the line down towards Irkutsk.'

'But who exactly is dictating the strategy?' asked Pavel. 'Is it the Czech-Slovaks, or us? What about the leaders of our new volunteer regiments?'

'That's the problem,' Mikhail pointed out. 'They're starting to form a Siberian government, as they call it, but you can't have a committee of politicians running the war. We desperately need someone in over-all command.'

'Technically,' proffered Sergei from his armchair, 'the Czech-Slovak Legion is under French Command – a General Janin. But I'm not sure how much influence the French have, other than they want the Czech-Slovaks out as quickly as possible and around to the Western Front. I agree with Mikhail, we're going to need our own man in Siberia.'

'It certainly can't be Kornilov,' answered Mikhail, 'he's thousands of *versts* away fighting in the Don, and God help us if they appoint the Ataman.'

'Mikhail, what about that Count Lebedev chap?' asked Sergei. 'You know, the brother of . . .'

Mikhail glared at him and abruptly cut him off. 'I keep asking where the hell he is; I was given the impression he would be a key figure in the creation of the Siberian Army, but he's yet to be seen.'

Sergei waved his glass towards Pavel. 'You should ask your English friend when you see him tomorrow. He seems to know everything that's going on.'

Pavel was joining them in the ride to Novonikolayevsk the next day. Anton had brought back a cryptic message for Pavel from Captain Spencer.

"Come Novonikolayevsk soonest. Few maps. Cptn. S."

Mikhail had frowned when Pavel had shown him the note. 'You need to be careful with that man. He calls himself a simple military observer, but the reality is probably very different. I think he's up to a lot, behind the scenes, if you know what I mean.'

'But he's been helping our cause – isn't that good?'

Mikhail shook his head. 'Only while Britain's objectives happen to coincide with ours. As soon as they don't, they'll walk away. And remember, if there are problems, you could be implicated.'

'But,' said Pavel, tapping the note with his finger, 'he's asking for my assistance. If it's just maps he's after, then that's hardly going to put me in harm's way, is it?'

'Just be very careful; he may only have one arm, but he's a puppet master, and he's extremely deft at it.'

Pavel, Mikhail and Sergei had busied themselves during their final day packing kit bags, cleaning weapons, and checking their horses, saddles and harnesses. Maria and Katrina helped the cook prepare provisions. For each man they filled a small calico bag with frozen *pelmeni* brought up from the cellar dug deep under the house. The permafrost kept the cellar at ice-chest coolness for most of the year. The spicy meat-filled dumplings could be quickly cooked by throwing them into a pot of boiling water and were ideal provisions to take away on campaign.

The old cook also busied herself making her specialty – fresh *blinis* of rolled-up pancakes filled with strawberry jam and sour cream.

'These won't last long,' said Pavel, as Maria slapped his hand away while he was in the process of pinching one from the kitchen table. 'Remember an army marches on its stomach,' he joked.

'And,' responded Maria, bustling him out of the kitchen, 'your stomach can wait.'

Alexei had agreed to stay behind at the stud. 'Dmitry, Galina and I will look after the new foals and keep an eye out for strangers,' he told Pavel. 'And you can tell your friend and the Ataman I'll bring in another forty horses or so in a few weeks' time.'

'Just make sure Galina stays here this time,' warned Pavel. 'Chain her to the yard rail if you have to.'

Sergei lay on his bed and listened to the old house creak in the wind. It was pitch black outside but, although it was not late, everybody in the house had retired early since they would be starting out for Novonikolayevsk at first light, in an attempt to ride all the way in one day.

Sergei reached down and pulled up the heavy winter eiderdown. It was cold in the house, and it made him wonder how he would adapt to sleeping rough again. The time he spent in Petrograd, and now back at the stud, had made him appreciate a warm bed, a soft mattress and, sometimes, someone to share it with. His mind immediately conjured up the picture of a warm, naked Tanya next to him, their arms and legs entwined. But he forced himself to push the image away, and rolled over to face the wall. He needed to get to sleep, but his mind was still active – full of nervous anticipation, and not without some trepidation.

Even the ride across to the newly liberated Novonikolayevsk would have its risks. The defeated Red forces, rather than surrender, had withdrawn into the *taiga* to form and operate partisan groups. Encounters with these groups hiding out in this thick forest could happen at any time, and anywhere along the trail. And, in all likelihood, the group of three horsemen would be watched from the moment they left the stud.

Sergei was finally starting to drift off to sleep when there was a soft rap on the bedroom door. He was fully awake in an instant, and propped himself up on one elbow. 'Who is it?'

The door slowly creaked open. 'Are you awake?' Galina whispered, as she quietly closed the door behind her. 'I just wanted to say goodbye.'

Galina was carrying a lighted candle in a brass candleholder in one hand. Her hair was tied back with a ribbon, and she was in her dressing gown and slippers.

'I wouldn't have gone without seeing you in the morning,' said Sergei. 'You know that.'

'But there'll be all the others around,' she replied, as she rested the candleholder on the bedside table and sat down on the edge of the bed. 'I wanted to find out if you've spoken with your father?'

Sergei looked puzzled. 'About what?'

'You know, about us. We're sort of engaged, aren't we? It would be nice if your father knew before you went away.'

Sergei went to say something but stopped himself. Instead he gave her a cheeky grin. 'This doesn't sound much like the Galina Sukhov I know.'

Galina rocked back and laughed quietly. 'You kissed me therefore you love me – anyway, that's what Iya told me.'

'So your sister has put you up to this?'

Galina averted her eyes and studied the wallpaper above the bed head.

'Look,' said Sergei, 'I'm not trying to be prudish, but your mother and father would kill me if they knew you were in here. If someone hears us, or finds us like this . . .'

Galina reached behind her head, pulled off her hair ribbon, ran a hand through her hair, and tossed the ribbon across to Sergei. 'We can discuss the bride dowry later.'

'The bride dowry?'

Galina stood, took off her dressing gown and pulled her night-gown over her head. 'Well, since the Bolsheviks have confiscated all our property, I won't have one.'

Sergei gave a quiet chuckle and reached a hand out for her. 'You're right, we can discuss that later.'

'And remember,' she whispered, as she slid her naked body between the sheets next to him, 'this will be my first time.'

'And mine,' answered Sergei, giving her a boyish grin.

Galina poked him playfully in the ribs and laughed. 'Liar.'

Chapter 31
THE CZECH-SLOVAK LEGION

Novonikolayevsk, Early June 1918

PAVEL PICKED HIS way through the town. Anton had been right – the place was a mess, with debris from shelled-out houses scattered everywhere. There were broken water pipes and the stench of raw sewage, and every step of the way, broken glass crunched under Pavel's feet. Only the area around the railway station seemed relatively unscathed; Pavel guessed this was a deliberate strategy of the Czech-Slovak artillery. Everywhere else had been shelled, but they had obviously wanted to keep the railway intact.

He had to ask directions several times, and finally found his way to an office tucked away at the back of the rail yards. He knocked on the door and entered what turned out to be an adjutant's room. 'I'm looking for Captain Spencer, the Englishman,' he said to the army clerk sitting behind the one desk in the small, austere room. 'I was told he would be here.'

The young clerk looked Pavel up and down with that certain disdain reserved for civilians, grunted something unintelligible, and pointed towards one of the chairs in the corner.

Pavel sat down and waited while a stream of officers and clerks, with files tucked under their arms, entered the room and proceeded straight past the clerk into an adjoining meeting-room. Every time the door was opened Pavel could hear the thrum of subdued conversation from the room's occupants, and catch a waft of warm air, thick with cigarette smoke.

Pavel checked his fob watch. Twenty minutes had elapsed since he had arrived. He got up and walked over to the clerk's desk.

'Can you at least tell me if the English captain is here?'

'Yes. Do you have an appointment?' The clerk spoke stilted Russian with a thick Slovak accent. Pavel knew from his accent, the broad face with flattened features, and tan-colored uniform, that he was part of the Czech-Slovak Legion.

'He sent me a note.' Pavel pulled it from his pocket and showed the clerk, who impatiently brushed it aside. 'He wants to see me urgently.'

'Meeting,' was all he said, gesturing towards the door. His Russian was obviously very limited. 'You wait.'

Pavel returned to his seat and waited. Finally the door from the back room opened and a group of four Legion officers, immersed in deep conversation, walked out and, without a glance in Pavel's direction, exited the building. There was something about their demeanour, the way they walked and spoke to each other, that conveyed a sense of purpose and optimism. Even though their Slovak was mostly unintelligible to Pavel, he guessed it had been a planning meeting, and something important had been agreed and decided.

A number of clerks, burdened with files, followed the officers out. Captain Spencer was one of the last to leave.

'Ah, Pavel Dmitrievich,' he said with a wave of his one good arm, 'you obviously got my message.'

'Yes, and I came as quickly as possible. I have been waiting here for over an hour.'

Captain Spencer nodded in the direction of the clerk and grinned.

'Military clerks are the same the world over; they are put on earth to obstruct and preserve us from interruptions. He's only doing his job. Please forgive him.'

'Your message – I don't really understand what you want me to do.'

Captain Spencer laughed. 'Forgive me. Writing cryptic messages comes naturally to me; it's part of the job. But I'm glad you're here.'

The captain had a relaxed look about him, even slightly jovial, which was far from his usual serious demenour. 'And, how is the family?' he asked, in an off-handed sort of way.

'Safely back at the stud farm. They'll stay there until the fighting is over.'

'Your daughter is with them?'

Pavel gave a chortle. 'Under lock and key, I hope.'

The captain looked surprised.

'It's the only way I could stop her joining in the fighting,' added Pavel. 'But, I'm only partially joking – she now accepts the need to be there to protect the family while the men are away.'

'Then, we'd better not detain you for long.' The captain took Pavel by the elbow and led him over to a corner of the room. 'The problem is that we don't have any accurate maps of this region. Either they don't exist, or the Bolsheviks have taken them, or they've deliberately destroyed them. So, we need people who know this area, and also Barnaul, and that, Pavel Dmitrievich, is where you come in. You were the first person to come to mind. I hope you can help us.'

'But there should be locals who know this area better than I, and also the region where the line runs through to Irkutsk.'

'Yes, there are, but not so much the Altai-Turkestan railway running out from Novonikolayevsk through Barnaul. And then, there's the area around Barnaul itself.'

Pavel gave the captain a puzzled look. 'But what's Barnaul got to do with it? Surely the Legion's plan will be to continue pushing east along the Trans-Siberian and liberate Irkutsk?'

'The Legion don't make all the decisions and, even if they think they do, there are always some of them who can be persuaded to take a broader view of things. Their desire to depart from Russia does require a certain amount of international cooperation from the Allies, if you understand what I mean, and their commanders know that they need to acquiesce to others' wishes every now and then.'

'Is it in their interest to take Barnaul?' Pavel was barely able to suppress a grin. 'Not that I'm complaining.'

'Yes, it is, but probably not for the reason you think. It's about the Altai-Turkestan line that runs through Barnaul, not Barnaul itself. Turkestan grows cotton, and from cotton you make gun cotton. Gun cotton propels artillery shells, and artillery helps win wars. Currently this cotton is accessed by Germany. The Allies take control of the line into Turkestan, we gain the cotton fields, and stop the supply to Germany.'

Pavel nodded thoughtfully. 'That all makes sense.'

Captain Spencer hesitated. 'There's another compelling reason that's specific for my country – Great Britain. You just need to look at a map to understand why it is so important, so I'm not telling you any secrets. Turkestan is the gateway to the North-West Frontier and India. If we manage to get the Germans out, then the last thing we want is the Bolsheviks taking control of Turkestan. India is a key target in Lenin's quest for global revolution. My government is highly sensitive to any move that might encourage the peoples of India to rise up against British authority. It is part of the British Empire, and will remain so. Already the Bolsheviks are attempting to subvert the tribes on the frontier, and then it is just a small step to spread trouble throughout the country.'

'So, if you don't mind me asking, what is the plan exactly?'

'Once we've captured Novonikolayevsk we want to push south and take Barnaul. From there we can secure the line through to Turkestan, and the Legion will be free to resume their operations towards Irkutsk.'

'And the Czech-Slovak Legion is happy with this?'

The captain smiled. 'Not without a few arms being twisted, but fortunately your old friend, Comrade Tsaplin, helped convince them. The other day he rather stupidly, in my opinion, declared sovereign rights over the Altai-Turkestan line, and his partisans have begun staging raids and sabotaging parts of the Trans-Siberian. In response the Czech-Slovaks sent one of their armoured trains up the track towards Barnaul but they only got as far as a small station called Evsino. Do you know this place? You can see, without maps we are operating blind.'

Pavel nodded, 'It's not very far from Novonikolayevsk, maybe just twenty *versts*.'

'Anyway,' continued the captain, 'at Evsino the Czech-Slovak train met a Bolshevik armoured train coming the other way. There were only a few shots fired, and then the Bolshevik train retreated, but they tore up a piece of the track so the Czech-Slovak train couldn't follow.'

'So, is that the end of any attempt to take Barnaul?'

Captain Spencer shook his head. 'If there's one thing an army commander can't abide, it is to leave a flank exposed, and Tsaplin's Bolsheviks remain a threat. So, with a bit of friendly persuasion from their British ally, combined with the antics of Comrade Tsaplin, the Czech-Slovaks are now committed to taking Barnaul, and I will keep them to their promise.'

Pavel recalled the warning Mikhail had given him about the captain, and wondered what "friendly persuasion" entailed, but pushed the thought aside as the captain ushered him into the back meeting-room.

'Come, there is someone I would like you to meet.'

The man in the Czech officer's uniform looked up from behind his desk as they entered. Pavel was a bit surprised how young he looked for a senior officer, and guessed he was in his late thirties. He had a flop of brown hair swept to the side, a slightly thin face with thick lips, and a small strip of a moustache. But what was most striking was a set of icy-blue eyes that seemed to bore straight through you.

'This is the man I talked to you about,' said Captain Spencer, nodding towards Pavel.

'Pavel Dmitrievich,' said Captain Spencer, 'I would like to introduce you to Colonel Gajda of the Czech-Slovak Legion. Colonel, this is the man from Barnaul.'

'So, you know Barnaul,' the officer spoke Russian with a strange clipped accent, 'and the Captain said you can be trusted; that is indeed a rare commodity in Russia these days.'

The colonel stood and strode across the room to a table cluttered with several rolls of maps.

'Come over here,' he waved Pavel forward. 'They're probably all inaccurate, but it's all we've managed to find.'

He unrolled one of the maps and flattened it out on the table, holding it down with his elbows while he placed paperweights on the four corners.

'Can you read a map?' the Colonel asked, bluntly.

Pavel nodded. "Yes, of course I can.'

'That's good,' said the Colonel. 'It appears not all your countrymen are capable of doing so. Now look at it and tell me if you think it's accurate.'

The Colonel stepped aside to let Pavel study the map. Pavel oriented himself by locating Novonikolayevsk and tracing the line of the Ob River up towards Barnaul.

'Is there a scale?' he asked.

Captain Spencer leaned over and indicated a rough scale bar at the bottom corner. Pavel used two fingers to measure out the distance.

'It's nowhere near scale and half the towns and stations are missing, and it hasn't even got the Chumysh marked.'

'What's the Chumysh?' asked the Colonel.

'It's a main tributary to the Ob and it enters about here,' Pavel said, indicating with his finger a place on the map. 'The Altai line crosses it before it gets to the Ob Bridge leading into Barnaul.'

'Is it defensible?' demanded the Colonel.

'Pavel Dmitrievich is not schooled in military art,' intervened Captain Spencer.

The Colonel, with a wave of an arm, swept Captain Spencer's interjection aside. 'But he should know the difference between a brook, a stream, and a river.'

The Colonel looked at Pavel quizzically and waited for an answer.

'It's a river, wide in places, with some steep forested banks. Sometimes fordable in places but, at this time of year, who knows? It depends whether the spring run-off has finished.'

The Colonel walked back to his desk and sat down, picked up a pencil and started nervously tapping away at his desk blotter.

'Has the Captain told you of our intentions?'

Pavel glanced across to Captain Spencer, who nodded.

'The Captain has told me you intend to capture the line to Barnaul and push the Reds out.'

'No,' came the blunt reply from the Colonel. 'We don't intend to push them out; we intend to destroy them. If all we do is push them back they'll just fade back into the forest, form into partisan groups, then continue to attack us and sabotage the Trans-Siberian. I want us to encircle the Red force in Barnaul and crush them. Leave them no avenue of escape.'

'If I'm permitted to offer an opinion?' asked Pavel.

The Colonel nodded his assent.

'If you only attack up the train line, all they have to do is to retreat across the Ob rail bridge back into Barnaul. There are heights overlooking the bridge on the Barnaul side of the river. The bridge would be easy to defend from the heights, or they could blow it up, and anyway it is long and narrow and exposed, and it would be almost suicidal to attempt to storm it by force.'

The Colonel permitted himself a wry smile. 'I thought you said your man didn't have a military mind, Captain Spencer.' He leaned back in his chair and clasped his hands behind his head. 'And this is exactly why we've decided to move up troops simultaneously on both sides of the river. The main force will be led by armoured trains on the rail line up the east bank, while another force moves overland from here along the western bank of the Ob. This way we can attack Barnaul from two directions and close the trap. Is there anything that the maps don't show us which would prevent us from doing this?'

'For the same reason they built the railway on the east bank, not the west bank,' answered Pavel. 'The land is low over there, and you would have to wade through two hundred *versts* of muddy tracks and swamps, or you would need to make a big diversion. Remember the river is in spring flood at the moment, making matters worse. You need to use the railway and the east bank, or you'll never get there.'

The Colonel stood up and started pacing the room. He suddenly swung around and confronted Captain Spencer.

'So, what does our military observer suggest now? I agreed to your plan, but it does not include sacrificing the blood of the Legion in a frontal assault on a long, exposed rail bridge. There must be another way.'

'By ferry.'

There was a moment's silence as both officers turned and stared at Pavel.

'By ferry?' asked the colonel.

'Downstream from the bridge there are ferries. It's not marked on this map, but there's a village and they've ferry boats that can cross, even at this time of year.'

'What if they've removed all the ferries to the other side of the river?' asked the Colonel. 'That's what I would do in their position.'

'You're possibly right,' answered Pavel, 'but I am guessing there are still people on the east bank who'll have their small boats. Perhaps a few of your men could cross the river at night. If you choose your time and place correctly you may be able to get across undetected. And if the ferries are not heavily guarded you may be able to take some and use them to transport a larger force.'

The Colonel walked over to his desk and returned with a pencil. 'Here, mark it on the map. What's this village called?'

'Gonba,' answered Pavel.

Colonel Gajda strode to the office door and pulled it open.

'Orderly,' he barked. 'Find Lieutenants Czesnovsky and Gusarek and tell them I want them here urgently, and tell the two Russian commanders, Sergeev and Travin, to come also. And, when you've done that, I want you to take this gentlemen to the cartography section.' The colonel walked back over to the desk, rolled up the spread-out map, and handed it to Pavel. 'Here, you can take this piece of rubbish with you and help them draw up some decent maps, even if they're rough.'

'And after I've done that,' asked Pavel, 'am I permitted to leave?'

The colonel shook his head. 'No, you come with us. Our engineers are replacing the tracks now, and we will send our armoured trains up the line tomorrow. At the place that you designate, you will leave the train and guide a detachment of men to this village called Gonba. Can you do this?'

Pavel hesitated. 'I think so.'

Colonel Gajda clapped his hands together and looked at Captain Spencer. 'Well, that's all done then. We just need a bit of luck in finding some boats.'

Captain Spencer touched Pavel's arm. 'The colonel was asking me about Matvei Tsaplin, the Bolshevik commander. What can you tell us about him?'

Pavel hesitated. 'I've only spoken with him a couple of times. We didn't get on that well – in fact, not at all.'

Colonel Gajda looked Pavel directly in the eye. 'But what sort of man am I dealing with here? I want to know what he's like, whether he's capable, what sort of commander is he?'

'Well, he's not a military man, he's actually a weaver by trade, but he is a committed communist. He was a delegate to one of the early Bolshevik conferences, one of the party faithful, and he's head of the Barnaul Revolutionary Soviet.'

'And he will be directing the Barnaul defense?' asked the colonel, raising an eyebrow.

'Barnaul is full of army deserters and I'm sure there will be a few among them who will be giving him advice.'

'That's useful, but only as long as it's good advice.'

'And that he heeds it,' added Captain Spencer.

'So,' asked the colonel, 'what is it that you don't like about the man?'

Pavel took a deep breath. 'He had my brother killed.'

Captain Spencer accompanied Pavel out of the adjutant's office. It was good to get outside into the sunshine and fresh air. Pavel had been uneasy in the colonel's presence; it felt as though he was before a board of examiners who were picking over every detail and nuance of what he said. 'I'm not sure what's expected of me,' he told the captain. 'I've never had any military experience.'

The captain clapped him on the shoulder. 'Leave the soldiering to the soldiers. Just lead them to Gonba, or whatever you call the village, and leave the rest to them. Don't try to win any bravery awards, and don't put yourself in harm's way. We need guides, and you're much more useful alive than dead.'

'What I cannot understand,' Pavel replied, 'is why the Bolsheviks are making it so difficult for the Legion to get out of Russia? Anyone would think they would be well served to see the backs of them, and as quickly as possible.'

The captain smiled. 'You're right, and I think Messrs Lenin and Trotsky would agree wholeheartedly with you. What we're finding is many of the Bolshevik partisan groups, up and down the line, are little more than bunches of bandits run by local warlords. They control sections of the line as if it is their own territory and, like gatekeepers, they want to extract as much as they can from those who wish to pass. What it also tells us is the Bolshevik hierarchy sitting in Petrograd has little control over what happens here in Siberia, even if the partisan group is truly Bolshevik. The distances are too vast, and the communications too poor.'

'I can see the problem.'

'Problem!' the captain put his head back and laughed heartily. 'It's exactly what I've wanted. The Bolshevik partisans attack the Legion, the Legion fights back and then they fight up and down the line to join up their various army groups, and, in the mean time, they secure the Trans-Siberian which means the armaments get through to your forces. What else would you want? They've just become your most important ally in your war against the Bolsheviks.'

'But they're not Russian, and this isn't their civil war – it's ours.'

'You're exactly right, and the White leaders, whoever they are, should never forget it. At the moment the goals of the Czech-Slovak Legion and your Siberian Army coincide. But that will not last forever, so take advantage of it while you can.'

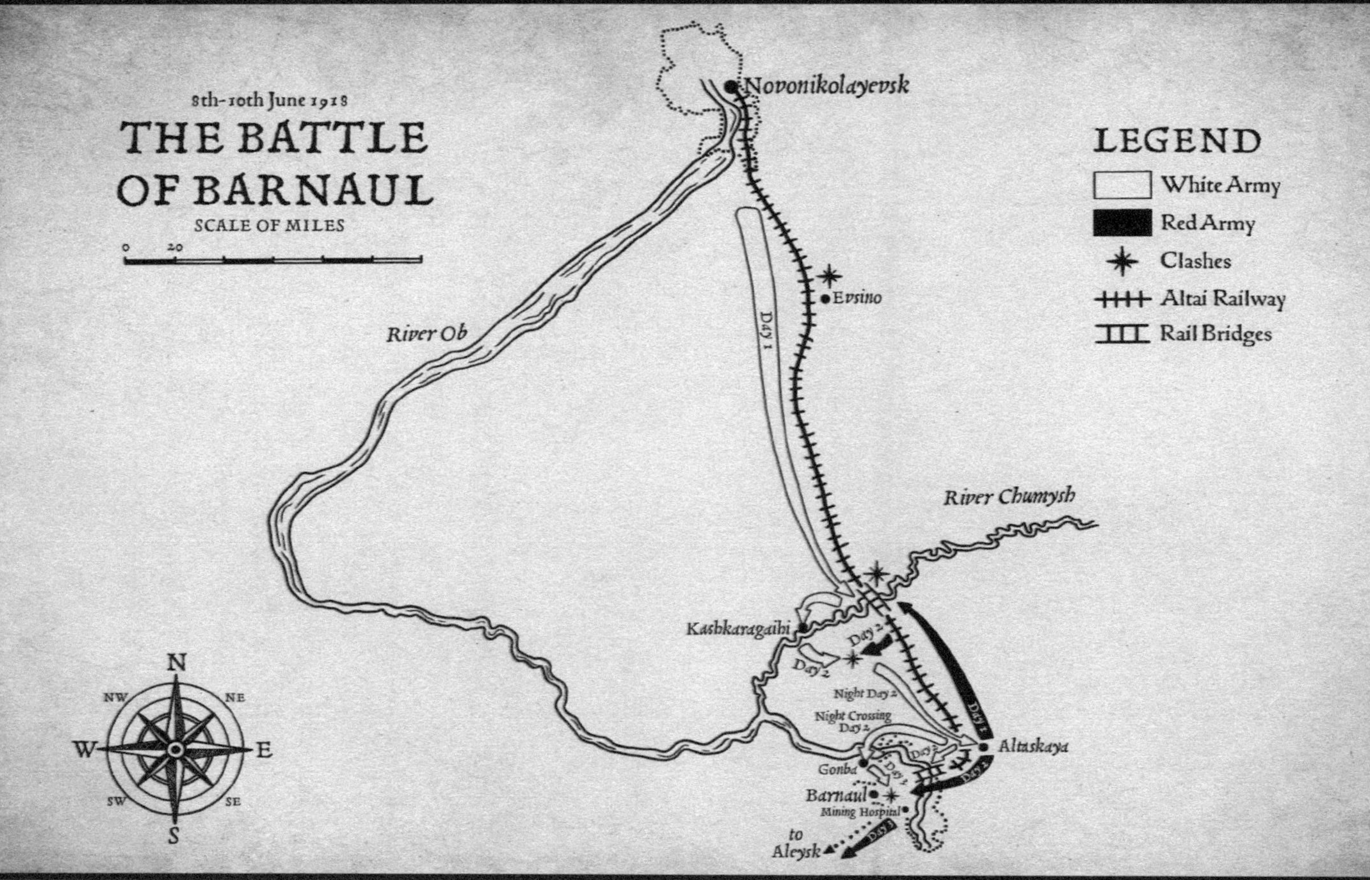

8th-10th June 1918
THE BATTLE OF BARNAUL
SCALE OF MILES
0   20
LEGEND
White Army
Red Army
Clashes
Altai Railway
Rail Bridges
Novonikolayevsk
River Ob
Day 1
Evsino
River Chumysh
Kashkaragaihi
Day 2
Day 2
Night Day 2
Night Crossing Day 2
Day 2
Gonba
Day 3
Day 3
Altaskaya
Day 3
Barnaul
Mining Hospital
to Aleysk
Day 3
N
NW
NE
W
E
SW
SE
S

Chapter 32

THE CHUMYSH RIVER

June 8 1918

THE ARMORED TRAIN stood alongside the platform at the Novonikolayevsk station. It was a long, ugly brute of a machine, its sides covered with blackened armor plate with narrow slots for windows and firing points. It had one flatcar in front of the locomotive, and hauled another two immediately behind the coal tender. The perimeter on each flatcar was stacked high with sandbags that shielded the heavy machine guns on tripods. On another flatbed sat a large howitzer, surrounded by armor shields on all sides, and held in place by thick chains. There were a number of armor-sided boxcars bringing up the rear with light machine guns positioned on their roofs. The whole train had the menacing look of an impregnable, fortified arsenal on rails.

Pavel glanced up at the sky. The sun was just rising in the east, the first light spreading rays against the underbelly of low clouds, turning them orange-pink. Pavel shivered and buttoned up his coat. The morning remained slightly chilly, but the rising sun would soon burn away the cloud and the temperature would quickly climb.

He glanced over at the machine-gunners on the flatbeds. The Czech-Slovaks appeared immune to the cold. They were all sitting around in open shirts with their sleeves rolled up, wearing their soft-peaked khaki caps. They were laughing and sharing cigarettes, seemingly uncaring about what might lie ahead. With their joviality and light-hearted banter it was as though they were about to head off for a picnic in the country.

Further to the rear of the train, the line of *teplushkas* was packed to overflowing with Czech-Slovak soldiers and White Russian volunteers from the newly formed Novonikolayevsk Regiment. The boxcars all had their doors open with soldiers sitting in the doorways with their legs dangling out, while others stood behind them, chatting and smoking. Every one of them seemed to be in a buoyant mood and itching to get the train convoy underway.

Pavel had spoken to a number of the volunteers, including a few of the Czech-Slovaks who could speak rudimentary Russian. They all exuded the same confidence based on self-belief that the Bolshevik force they were facing was nothing more than a hastily organized rabble of deserters and civilian militia that would be easily swept aside.

A large part of this confidence was built on the belief in themselves – the White Force comprising the battle-hardened Czech-Slovak veterans and the Russian Volunteer Regiment made up of a preponderance of seasoned regulars, including professional officers and NCOs.

'There may be some truth in what you say,' Pavel said to one of the officers in the Volunteers, 'but don't totally dismiss the force you're facing in Barnaul. Many of the deserters are battle-hardened, and the militia is committed, if nothing else, and will likely be led by veterans. I expect they'll put up a fight and, after all, they're in a strong defensive position which puts us at something of a disadvantage.'

The Volunteer officer laughed, and dismissively waved his comments away. 'They'll run like damned hares, just you wait and see.'

Pavel felt a touch on his shoulder and was startled to find Captain Spencer standing alongside him. He had not heard the captain approach along the platform and wondered how such a tall man could move so quietly and quickly.

'Remember what I told you,' said Captain Spencer. 'You're going as a guide, and a dead guide is no use to anybody and can jeopardize the whole operation. So keep your head down and stay out of trouble.'

'How will I know what they want me to do?'

'Don't worry, they'll let you know when they need you.'

'Will you be coming too?' asked Pavel.

The captain shook his head. 'I'm needed back here. There's a lot of telegraph traffic coming through from Vladivostok needing urgent answers. Good luck and stay safe.'

The captain went to walk away, but turned. 'Oh, there's one more thing. You may be asked to go into Barnaul ahead of the attack. We've information there's a group of anti-Bolsheviks in town who are prepared to come out in support when we launch the assault. It would be useful if they stirred up trouble and had the Bolsheviks looking over their shoulder. We suspect there's a good chance you may know some of these people.'

Pavel felt a knot of fear form in the pit of his stomach. 'It's been a long time,' he answered, after some hesitation. 'I just don't know who may be left, or even how to locate them. If they've managed to survive for this long it means they would've all been in hiding. And anyway, how would I get into the town?'

'We've some people who can probably get you through the lines, so the question is, would you be prepared to give it a try? We don't underestimate the danger but, if you can succeed, it could make the difference between winning and losing.'

Pavel stood and thought for a moment. On the one hand the captain was telling him to stay out of harm's way but, on the other, he was asking him to volunteer for something that was clearly dangerous. The captain didn't seem to be concerned about the contradiction, and

Pavel didn't want to ask, so he finally nodded. 'If you're certain it will help us win.'

The captain gave a smile and clapped Pavel on the shoulder. 'I knew I could rely on you.'

The armored train moved cautiously along the track towards Barnaul, often at little more than walking pace, and regularly stopping while engineers went ahead to check bridges and culverts for mines. So far, everything seemed clear, but there were several places where trees had been felled across the line, or spikes had been removed that had held the rails to the sleepers. The clearing of trees and repairs to the rails all ate away time. What should have been a relatively short journey of just a few hours was taking an excruciating length of time.

Exacerbating the situation were snipers. Whenever the train passed through a densely wooded section of the line, more often than not, a shot rang out. The lone sniper would fire once, and then slip quietly away into the forest before a detachment could locate them. The snipers were more than just an annoyance; their shots were usually from close range and, with frightening regularity, the sniper's bullet found its mark.

Pavel had been instructed to ride in one of the medical boxcars that were located right at the rear of the line of carriages. One boxcar had been fitted out as a mobile operating theatre, while the others served as medical wards with tiers of stretchers for the wounded. An army surgeon and three assistants, all wearing long, white rubber aprons and gumboots sat around in the operating theatre, waiting for their first patients. Pavel's stomach heaved when he looked over the array of scalpels, pliers, long pincers, sewing kits and hacksaws set out on a long scrubbed metal table close to the operating table.

When the first stretchers carrying the wounded from the sniper fire were brought back, Pavel was put to use helping the medical staff, handing them rolls of bandages, ladling out water to the wounded, or lighting cigarettes for them. He was happy to be busy in the wards, since it kept him away from the operating theatre, and out of sight of the associated blood and gore. The surgeon and his team worked quickly and efficiently to stem bleeding and stitch up wounds but, even then, the carriage floor quickly became slippery with blood. Additional orderlies were kept busy sluicing the floor with buckets of water and sweeping the pools of crimson-colored water out the door.

Most of the wounded men stoically endured the pain of the operation. There were only rudimentary procedures used – first, a liberal dose of brandy given to each man, and then raw alcohol to clean the wounds. In extreme cases, when the soldier was in intense pain, opiates were used, but supply was limited and the drug was dispensed frugally. Generally the men remained cheerful and did not complain, most being thankful they had somehow cheated death and survived.

The foliage on each side of the track gradually thinned out as the train progressed, and there was a respite from the sniper fire. The delivery of stretchers to the boxcar trickled to a halt and, much to Pavel's relief, he was released from his duties and was able to sit at the open door of the boxcar, smoking a cheroot, and watching the countryside slide by.

Pavel mentally ticked off the familiar landmarks as they passed. They were now well past the Evsino station where the two armored trains had met, and Pavel guessed they were getting close to the Chumysh River.

The train was managing to keep up good progress without the continual stoppages for snipers, and had picked up some speed, when suddenly, without warning, there was a sudden lurch as the brakes screeched, the wheels locked, and the train juddered to a halt. Pavel had to grab the door handle to prevent himself being catapulted out of the boxcar, and all the operating instruments on the table clattered onto the floor, amid a great deal of swearing from the medical staff, and cries of pain from the wounded.

Officers' whistles pierced the air, and boots crunched on gravel as soldiers jumped out of the boxcars and ran towards the front of the train. A heavy machine gun had opened up from one of the flatbeds at the front of the train. Pavel could feel the reverberation from the firing run through the carriage.

Soldiers were starting to fan out on both sides of the track and a ferocious exchange of rifle fire had begun. Pavel flinched as bullets hit the armored sides of the boxcar and ricocheted away.

'Close the fucking door,' one of the medical staff shouted across to Pavel. He was reaching for the door handle when there was a sudden crash of couplings and a jolt. Then the wheels screeched and spun, and the train started to reverse, slowly backing up until it had retreated around a bend and out of the direct line of fire.

'You can open that door again,' Pavel was told, 'they'll be starting to stretcher back wounded in a few minutes.'

A soldier's face appeared at the door of the boxcar. He looked around and pointed at Pavel. 'You over there, come with me.' He had a heavy Slovak accent and had to shout to be heard over the gunfire.

Pavel jumped down from the boxcar and followed the soldier forward. On both sides of the train Czech-Slovak soldiers and White Volunteers were falling back and regrouping out of the direct line of fire. Meanwhile, the heavy machine guns were being dismantled from their mounts on the flatcars and moved into positions amongst the trees on both sides of the track.

An officer from one of the volunteer regiments stopped Pavel and pulled him aside, just as one of the re-positioned machine guns opened up close by. The noise was deafening.

'There's a river up ahead,' yelled the officer, 'and they've pulled up the track and sandbagged the bridge. They've set up positions on the other bank from where they can enfilade our troops.'

'What's enfilade? I don't understand.'

'Flanking fire – they'll cut our troops to ribbons if we try to force the bridge. And this isn't a just a bunch of local militia, we're facing damned regulars if you ask me.'

'So what do you want me to do?'

'Come with me.' The officer waved him to follow, and they ran forward to the first boxcar behind the flatcar where the howitzer was mounted. Hands reached down and roughly hauled Pavel up into the boxcar where a huddle of officers crouched in a circle. One of Pavel's maps had been spread out on the floor.

The officers moved aside to let him join the circle. 'This is Commander Gusarek,' one of the Russian officers said, indicating a short officer with dark eyes, a thin moustache, and a worried look on his face. 'He wants to know where we are.'

'If it's a decent-sized river then it has to be the Chumysh.' Pavel pointed to it on the map. 'Which means we're still about eighty *versts* short of the Ob River Bridge and Barnaul.'

The heavy machine gun had started up again, making it almost impossible to hear. 'We guessed that,' the officer shouted into Pavel's ear, 'but what can we do? Are there any fording points close by so we can get around their position?'

Pavel took the map and twisted it around to face him. He found the Chumysh and traced the river to its confluence with the Ob.

'I didn't mark it because it's really just a few huts, but there's a small village near where the Churmysh joins the Ob. It's called Kashkaragaihi. Here the Chumysh widens and shallows. In summer you can easily wade across near the village. The question is whether we can get across with the spring thaw.'

'How long would it take to get there?' asked an officer.

'I would think about two hours' march,' replied Pavel, 'assuming you don't meet any resistance.'

'Nothing closer?' asked Commander Gusarek.

Pavel shook his head. 'It's the thaw.'

Gusarek heaved himself upright with a grunt and looked around at his officers. 'We can't storm the bridge without heavy losses, so our only option is to try to get around them.'

He looked at his watch. 'We've only a few hours of daylight left. We need to keep pressure on them here and pin them down. Hopefully we can get some troops down to this village and across the Chumysh before dark. Then we can hit them in the flank and rear tomorrow morning.'

There was a murmur of agreement among the officers. Commander

Gusarek singled out one of the Czech-Slovak officers. 'Kapitan Czesnovsky, we'll keep your unit here and use them to pin down the Red force guarding the bridge. Where's Kapitan Sergeev?'

A tall, thin man with a boyish face in a crumpled Russian uniform stepped forward and snapped a salute.

'Take this man as your guide and get your Novonikolayevsk Regiment down to this village and across the Chumysh as fast as you can. We expect you to mount an attack, even if it's just a demonstration, on the bridge defenders by mid morning tomorrow.' The commander looked at his watch. 'Let's say 10.00am – that should give you enough time to move up. Your objective is to force them back so we can get men across the river from here and put a repair crew onto the bridge.'

Pavel, Mikhail and *Kapitan* Sergeev lay on their stomachs on a small rise overlooking Kashkaragaihi. The village was nothing more than a small collection of rough-hewn log huts with thatched roofs, close to the muddy bank of the river. There was a single fenced vegetable garden and a bramble-fenced corral for animals.

Sergeev had his binoculars out, and had been studying each of the wooden huts and both riverbanks now for several minutes. He shook his head and handed the binoculars across to Mikhail.

'I've scanned the village and the banks a dozen times, and I can't see any movement. Here, you have a look.'

'It's strange,' commented Mikhail, as he raised the binoculars to his eyes, 'the village seems totally deserted. There's not a single animal or person in sight – absolutely nothing. It doesn't feel right.'

'And there's no smoke coming from any of the chimneys,' pointed out Pavel, 'and it's nearly dusk. The villagers would normally be cooking their evening meal by now.'

'We need to send someone down there to check it out before it gets dark,' said Sergeev. 'I'll go back and organize a volunteer.'

'Do you want me to go?' asked Pavel. He wasn't at all keen on the idea, but he was the only one in civilian clothes, and that might raise less suspicion if he was spotted.

Sergeev shook his head. 'I've been told to keep you alive, or it'll be my head on the chopping block. No, I'll find someone else.'

'Then I'll go,' offered Mikhail. 'At least I'm a local of sorts, and know what to look for.'

Mikhail edged his way forward, crawling on hands and knees through the underbrush down the short slope towards the village. Sergeev had brought up some riflemen and had positioned them along the crest to give fire support if required.

When Mikhail got close enough, he raised himself up, and dashed across the bare ground towards the wall of the nearest hut. Holding his rifle ready, he kicked at the door of the hut and then jumped to one side. The door swung open. Mikhail waited a few moments, and then cautiously peered inside.

It took time for his eyes to adjust, and then he could see the hut was empty, devoid of any occupants. However, there were signs of recent habitation. A stack of dirty plates sat on the table, some with uneaten food still on them. It was as though the occupants had suddenly dropped everything and run.

Mikhail knelt and touched the ash in the hearth. The top layer was damp and cool to the touch, but when he scraped the sodden ash away, underneath remained glowing embers.

Mikhail moved from hut to hut and repeated the exercise. It was a similar scene in each, and he could only conclude the villagers had got warning of their approach, had dropped everything, doused their fires and fled, taking with them whatever possessions and animals they could manage.

Mikhail came out of the last hut and waved up at Sergeev and Pavel to come down.

'There's not a bloody soul,' Mikhail told Sergeev, 'but everything points to them finding out we were coming and getting out, maybe just half an hour before we got here. I suspect they're not too far away, probably hiding close by in the forest.'

'Then they'll be watching us,' said Sergeev. 'Let's get all the men down here and set up a defensive perimeter around the village. Then we find out if we can ford this river.'

Sergeev turned to Pavel. 'Do you have any idea why they would run? We're not exactly any threat to them.'

'How would they know that? They're peasants after all – always distrustful, whether we're White or Red. But I don't think we should be worried. My guess is that they'll hide in the forest and watch us until we leave.'

'But will any of them inform the Bolsheviks up at the bridge that we're here?' asked Sergeev.

'You'd be wise to assume the worst.' answered Pavel.

'Then let's get down and have a look at this river crossing. I want to see if we can get over to the other side before nightfall.'

Sergeev and Pavel made their way down a slippery path to the bank of the river. They moved cautiously, using the protection of any cover available, mindful they were exposed and could come under fire at any time.

The Chumysh was flowing strongly with the spring melt and was running high. Fording would be difficult.

'Holy Christ,' exclaimed Sergeev, 'how are we going to get across?'

Pavel looked around. There was a partially collapsed part of the riverbank next to an old willow tree. He went down and studied the mud near the water's edge. There were faint signs of footprints of men and some animals that someone had tried to obliterate but a few slight imprints still remained.

Pavel searched through the briars at the base of the thick willow trunk until he located a thin rope tied around a surface root. He tugged the rope free from where it had been buried, and followed the rope down to the water's edge. He pulled gently on the rope, careful not to put too much strain on it. Slowly, hand-over-hand, he hauled in the end of a much thicker sisal hawser from the river.

'Can you get some men to give me a hand?' he called over to

Sergeev. 'It's bloody heavy and we need to pull it in as tight as we can and tie it around the base of this tree.'

Mikhail was first across. He had removed his trousers, and waded across in his long underwear and boots, carrying his clothes in a bundle and his rifle slung across his back while his other hand held on to the slippery cable. At first the icy water made him gasp as he waded deeper into the river, and he grimaced as the water reached his groin.

The riverbed was strewn with large, slippery boulders but, if he steadied himself with the hawser, he could brace against the fast-flowing current. Numbed and saturated, he finally struggled up the far bank and signaled for the rest of his men to follow.

His company took almost an hour to get across the river, since the fast-flowing current allowed only a few men at a time to cross. Those reaching the far bank pushed out to form a perimeter and started digging themselves in. The last of Mikhail's company barely made it across before darkness fell.

'It's far too risky to get more men across in the dark,' Sergeev told Pavel. 'At least we've now established ourselves on the other bank so we can protect the ford in case the Reds mount an attack. We'll get you and the rest of the men across at first light, and then you need to lead us back up to the bridge.'

Sergeev grinned, and patted Pavel on the back. 'You did well today. How did you know about the rope across the river?'

Pavel smiled. 'I didn't, but it's an old local trick, and I just got lucky.'

Chapter 33
THE ADVANCE FROM KASHKARAGAIHI

9 June 1918

A LOW MORNING RIVER mist hung over the Chumysh, shrouding the river crossing in a thin, diaphanous veil of white. But the mist was limiting the penetration of the pre-dawn light, and Pavel still could not make out the far bank where Mikhail's company had positioned themselves overnight. The air was still, and apart from birdsong heralding the breaking dawn, there was almost complete silence on the riverbank.

The night had passed quietly for the regiment, including Mikhail's group on the far bank, but it had been a nervous wait. While there was neither sign nor sound of the village's inhabitants, everyone assumed they were out there somewhere, remaining well hidden and watching their every move.

Pavel had stayed in the deserted village along with the 2nd Company, which was commanded by Sergei. He was thankful he hadn't been required to ford the river with Mikhail's unit. He worried about Mikhail, but the thought of spending the night isolated on the far bank, while attempting to sleep in cold, wet clothes, did give Pavel cause to count his blessings.

Sergeev and Sergei came looking for him before first light, and together they made their way down to the water's edge. The far bank wasn't yet visible, but they checked that the hawser across the river was still in place.

'We can't wait,' Sergeev told Sergei, 'we need to start getting more men across now.'

Sergeev turned to Pavel. 'They sent a messenger down to us last night. They're still bottled up at the bridge but will try to storm it as soon as there's any sign of us attacking, so we need to get going urgently. I want you to go across the river with the first men of the 2nd company, locate *Kapitan* Mehenov and the 1st Company, and start guiding his men back up towards the rail line. The 2nd Company will follow as soon as we get all the men across. But don't get too far ahead. You need to allow them to catch up so we don't get too strung out.'

Pavel took off his trousers and socks, carefully rolled them up into a ball, and pushed them into his small haversack. Then he pulled his boots back on and slung his rifle over his shoulder.

The sisal hawser was slimy and cold to touch. As soon as he took his first steps the icy water filled his boots, but he needed them on to maintain his footing on the slippery rocks of the ford. The water was close to freezing, not much more than melted ice. After the initial shock he was surprised how quickly his body adjusted, and the sharp pain he felt initially quickly became tolerable as numbness set in.

He was the third man in line to cross. They were spaced out to avoid putting too much strain on the hawser and, save for the sound of the other men's splashes and curses, he could barely make them out ahead. He caught up with the two of them when he reached the muddy riverbank on the far side. Together they found a log in a nearby clearing and sat down to tug off their boots, pour out the muddy water, and rub their feet vigorously until they got some feeling back again.

After Pavel had dried himself and dressed, he looked about. The first crack of dawn was yet to appear, but he could make out vague human forms dotted about on the edge of the clearing. He just hoped they were Mikhail's men.

They were, and they had dug a series of shallow foxholes forming a rough semi-circular perimeter to protect the crossing. Pavel found Mikhail sitting off to one side of the clearing with his back against a large fallen tree. He looked up and grinned. 'How did you like your early morning swim?'

'A little too brisk for my liking.'

'Welcome to a soldier's life.'

'*Kapitan* Sergeev sent me across with the first men. He wants you to start heading back towards the bridge and not wait for the 2nd Company.'

Mikhail frowned. 'I can understand his haste, but I don't think that's a particularly good strategy. If the villagers have contacted the Reds, they would have had time to move troops into position during the night. We should be staying together in case we walk into an ambush.'

'I'm only repeating what Sergeev told me. He got a message last night saying they need us there urgently. Sergeev was insistent you start to move out but, to be fair, he did say we shouldn't get too far ahead so we give the 2nd a chance to catch up.'

Mikhail heaved himself up. 'Well, he's the boss so we'd better get on with it then. I'll get the company ready to head out but, in the meantime, you could try to locate a path that will lead us back towards the bridge. I suppose we just need to follow the river bank, isn't that right?'

Pavel shook his head. 'No, the Chumysh winds about all over the place. The river has changed its course over time and there are several cut-off parts we call "bow lakes". It can be very confusing and you need to know when you can cut off a loop and when you can't. Trust me, I've hunted this area before.'

Commander Gusarek had slept fitfully on a canvas stretcher in the forward boxcar. He had left orders to wake him at any sign of trouble but, even though nothing was reported, he had lain awake for most of the night nursing an uneasy feeling. It was unusually quiet over on the Bolshevik side of the river – too quiet.

The distance between the opposing forces was the width of the river and, where the bridge crossed, it was quite narrow. Under the cover of darkness Gusarek had managed to get some men down to the bank. Hidden by bridge supports, they had set up a listening post, trying to detect any movement of the Bolshevik troops.

All soldiers manning a line, no matter how silent they try to be, make some noise – perhaps a discreet cough, a whispered conversation, or the strike of a match. Sentries are also changed over. In the still air of the night, the smallest sound can carry a long way, and yet there had been deathly silence from the Bolshevik position.

'Apologies, Commander.'

Gusarek grunted, rubbed his eyes, and was immediately alert. He swung his feet to the floor and looked at the Czech-Slovak corporal. 'Is there trouble?'

'Compliments from *Kapitan* Czesnovsky, sir. He would like to you meet him near the entrance of the bridge.'

Gusarek reached for his cap and pulled on his greatcoat. He jumped down from the boxcar and, stepping on the wooden sleepers to avoid crunching the gravel bed, carefully followed the corporal forward. A waning moon gave just sufficient light for them not to need a lantern.

Czesnovsky met him part way there. 'Sorry to disturb you Commander,' he whispered, 'but I thought you should be informed.'

'What is it?'

'There's still no sound coming from the other side but, every now and then, the moon casts enough light and we can just make out their positions. Then a cloud masks the moon, and we can't.'

'So?'

'One moment we can see the parts of their trenches that are manned, and then they're gone.'

'What do you mean, gone?'

'It seems every time the moon clouds over, they're moving men.'

'Which direction?' asked Gusarek.

'We're not totally sure but, by the look of it, we suspect they're starting to send detachments downstream. That would be heading towards *Kapitan* Sergeev's column.'

Gusarek stared at the ground for a moment. Then he gripped Czesnovsky's arm. 'I'm not waiting any longer. Let's get all our troops up here. We're going to stage an assault on the bridge. If they're shifting men to block Sergeev, then he may never get here. However, it may also mean that they have been forced to weaken their defences here.'

'But it's still not going to be easy. We're going to get quite a few casualties.'

'What's the choice? Take casualties here, or sacrifice Sergeev's two companies? And, whatever happens, we still need to take this damned bridge.' Gusarek looked around. 'Have we brought up that field howitzer yet?'

Czesnovsky pointed towards a dark shape off to one side of the bridge. 'It's only a 4 inch, but it'll give them a bit of a fright.'

'Get them to position it so it can target the Bolshevik machine gun positions at the end of the bridge.'

Gusarek looked towards the east. 'Dawn's not that far away, but we're not going to wait for it. I want the first assault to go in on my signal.'

Mikhail's company was assembled and ready to move. Mikhail came up to Pavel at the head of the column and took him aside. 'As soon as you show the men the right path, I want you to drop back. We don't know what's out there, and there'll be plenty of spots where we could walk into an ambush. I need to keep you safe so you can get us to that bridge.'

Pavel nodded solemnly. 'I don't need any convincing.'

He showed Mikhail his compass and pointed towards the small

gap where a rough path entered the forest. 'We need to take that and head north-east until we get past the next bend in the river. Then we can head due north until we meet up with the river again. It'll save a lot of time.'

Mikhail had been going back and forth to the ford, regularly checking on the progress of the 2nd Company. 'Sergei is just coming across now,' he told Pavel, 'but it's slow with just three men at a time. Before we head out I want you to show him the path we're taking. Tell him we'll halt at the first river bend and allow them to catch up. When we see the first of their men moving up, only then will we strike out for the next bend. Do you understand?'

The forest comprised a mixture of spruce, birch and larch. They were mostly tall, mature trees with few low branches and with little undergrowth on the forest floor, apart from leaf litter and some fallen branches. The openness of the forest made the path easy to follow, even in the semi-darkness, but the scant cover meant they could easily be watched and were vulnerable to attack.

They had been making steady progress up the track for about half an hour when they heard the *crump* of artillery from somewhere up ahead of them. Then came the sound of rifle fire and the distinctive rattle of machine guns.

It was still quite dark, but the first thin shafts of sunlight were gradually starting to penetrate the canopy. However, the mottled light reaching the forest floor was still faint, and left much of their surrounds in dark shadows. Mikhail felt compelled to move on quickly despite not knowing what was out there, or what they could blunder in to. He kept pushing the pace of his men as much as he dared, while trying to avoid taking too many unnecessary risks.

They halted as planned at the first major bend, and the company fanned out on both sides of the track to take up a defensive position and wait. Mikhail dispatched a couple of men part way back down the track to see if there was any sign of the 2^(nd) Company, but when they returned the answer was a quick shake of the head.

As the distant gunfire intensified, Mikhail kept nervously checking his watch. 'I don't know what the hell is holding them up, but I don't think we can wait any longer,' he finally told Pavel. 'I want you to lead our scouts out and show them the way towards the next bend. We need to get moving, with or without Sergei's company.'

Mikhail had ensured those soldiers leading the column were all experienced scouts, men well versed in moving with stealth through the landscape, who would carefully probe forward to check the path ahead was safe before signalling the main column to follow. The further they moved upriver the more dense the forest became, and that afforded more opportunities for an ambush.

The prospect of ambush weighed heavily on Mikhail's mind, but he was heartened by the sound of the distant gunfire, hoping the enemy would be preoccupied with defending the area around the bridge. Perhaps, he thought to himself, they were yet to become aware of his advancing column.

Mikhail's training and experience had taught him it was unwise to feed men into battle in a piecemeal fashion, instead of building numbers until you had sufficient force to prevail. Yet he was aware Gusarek would be desperate for him to launch an attack, even a token demonstration, against the enemy's flank at the first opportunity. Frontal attacks against defended bridges were usually brutal and bloody affairs, and by the sound of the gunfire coming from that direction, Mikhail could only assume that Gusarek had decided not to wait but to take the risk anyway.

So it was with some trepidation, and against his better judgement, that Mikhail continued to move his small company of men forwards without the 2^(nd) Company. He worked his way up towards the head of the column to find Pavel and pulled him aside to let the other soldiers move through. 'How close are we getting to the bridge?'

'I think we're about halfway there. Maybe just half an hour away at this pace.'

Mikhail looked back down the track and shook his head.

'How far back do you think they are?' asked Pavel.

'I've sent men back to guide them up to us, and I hope to see the first of their platoons soon. Because they're not leading, they should have been able to move faster than us.'

Just then, the front of the column came to a standstill and the men bunched up. These stops weren't unusual, and occurred frequently, as the scouts halted the column while they probed forward into what they considered was high-risk territory. The men in the column would usually take the opportunity to fall out and have a welcome rest until the order came down the line for them to move. The men had been expressly forbidden to smoke during any breaks; the distinctive smell of tobacco could easily pinpoint their location.

This stop, however, went on a bit longer than usual, and Mikhail was getting nervous. 'I'm going up to check what's happening,' Mikhail told Pavel. He was just about to set off when one of the scouts came jogging back down the track.

'We want you to come up and have a look, sir,' he told Mikhail. 'Something's not quite right up ahead. We think it could be a trap.'

Mikhail told Pavel to stay where he was, and instructed the men to stay alert while he went to investigate.

The track ahead followed a curve in the river and narrowed, leaving just a narrow pathway between the riverbank and a low escarpment. A tree had fallen down from the escarpment, partially blocking the track. The tree wasn't a huge impediment, but it did block the view around the bend.

'What's the problem?' Mikhail asked the scout who had led him up. 'We could easily get around it, or just climb over it.'

The scout had crouched down behind a low bush. He carefully parted the bush and pointed towards the fallen tree. 'When it fell, it clipped some branches from adjacent trees. But look at those broken branches; those breaks are still raw. There's no wind to speak of, and trees just don't fall by themselves, unless of course they're pushed over or chopped down.'

'What are you suggesting?' Mikhail trusted his scouts' judgement, and usually sought their advice.

'This, if you ask me, sir, is a perfect place for an ambush and, if I was setting it up, I would position men behind the tree, and on top of the escarpment. As we move forward our men will be funnelled into that narrow area and they can hit us from the front and the side from above, and we'd have nowhere to run.'

'Have you seen any movement?' Mikhail asked.

The scout shook his head. 'Not a sign, but neither would I expect to see anything if it's a properly set up ambush. There's only one way to find out; either we try to flush them out, or cut inland to get around it.'

Mikhail thought for a moment. 'We're so close and, we can't afford to lose any more time by cutting inland. On the other hand, if we get into a fight, they will hear it up at the bridge, and it may be enough to get the Reds worried about a threat to their flank. I'll go back and get the men into position.'

'So, we're going to try and flush them out?'

Mikhail took another look at the fallen tree. 'Can you get a man close enough to lob a grenade over that log?'

Chapter 34

THE BATTLE FOR
THE CHUMYSH

9 June 1918

COMMANDER GUSAREK WAS also studying the sky in the east for the first crack of dawn. He had been over to speak to the gunners manning the howitzer and had personally checked the gun alignment. The gun had been positioned back from the entrance to the bridge, straddling the rails and pointing directly at the sandbag emplacement the Bolsheviks had built at the far exit of the bridge.

They had secretly manhandled the gun into place under cover of darkness, and had covered it with netting to camouflage its outline. The short distance across the river meant they would be firing at almost point-blank range. It should be difficult for them to miss.

Gusarek had instructed the howitzer to be loaded with a low-intensity explosive round. He prayed the blast would be sufficient to destroy the emplacement, and those in it, without seriously damaging the bridge's steel structure. In theory, the force of the blast should be mostly projected forward, not sideways, leaving the main bridge structure intact. It was a gamble he was prepared to take to minimise casualties.

'Just make sure you hit the damned emplacement the first time. You've only got this one chance,' Gusarek repeated to the gun captain. ' And wait for my signal before you fire.'

Gusarek checked the infantry were ready. They had drawn lots, and a company from the Tomsk Regiment would be first on to the bridge, immediately after the howitzer had fired. They had removed their backpacks and other superfluous equipment that could slow them down. The eighty-meter distance to the other side would be like a sprint race, with every second counting, and potentially marked in their blood. The group huddled together in the shadows, back a little way from the bridge, and waited nervously. Their faces were smeared in charcoal, bayonets fixed on their rifles, and each man carried a stick hand grenade in his hand.

Gusarek looked across to the howitzer crew. The round was in the chamber, the gunners were standing back with their hands over their ears, while the gun captain stood clear of the recoil zone with the long lanyard in his hand, looking over to the commander, and waiting for his signal.

The Tomsk Company quietly moved up as close as they dared to one side of the bridge's entrance. They could only just make out the Bolshevik sandbag emplacement at the far end of the bridge and knew the machine gun team would, if they survived the howitzer shot, be firing at them with deadly effect, straight down the narrow confines of the bridge. There would be no place to hide for the attacking force. It would take a combination of surprise, the accuracy of the howitzer crew, and their own sprint across the bridge, to give them their best chance of survival.

Another company of infantry also stood nervously waiting in the shadows, further back from the bridge. Their task was to follow the

Tomsk's charge onto the bridge – either to provide reinforcement, or to take over if the initial charge faltered.

The rest of the infantry and the machine-gunners were spread out along both sides of the bridge. They were to provide a concentrated covering fire against the rest of the Bolshevik position, hopefully forcing them to keep their heads down and preventing them from moving up to help defend against the attack.

Gusarek had one arm raised and his whistle in his mouth. He closed his eyes briefly, took a deep breath, and blew a long, shrill note. The gun captain yanked the lanyard and jumped back. The howitzer barked once and, almost simultaneously, the shot exploded in a cloud of black smoke at the base of the sandbag emplacement, sending a hail of dirt, gravel and sand high into the air. The officer in charge of the attacking force blew his whistle and waved the men forward.

Before the smoke had cleared, and with debris from the blast still clattering to the ground, the Tomsk infantry rushed onto the bridge and ran as hard as they could towards the far side. The men leading the charge paused two-thirds of the way across the bridge, pulled the pins from the handles of their stick grenades, and lobbed them towards the tattered remains of the emplacement. They then ducked as the grenades exploded, scattering shrapnel in all directions.

The Bolshevik forces were initially taken by surprise but were reacting now with concentrated machine gun and rifle fire. They tried to target the infantry now swarming across the bridge, but their oblique fire coming from either side of the bridge was largely thwarted by the steel structure that gave the attackers some cover.

But men still went down, and the bodies of dead and wounded started to pile up on the bridge, impeding those at the rear of the charge. Still, the momentum of the survivors at the front continued to carry them forward, over the destroyed remains of the emplacement, and into the forward trenches on the Bolshevik side. The attackers were now fanning out on both sides of the bridge as Gusarek, waving other companies forward, pushed more and more men onto the bridge to reinforce the gains.

The Bolshevik defenders put up a stout resistance, but they were now outnumbered. Some threw down their weapons and surrendered, while the major portion of their force started a frantic withdrawal back down the rail line.

Mikhail heard the intense fighting start up at the bridge as he was working his way back down the track from the site of the fallen tree. He was looking for Pavel, and found him lying down on the forest floor with his eyes closed. Mikhail leaned over and gave him a gentle nudge.

'Just taking a quick nap,' Pavel explained, rather apologetically. 'I've found it's useful to grab one when you can.'

'Not when we're in trouble.' Mikhail responded, a bit more gruffly than he intended.

He explained the situation by drawing a rough map with a stick in the dirt. 'If it's a trap, like we think it is, we'll be cut to ribbons. The escarpment overlooks us, and they can fire down from above. We won't be able to hold position there, so we're going to need to pull back somewhere more secure.' Mikhail looked at Pavel, 'So?'

Pavel thought for a moment. 'There's a bow lake just back down the track here in the loop of the river.' He borrowed Mikhail's stick and marked the spot with an "x". 'You would have your back to the river, but I think it's better than being stuck out in the open.'

Mikhail waved a corporal over and gave him instructions. 'If it's a trap we're going to adjust our position, so get ready to move men back and dig in. If you hear gunfire, Mr. Sukhov here will show you where I want you to go. Meanwhile, I'm going back to poke the bear and see what happens.'

Mikhail returned to the head of the column. One of his men had managed to squirm his way forward using a line of low bushes for cover. He had crawled almost halfway to the log.

'It's still a long way for him to throw,' Mikhail whispered to the lead scout.

'Don't worry. He can do it, but he's going to have to stand up to throw. That's when we'll find out.'

Mikhail looked around at his men. 'You three take sight on the log, and the rest of you aim for the top of the escarpment. If we stir up something, then we need to give him covering fire.'

They took up position and waited. The scout had managed to wriggle another few meters forward, and then stopped. Any further would take him out into the open. He had not taken his rifle, and had left his helmet behind. He clutched a stick grenade in one hand, and had a spare stuck under his belt in the small of his back.

He remained lying motionless on the ground, and then slowly moved his arms, bringing the grenade forward in front of him so his free hand could grip the pull-ring at the end of the stick.

'Get ready,' Mikhail whispered to the men around him, 'I think he's going to throw.'

The man tensed, sprang to his feet, and yanked the pin out. His arm came back, and then forward, lobbing the grenade in a high arc towards the log. The grenade hit the top of the log, bounced in the air, and then exploded. Mikhail heard screams coming from behind the log just as the top of the escarpment erupted in a fusillade of rifle fire. The grenade-thrower had turned to run back, but the fire from the escarpment instantly cut him down.

Bullets split the air around them, smacking into tree trunks and showering them with splinters of wood. Mikhail waved at his men. 'Pull back,' he shouted.

A corporal looked at him. 'We're going to leave Boris just lying there?'

'What do you want, two people out there dead, or more? We'll get him later, now move!'

They ran, weaving their way back through the forest, until they reached the main group, who were already in the process of pulling back. The Bolshevik rifle fire had stopped now they were out of sight, and a temporary hush settled over the forest glade.

Mikhail counted heads. Apart from the grenade-thrower, they had all made it back intact. There were some with minor wounds, but these were mostly the result of flying wood splinters. Only one man had a bullet flesh wound to his arm.

'What happens now?' Pavel asked, once Mikhail had regained his breath.

'We wait. The Bolsheviks will be wondering where we've gone, and they can't find that out by sitting on top of an escarpment. They'll also be worried that we'll try to circle around them. I bet they'll send a patrol to locate us, and this time it will be our turn to be the ambushers.'

'The 2nd Company must have heard the gunfire, surely.'

Mikhail nodded. 'I'm also hoping it sends a signal to Gusarek at the bridge that there's a fight going on down here.'

Mikhail waved a corporal over. 'I want five forward lookouts stationed in those trees to our front. As soon as they see anything, they're to fire just one shot, and then pull back. I want them to draw the enemy towards us and let them know where we are.'

The corporal gave Mikhail a puzzled look, but did not question the order.

'And when you've done that,' he told the corporal, 'I want you to go back down the track, locate the 2nd Company, and lead them here.'

'I could do that,' offered Pavel. 'It's what I'm here for.'

'No, I want the corporal to go. I need him to give them instructions about what I want them to do. I'm sorry, but you're a civilian, and it will carry more weight from the corporal. We've only got this one chance to get it right.'

Mikhail took the corporal and pointed to a line of trees to their right. 'Our right flank can't be stretched all that distance since we don't have enough men, so there'll remain a gap between the bow lake and those trees. When you bring them up, I want the 2nd to position itself so they are at right angles to our line, but I want them to stay hidden in those trees. I'm planning on the Bolshevik commander spotting the gap, and then trying an outflanking move there. If he does, he'll have to swing his attack down that line of trees. If the 2nd stays hidden then, at the right time, they hit them on their flank. The timing is crucial. Do you understand?'

The corporal nodded. 'Yes sir, I'll explain this to Commander Sergeev.'

'Lieutenant Vinokurov is the one leading the 2nd. Please make sure he is clear on this as well – it's critical.'

The corporal looked uneasy. 'But, *Kapitan* Sergeev is the commander.'

'No disrespect to the commander, but the lieutenant and I have fought alongside each other for years. If he hears it from you, he'll know exactly what to do.'

As the fighting at the bridge started to subside, Gusarek detected the sound of gunfire coming from down the river. He looked around and spotted Czesnovsky near the exit of the bridge directing the pursuit of the retreating Bolshevik force. 'Don't worry about them,' Gusarek shouted to Czesnovsky as he ran up to him. 'Collect your men together and head down river. You can hear the gunfire – they're attacking Sergeev's column. You need to get to him before he's overrun.'

'But someone needs to be chasing them,' protested Cvesnovsky, pointing towards the retreating Bolshevik force. 'We need to know where they're heading.'

'They'll be pulling back to Altaskaya, the next station on the line before you get to the Ob Bridge. We've had intelligence they've dug fortifications around the town.'

Cvesnovsky shook his head. 'Another damned town, and another fight. When does it end?'

'Unfortunately, when you are fighting along a railway line, that's the way it is, and that's why you need to save what you can of Sergeev's men – we're going to need them if we have to fight our way into Altaskaya. I want you to link up with whatever remains of Sergeev's column, help them beat off the Reds, and then head straight to Altaskaya – that

Russian guide with them should know the way. Meanwhile, I'll get the rail line repaired and push on. We'll join up again in front of the town.'

They both stood for a moment, listening to the sound of gunfire coming from down the river. Cvesnovsky gave a quick, casual salute. 'As fast as I can, sir.'

The waiting game had begun, and Mikhail was comfortable to wait. The company occupied the time by digging foxholes and clearing zones of fire to their front. The left flank extended to the bend in the river, while his main force was dug in behind the bow lake. It was a good defensive position. Only the right flank was unprotected. 'Like mother's washing flapping around in a gale,' Mikhail quipped to his sergeant. 'Let's hope the Reds see it too.'

Mikhail grabbed Pavel and led him back down to the riverbank to their rear. 'This isn't your fight – it's ours. Find yourself a protected spot close to the water's edge and keep your head down. If by chance we get overrun, then strip off and swim for it. Whatever happens, don't let yourself get captured. I don't think this lot will be inclined to take prisoners.'

Pavel felt a mixture of relief and guilt but didn't argue. 'I've got my rifle, so don't worry about me,' he told Mikhail. 'I'm capable of looking after myself. Just you stay safe.'

For Mikhail it was like a game of chess. He had moved a sacrificial pawn forward in a feint towards the enemy, had drawn the reaction he had expected, and then shifted the rest of his pieces into a defensive position. It was now up to the enemy to make its move. Mikhail always tried to put himself into the mind of his opponent – to visualize what he would be thinking, and the thought process he would be going through. If he indeed was facing a Russian officer, then they would have undertaken similar training and have read the same textbooks. But he could not be certain of this. He knew for certain that the man commanding the Bolshevik troops would be nervous and would hate making decisions when he lacked information. Commanders want to know what the enemy is doing and where they are. If they don't know, they want to find out. Mikhail was expecting this, in fact relying on it, but it was now up to his opponent. He didn't know the calibre of the man he was facing, or what his training had been, but what he did know was the next move was his opponent's, and something unpredictable could always happen.

Mikhail was relieved when he heard a rifle shot fired somewhere to their front, and then another, and another. Soon the lookouts appeared, scampering back towards them through the trees. Mikhail went over to question them. 'There's a line of men moving through the trees,' one of them said.

'Just a patrol or a larger force?'

'Hard to tell, but there's quite a few of them, and they're heading this way.'

Mikhail would have preferred a better idea of numbers but couldn't blame them for not holding on. They had followed their orders. He grunted with satisfaction. Whatever the numbers, he had drawn the enemy towards his position. He still harboured concern about the vulnerability of his right flank, but he had planned it this way and, in the end, he desperately hoped this would be his salvation. But this heavily relied on his corporal locating Sergei and getting them here on time.

Mikhail worked his way up and down his defensive line, talking to his men constantly, buoying up their courage, and making sure they understood their task. Wait for my signal to fire, and preserve your ammunition, he kept telling them. Only fire when you have a clear target. Make sure you have your spare magazine clips within easy reach. Have your bayonet out of its sheath, stuck into the ground next to you, and ready to clip on. Is your water bottle filled? To the men on the far right he gave instructions to hold on for as long as they could, and only pull back if they were in real danger of being outflanked and, above all, to keep an eye out for the 2nd.

There were now the first signs of the approaching Bolshevik force

–vague, fleeting human forms cautiously working through the forest from tree to tree. It was still difficult to tell their numbers, but Mikhail was optimistic it was more than just patrol strength. Even though his force was just one company strength and would be outnumbered, he preferred that the bulk of the enemy was brought out into the open, and he was not left to deal with separate units scattered through the forest and attacking him at various points in a piecemeal fashion. He wanted to see what he was dealing with. He was quietly confident that, with their defensive position behind the bow lake, they had a chance to fend off one main attack. But, after that, he was doubtful they could avoid being overrun without help arriving.

Through his binoculars he could see the enemy taking up position at the edge of the trees directly to their front where the cleared ground started. He waved at his men to keep their heads down. He still wanted his opponent to be uncertain of the numbers he was facing and tempt him to push men forward. It could be an all-out attack, or he could send a smaller group to probe their defences. But, better still, would he spot the weakness on the right? 'Come on you bastards,' Mikhail muttered to himself, 'do something.'

Finally, his Bolshevik opponent answered. From the edge of the trees, his men opened fire from long range. A hail of bullets slammed into the earth mounds that had been pushed up at the front of the foxholes they had dug behind the bow lake. The bullets kicked up dirt and stones, showering Mikhail and his men in debris. But, from that range, many of the bullets passed harmlessly overhead.

The men cowered in their foxholes, covering their heads with their hands. Mikhail kept yelling at them to keep their heads down. It was hard for him to be heard, but his men's own survival instincts kept most of them safe.

Mikhail counted at least two light machine guns, together with any number of rifles. The fire was relentless and frightening, but mostly ineffectual. As he lay in his foxhole listening to the hail of bullets flying over their heads, Mikhail was comforted that they were expending so much precious ammunition for so little gain.

He crawled out of his foxhole and tumbled into the next one occupied by his senior NCO. 'If I've guessed right, they're trying to pin us down,' he shouted in the corporal's ear. 'Pass the word – expect them to attack us on our right flank.'

'What should we do?' the NCO shouted back. 'Start pulling back our flank?'

'No, leave it where it is for the time being and send a few men from here to reinforce it. They've got to hold on for as long as they can.'

The corporal gave Mikhail a puzzled look and went to protest, but Mikhail stopped him. 'I've got a plan. It's an order.'

Mikhail slithered back into his foxhole and checked to his front again. The Bolshevik force remained dug in at the edge of the forest, but they had reduced their rate of fire. He looked right and could see a gathering concentration of enemy numbers. The attack Mikhail was hoping for, if he was guessing correctly, was about to be mounted.

He scanned the forest to his right. Still no sign of the 2nd, but this was not a bad sign – if he couldn't see them, then neither could the enemy. His main concern was if the enemy also sent troops into the forest and blundered into the 2nd as they were moving up. That could become messy, but as yet, there was no gunfire coming from that part of the forest. As every minute ticked by, he became a little more confident that his ruse might work. He now just wanted to get on with it. 'Come on, come on,' Mikhail kept telling himself. 'Attack, you bastards!'

As if in answer, a far-off whistle blew, and the Bolshevik attackers started moving forward. To Mikhail's relief, it was clear they were sending a column of men to turn his right flank. At first, the Bolsheviks moved at walking pace to keep their men consolidated, but as they came closer, the front of the column started breaking into a jog.

Mikhail had witnessed charges before. The officers tried to control the pace of the charge to keep the men bunched so they would hit the defence as a solid phalanx, but usually group instinct took over, with those in the lead wanting to close with the enemy as quickly as they could. Sustained rifle fire against the head of a column always drove them to splinter into smaller groups, then to close with the enemy quickly, running like desperate madmen against the enemy line.

Crouching low, he ran over to the right flank. His men there were continuing to hold their position, but he could see they were becoming more fearful as the attackers closed and were starting to waver. They had maintained a steady rate of fire, but it was having little effect in arresting the momentum of the charge. The Bolshevik column, just a distant mass of men when it had started out, was now distinct, close and threatening. Men, with bayonets fixed, were yelling and howling like wild animals, and running straight at them.

'Hold the line!' Mikhail kept shouting, as he physically shoved some men back into position. 'Keep firing!'

The attackers were now just meters away, and the flank would be overrun within seconds.

'Please, Sergei! Now!' Mikhail prayed.

As though, in answer, a volley of rifle fire erupted from the forest on the right. It caught the Bolshevik charge by surprise as bullets hit them on their exposed flank. Attackers fell in numbers as concentrated fire poured into their column, simultaneously from the front and side. The charge faltered just a few meters out from Mikhail's troops, and then stopped. Some individual attackers had kept running forward, but they were quickly cut down. The main attacking force, now confused and frightened, at first bunched together for protection, and then started to fall back, pulling their wounded with them. Then, as if by some signal, they dropped everything and started to run.

The remaining Bolshevik force in the trees to their front saw what was happening and picked up their firing rate, desperately trying to provide protection for their retreating comrades. But the retreat was now exposing their own position, and the firing quickly died down as they also started pulling back.

One of Mikhail's men ran up to him. He was panting hard and had a look of panic on his face. 'We've spotted soldiers moving through the trees away to our left. You need to come quickly!'

Mikhail sprinted across to the left and jumped into a vacant foxhole. Crouching low, he steadied himself with his elbows on the dirt parapet, and carefully scanned the trees with his binoculars. He finally spotted them – there was a group of soldiers moving through the forest. Then Mikhail looked harder and spotted the familiar khaki forage caps. He stood up and laughed with relief. 'Don't worry, they're the Czech-Slovaks.'

Chapter 35

ALTASKAYA

10 June 1918

PAVEL SAT BEHIND the log next to the riverbank as he listened to the battle gradually subside. There was still rifle fire, but the sound of fighting was diminishing and becoming more distant. He had heard the shouts of jubilation at the arrival of the Czech-Slovak troops, and guessed the gunfire was from their pursuit of the retreating Bolshevik forces.

He looked at his hands. They were trembling almost uncontrollably, so he tucked them tight under his armpits, hunched himself over, and hoped it would stop soon. He thought about the battle. Nothing had prepared him for this. He was in awe of Mikhail's cool, rational and meticulous method of devising strategy and the way he organized and motivated his troops, but whenever he had been brave enough to raise his head above his log parapet, all he saw was confusion, bordering on chaos.

Bullets filling the air, violent grenade explosions, men running in all directions, shouts and screams, and clouds of stinging cordite that had made his eyes weep. He wasn't quite sure what had happened, but was vaguely aware they had somehow been victorious over the enemy. They were still here, he was alive, and the enemy had gone. That was all he could understand.

'Are you all right?'

Pavel's ears were still ringing from the explosions, making hearing difficult. He only just managed to comprehend the question, and took a moment to realize it was directed at him. He looked up and saw Mikhail standing on the bank above him.

Pavel slowly nodded. 'I, I think so.'

'Good, we need you to show us the way to Altaskaya.'

He went to stand, but found he was unsteady on his legs, and had to use the log for support. He held up his rifle to show Mikhail. 'You know, I never fired one round. Every time I looked, I couldn't make out who was who.'

'I'm glad,' laughed Mikhail, 'you probably would have shot one of our own.'

'But I feel guilty, I was never really any help.'

'You stayed alive, and that's all that counts. And now you can help us get to Altaskaya. We don't want to go all the way back to the rail line. Is there a more direct route from here?'

'Of course, but I'll need to scout around for it.'

Mikhail leaned over, held out a hand, and helped Pavel climb over the log. 'Let me know when you've found the track. Just don't wander off by yourself into the forest. There'll still be a few strays out there.'

Mikhail went off to organize his troops and left Pavel to locate the path. Pavel looked around. The horror of the aftermath lay around him – bloodied and mutilated bodies of the dead and dying, and the grotesque sight of body parts scattered around everywhere. It seemed everything around him was drenched in blood, reminding him of a slaughterhouse. The sight made him want to gag.

The whimpering, the desperate cries for help, and screams of agony from the wounded assailed his ears, and the all-pervasive smell of death was inescapable. A rancid cocktail of smells – raw earth mixed with blood, intestinal juices, excrement, and cordite clawed at the back of his throat and made him yearn for fresh air. He staggered down to the river, knelt, and sluiced water over his face. Then he took out a handkerchief, soaked it, and tied it over his mouth and nose.

Mikhail's men were moving about the battlefield, picking over the remains. They were collecting discarded weapons, and searching both the dead and the wounded, patting their pockets and digging through their haversacks; for food, ammunition, or other items of value. Clothing, particularly greatcoats or boots in good condition, were a prized find.

The wounded were being collected and taken to a rudimentary casualty station where medics roughly cleaned and bandaged wounds. The worst cases were left untreated, particularly if they were Bolsheviks, and left to die. Pavel could not see any prisoners being held and presumed none had been taken.

He walked back up the track towards the original ambush site. He was alone, and disobeying orders, but was thankful to distance himself from the sight and smell of the carnage. It was quiet, almost serene in the forest, and he could remove his mask and breathe fresh air at last.

He found the fallen log and the escarpment. The log was blackened and scarred from the grenade explosion, and the trees were chipped by the gunfire, but there were no bodies to be seen. Pavel searched along the track at the base of the escarpment. It was difficult to pinpoint the entrance, but there was a narrow path leading off the main track around to the right. He followed it for several meters until he was satisfied, and then returned to the main track and tied his handkerchief onto a branch.

Dusk was starting to fall when they first spotted the distant lights of the Altaskaya Railway Station through the trees. Pavel had led the group from the Chumysh along a narrow forest track and got them as close as he dared to the edge of town.

He stood aside and let the soldiers file past him. There were Czesnovsky's Czech-Slovaks, Sergei and the 2nd Company, followed by Mikhail and the 1st Company. Then came the walking wounded, mostly from the 1st, followed by a line of stretcher-bearers making up the rear of the column.

The Czech-Slovaks had pursued the retreating Bolsheviks for a short while, but it was difficult in the thick forest, and contact was quickly lost. Czesnovsky was also mindful that Gusarek wanted him to rejoin the main group in front of Altaskaya, and decided to call off the pursuit.

The Bolsheviks had splintered into small groups, which made pursuit even harder, and they appeared to be pulling back in a direction that would take them towards the rail bridge over the Ob, rather than joining up with their force at Altaskaya.

Pavel was thankful they met no resistance as he guided the column forward along the narrow forest path. The leading soldiers ahead of him remained vigilant, expecting to run into an ambush at any turn of the track, but they encountered no enemy. The path towards Altaskaya had been surprisingly clear.

Once the Altaskaya Station came into view in the distance, the column halted, and the men fell out to rest on the side of the track. Mikhail had come up from the rear, and stood conferring with Czesnovsky and Sergeev in a forest clearing where Pavel had taken a rest. He couldn't hear what they were saying, but they seemed concerned and puzzled. Mikhail broke away from the group and came over to talk to Pavel.

'How well do you know this town?'

Pavel shrugged. 'Well enough – it's just a station and a few houses.'

'There's something strange about it, but we're not sure what it is. There are a lot of earthworks where they've obviously dug trenches around the town, and we have spotted soldiers moving about. But what's puzzling is the place is lit up like a damned Christmas tree.

There are lights on everywhere. You've seen the place before, so we want you to go up and have a look for us. See if you can work out what's different.'

Pavel and his armed escort carefully worked their way through the dark forest without incident. For the last part, they crawled on hands and knees until they felt they were close enough, but still far enough away not to run into enemy lookouts. One of the soldiers handed Pavel a pair of binoculars.

Mikhail had been right. There were a number of lights on in the town, particularly towards the centre where the station platform was located. It was difficult to see past the earthworks, which surrounded and shielded most of the town's outskirts, but there were a few gaps. Pavel focused the binoculars and carefully scanned the town.

The distinctive *"chuff"* of a locomotive, followed by a plume of white steam that rose into the cool night air, came from somewhere close to the station platform. Pavel had to concentrate. Even with lights illuminating part of the town, it was difficult to get a clear focus on anything, but through one of the gaps he managed to spot a large black object.

He handed the binoculars back to the soldier beside him. 'Here, you take a look, I think it's an armored train.'

The soldier took his time. 'I think you're right,' he finally said, 'but is it ours or theirs?'

'The locomotive is pointing in the Ob direction. There's no turntable at this station, so it must be ours.'

Czesnovsky led his men the way through the maze earthworks on the outskirts of the town. They had sent a couple of men forward to make contact with the sentries, who fortunately turned out to be fellow Czech-Slovaks. They had been expected and didn't need the password to enter.

An elaborate system of trenches had been dug, and many of the outlying buildings fortified, but there was no evidence of any fighting. Everything was intact. Gusarek and his Czech-Slovaks had been able to walk into the place without a shot being fired. What had been anticipated as a dangerous and costly assault against a well-prepared defence had come to nothing. After all of the Bolsheviks' hard work to build the defence works, they had surrendered the town, and nobody had bothered to stay and fight. And it appeared that all the inhabitants had also fled. The place was a ghost town.

'Why would they do this?' Pavel was sitting opposite Mikhail at a long trestle table in a canteen that had been set up in the main station waiting-room. Pavel was hungry, and had wolfed down the plate of stew. He was now wiping his enamel plate with a large piece of buttered bread. 'All this work, for what?'

Mikhail aimlessly pushed a lump of meat around his plate with a fork, and didn't seem that hungry. 'It's what I would've done. Altaskaya would only have been a delaying tactic while they pulled their troops back over the bridge into Barnaul. But, if they're already all back there, then there's no point using up resources to defend this place. There's no strategic value.'

A Czech-Slovak soldier approached their table and indicated that he wanted Pavel to accompany him.

'They'll be wanting you to guide them to those ferries,' said Mikhail. 'Are you up to it?'

Pavel patted his stomach. 'I would have preferred a nap but, now I've eaten, I'm okay to do it. One last step.'

Mikhail, a grim look on his face, leaned over the table and grabbed Pavel's arm. 'Don't trust them.'

'Who?'

Mikhail nodded in the direction of the Czech-Slovak soldier. 'This lot, they're a bunch of murdering bastards.'

The soldier was becoming impatient and beckoning Pavel to follow. Pavel ignored him. 'What do you mean?'

Mikhail looked around and leaned closer. 'When they stormed the Chumysh they captured a lot of prisoners.' Mikhail took a deep breath. 'It turns out there were a couple of hundred Austro-Hungarians mixed up with them. They had signed up to fight for the Bolsheviks. Whether they were true communists or mercenaries, we'll never know.'

'Why will we never know?'

'Because these murdering bastards executed the lot of them – two hundred men, buried in a mass grave somewhere out there in the forest.'

Pavel pushed his plate away and stood. 'Why are you telling me this? We know they hate the Hapsburg Empire, and isn't this what happens in war?'

Mikhail wiped his mouth with the back of his hand. 'It's this sort of stuff that'll provoke a reaction. What they've done is bound to get out. Live by the sword, die by the sword. The Czech-Slovaks have now set the precedent in *our* Civil War for both sides – take no prisoners.'

'Isn't that what we did today?'

'In a fight maybe, but this was straight execution.'

Pavel shook off Mikhail's grip on his arm. He felt numb. He had seen too much death today without trying to comprehend the magnitude of the execution of two hundred men.

'I just want to get this horrible war finished and done with.' said Pavel, suddenly feeling a crushing weariness. 'I just want to get home, back to Barnaul.'

Chapter 36

THE NIGHT CROSSING

9th/10th June 1917

PAVEL WAS LED to the armored train and ushered into one of the carriages where he found Commander Gusarek alone, sitting at a desk and hunched over a map. A hanging kerosene lantern cast a dim, flickering light over the walls of the carriage. Gusarek looked tired and ill tempered. He didn't look up when Pavel entered, just waved him towards a chair at the front of his desk. He sat, tapping away at the map with a pencil until he finally pushed back his chair and ran his fingers through his hair. He shook his head in exasperation. 'Another damned bridge to cross.'

Pavel wasn't quite sure whether he was being addressed, or Gusarek was talking to himself, so he continued to sit there in silence.

Gusarek shot Pavel a glance. 'What do you know about this bridge?'

Pavel assumed he was referring to the bridge spanning the Ob. 'It's long, six or seven times the length of the Chumysh bridge. The Ob is deep and fast running underneath the centre spans. It can take large boats and barges. The ground is flat on this side of the bridge but, on the Barnaul side, there's a bluff overlooking the bridge.'

'And that's where the bastards will be, waiting for us.'

Pavel just shrugged, but stayed silent.

'What about this village called Gonba?'

Pavel leaned over the desk and pointed to a spot on the map. 'It's marked here. The bridge is just for rail traffic. The big ferries cross to the River Station that's right on the edge of town under the heights, but there are smaller ferries which cross the river to Gonba.'

'But nothing's crossing at the moment.'

'I doubt it. I think they will have withdrawn all the ferries to the other side.'

Gusarek threw the pencil onto the desk and drew a deep breath. 'So, you think we can still cross?'

Pavel leaned forward and put his hands between his knees. He was now wary of Gusarek, even a little afraid of him. He chose his words carefully. 'The villagers on the river are all fishermen. They have rowboats, skiffs, and that sort of thing. Perhaps some of them are still there.'

Gusarek gave Pavel an accusatory look. 'But you don't know, do you?'

Pavel just shook his head.

'And can these boats be rowed across the river?'

'You will need a strong crew who know what they're doing, and they can't overload the boats. There's a sandy beach on the other side below Gonba that is a good landing spot, but you will need to aim above that, and let the current carry you down.'

Gusarek swivelled in his chair and shouted for an orderly. He then turned back to Pavel. 'You're leaving in half an hour. I'll detach officers and a hundred men for you to guide to the river and find a way to get across. You need to be on the other side before dawn.'

'What if we can't find any boats?'

'Then find another way.'

The night was clear and a crescent moon had risen. Finding and following the right track to the river was relatively easy. It was wide enough to take wagons, and ran in a southerly direction towards the big river. The Czech-Slovak force didn't really need Pavel for this part, but he knew they were relying on him to locate some boats and, if successful, direct them towards the landing place on the far side.

'I suggested bringing a pair of bolt-cutters.' Pavel was walking next to one of the officers, a young lieutenant with a badly pockmarked face.

'We have them,' the officer replied. 'But why?'

'If there are any boats there, they'll have them chained to trees. Then we need to find where they've hidden the oars and rowlocks.'

Pavel did not express it, but he was worried. They would need to be lucky, very lucky. His one hope was that he knew the villagers would have been extremely reluctant to give up their boats if the Bolsheviks had tried to confiscate them. It was their one source of food and income. But then, the Bolsheviks could be brutal too, and the villagers could have been coerced to take their boats across to the other side of the river.

And, if they couldn't find any boats, then exactly what did Gusarek mean by, "find another way"? This was the man who, in Pavel's mind, had probably ordered the massacre of the prisoners, and was unlikely to take failure lightly. He might just be the guide, but Pavel felt a crushing weight of responsibility on his shoulders.

One of the lead scouts returned and spoke to the officer walking next to Pavel. 'We've just hit a stretch of water, so we guess it is the Ob. It's flowing strongly and is so wide you can hardly see the other side. What do you want us to do now?'

Pavel had already briefed the officer.

'Split up and search the fishermen's huts upstream and downstream,' the officer told the scouts. 'See if you can find anyone but, for Christ's sake, capture them, don't kill them. We need to know where their boats are.'

The men in the main column rested while the search was underway.

Soon reports came back from the scouts that they had found all the huts empty.

'They've pulled everyone across to the other side,' Pavel advised the officer. 'Unless you can swim across a wide river in freezing temperatures, this is going to be difficult.'

The officer sat in silence, staring at the ground. Pavel guessed he was also worried about delivering the news back to Gusarek.

Another scout came back. 'We've found a boat, but it's a bit of an old hulk. By the look of it, it's been sitting behind one of the huts for years.'

'Let's go and have a look,' said the officer.

It was a rowboat, an old fisherman's skiff, and its weathered planks showed its age. It was on blocks, hidden in trees at the back of one of the huts, which was probably why the Bolsheviks had overlooked it. If they had found it, they would have simply put an axe through the ancient hull, rather than try to take it across the river. There was a set of old oars, a bit split in places, but useable if they were carefully bound up by twine. However, there were no rowlocks. Pavel hunted around the huts until he found some wire and they wrapped this around each oar and through the rowlock hole.

The boat was manhandled down to the river's edge and checked for leaks. There were some minor ones, but someone had found a bucket in one of the huts that could be used as a bailer.

'Two rowers, five others,' said the officer.

Pavel pointed to a faint far-off sliver of white on the other bank. 'That's the beach you have to aim for, but start by heading upstream in that direction.' He pointed to a spot on the far bank close to the rail bridge foundations. 'The current will push you down. You'll find the village of Gonba on the bank, above that beach.'

'Thanks,' said the officer. 'You can sit in the prow and direct.'

Pavel looked at him incredulously. 'You want me to go in the first boat? They may have posted sentries on the beach.'

'Then our friends here will deal with them.' The officer indicated two men standing well back, almost hidden in the shadows of the trees. The men were both dressed in black, their dark faces smeared with charcoal, and their shirtsleeves were rolled up. Leather bands were worn around each wrist, their long hair was tied back into a ponytail, and both wore a single gold ring in one earlobe. They had no rifles, but each carried a long stiletto knife tucked into their belt.

'Roma gypsies,' said the lieutenant, as though that was all the explanation required. 'Twin brothers.'

'And who else will go?'

'Besides the rowers, the gypsies, and you, there'll be two others who can handle boats. We hope we can find some over there and bring them back. Then we can get more men across.'

'And if we don't?'

'Then it's going to be a damned long night with just one boat.'

The bow of the boat crunched softly into the coarse sand. Almost instantly the two gypsies jumped onto the beach, and ran across to the embankment where they quickly disappeared from sight.

'Stay here until they check it's clear,' one of the rowers whispered to Pavel.

From somewhere on top of the embankment came a muffled curse, a grunt, and then silence. A few moments later the gypsies reappeared and waved for them to follow.

Meanwhile, Pavel had noticed some dark, long shapes high up on the sand at one end of the beach. 'There are your boats,' he pointed out to his companions.

'Just leave it to us,' he was told. 'You go with the gypsies.'

'Go where?'

The soldier gave him a surprised look. 'We were told you're going into Barnaul to make contact with your friends.' He nodded towards the gypsies. 'They're going with you.'

Pavel hadn't forgotten Captain Spencer's words to him but, since Gusarek never mentioned this as part of the plan, he had hoped he would never be asked. What exactly was he expected to do? Who was still there and how could he locate them? He had thought about this a lot, and had only one option, but it was a long shot.

'Remember the Commander is relying on you,' said the lieutenant, 'and the attack starts at 0600 hours tomorrow.' He looked at his watch. 'That doesn't leave you much time, so you'd better get on with it.'

Pavel and his two companions made it into the outskirts of Barnaul more easily than they had anticipated. Pavel suspected the Bolsheviks were giving their attention to preparing their defenses on the heights near the rail bridge, and considered that the prospect of the enemy getting across the river and approaching from the Gonba direction was low.

That is until dawn breaks tomorrow, Pavel thought, *and then they'll realize.*

They had seen the occasional patrol from afar but, by keeping away from the major streets, had easily managed to avoid them. There were also guard posts at all the major road entrances into the town, but these were easily spotted. The cool night air meant most of the guard posts had braziers lit to keep the men warm. This made them highly visible from a distance, and the light from the fires reduced the guard's night vision, which allowed them to detour and slip by without being challenged.

Pavel knew where he was heading, and therefore took the lead. But the two gypsies followed him so closely they were like his own shadow. They moved silently, rarely speaking a word to each other, but intuitively knowing what the other would do.

Using a crude form of sign language, Pavel had managed to learn their names – Joric and Stefan – but this was all he gleaned. They spoke to each other in a Roma dialect that was unintelligible to Pavel, however they did know a few words of Russian and Slovak. Although they didn't know the town layout, they seemed to have a natural sense of direction in the dark, and a sixth-sense seemed to steer them away from trouble spots before they were even encountered. But it was the way they could move silently, and almost invisibly, that amazed Pavel. Like cats stalking prey, they used every shadow cast by a fence line, a building or a tree to move through the town without being seen. Several times Pavel stopped when he lost sight of them, only to be surprised to find them standing right behind him. At first it unnerved him, but after a while he grew accustomed to their stealth, drawing comfort from knowing they would always be there, always somewhere close.

Pavel lay hidden in the shadow of the fence line studying the tumbledown dacha closely. It was hard to be sure in the dark, but it definitely looked familiar. A lot more dilapidated than when he had visited it last, but he had checked the location and was convinced it was the right one.

He handed his rifle over to one of the gypsies. It was a risk to go unarmed, but he thought it better that way. Crawling around in the dark trailing a rifle was one thing, but turning up armed at someone's door invited a greater risk. If they saw you were armed, there could be an inclination to shoot first and ask questions later.

For one final time he checked up and down the lane to make sure nobody was coming and then, as quietly as he could, he pushed aside some broken fence palings. He crept forward on hands and knees, through the gap, and into the long grass and wild brambles of the unkempt garden.

Joric and Stefan remained in the lane to keep a lookout and guard his back while he worked his way alone towards the small log dacha. By holding up two fingers, he had signaled to them to allow him a head start of a few minutes before following. If the place was occupied, and he hoped it was, he felt first contact was best left to him. The sight of two gypsies with long knives would be enough to panic anyone.

The wooden shutters were closed and bolted from the inside, but there were chinks of light at the edges. Pavel could hear the faint murmur of conversation coming from inside the dacha, and he caught a whiff of fried cabbage and bacon.

Without warning, a nearby dog gave a low growl and then started barking. Pavel couldn't see the animal, since the barking was coming from the neighboring yard. Pavel froze and held his breath. A door creaked open, a man shouted at the dog, and the door slammed shut. Pavel could hear the rattle of a chain, probably as the dog retreated to its kennel, and then everything went quiet again.

Pavel crawled to the side of the dacha and slowly raised himself into a standing position, being careful to keep in the shadow of the eaves.

Pavel got as close to the rear door as he dared and stood there, listening carefully to every sound from within. The muffled voices were still there, undeterred by the dog's barking, and there was the faint clink of crockery, as though someone was clearing up after dinner. Pavel thought he could discern just two voices, one an older man and the other a young girl, and this puzzled him. Had he made a mistake and chosen the wrong dacha, or was somebody new now living here? He was certain this was the right place, but though the voices he'd heard made him uneasy, he didn't have the time to wait for daylight to find out.

Pavel stood alongside the back steps, back pressed against the wall. He leaned over, gave a quiet rap on the door, quickly pulled back, and then waited. The voices inside stopped, and then came the sound of chairs being scraped back on the wooden floor. The chink of light through the shutters suddenly went black as someone extinguished a lamp. Then Pavel heard the unmistakable *clunk* and *click* of a rifle bolt being worked – a cartridge being pushed home into a rifle breech.

'Whoever you are, go away,' a man's voice hissed from the other side of the door.

'Is that you Nikifor?' whispered Pavel. 'It's Pavel Dmit . . .'

'I don't care who the fuck you are. We don't open the door for anyone. Now get the hell out of here before I put a bullet through you.'

'Nikifor, it's Pavel. I need your help. For Christ's sake let me in.'

Pavel could hear the sharp, shallow breathing of the man behind the door. He waited. If the man fired, he might splinter the door, but he would have to open it and step outside to direct a shot at Pavel. But then the whole neighborhood would be alerted, and Pavel would have to run.

Seconds ticked away in silence. Then came the sound of the woman's voice, a whisper, terrified and urgent. Silence again, and then the man telling her bluntly to shut up and keep back. 'Who did you say you were again?'

It was almost indiscernible, but Pavel sensed a subtle shift in demeanor. He suddenly realized he had been holding his breath for all this time. He slowly exhaled, and felt his body relax.

'Nikifor, you old bastard, it's Pavel Sukhov. Surely you remember me.'

'You're supposed to be dead.'

Pavel laughed quietly. 'So are you.'

Chapter 37
THE EVE OF BATTLE

Night of 10/11 June 1918

PAVEL SAT STARING at the man sitting across the rough wooden table. The man's loaded rifle lay flat on the table between them, just out of Pavel's reach. The person he once knew as Nikifor used to be large and robust, with a shock of black, unruly hair, and a thick, luxuriant beard. This person was clean-shaven and had pallid, sagging jowls hanging from a thin skeletal face. His hair was stark grey, cut in short tufts, as though it had been hacked with a pair of blunt scissors. Only the voice remained vaguely familiar.

'Nikifor Trevanovich, is that really you?' Pavel struggled to find the right words without sounding uncomplimentary. 'You look different from what I remember.'

'Nikifor Trevanovich is now dead. My name is Milan Milosovich, and I can show you my Bolshevik-issued papers to prove it.'

'But you used to be Nikifor, isn't that right?' Pavel pointed to his own face. 'Do I still look like Pavel Sukhov, or am I someone else?'

Nikifor shifted uncomfortably in his chair. 'You obviously didn't have to survive living in a town run by the Bolsheviks. They'd kill me if they knew who I really was.'

'So, who is Milan Milosovich?'

Nikifor shrugged nonchalantly. 'Just someone I found dead in a ditch. I stole his papers.'

Pavel nodded towards the girl huddled on the floor in the corner of the room. She sat clutching her arms around her knees, visibly shaking, and staring wide-eyed at Pavel. She was young with a ruddy face and plaited blond hair. She wore a rough woolen peasant skirt and a shawl pulled tight around her shoulders. Pavel guessed she probably was no older than sixteen, even younger than Mara. 'And who's she?'

'I found her in the *taiga* close to where I've been hiding out for months at my brother's hunting cabin. She told me her parents had been murdered, but the bandit group took her with them. You don't have to guess why. One day she managed to escape into the forest, and that's where we accidentally stumbled into each other. She was starving, and I had food, but she was still terrified. It took quite a few days before she would trust me, but now we look after each other.'

'But then you moved back into town. Is that when you took on a new identity?'

Nikifor rubbed his hand over the stubble on his chin. 'We wouldn't have survived another winter in the *taiga*, so I decided to risk it. You'd be surprised, there's a number around here like us, and we look out for each other. We avoid the main part of town and keep to ourselves as best we can. There are informers everywhere, and it takes only the smallest thing to warrant a visit from the *Cheka*.'

'The *Cheka*?'

'You're obviously out of touch. They've replaced the Tsar's secret police with one of their own. It's called the *Cheka* for short.' Nikifor reached over and laid his hand on his rifle. 'But, enough about me

– what the hell are you doing turning up at my door in the middle of the night?'

'Before we get on to that, you need to know something. I've a couple of colleagues waiting for me out in the back alley.'

Nikifor's eyes narrowed. 'Is this some sort of threat?'

Pavel shook his head vigorously. 'It's just that they'll be worried I've been gone for a while, and then there's always a chance a patrol may spot them.'

'Colleagues? What exactly do you mean by colleagues?'

'We've come across the river.'

'You've what?' Nikifor looked startled.

'There are regiments of volunteers, and the Czech-Slovak Legion across there.'

'Of course we know they're there. The whole fucking town, including Comrade fucking Tsaplin, knows they're there.'

'We've come from them.'

Nikifor sat back and took his hand back off his rifle. He pushed back his chair, went over to the girl and knelt next to her. He put an arm around her shoulders, and they had a whispered conversation. Then Pavel saw her nod.

'You'd better bring them in before a patrol finds them and comes storming through the door. As you can imagine, they're likely to be somewhat on edge tonight.'

'There's another thing you should know first.' Pavel hesitated. 'They're Roma gypsies.'

Joric sat on the floor in the far corner where he could keep an eye on the door, while Stefan elected to stay outside, hiding in the garden to keep a lookout.

Nikifor had taken the rifle off the table, put the safety catch back on, and propped it against his chair. But it remained within easy reach. He was still tense and eyed Pavel with suspicion. 'So, tell me again, what are you asking me to do?'

'You said you have contacts, people around here that look out for each other – they were your words.'

Nikifor nodded.

'Are they prepared to fight – in other words, can they help us?'

'Maybe.'

'Can you get in contact with them, and, I mean tonight?'

Nikifor's eyes narrowed. 'You mean now?' He asked incredulously.

'Yes, I'm afraid I do,' answered Pavel. He leaned forward across the table and looked Nikifor in the eye. 'Look, if we're going to retake this town, then we need their help, and we need it now.'

'Now being when?'

'We need to get them to assemble at first light tomorrow, at some place that is safe. Is it possible you can contact them?'

Nikifor leaned back, ran his hand through his hair, and blew a noiseless whistle into the air. 'There is a way, but first you need to tell me exactly what we're expected to do.'

Nikifor left Pavel and the gypsies at the dacha and hurried off into the night to start contacting the group. Pavel was nervous. There was always the possibility Nikifor could turn them in to the *Cheka* if it meant he could save himself and the girl. But, while Pavel still harbored some doubts, in reality he didn't have any option but to trust him.

The girl had reluctantly stayed behind to cook some food for them, and her presence did partly reduce Pavel's anxiety. In some ways she was Nikifor's surety, and he couldn't imagine Nikifor wanting to put his young companion at risk if the *Cheka* raided the place. Pavel tried to strike up a conversation with the girl, and even tried to learn her name, but was met every time with a shake of her head and a stony silence.

He had given up trying to converse with her and, once he had food in his belly, decided to spread out his coat on the floor and grab a few hours' sleep. Joric and Stefan had eaten as well and each took turns keeping watch while the other snatched some sleep.

Nikifor finally returned in the early hours of the morning. He woke Pavel to inform him that the word was being spread, and the group would meet at the designated place at 5 o'clock in the morning.

'How many?' asked Pavel.

Nikifor just shrugged. 'How many turn up.'

Nikifor led Pavel and the gypsies across town to the old hospital well before dawn. The route took them through a labyrinth of narrow alleys to the rear of the building.

Even though it was familiar territory for Pavel, it was also unnerving, and he wasn't prepared for the wave of emotion that he felt seeing all the old places again. Quite some time ago he had reconciled himself to the fact he might never see Barnaul again, let alone his own store.

The disused miners' hospital fronted the open square – Demidovsksya Place. On the other side of this open public space, with the view from the hospital only interrupted by a stone obelisk in the square's center, sat the imposing brick building of the D.N. Sukhov & Sons store. Close by the store, the church was also clearly visible, the gold of its domes glinting in the first rays of the dawn.

He had only ever seen the disused hospital from the outside, either from the distance of his store, or when he sometimes cut through the square on his way down to the ferry terminal at the waterfront, but he'd never had the need to enter the building.

It was two-storied with thick, rendered walls, a clay-tiled roof, and lines of small windows overlooking the square. When the mines closed, the hospital had been allowed to fall into disrepair and most of the windows had long since been broken.

The room on the bottom floor was long, with low ceilings and bare, wooden floors. There was a pile of old, rusting bed frames stacked up in one corner. The place stank of mildew and pigeon droppings. The whitewash was flaking off the crumbling walls, and countless years of grime and dust covered everything. There was one rickety, wooden staircase that connected to the upper floor.

'Why did you choose this old place?' Pavel asked Nikifor.

'The Bolsheviks use Demidovskaya as a troop assembly point and, anyway, have you seen how thick the walls are?'

There was already a large group of men in the building when they arrived, and more were trickling in all the time. Pavel was surprised as he looked around. 'How did you manage to contact so many in such a short space of time?'

'I've never seen most of these people before. We developed this communication system; it's quite efficient. I know four people and pass the message to them. They each know four people and get the message to them, and so on, and so forth. It also helps with security – if the *Cheka* ever picks one of us up, we can only give them four names.'

Pavel scratched his head. 'But that only works if the *Cheka* doesn't follow each rabbit down each burrow.'

'Thank God we've never had to test it,' grinned Nikifor, 'but look, here's someone you need to meet.'

He was the archetypal retired army officer – full of his own self-importance, with a bulbous drinker's nose and mutton-chop whiskers, and wearing a tweed jacket with leather patches on the shoulders.

'We don't use names,' Nikifor explained to Pavel, 'but you may recognize each other.'

Pavel and the retired officer shook hands. 'So, you're the chap who came across the river last night.'

'Me and my companions.' Pavel nodded in the direction of Joric and Stefan, who were standing off to one side, keeping their distance from the other men in the room.

The retired officer eyed them suspiciously, and then turned back to Pavel. 'So, what's this all about, then?'

'The Czech-Slovaks and the Volunteers have moved up from Altaskaya and will be attacking the Ob bridge this morning. They'll probably start with a bombardment of the defenses on the heights overlooking the bridge. What the Bolsheviks don't know, but are about to find out, is that they've been ferrying men all night across to Gonba and there'll be an attack mounted from that direction as well.'

The retired officer nodded thoughtfully and tugged his nose. 'They'll need to reposition their troops – pull some back from the heights, and get a new defensive line formed to stop the Gonba attack. So is that where we come in?'

'Exactly,' said Pavel, 'and this may be the ideal place to do it from. Nikifor tells me they use the square here to assemble troops. If they need to relocate men towards Gonba I assume they'll load them on to trams at the terminus over there, or perhaps onto lorries. If we hit them at the right time, we can disrupt the moving of their troops and that gives ours a better chance. Suddenly the Bolsheviks may find they are fighting on three fronts and feel like they're trapped in a triangle. Also, if we can divert their attention away from the bridge, even for just a moment, then it may give the Czech-Slovaks a chance to get men across.'

'And when is this all supposed to happen?'

Pavel looked at his fob watch. 'In about one hour's time.'

Chapter 38

THE BATTLE FOR
THE HOSPITAL

12 June 1918

PAVEL CHECKED HIS watch again; it was 5.45am. He sat on the floor, holding his rifle across his lap, and leaning against the wall. Nikifor was next to him.

'Fifteen minutes to go', he told Nikifor. 'Nervous?'

'Petrified. I've never done anything like this before.' He looked across to Pavel and lowered his voice to a whisper. 'Tell me, have you ever killed a man?'

Pavel shook his head. 'I've only acted as a guide. They kept me out of any fighting. Not that I haven't been scared out of my wits with all the bullets flying around.'

Nikifor gave him a quizzical look. 'But doesn't it make you think about killing someone else? We may call them Bolsheviks, or "the enemy", but that doesn't mean they're not real folk. They're Russian flesh and blood like us, and there are people over on that side we would probably know – maybe they've even visited our stores and bought stuff from us. And look at us now, we're prepared to kill them.'

Pavel didn't answer immediately, but looked around the room. There were nearly one hundred men, split between the ground floor and upper level. Everyone was carrying a firearm of some sort. He recognized various people; however, nobody came up and talked, although sometimes they gave him a quick nod of recognition. Each one of them knew why they were there, and each one probably had their own reasons and motivation. While many of the men kept to themselves, some were huddled in groups, smoking and talking quietly.

'But what makes it different,' said Pavel, 'is that a lot of those we are fighting, like those army deserters, are actually not from here, that is, leaving people like Tsaplin aside. And it wasn't any of us who stole properties, closed businesses, burnt farmhouses, or murdered and raped other people's loved ones. I guess we're all here to simply take our town back, and this isn't Petrograd or Moscow. We don't have the big factories with the big unions; we're a small town of traders, shopkeepers and farmers stuck out in the middle of Siberia, thousands of *versts* from anywhere.'

Nikifor paused for a moment in thought. 'So that makes a difference, the fact that we don't know the Russians we are killing? So then tell me what happens when one side wins and the other loses? Are the losers put up against a wall and shot, or are they forgiven their transgressions?'

Pavel hadn't mentioned the execution of the Austro-Hungarian prisoners to anybody, and didn't want to raise it now. 'I can't really answer you. All I know is it's a case of kill, or be killed. What happens after, I don't know. But look at the time, it's about to turn six o'clock.'

'And then what's supposed to happen?'

'We're just about to find out.'

Right on cue, a distant rumble of artillery fire commenced. After a few seconds' delay, came the *crump, crump, crump* of shells exploding on the heights above the rail bridge.

'The poor bastards,' someone said, 'I wouldn't fancy being there.'

The artillery barrage went on and on, without respite. Though the heights were some distance away, the hospital shook, the windows rattled, and years of accumulated dust was shaken from the rafters. The men inside the hospital sat and waited, in nervous silence. Everyone had been instructed to stay away from the windows to avoid revealing their presence, but a couple of men had been posted to keep a surreptitious watch on the square.

Nikifor leaned across to Pavel. 'Where are your gypsy friends? I haven't seen them for a while.'

Pavel looked around the room and spotted Joric and Stefan, just as they were coming through the back door. They had been outside somewhere and had returned, both carrying rifles.

'Where did they get them from?' whispered Nikifor.

'You should never ask.'

One of the gypsies waved towards Pavel, beckoning him to follow them out the back. Pavel pushed himself off the floor, and ran in a crouch over to them. They took him out into the back alley and pointed to several buildings and roofs on both sides of the narrow-walled pathway.

'No good,' one of them said in rough Russian, and mimicked firing a rifle. 'No good.'

'What did they want?' Nikifor asked, on Pavel's return.

'I think they were trying to tell me our line of retreat is far too dangerous if we have to pull out of here. We could be easily surrounded, and there are lots of places they could position snipers.'

'Who says we're going to pull out?'

There was a moment's lull in the artillery fire, just enough for the men in the hospital to hear the far-off rattle of machine gun and rifle fire. Pavel got up and ran over to the officer. 'Gonba,' he told him. 'It's coming from the Gonba direction. The attack has started.'

The officer nodded. 'The Bolsheviks will have to start moving troops urgently. I'll go and look for myself.' He ran over and climbed the staircase leading to the upper level.

Pavel, against orders, went over and had a quick glance out of a window. There were already troops milling about near the church on the far side of the square, and more arriving. Some lorries could be seen driving down the boulevard and were about to enter the square.

'What's happening?' asked Nikifor.

'They're doing what we thought they would do. We should get ourselves ready.'

Pavel and Nikifor crouched down below a window and waited for a signal. Pavel patted his pockets, withdrew some spare ammunition clips, and carefully laid them out on the inside sill of the window.

'Do you have much ammunition?' he asked Nikifor.

'Some.'

'Just don't shoot it off all at once. The worst thing we could do is run out.'

Pavel had long since swapped his hunting rifle for a Mosin-Nagant standard army-issue rifle. It wasn't as good as his rifle in terms of quality or accuracy, but there was always a chance of finding more ammunition for it. Most of the men had brought their own firearms, all varying calibers, and would struggle if they ran low.

The officer came back part way down the stairwell. 'Get ready,' he called out. 'Fire on my command.'

Pavel and Nikifor stood side-by-side at the narrow window. There was just enough room for the two of them. Across the square the open-top lorries were now parked, and troops were lining up ready to load. Pavel rested his left elbow on the sill and took aim at the assembling infantry. They were too far away to aim at any individual – they were just a solid grey mass of men that stood out against the stark, white-washed walls of the domed church.

'Fire!'

Pavel held his breath, squeezed the trigger, and fired. He worked the bolt to load another cartridge, took aim, and fired again. He didn't think about what he was doing. It was mechanical and without emotion, and he didn't check whom he hit, or whether he hit anyone – he just kept firing into the mass of men. Suddenly the five-cartridge magazine was finished. He went to load another magazine, but then stopped himself.

A lot of bodies lay about the square, wounded men were trying to crawl away to cover, and others were running in all directions. Some had sought shelter behind the cenotaph, while most had jumped the low wall surrounding the church. The empty lorries sat, stranded in the square. One of the drivers had attempted to drive his vehicle away, but in his panic had crashed it into one of the bollards surrounding the square.

Once the Bolshevik troops had taken cover, the targets were few, and the firing died down from those in the hospital. But this was short-lived. Soon the enemy regained their composure and started to organize themselves. The hospital was the obvious origin of the attack, and they opened fire, mostly aiming for the windows. It was intense but indiscriminate fire. Everyone in the hospital ducked for cover as bullets smacked into the thick walls of the exterior. Plaster dust was falling and coating everything as bullets flew through the windows and buried themselves in the back wall of the room.

Gradually the firing from the Bolshevik side subsided when they realized their rifle fire against the solid hospital walls was futile and a waste of ammunition. Under a white flag they sent out stretcher teams to bring in their wounded, and the men stranded behind the cenotaph took the opportunity to scamper back to better cover with their comrades in the churchyard.

The fight had reached an impasse, but not a truce. While the Bolsheviks in the square had lost many men, the White force in the hospital had suffered very few casualties; the thick walls had shielded them well. Now they waited, relieved and buoyant that they had successfully hemmed the Bolsheviks in and impeded the movement of troops towards Gonba.

But Pavel worried that they would not be sitting over on the other side of the square doing nothing. They might have lost their transport terminus and assembly point, but they would be able to find other ways and a different route to get troops across town to reinforce the Gonba front.

Then there was the hospital, and the threat it posed to the enemy. It wasn't so close to the river that it absolutely cut off their line of retreat if they had to pull out of Barnaul, but it would make any troop withdrawal back up the river difficult. Pavel knew they would have to do something about it, but what?

Nikifor was sitting on the floor next to the window, with his back leaning against the wall. He was grinning. 'Like ducks in a bloody shooting gallery.'

'Don't get too damned confident,' Pavel replied. 'The Reds are hardly going to sit on their backsides and let us control their troop movements. They'll be up to something, for certain.'

Pavel thought a full frontal assault on the hospital was unlikely. The Bolsheviks had already lost a lot of men, and they would have to attack across the open square under a hail of bullets. 'I reckon,' continued Pavel, 'they're more likely to try and hem us in, then sit back and wait for our ammunition to run out.'

Pavel's words were hardly out of his mouth when there was a hollow popping sound, followed by a high whistle, then a blast that peppered the front of the building with shrapnel. Pavel looked around, spotted the old officer, and ran over to him. 'They've brought up mortars,' he shouted to him above the following explosion. 'They'll destroy this place, and us in it!'

'Don't worry, we've got thick walls,' shouted back the officer.

Pavel pointed upwards. 'The walls don't matter a damn if they start lobbing shells onto the roof.'

The Reds were thinking along the same lines, and the very next mortar shell exploded on the roof at one end of the building. Sharp, tiny pieces of shattered tiles flew about the room. A wooden beam crashed through the floor from above and plaster cascaded from the walls. When the dust cleared there was a gaping hole in the roof through to the first floor.

Pavel looked around. Everyone was coated in a thick layer of plaster dust. There were some men killed, but many had received wounds from the flying tile shards, some serious, but many minor cuts. Their plaster-whitened faces and clothes were speckled with their own blood.

The officer was standing there, looking up and gazing blankly at the hole in the roof. It was as though he was mesmerized. Pavel grabbed the officer by the arm and shook him. 'Don't you realize, they've now got this place ranged. If we just sit here, we'll all die.'

Another explosion. Pavel felt himself lifted off his feet by the concussion wave and thrown, like a rag doll, against the wall. He blacked out.

As he regained a degree of consciousness, he became vaguely aware of someone dragging him across the floor and out into sunlight. The glare startled him, and he lay on the ground with his head pounding and his entire body aching. Someone sluiced his face with water, but his vision remained blurred, and his ears still rang. He shook his head and tried to sit up, but somebody pushed him flat again.

He lay still, sucking in deep breaths, trying to force away the pain and clear his head. The faces of the people surrounding him swam in and out of his vision.

Nikifor looked down at Pavel, grim-faced. 'Is he going to live?'

The two gypsies were kneeling over him, feeling his bones for breaks.

'For Christ's sake, let me up,' mumbled Pavel, as he tried to shake off their probing fingers. 'What the hell happened?'

'A mortar bomb,' answered Nikifor. 'You were lucky, that old officer chap shielded you from the worst of the explosion.'

'What happened to him?'

'He's dead,' replied Nikifor, in a matter-of-fact way.

Pavel lay there trying to slow down his pulse and clear his head. He gradually started taking in his surroundings. They appeared to be in the backyard of a house since all he could see were tall wooden fences, a woodshed, and an outhouse. Around him were Nikifor, the two gypsies, and a small group of men – perhaps there were six or seven of them.

'Where are we?' he asked.

'The hospital's been abandoned,' answered Nikifor. 'It was a wreck anyway. The main group headed out the back and straight down the alley, but they've obviously run into stiff opposition. The Bolsheviks had moved men around to cut off the retreat.'

'So what are we doing here? Why aren't we all sticking together?'

'Your two gypsy friends refused to go with our main force. If you listen to what's going on down there, they probably saved our lives. The others are likely trapped in the alleys fighting for their lives, and I hate to say it, we don't fancy their chances.'

Pavel could hear rifle fire and exploding grenades. It sounded close by, and the noise was fearsome.

'Then how do we get out of here?'

Nikifor pointed over to the gypsies. 'That's the easy part. They've found an axe.'

Chapter 39

THE RETREAT

12 June 1918

FROM WHERE THEY were, in someone's backyard, the fighting of the main group in the alley sounded alarmingly close. Narrow alleyways bunch men together into a tight group. They don't have any room to maneuver, and they present an easy, vulnerable target. Pavel hated to hear the gunfire and the explosions from grenades – that meant their colleagues were dying – but there was nothing he and his companions could do about it other than to sacrifice their own lives with little chance of success.

'We can't worry about them,' Nikifor said to Pavel. 'It was their decision, not ours. Let's just get out of here before they find us as well.'

Pavel nodded in agreement. The Bolsheviks would have taken what remained of the hospital by now, and would know they had the retreating White force bottled up. The Bolsheviks would want to follow up quickly, and would be sending men down the alleys to attack any survivors from the rear. If Pavel's group didn't move soon, they could be easily be trapped, with little hope of escape.

'We need to move laterally, away from this fighting,' suggested Pavel, looking around. 'That means we need to start scaling fences.'

'We agree,' answered Nikifor, waving a hand towards one of the gypsies, 'hence the axe.'

Joric waited for the next sharp burst of rifle fire to mask the noise, then hit the fence with the axe. It took three blows before he had punched a large enough hole. The men got together, carried Pavel over to the fence, and bundled him unceremoniously through the gap.

'Thanks, but next time,' Pavel told Nikifor, 'I'll manage myself.'

Another tall wooden fence bordered the next yard, and that pattern continued for the next five houses. However, they were gradually moving away from the fighting.

'Do we know where we're heading?' Pavel asked, as they were preparing to cut their way through another fence.

'Kazyonnaya Zaimka, to the northwest of us,' answered Nikifor. 'We think that's where our force would be advancing towards. It's in a direct line from Gonba towards the bridge. We guess it's only about two to three *versts* from here.'

'But that means we're going to need to get across Moskovsky Prospekt without being seen. You can bet the Bolsheviks will have men stationed there – it's the main street down to the river.'

'What option do we have?' replied Nikifor. 'If we just sit here, all it takes is one person to spot us and inform on us, and then we're done for.'

Pavel glanced over towards the rear of the house of the yard they were in. They had already tested the back door. It was locked, but Pavel was sure he had seen a curtain in an upstairs window move, ever so slightly. Perhaps the occupants were hiding there.

But Nikifor was right – there was a high chance of someone seeing them and informing on them. A betrayer would just have to walk out the front door and tell the first person they saw on the street. The civilians who had remained after the Bolshevik takeover would either be sympathizers, or those who had worked out how to survive. Informing on fellow citizens had become one such method of survival.

Pavel was able to move more easily now and, even though he still ached all over, he found he could crawl and even walk unassisted. He didn't know this part of town well, but he knew they couldn't keep jumping from backyard to backyard without coming to a major street. Sooner or later they would have to take their chances crossing Moskovsky Prospekt.

In the end the decision was made for them – they had crawled through the last wooden fence and were faced with a brick wall on the far side of the yard. Stefan gave Joric a leg-up to have a look over the top, but he quickly ducked his head below the parapet and jumped back down. He vigorously shook his head and indicated by a hand signal that there were soldiers on the other side.

Fortunately, the nearby fighting must have masked the noise they had made breaking through the last fence, and the soldiers on the other side of the wall seemed unaware they were there. Their survival relied on the mere width of brickwork that stood between them.

It was too risky to stay, so they retraced their steps back through two yards until they were confident they would not be heard. Pavel recognized the house where he had seen the curtain twitch. Joric checked the back door – it was still locked. He stood by the door and waited, with axe poised.

There was an explosion some way off, possibly a stick grenade, followed by scattered rifle fire. He quickly swung the axe, and the door splintered and swung inwards. Joric led the way through the door. The kitchen was the first room they entered at the rear of the house. A family of four – a husband and wife, with two young children – cowered under the kitchen table. There was terror etched on their faces. The father tried to stand, but Nikifor roughly pushed him back down, and put a finger to his lips. 'Shush.'

Pavel ran up the hallway to the front parlor and carefully lifted the lace curtain. 'Fuck,' he cursed.

He recognized the broad avenue with the linden trees planted up the center strip. The house fronted directly on to Moskovsky Prospekt and the street-frontage was just two steps away from the front door. Looking out the window at an angle, he could see Bolshevik soldiers busily building sandbag emplacements in the center of the boulevard, facing away from them, towards the direction of Kazyonnaya Zaimka.

Pavel left one of the other men as a lookout and went back to the kitchen. 'We can't go any further,' he told Nikifor. 'It's Moskovsky Prospekt out there and there are groups of soldiers building emplacements, literally a few paces away from the front door, and more soldiers are arriving all the time. It looks like they're pulling back and setting up a new defensive line right here. If we put our nose outside the front door, we're dead.'

"Then we need to forget about making it to Kazyonnaya.' said Nikifor. 'Any sign of our troops?'

Pavel didn't answer, but stood quietly, listening to the distant sound of the gunfire. But where was it coming from – the river, or back towards the alleys behind the hospital, or from the Kazyonnaya direction? Perhaps all three, but it was unclear and confusing.

'We don't have an option but to wait here and see what happens,' he told Nikifor. "We'd better pray we don't get discovered before our troops arrive.'

'What about the alley at the rear of the house?'

The alley at the back was narrow and cobblestoned – a lane that divided the yards of houses that backed on to it, probably used by the night carts.

'There's only one way out of that alley, and it just leads us straight back to that main street,' answered Pavel. 'We already know there are troops there.'

'Then we're trapped,' shrugged Nikifor.

Pavel nodded in the direction of the family group. They were still sitting under the table, huddled together, their arms clasping their knees. 'We need to keep a close eye on this lot. Don't let any of them go anywhere near a window. It would take just one small signal, and we'd have every Bolshevik out there charging through the front door.'

'What if one of them wants to go to the toilet?'

'Grab a chamber pot from one of the bedrooms. They're bound to have one under their beds.'

With nowhere to go, they decided to fortify the house as best they could. The broken back door was closed and barricaded with heavy furniture, as were the front door and windows. The men spread themselves through the house, including upstairs, from where it was easier to keep an eye on the street. Some of them kept watch, while the others rested, waited, and listened to the distant fighting.

Some of the men had brought food and they shared it around, including with the family, who had been allowed to crawl out from under the table, as long as they stayed within the strict confines of the kitchen. They were still very anxious and the young children remained terrified, but at least the mother and father had now realized they would not be harmed if they continued to cooperate. They mostly sat on the floor in sullen silence, broken by an occasional sob from one of the children.

Nikifor had opened a cupboard in the hallway and was rummaging around in it.

'What are you looking for?' enquired Pavel.

'Something red we can tie around our arms. It might just fool them if they decided to break into the house.'

'I'm not sure it would fool them for very long and, anyway, if it also fools our own forces then we could be mistaken for Bolsheviks. I'd prefer to take my chances.'

Nikifor stopped his rummaging. 'You're probably right and, besides, I can't find anything red.'

He walked back into the kitchen. 'Aha!'

He pulled the white tablecloth off the table and started ripping it up into strips. The woman glared at him, but didn't say anything. Nikifor smiled at her. 'I'll buy you a new one, I promise.'

He went round and handed each man a strip. 'Stick it in your pocket for now but, if you see our troops, tie it around your arm.'

He kept one larger piece of the tablecloth that he attached to a broom handle and propped in the corner. 'It may come in useful at some stage.'

It was now several hours since the retreat from the hospital, and the sound of any fighting from that part of town had finally ceased. They could only fear the worst for their fellow fighters from the hospital. Each one of the survivors nursed some residual guilt, despite the clear futility of going to their help. Perhaps, just perhaps, they could have made a difference.

The artillery bombardment of the river heights had significantly reduced but, from the upstairs windows of the house they could still see a grey-brown cloud of dust and cordite hanging over the heights.

'Maybe they're running low on shells,' suggested Pavel.

'Or maybe they've managed to storm the bridge,' responded Nikifor.

'I think you'd hear the fighting if they had. Maybe they're just sitting back and waiting for the force from Gonba to make their way into town.'

The only sound of fighting they could hear was coming from the direction of Kazyonnaya. It may have been a hopeful conjecture, but Pavel was convinced it was gradually moving closer, and they could see the activity of the Bolshevik soldiers out on the street had taken on a new urgency. A steady trickle of Bolshevik infantry could also be seen pulling back from the direction of Gonba, and they had started digging trenches across the width of the boulevard.

'It's going to get dark soon,' Pavel said to Nikifor. 'We'd better pray they don't decide to use this place to billet troops.'

Nikifor gave an ironical laugh. 'Perhaps we should hang a "No Vacancy" sign on the front door.'

'I'm serious,' answered Pavel. 'If they come banging on the door, what the hell are we going to do?'

Pavel and Nikifor agreed it was best to move the furniture blocking the back door to at least leave a line of retreat open. They had one of the men sit and guard the door in case anyone tried to come through the back entrance, and also to stop the family attempting an escape.

'We'd better pray our troops keep those Reds manning the trenches occupied for the night,' said Nikifor. 'If there's a lull in the fighting, then some of them could come looking for a bed.'

They had heard sounds from houses further up the street of a sledgehammer being used against a brick wall, and of breaking glass. 'I bet they're starting to fortify houses and create fire holes,' Pavel told Nikifor. 'I'll go upstairs and check.'

He was right – from an upstairs window he could see houses close by being fortified with sandbags and occupied by troops. Pavel was thankful the house they were in was sufficiently back from the front line, and perhaps would remain distanced from any fighting. But this, as Pavel had seen for himself, was by no means guaranteed. A battle was a very fluid and unpredictable event.

Still nervous about their prospects, he kept checking regularly. The soldiers below had completed the sandbag emplacement and were manhandling the machine guns forward. Pavel could hear them being pulled up the road. He frowned and pulled back a tiny section of the curtain, then let it quickly drop back. 'Shit!'

Sheltered behind the sandbag emplacement, the two heavy-caliber machine guns were now wheeled into position. They were facing directly up the boulevard, giving them a firing zone that would allow the guns to rake the street to their front with deadly effect. Long belts of ammunition lay stretched out over the sandbags, and wooden boxes of spare belts were stacked up outside the emplacement. The machine gun crew were sitting around on their haunches, talking, smoking, and waiting. They exuded a nonchalant confidence.

'What's wrong?' asked Nikifor, who had come up the stairs.

Pavel didn't answer immediately; he just sat there, with his back against the wall, staring at the ceiling. 'We've got a problem. *Pulemyot*

Maksima heavy machine guns, and there's two of the bastards. There's no way our troops are going to get past those.'

Nikifor went over to the window and had a quick look. 'Fuck, I see what you mean. Those things look deadly. What did you call them?'

Pavel shook his head. 'It doesn't matter; I've seen them before. It'll be a slaughterhouse.'

Nikifor gave Pavel a quizzical look. 'You're not suggesting, are you?'

Pavel shrugged. 'Do we have any other option? Of course we could just sit here and do nothing, apart from look on as our men get massacred.'

Nikifor thought for a moment. 'There's got to be something we could do. Maybe your gypsy friends, I wonder if they've got any ideas? Just wait here a minute.'

Nikifor hurried down the stairs, returning a few moments later with Joric and Stefan, and took them over to the window. The two of them had a brief look, stepped back from the window, and started fervently whispering to each other. Then they nodded, having seemed to reach some sort of agreement.

Joric came over and crouched down next to Pavel. He pointed towards the window. 'Bad, very bad,' he said in a mixture of guttural Russian and Slovak. He pointed to his brother, and then to himself. 'Joric, Stefan, we leave.'

'What's he saying?' asked Nikifor.

Pavel shrugged. 'I'm not sure, but they want to leave the house. I can't be certain, but I think they have a plan.'

'And leave us just sitting here? Do we trust that they won't make a run for it?'

Pavel looked across to Nikifor. 'There's something about them I trust and, anyway, do you have a better plan?'

The gypsies stayed with them until it was dark outside, and then crept out the back door and disappeared silently into the night. None of those who remained knew how long they would be away, or whether they would return. All they could do was sit and wait out the long night, and hope.

The sound of machine guns woke everyone with a start, just as dawn was breaking. It wasn't the harsh, deafening sound of the heavy machine guns positioned out on the street, but the rattle of light hand-held machine guns coming from a few blocks away. Pavel ran to the window. The Bolshevik machinegun crews were scrambling to their positions and loading the heavy ammunition belts into the gun breeches. Everywhere, Red infantrymen were running to man the trenches that spanned the width of the boulevard.

'They've got to be our troops,' said Nikifor, excitedly. 'They must have moved up undetected during the night. Have your gypsies made it back yet?'

Pavel shook his head. 'If they haven't made it back by now, then I'm afraid they're going to be stuck out there.'

'If the bastards ever had any intention,' scoffed Nikifor. Even Pavel had lost hope, and felt a level of responsibility for letting them go in the first place.

The heavy machine guns started firing, first one, and then the other. They were firing large, heavy caliber rounds, and the noise was overpowering and shook the house. The guns each fired in short bursts, allowing time for the water coolant in the jacketed barrels to keep the temperatures down, and prevent the guns from jamming. But between the two guns, the noise of the firing was relentless.

'Nobody is going to get past those,' Nikifor shouted, over the noise of the gunfire. 'Our side is going to have to call off the attack!'

'Then it's up to us to do something about it,' shouted back Pavel. He crouched at the window and looked out. 'We just have a line of sight into the back of the emplacement. Get everybody ready, and on my signal we break the windows and try to take out the gun crews.'

'We don't have much ammunition,' shouted back Nikifor, 'maybe just enough for a few minutes.'

'Then, don't waste a shot.'

Pavel called down to the men below on the ground floor. 'Are you ready?'

'No, wait a minute,' someone yelled back. 'There's a couple of soldiers running up the street. They're bringing more boxes of ammunition for the gunners and they'll block our line of fire. Let's wait for them to get past.'

Pavel lifted the lace curtain a fraction, just in time to see the ammunition carriers run past. They wore helmets and greatcoats. Pavel thought, *greatcoats, unusual for this time of day*. They hoisted the heavy wooden box onto the stack already there and levered off the lid. Both men then reached into the box, pulled out a stick grenade, yanked the pin, and casually rolled the grenades into the emplacement. They then dived for cover behind the nearest stack of sandbags.

'Everyone duck,' yelled Pavel, as the grenades exploded, sending out shrapnel in all directions, breaking their windows, and showering them with shards of glass. Pavel brushed himself down and scrambled back to the window. The two machine guns, twisted and blackened by the explosions, lay on their sides and pointed at a crazy angle towards the sky. Split sandbags oozed sand, and lacerated bodies littered what remained of the emplacement.

'Fire on the troops in the trenches,' Pavel yelled, 'and for fuck's sake, try not to hit Joric and Stefan.'

With their own machine guns out of action, the fire coming in from the attacking White troops to their front, and now being under fire from the rear, the Red troops' will to stay and fight quickly evaporated.

'Rabbits,' laughed Nikifor, 'just like your officer predicted. They're running like fucking rabbits.'

Pavel grinned back. 'For the record, he actually said hares, not rabbits.'

'Who cares,' said Nikifor, fishing for something in his pocket and then pulling out the strip of white tablecloth. 'Give me a hand to tie this on, then I'll do yours. Now, where's that white flag of mine?'

Chapter 40

THE PARADE

July 1918

PAVEL PULLED ON his frockcoat and checked himself in the hallway mirror. He adjusted his cravat and ran a hand through his hair, before putting on his top hat and then reaching for his silver-topped cane.

'Won't you be too hot in that?' asked Maria. She was brushing the back of his coat with a clothes brush. 'It's the middle of summer after all.'

'Mushka,' answered Pavel, 'today is not just a victory parade. It's much more than that – this is to show we have returned to normality. This is what a peaceful town should be like, a beautiful Siberian summer's day, and people out enjoying themselves.'

'And that happens to ignore the fact that half the town is now destroyed. What the fire didn't get the first time, the shelling did later.'

'How many times have I said, that you can't make . . .'

'I know, I know. You cannot make an omelet without breaking eggs. But this is horrible; the poor people out there, I don't know how they survive.'

Pavel turned and brushed away an invisible fleck from his coat. 'Just count yourself lucky we found this house to rent, or we could also be living in a tent, or something a lot worse.'

'Like those hiding out in the *taiga*.'

'That's their problem, not ours. They sided with Tsaplin and lost, and then they ran. It was a damned close thing, and it could have just as easily been us. But, mark my words, hiding in the *taiga* might be okay for now, but just wait for winter and see what happens. They'll be pleading with us to let them back into town.'

Maria set the brush down on the hall dresser and stepped around Pavel so she could see herself in the mirror and adjust her hat. 'And, in the meantime, we are trapped. It's like living inside a prison of our own making, an island surrounded by a sea of red. We don't dare to take one step outside the town's cordon.'

'Just you wait and see,' Pavel snapped back. He regretted sounding so terse, but he had little patience for peoples' complaints about life in the town. 'We have our own Volunteers, besides the Czech-Slovaks and the British. Besides, we've got our town back – and we'll keep it.' He impatiently tapped his cane on the floor. 'Now, where are those girls? It's time we were leaving.'

There was a faint tinkling of bells from the street outside their front door. 'That sounds like Dmitry,' said Pavel. 'I asked him to bring the troika round to the front.'

Maria went down the hallway and called the girls. They had been up since early morning, bathing, doing each other's hair, and helping the maid iron their white cotton summer dresses. They filed down the stairs, with radiant smiles, laughing amongst themselves. They held a straw boaters, and playfully jostled each other in front of the hall mirror while they adjusted their hats.

'Now, we're all ready' announced Maria. 'And I've packed a picnic hamper so we can go down to the riverbank after the parade. There's going to be a band playing in the rotunda.'

Pavel smiled to himself. *This is finally like old times.*

Maria and the three girls sat in the troika and unfurled their parasols to shade themselves from the bright sunlight, while Pavel climbed up on the driver's bench alongside Dmitry.

'Let's get a move on,' Pavel told him. 'We can't be late.'

Dmitry cracked the whip with a flourish and flicked the reins.

The street was full of carriages, all heading down the broad *Prospekt* towards the river where the Town Hall was located.

Everywhere there were visible signs of the battle. Half-destroyed buildings, smashed windows and walls pockmarked with bullet holes. When Maria and the girls had first returned from Alexei's stud, and had seen the destruction, they had considered moving out to the farm. But one visit was enough to convince them otherwise. Maria had cried when she saw the state of the homestead. The house was almost a shell. Everything of any value had disappeared, floorboards had been pulled up to fuel fires, and rubbish was strewn throughout the house. People had even defecated in rooms.

The farm itself had fared little better. The animals were all gone, the fences destroyed, the barns and outbuildings in disrepair, and almost every piece of equipment broken. It looked like the outcome of a senseless vendetta, deliberate vandalism that was more about revenge than appropriation. They had destroyed the very things they had always coveted.

'It's all the pent-up anger,' suggested Iya. 'Centuries of oppression.'

'We never oppressed our workers,' snapped Maria, 'we treated them like family.'

Iya thought for a moment about mentioning they had left their "family" of workers to their own fate when they had fled to Alexei's stud, but decided today wasn't the time and place to start another family argument.

In the end, it was the danger of the countryside that convinced Pavel and Maria not to attempt restoration of the farm. Living outside the town's protective cordon would be almost suicidal. However, finding a largely intact and empty house in town had also been difficult, and it had cost Pavel a substantial amount in Mexican dollars to obtain it, and then find the scarce materials to have it fixed up. Window glass replacement had been the biggest challenge. The shelling of the town had left very few windows intact. Even if a building had not received a direct hit, the concussion waves from the explosions had broken almost every pane of glass, and they had had to hunt through the ruins of the town to find the rare unbroken window.

Despite the problems, the town was gradually being brought back to life. An effort had been made to get the streets cleared of rubble so traffic could resume. Electricity had been restored to some areas, the main broken sewer pipes were being repaired, and there were even the beginnings of construction of several new buildings along the *Prospekt*.

But it was the unsanitary conditions in the large shantytown of tin, tarpaulin and cardboard shacks that were the cause of most concern. The ever-present threats of cholera and typhus spreading among the homeless families weighed heavily on everyone's minds, and people lived in dread of an outbreak.

Since coming back to Barnaul, the family had debated whether to stay or go. It was a sensitive topic for Pavel, and the whole family was aware of it. He still nursed a sense of guilt that it was primarily his decision not to leave when Tsaplin's Bolsheviks first took over, when many other families were fleeing for Harbin, or beyond. He had put the family in danger, and he knew it. The victory had gone a long way towards vindicating his decision, but the state of the town, and the lurking menace of the Bolshevik partisans in the forest did temper his optimism for the future.

'There's a large Russian émigré community already in Paris,' Mara had enthusiastically pointed out, 'and I could study piano at the *Conservatoire de Paris*.'

Iya laughed. 'Frankly, the French are way too *"Ancien Regime"* for me. If we want to get as far away as we can from Russia and its poli-tics, there's the New World: America, Canada, or even, God help us, Australia.'

'And there's still Harbin,' suggested Galina. 'China is a lot closer to Siberia than the other side of the world. Then, at least, if we manage to get rid of the Bolsheviks, we can always come back.'

'You,' said Mara, playfully poking Galina in the ribs, 'just want to stay as close as you can to Sergei.'

Galina flushed red. 'It's just while the men are fighting, we should all stay and support them.' She looked across to the heavily pregnant Iya. 'And that especially goes for you and Mikhail.'

Pavel turned in his seat. 'Whatever we do, we're not about to start scattering ourselves all over the world. The family stays together, and that is not for discussion. But, speaking of Mikhail and Sergei, we need to get a move on, or we'll miss seeing them marching.'

Mikhail and Sergei had left the house earlier, going off to join their troops of the Novonikolayevsk Regiment for the march-past. They were wearing their dress uniforms, washed and freshly pressed, with their high cavalry boots polished to a mirror finish. It was a bittersweet moment for the two of them. A new regiment – the 1st Barnaul Rifles – was in the process of being formed; Mikhail had decided to switch regiments, and then Sergei had agreed to also move. The two of them had fought together for too long. 'We're each other's lucky charm,' Sergei used to joke.

The parade was a poignant moment for both of them – it would be the first and last time they would march with the men they had fought alongside in the battle.

A steady stream of pedestrians hurried along the sidewalks, all of them eager to gain a good vantage point along the parade's route. It seemed everyone in the town had come out and was heading down to line the streets by the Town Hall. There was a festive mood in the air, and people were dressed in their Sunday-best clothes, except for the usual collection of barefoot, grubby-faced urchins, dodging and weaving their way through the gathering crowd.

'Where have all these people come from?' asked Galina, incredulously. 'It's as though the whole town's come out of hiding.'

'What you don't see anymore,' pointed out Pavel, 'are those gangs of deserters loitering about everywhere.'

'They probably ran into the *taiga,* along with their Bolshevik friends,' said Mara.

'Bolsheviks, deserters, what's the difference?' said Pavel. 'If you ask me, it was the Bolsheviks who got them to desert in the first place.'

'Let the past be the past,' insisted Maria. 'Just be grateful they're not here, and let us enjoy the day.' She waved at a family of fellow travelers in another carriage. 'Look, there are the Borodivichs.' The Borodivich family cheered and waved back, and the men tipped their hats.

Another large fancy carriage drove past drawn by four glistening black stallions. Three beautiful girls in pretty dresses with flowers in their braided hair sat together in the back seat, while the men, in tails and tuxedos, were standing up in the carriage, gripping a rail with one hand and a glass of champagne in the other.

'How wonderful. It's like they're all off to a ball,' laughed Mara, as she waved at them.

But Pavel clicked his tongue disapprovingly. 'I'm not sure if that's appropriate, given the town's circumstances, and what some folk are having to endure. Besides, there are men who have fought bravely and died, and that's on both sides.'

'Papa,' said Iya, 'you surprise me. I think it's the first time for a while we both agree on something.'

Pavel had reserved a spot for the family on the Town Hall steps in the shade of the hall's portico, not far from the reviewing dais. 'We'll have a good review of the parade and should be able to see all the dignitaries from here.'

The day was hot and cloudless, with only a faint breeze to stir up the dust on the avenue. Despite their having a reserved place, people were crammed around them, jostling for space and a vantage point. Several people recognized Pavel. They doffed their hats to him and the family, and made room for them on the steps. One man went into the Town Hall and returned with a chair for Iya.

'You're most kind,' said Pavel.

'It's the least we could do,' the man answered graciously, with a small bow.

'Who's that person on the dais?' Mara asked, pointing towards a slim, distinguished-looking man in his forties with a bushy moustache. His Russian-style military jacket was bedecked with rows of medals.

'That's General Diterikhs,' answered Pavel. 'Chief of Staff for the Czech-Slovaks.'

'But his name sounds German.'

'I'm told he has a Russian mother and a German father.'

'And he's with the Legion?'

'He was fighting for us on the Eastern Front when the Bolsheviks took over. He made his way to Siberia and was recruited by the Czech-Slovaks.'

'And the general in the pillbox hat with all that braid on the peak?' asked Galina.

'That's a French kepi. The Czech-Slovaks are nominally under French command. I think that's General Janin.'

Galina laughed. 'The Czech-Slovak Legion with a Russian-German Chief of Staff and a French general in command – it's very confusing.'

Pavel shook his head. 'See that officer with the dark features standing off to one side; the one with a serious look on his face.'

Both Galina and Mara stood on tiptoes and craned their heads to see.

'That's Colonel Gajda. He's the main Czech-Slovak commander, and he *is* actually Czech-Slovak. I know, I was once introduced to him.'

From a few blocks away at Bavarina Place down near the River Boat

Station, the strains of a military band could be heard striking up. First came the rhythmic beating of drums, followed by the sound of massed accordions. Then, rising above the instruments, Russian soldiers singing in unison.

From taiga, dense taiga
From Amur, from the river
Like a silent, terrible cloud
Siberians go to battle

'Listen,' said Pavel. 'They are singing the March of the Siberian Regiment.'

Men removed their hats and held them over their hearts, and many women reached for their handkerchiefs to wipe their eyes. Some onlookers joined in with the chorus, and unashamed tears flowed down many faces.

Free Russia will rise again
Shining with our faith
And this song will be heard
By the walls of the ancient Kremlin

Maria put her arm though Pavel's and squeezed his hand. 'You don't regret not marching?'

The surviving "rebels" from the battle, (as those who staged the uprising in the town had been dubbed by the Bolsheviks) had been invited to join the parade, along with the regular troops of the Volunteer regiments and the Czech-Slovak Legion. Pavel was asked, but had declined on the advice of Captain Spencer.

'Better to keep out of it,' the captain had warned him. 'You can rest assured the *Cheka* will have people in the crowd taking photographs. You will be a marked man.'

Four bearded priests in long black cassocks led the parade as it rounded the corner down by the riverbank, and started up Moskovovsky Prospekt. Each of the priests was helping hold up the large gilt icon from the local church. They were flanked on both sides by altar boys in white smocks, carrying the smaller church icons.

'It's a wonder the icons survived,' commented Maria, 'when you see how the Bolsheviks desecrated the church.'

'The priests hid them,' answered Pavel, 'just before they fled themselves.'

Following closely behind the priests were the flag-bearers. A cheer went up from the crowd. There was the unmistakable double-headed eagle of the Russian Imperial Flag; taking central place however, and proudly held aloft, the green and red flag of Siberia.

The Volunteer regiments of Novonikolayesk and Tomsk came next, marching ten men wide up the dusty boulevard. Pavel recognized the figure of *Kapitan* Sergeev marching at the head of the column, his sword drawn and held aloft.

'Where are Mikhail and Sergei?' asked Maria, trying to find a gap in the crowd to see through. A large man in front of her was blocking her view.

'I think I can see them,' said Galina. She had gone back into the hall to find a spare chair, and was now standing on it, much to the annoyance of her mother. 'Look, there they are, they're about to pass the dais.'

'Eyes, left!', shouted the commander of each company as they approached. The soldiers' heads snapped around, and the company officers raised their sabers to the peaks of their caps. The flag bearers lowered the regimental standards to horizontal, and then, once they had passed the dais, raised them to vertical again when the 'Eyes, front!' command rang out.

Cheer after cheer met each company of infantry, each cavalry squadron, and each battery of horse-drawn artillery.

Then came the khaki-uniformed Czech-Slovaks. Commander Gusarek was at the front, leading the massed ranks that stretched all the way back down the *Prospekt*, almost to the river. The cheering was a bit subdued compared to that for the Volunteer regiments, but it swelled, and then reached a crescendo, when the Barnaul "rebels' came into sight. With their rag-tag collection of uniforms, and many in civilian clothes, they looked out of place compared to the regular troops.

They made little effort to stay in line or in step, but proudly marched along the boulevard waving to friends and family in the crowd. Pavel managed to pick out Nikifor amongst the marchers. He lifted his hat and waved to him, and Nikifor grinned, gave Pavel an informal salute, and waved back.

The final units had marched past and had been lost to view as they turned off the boulevard. The band had stopped playing, and the senior reviewing officers on the dais were busily saluting each other and shaking hands before returning to their waiting vehicles.

'It's over,' Pavel told Maria. 'Let's wait for a moment for the crowd to clear.'

Pavel felt a light touch on his elbow, and turned to see Captain Spencer. He was dressed in civilian clothes. The captain gave a slight bow towards Maria. 'Madame, will you excuse your husband for a moment?'

Captain Spencer led Pavel through the crowd, and back into a room at the rear of the Town Hall. He closed the door behind them.

'I need to go away again, but I wanted a quick chat before I leave.'

'What is it?' asked Pavel.

'Thanks to your help we won the battle, but it's far from over. We think Tsaplin, and what remained of his men, managed to slip away to Aleyesk. It was our worst fear, but in the end, we could have done little to prevent it. We are just going to have to live with his partisans attacking the Turkestan line every now and again. Hopefully we can stop them. I've managed to convince the Czech-Slovaks to station some troops here. They will be a big assistance, but they will need help.'

Pavel nodded. 'What do you want me to do?'

Captain Spencer looked at him. 'More than ever I need your reports on the local situation, in particular, whatever you can find out about what Tsaplin is up to. I'll be getting reports from the Czech-Slovaks, and it isn't that I don't trust them, but I want an independent view of the situation here.'

'The usual arrangements?'

The captain nodded, 'Of course.' Then he reached into his pocket.

'I really must get going, but there's one more thing. You are a civilian and we can't award medals for what you did but, at the same time, I don't want you to go unrecognized.'

'It's not necessary,' stuttered Pavel, feeling a bit embarrassed. 'We've got our town back, and that's all that matters.'

Captain Spencer smiled. 'Nonsense,' he said. 'I can't exactly give you a British decoration, since we're not supposed to be here, so I'm giving you something that's distinctly Russian. It's a sort of memento, something I picked up during my travels.'

'You don't need to.'

The captain thrust an oblong leather-bound case into Pavel's hand. 'Put it in your pocket and look at it later.'

Then he turned and hurried out the door before Pavel could say anything else.

'What was that all about?' asked Maria.

Pavel had rejoined them back on the Town Hall steps. 'It was nothing really. Let's find Dmitry and the troika.'

Many of the townsfolk had already gone down to the riverbank after the parade. Rugs had been spread out on the grass, hampers unpacked and bottles uncorked. The military band had set up in the rotunda and started to play light waltz music. Birds wheeled in the azure blue sky above the embankment as a light, cooling breeze floated in across the Ob.

'Let's go for a walk,' Maria suggested to Pavel after they had set up their picnic spot. Mikhail and Sergei had joined them and the young people were all sitting around on the rug, laughing, drinking and eating.

Pavel and Maria strolled along the top of the river embankment. There were other couples walking along the embankment; everyone being polite, smiling and nodding greetings, and the men tipping hats. It reminded Pavel of the May Day Parade, the one before the big fire.

While it was not that long ago, it felt to Pavel as though it was from another life – a past existence – and he found it strangely unsettling.

'Now you can tell me what Captain Spencer wanted,' insisted Maria.

'He has to go away again, and he just wanted to ask me to do something.'

'More of those reports?'

Pavel nodded.

Maria glowered. 'You know they could get you into trouble. They'll think you're a British spy.'

'It's only local gossip he's after.'

'If it wasn't important, he wouldn't be asking. And anyway, what's local gossip got to do with the British?'

Pavel looked around to check nobody was in earshot. 'He mentioned the British have just landed an expeditionary force at Murmansk.'

'What's an "expeditionary force"?'

'I'm not sure,' whispered Pavel, 'but it could mean the British are about to enter the war.'

Maria stopped and turned to face Pavel. 'Murmansk is a long way from here, and anyway, I would have thought the British have enough on their hands in their own war against the Germans.'

'The Americans have arrived now. The captain believes the Germans will be beaten by Christmas.'

Maria looked at the bulge in Pavel's coat pocket. 'And what do you have in there?'

Pavel flushed red. 'Just something the captain gave me. It's a sort of award, I guess.'

Pavel got out the slim case, checked nobody around them was looking, and opened it up.

Maria put her hand to her mouth. 'Oh, my goodness.'

In the slim, leather case, embossed with the Imperial Double-Eagle, lay a large silver Russian Orthodox cross nestled on a red velvet pillow.

She carefully picked it up. 'You should feel the weight – it's solid silver.' Maria turned the cross over in her hand and gasped. 'Look, the

Tsar has had his initials engraved on the back. It says "NII" – that's Tsar Nicholas.'

'Good God,' said Pavel, taking back the cross, placing it back on its velvet bed and snapping the case shut. 'It must be valuable and I can't believe he's given it to me. We shouldn't let anyone see it, and let's not tell the others.'

Maria put her arm through Pavel's. They turned, and started walking back towards the family. 'Speaking of the Tsar, what do you think has happened to him, do you think he's still alive?'

Pavel stopped, put his hand in his pocket, and felt for the cross in the case. 'I really couldn't tell you.'

Epilogue
BARNAUL

September 1918

PAVEL WAS LEANING on the counter of his store, reading the broadsheet newspaper spread out before him, when the bell on the main door tinkled. He looked up and smiled.

'This is a pleasant surprise,' he said, walking around to the front of the counter. 'I hope you didn't walk down from the house alone.'

'No,' replied Iya, 'Dmitry acted as my bodyguard. He's just outside. It was such a beautiful day, and I thought we could both do with some fresh air.'

'And how's my little Vera?' asked Pavel, bending over the wicker perambulator. He went to waggle his finger at the baby, but Iya stopped him.

'Leave her alone, she's asleep.'

Pavel remained, admiring the serene sleeping face of the newborn, with her ruddy cheeks and wisps of blond hair. She was wrapped in a woolen shawl and well tucked in.

'She's going to be a tall one,' whispered Pavel. 'It must be from Mikhail's side of the family.'

The shop doorbell rang again. Nikifor was standing in the doorway, in his white shopkeeper's apron and his typical grin on his face. He looked excited and started to speak.

'Shush,' hissed Iya, pointing at the pram. 'She's asleep.'

Nikifor beckoned Pavel over towards the door. 'Quick, you've got to come and have a look at this. It'll only take a minute.'

'You go, Father. Vera and I can look after the shop.'

Pavel took off his apron and hurried off up the street after Nikifor.

'Come on, it's just over here,' said Nikifor, as they walked briskly over towards the group of people gathered near the steps of the Town Hall.

'Mr. Sukhov will know,' someone said, as the crowd parted to let Pavel through.

In the middle of the crowd, a scraggy-looking mule stood tethered to a rough wooden sled, with the mule's driver standing alongside the animal, holding the bridle.

A bloodstained piece of canvas barely covered the body lying face-up on the sled. Pavel bent over for a closer look and pulled back the canvas from over the corpse's head. He took a sharp inward breath.

The pale face stared up at him, with open, blank eyes that had rolled up into their sockets. The skin was stretched taut over the cheekbones and had turned a waxy yellow. Pavel could smell the start of decay, the smell of death. He dropped the canvas and stepped back.

'We got him in an ambush out towards Aleyesk,' said the mule driver. 'They were trying to rip up the train line again. I was told to bring the body back into town so we could identify him.'

Pavel remained silent, staring down at the corpse, and the bloodstained canvas. He felt numb, not knowing what to think, not knowing what he felt.

'Can you identify him for us, Mr. Sukhov?'

Startled, Pavel looked up at the mule driver. He hesitated, and looked slowly around at the cluster of people.

'His name is Tsaplin; Matvei Tsaplin.'

The End

List of Characters

(REFER FAMILY TREE FOR THE SUKHOVS)

- Antonovich, Joseph – Neighboring farmer of the Sukhov stud farm
- Brusilov, General Alesksei – Commander-in-Chief of the Russian Army during the spring offensive of 1917
- Czesnovsky, Kapitan – Officer in the Czech-Slovak Legion in the Battle for Barnaul 1918
- Denikin, Anton – Commander of the White Army of the Crimea
- Diterihks, General Mikhail – Russian- born Chief of Staff for the Czech-Slovak Legion
- Gajda, Colonel Radola – Commander of the Czech-Slovak Legion
- Gorokhov, Lieutenant – Officer in the Volinsky Regiment during the retreat from Ternopol 1917
- Gusarek, Commander – Commander of the combined Czech-Slovak Legion and White Russian forces during the assault on Barnaul 1918

- Herzen, Lieutenant – Officer in the Russian 11th Division during the mutiny in 1917

- Janin, General Maurice – The French Commander-in-Chief of the Czech-Slovak Legion

- Katrina (surname not known) – Manageress of the Sukhov's Moskovsky Street store

- Kerensky, Alexander – Russian Prime Minister at the time of the coup by Bolshevik revolutionaries 1917

- Kornilov, General Lavr – Replaced Brusilov (see above) as Commander-in-Chief of the Russian Army following the failed spring offensive 1917

- Krasilnikov, Ataman Ivan – Leader of the Siberian Cossack *Host*

- Krymov, Lieutenant-General Alexander – Commander of the 3rd Cavalry Division, Russian Army

- Lebedev, Countess Vera – courier for the Officers' Union in Petrograd

- Lebedev, Prince – Elder brother of the above, and a senior organizer for the Officers' Union

- Lenin – aka Vladimir Ilyich Ulyanov, leader of the Russian Bolshevik Party

- Listnitsky, Major – On the General Staff of the Russian Army *Stavka* GHQ.

- Mehenov, Kapitan Mikhail – Husband of Iya Sukhov and officer in the 11th Division of the Russian Army

- Nicholas II, Alexandrovich Romanov – Tsar of Russia (abdicated 1917). Married to Alexandra of Hesse. Children: Olga, Tatiana, Maria, Anastasia, and Alexei

- Nikolayevich, Ivan – foreman on the Sukhov Barnaul stud farm

- Purishkevich, Vladimir Mitrofanovich – Russian politician and leader of the Black Hundreds, the ultra right-wing paramilitary group

- Sergeev, Kapitan – Officer in the White Russian forces during the attack on Barnaul in 1918

- Spencer, Captain – A British Army "military observer" stationed in Siberia. It is unlikely this was his real name

- Trifonovich, Nikifor – friend of Pavel Sukhov and fellow-merchant in Barnaul

- Trotsky, Leon – Leading revolutionary in the Russian Bolshevik Party and founder and organizer of the Red Army

- Tsaplin, Matvei – head of the Barnaul Bolshevik Soviet and commander of the Red force in the Battle of Barnaul

- Vinokurov, Alexei – Friend of Pavel Sukhov and owner of the Tyumentsevsky stud farm on the Pavolvsk Trakt outside of Barnaul

- Vinokurov, Lieutenant Sergei – son of the above and officer in the 11th Division of the Russian Army. Friend of Mikhail Mehenov

- Zhuravsky, Kapitan – member of the Officers' Union in Petrograd

Russian Patronymic Names

It was usual practice to give Russian children a patronymic middle name as part of their full name. The patronymic name refers to the father. As an example, Pavel "Dmitrievich" Sukhov denotes that Pavel Sukhov is the son of Dmitry Sukhov.

I have used patronymic names sparingly in the text since it often confuses non-Russian readers and makes the names cumbersome. Therefore, apart from a few formal greetings in the dialogue, I have used the shorter versions of people's names.

Acknowledgements
THE JOURNEY

Writing a book is a journey – there is the planning stage, the departure, and the arrival. But there are a lot of things that happen along the way; some are planned, but a lot is unplanned, haphazard and accidental, somewhat like chaos theory at work.

Firstly, we just happened to be living in Thailand. This is where my wife Bronwyn formed a friendship with Arlette, to whom this book is dedicated. I'm not sure which one of them it was, but it was suggested I write the book about Arlette's family.

Then came meetings with Arlette where I was given a mountain of family archival information that spanned three wars and two revolutions, in three different countries over several decades. We had to decide on a starting point – a place and a time in the family's history. By mutual consent it was Barnaul, Siberia 1917.

I discussed this with my long-time friend and ex-work colleague, John Hudson. He is an avid reader, a researcher of history, and was keen to help on the project. "Everyone writes about the Russian Revolution,' he told me, 'but who has written about the civil war in Siberia?"

Somewhere during the first drafts of the book, Bronwyn and I decided we needed to go to Russia, and John wanted to come too. Where to start, and where to go in a country that spans half the globe? How do you dive headlong into an unofficial research trip in a foreign country described by Winston Churchill as "a riddle wrapped in a mystery inside an enigma". Notwithstanding that the civil war is a shunned subject, deliberately expurgated from Russian history.

But we did have an idea, and asked Flower Travel for assistance. They are Australia's experts on travelling the Trans-Siberian Railway; however, this was never going to be a normal tourist trip. We wanted to start in Saint Petersburg, then on to Moscow to explore the crucible of the revolution, and then take the train journey across the Urals into Siberia where the major part of this story is located. There would be side trips to Yekaterinburg where the Tsar and family were executed, to Omsk where the White Russian Government was established, and to Barnaul, the home of the Sukhovs. After that, it was on to Novosibirsk, Irkutsk, and to Lake Baikal and beyond to follow their route of escape from Russia. The trip would end in Vladivostok, one month and 11,000 kilometres later.

On our trip we received local assistance organised through our travel agents. Our guides were generally all well educated young people, with excellent English, friendly, and very helpful. In particular we are indebted to Professor Sergey Manskov and his assistant, Maria Naumova of Barnaul University who hosted us in the hometown of the Sukhovs, showed us the locations, and gave us excellent information on the local history of the family.

Back in Thailand, rewrites were needed based on new information gathered on the trip, and my fellow-writers of the Pattaya Writers Group helped with reviewing and critiquing. John Lynham, one of the founding members, a retired English lecturer and Russian scholar, was a great support and did a superb editing job, but I also need to give an honorable mention to Chris Elliot, Carol Johnson, Martin Bower, Karyn Walker, and Darla Rice, who is writing a historical fiction novel of her own.

In Australia our neighbours and friends supported the project with surprising enthusiasm. As retired university academics, English literature and language experts, and published authors and playwrights, Gay Baldwin and Peter Fitzpatrick have both contributed enormously to editing and provided insightful comments, and have been in it for the long haul, despite both of them having their own projects to pursue.

Mention must be made of my late mother-in-law, Pattie Little, who read some of the early drafts, rolled her eyes, and wrote all over the manuscript in red pencil. But she thought enough of the book to buy me a MacBook Air as an encouragment to keep me writing.

Others have looked over the manuscript. Victoria, my sister in the U.S. has previously edited for other writers and provided useful and supportive comments. And I coerced Bronwyn into reading it and making notes, particularly on the mindboggling list of Russian characters requiring explanation and placing into context. Also to help the reader, Britt Wilson of Author Services Australia has created a family tree and a number of superb maps. She was also responsible for the cover design.

Honorable mention must go to Robin, Allison and Jan, my group of *beta* readers, who scoured the manuscript for the final time before it hit the printing press.

I do not list for acknowledgement either a literary agent or a publisher. I would have liked to, but in the risk-averse mainstream publishing world of today, I would have needed to financially mitigate the publisher's risks. Instead, I decided to spend this money on self-publishing – a great leap into the unknown, and a journey all in itself.

SJC
South Gippsland, Australia
September 2023

SIMON J. CAREY

SIMON CAREY, born and educated in New Zealand, moved to Australia to complete his tertiary education at RMIT in polymer technology. He then worked in the petrochemical industry in various locations throughout the Asia-Pacific.

When he retired from a successful corporate career, he was asked by a Sukhov family member to write their story. Having written for industrial and print media over many years, and coming from a long family line of journalists, editors, and newspaper proprietors, he readily accepted the project.

An avid traveler, snow skier, sailor and golfer, Simon and his wife, Bronwyn, live at their coastal property at Wilsons Promontory, Australia – the southern tip of mainland Australia. They also spend part of each year residing in Thailand and Canada.

The Siberians
THE SUKHOV SERIES

"The Siberians – Journey into the Unknown"

Covers the period from late 1918 – 1920.
The 2nd Book in the Series

The Sukhov family has re-established their home and businesses in Barnaul after the Bolshevik defeat. Mikhail and Sergei are away at war with their new unit that is steadily advancing towards Moscow. There is a coup, and a new commander of the White Army in Siberia takes control. The Imperial Gold is seized from the Bolsheviks, foreign troops are supporting the White Army in Siberia, and tentative moves are made towards peace talks despite victory for the White Army looking imminent.

And, then things start to go wrong – horribly wrong.

Once again the Sukhov family need to make a decision whether to stay or flee, as their world starts to crumble around them.

Follow the progress of this new book and release date on
www.simoncarey.com